Diana
W9-BRC-025

AN EXTRAORDINARY AMERICAN FAMILY—ITS BOLD IMMIGRANT FOUNDERS, THEIR TURBULENT INHERITORS . . . AND BARBARA LAVETTE, WHO DEFIED THEM ALL, DETERMINED TO BUILD A LIFE OF HER OWN . . .

DAN LAVETTE—Barbara's father. Son of an Italian fisherman. Life took him from rags to riches and back again. Undaunted, he would rise again to build a new financial empire from the ashes of the old.

JEAN SELDON LAVETTE WHITTIER—Barbara's mother. She had inherited her father's fortune and his genius for banking. Her marriage to Dan was doomed from the start, but beneath her icy beauty, fiery passion ached for fulfillment.

TOM LAVETTE—Barbara's brother. Ashamed of Dan's immigrant roots, he turned to his arrogant stepfather. Certain of his desire for wealth and power, he was torn between the love society demanded and the love it would never forgive.

MARCEL DUBOISE—Barbara's lover. His ties to Barbara were deep and intensely moving. Only war could shatter their dream of enduring love.

Books by Howard Fast

* *In Dell Editions*

SECOND GENERATION

Howard Fast

A DELL BOOK

For Jerry and Dotty

THIS BOOK IS PUBLISHED BY
SPECIAL ARRANGEMENT WITH ERIC LASHER AND MAUREEN LASHER

Published by
Dell Publishing Co., Inc.
1 Dag Hammarskjold Plaza
New York, New York 10017

Copyright © 1978 by Howard Fast

All rights reserved.
No part of this work may be reproduced or
transmitted in any form or by any means,
electronic or mechanical,
including photocopying and recording,
or by any information storage or retrieval system,
without permission in writing from
Houghton Mifflin Company.
For information address
Houghton Mifflin Company, Boston, Massachusetts.

Dell ® TM 681510, Dell Publishing Co., Inc.

ISBN: 0-440-17915-7

Reprinted by arrangement with Houghton Mifflin Company.

Printed in the United States of America

First Dell printing—September 1979
Second Dell printing—September 1979
Third Dell printing—November 1979
Fourth Dell printing—July 1980
Fifth Dell printing—September 1980
Sixth Dell printing—October 1980
Seventh Dell printing—November 1980

CONTENTS

Part One

HOMECOMING

Pete Lomas' mackerel drifter was an old, converted, coal-fired steam tug of a hundred and twenty-two tons, purchased as war surplus in 1919. It cost him so little then that he was able to sell its oversized engine for scrap and replace it with a modern, oil-burning plant. He named it *Golden Gate*, packed his wife and kids and household goods into it, and sailed from San Francisco Bay down to San Pedro. There he rented a berth for the tug and went into the mackerel business. His wife suffered from asthma, and her doctor determined that the San Francisco area was too damp. Lomas then decided to make the move to Los Angeles County, and he bought a house in Downey.

He laid out his drift nets with a three-man crew, and until the Depression came, in the thirties, he did well; and even after 1929 he managed to make a decent living out of his boat and to pay his crew living wages as well. Years before, he had worked for Dan Lavette as the captain of his fleet of crabbing boats on Fisherman's Wharf in San Francisco; and when, in 1931, he stumbled on Lavette on the dock at San Pedro, broke and hungry, he offered him a job. Now, in 1934, Dan had been working for Lomas steadily for three years.

Today, the first of June, 1934, Dan Lavette came off the mackerel boat at ten o'clock in the morning and got into his 1930 Ford sedan to drive to his home in Westwood, where he lived with his second wife, an American-born Chinese woman named May Ling, their son, Joseph, and her parents. Their small house was a few blocks from the University of California campus in Los Angeles, where May Ling worked at the library.

Dan was a big man, six feet and one inch in height, heavily built but without fat, broad in the shoulders, his skin tanned and weather-beaten by the sun and water. He had a good head of curly hair, dark eyes under straight brows, high cheekbones, and a wide, full mouth.

To the two men who comprised the crew of the mackerel boat along with Dan and Pete Lomas, Lavette was a plain, soft-spoken, easygoing, and competent fisherman. He never lost his temper and he never complained, regardless of how brutal or backbreaking the conditions were, and that in itself was most unusual among fishermen. Of his background, they knew only that years before he had fished with Pete Lomas in San Francisco Bay. One of them was a Chicano, the other an Italian who spoke little English, and they were not inordinately curious. As for Lomas, who knew a great deal more about Dan Lavette, he kept his peace.

The Chicano, whose name was Juan Gonzales, while only twenty-two years old, was alert enough to realize that Dan Lavette was unlike any of the other fishermen on the wharf. He said to him one day, "Danny, how come a man like you, he's satisfied to pull fish?"

Dan shrugged. "I'm a fisherman. Always been one."

"You'll be an old man soon. I'll be goddamned if I spend my life on a fishing boat, take home twenty, thirty dollars a week, and end up a poor bum on the dock."

"I've been a bum on the dock," Dan replied. "I like fishing better."

Driving home today, Dan thought of that. Did he actually like what he did, enjoy what he did? It had been a bad night, cold and wet out on the water, and he had wrenched a muscle in his shoulder. His whole body ached, and he thought longingly of the hot bath that he would climb into the moment he set foot in the house. He supposed he was as happy as a man might be. He had made his peace with himself. Nevertheless, he was still a fisherman who took home between twenty and thirty dollars a week, and he was forty-five years old.

The morning mist and overcast had cleared by the time he reached Westwood. His father-in-law, Feng Wo, was in the garden, tending his beloved rosebushes, and he greeted Dan formally as always.

"You are well, Mr. Lavette?" He had never broken his old habit of addressing Dan as Mr. Lavette.

"Tired."

"You have a letter. From your daughter, Barbara."

Dan nodded. "I'll have a bath first."

He soaked in the tub, and strength and comfort flowed back into his body. In a few hours, May Ling would come home, and he would sprawl in a chair and listen to her recitation of what had happened that day on the campus. She dispelled the common notion that nothing but whispers are heard in a library; everything that May Ling looked at or encountered took on a marvelous and enchanting dramatic shape. Her whole life, every day of it, was an adventure in newness. This past night, out at sea, one of their drift nets had parted. Dan hated the drift nets, which trapped the mackerel by their gills. This time he spent an hour splicing the break, soaked to the waist, the dying fish threshing around his hands; still, he could not put into words what he felt, yet with the most ordinary occurrence May Ling brought a whole world to life.

Out of the tub, he toweled himself dry, relaxed, delightfully weary. The *Golden Gate* would lay over until tomorrow morning while the nets were refurbished, so he had a long, lazy time of daylight ahead of him, and then a night when he could sleep himself out on a clean bed instead of huddling for an hour or two on the damp bunk in the cabin of the boat. He and his son would play a game of checkers. May Ling would be reading a book, looking up every now and then to catch his glance and smile at him. Hell, he thought, it was all and more than anyone wanted out of life.

Dressed in a clean shirt and trousers, he went down to the kitchen where the old woman, So-toy, his mother-in-law, had tea and cake waiting for him. The letter from Barbara lay on the table next to his plate. "You'll excuse me," he said to So-toy.

Still, after so many years in America, she spoke very little English. She simply smiled with approval as he opened the letter, then sat down opposite him at the kitchen table while he read. At first, he had been uncomfortable living with two people who worshipped him as uncritically as Feng Wo and his wife. Now he was almost used to it.

"Daddy," the letter began—always that single word, as if it conveyed a significance beyond what any adjective could, yet a word she had spoken to him only at one meeting, a year before—and then went on: "School's over, but I had to write to you before I leave New York for San Francisco, because you will remember that every letter I ever wrote to you has been from here over the past eight months, and I want this to complete our correspondence for this semester. You always tell me that you are not much of a letter writer, and it's true your letters are short, but I do treasure them. And if anyone ever asked me about my father, and they do, you know, I could have said that so much of what I know of him is from his letters, which is strange, don't you think?

"Anyway, school is over. It was such a good year and I do love Sarah Lawrence, but really, I don't know whether I want to go back. Isn't that a strange thing for me to say? For the past week I have been puzzling over the way I feel and trying to make some sense out of it. Have you ever been very happy, but with a little worm of discontent nibbling away at your insides? I shouldn't ask you that, because I saw you with May Ling and I know how happy you are and that there are no worms of discontent eating at you, and it's worse because I don't for the life of me know why. Can one be happy and so terribly dissatisfied at the same time?

"But now when I look at what I have written here, it occurs to me that happy is not the right word. Jenny Brown, who is one of my roommates, gets very blue, and she can't understand why I am always so cheerful, and I guess that's what I really mean. Cheerful is a better word than happy to describe how I usually feel, because even when I feel that something is deeply wrong about the way I am, I don't get depressed about it. But I am going to take two decisive steps when I get home. I shall tell mother that I want a place of my own, and I also intend to find a job, and the latter may have to take place before the former, since it's up to mother whether my allowance continues. Anyway, I feel a little ashamed writing to you about that, when my allowance is more than anyone deserves without working for it. All of this is just to tell you what to expect when I come down to see you, because it's so very long since my first trip to Los Angeles, and every time I think about that I get all wet-eyed and emotional. But I do promise you that very soon after I get home, I will drive down to Westwood.

"I can't tell you how much I want to see Joe again. It's so strange to have a brother you have only seen once in your entire life, and I liked him so much. How can one have two brothers as different as Tom and Joe? But of course I can answer that myself. I do love Tom, but he's such a stuffed shirt. You know that he's graduating from Princeton this year, and he's just furious at me because I wouldn't hang around with mother's family in Boston until the graduation, and I wouldn't because I don't think it would matter a bit for me to be there at the graduation and I don't intend to make that long train trip twice in one month.

"Anyway, two more weeks away was just too much. I am so eager to get home and to see San Francisco, and to see you and Joe and May Ling, who is just the loveliest person in the world, and her father and mother, who are just darling and much more like two people you read about in a book and don't ever meet in real life."

She signed the letter "Barbara," as if no term of endearment could add to what she had written, something Dan understood very well indeed.

"How is daughter Barbara?" So-toy asked him.

"Good. Yes, she's fine."

I have stepped into the pages of *Alice in Wonderland,* Barbara told herself; yet she had been here and lived in this San Francisco mansion before, and nine months away was not such a long time. She was playing a role, not they. She was having dinner in the pretentious dining room with her mother and her stepfather, John Whittier, and while it was true that the room was somewhat larger and more elegant than the dining room in the house where she grew up on Russian Hill, when her mother was still married to Dan Lavette, the difference was not all that great. The mahogany table was no longer. It was true that they had not had a butler on Russian Hill, but this was by no means her first dinner in the Whittier house, and the position she occupied between her mother at one end of the long table and John Whittier at the other was not particularly novel. Why then did she feel totally disconnected from this world, a stranger, an intruder? The plain fact of the matter was that she was a daughter of the very rich and had been from the moment of her birth, so how could she sit in judgment? But I am not sitting in judgment, she assured herself, I am simply very uncomfortable and filled with guilt, and I don't know why.

Jean was not an insensitive person, and Barbara realized that she had planned a simple but delicious dinner that would be quite different from the institutional food at

school: a clear soup, then a planked steak with scalloped
potatoes and asparagus, and ice cream for dessert, remembering Barbara's passion for ice cream. Knox, the
butler, brought in the ice cream, a gallon brick sitting in
a tureen of lovely pale ivory Limoges. He served a
portion of the ice cream to each of them and then put the
tureen down in front of Jean and left the room.

John Whittier was holding forth on the waterfront strike,
which had been called in San Francisco just two weeks
before Barbara's return. Whittier was not a conversation-
alist; he had small ability to listen to anything he was not
saying himself; and when he spoke, especially in anger, he
tended to be carried away and lose the threads of his discourse. It always helped him to be accusative.

"Don't tell me you can understand why they're striking,"
he said to Barbara.

"But I can."

"Because you don't understand one damn thing about
it," he went on. "That's the trouble with a place like Sarah
Lawrence. I told your mother that. It's not only a wretched
substitute for education, it's a communist substitute. It's
anarchy—and I'm not saying that because of what it has
cost your mother and myself personally."

"Leave me out of it, dear," Jean said softly. "I left the
bank this morning. I am through with business." She
smiled.

"Hardly, my dear," Whittier said. "Like it or not, this
family is the largest shipowner on the West Coast, and for
two weeks we haven't moved one damn pound of cargo
out of this port. Do you know what that has cost us?"

He directed this at Barbara. She shook her head, her
eyes fixed on the mound of ice cream in the Limoges
tureen. It was melting. No one noticed that it was melting.
No one cared that it was melting.

"Would a million dollars shock you? Or does a million
dollars mean absolutely nothing to you? What do they
teach you back there in school? That Karl Marx was a
saint? Or do we have our own living saint in Franklin
Delano Roosevelt? Do you know what longshoremen
are? Have you ever met a longshoreman? Have you ever
smelled one?"

"John," Jean said.

"The dregs of this city, and we've put the bread in
their mouths all these years, and this is our repayment—

to be destroyed! And you can understand why they're striking—"

Listening to this, Barbara watched the ice cream melt. In back of her mind, there was the memory of Professor Franklin's Sociology II, where he made the point that the rich are incapable of understanding the rich. It had been a non sequitur then, and now suddenly it made sense. A gallon of ice cream, melted, could only be thrown away.

"Mother," she said, "the ice cream is melting."

Jean's slight smile remained unchanged. She was watching her husband, and Barbara realized that her mother heard nothing Whittier was saying, nothing she was saying. The ice cream continued to melt.

"As for Harry Bridges," Whittier was saying, "if there were law and order in this city, he'd be behind bars. Oh, yes, behind bars."

Barbara was in bed, reading Gertrude Stein's *Autobiography of Alice B. Toklas*, intrigued, fascinated by a world so distant and different, when the door opened and Jean entered the room. She wore a dressing gown of pale pink velvet and she had removed her make-up, and as far as Barbara was concerned, it only enhanced her face. If she were as beautiful as her mother, she would never touch make-up. She put down the book, and Jean came to the bed and sat down beside her. Jean picked up the book and glanced at it.

"Like it?"

"I like to pretend I'm in Paris."

"The question is, darling, are you glad to be back in San Francisco?"

"I think so. Yes."

"You mustn't mind John. He's terribly upset. People in his position develop a tremendous feeling of power. I know the feeling, and now, with the waterfront closed down as it is, he's utterly frustrated. This is hardly the best side of him."

"Mother—"

"It used to be 'mummy.' "

"I know. I'm twenty years old."

Jean was smiling.

"So you mustn't laugh at me."

"I wouldn't dream of laughing at you. But you're so very serious."

"Yes," Barbara agreed. "I guess I'm forcing myself to be serious because I have been trying to get up the courage to talk about this—"

"Baby, we can talk about anything. You know that."

"We can't," Barbara protested almost plaintively. "You're my mother. It's just not true that we can talk about anything."

Jean stopped smiling. "Try."

"All right. I want a place of my own."

"What do you mean by a place of your own?"

"My own apartment. I can't live here."

Jean sighed. "The truth is, you don't live here—I mean in reality, my dear. Think about it. You're away at school. It's only the few summer months. And your horse is down in Menlo Park, and you can stay at the club there whenever you wish—and if I know you, you'll be practically living there. You do have your car, so I just don't understand what you mean."

"You don't want to understand what I mean."

"No, that's not fair. Put yourself in my position, Barbara. You tell me that you want an apartment of your own—but why? You're comfortable here. You have everything you could possibly want. You come and go as you please, and whatever you may feel about John, he certainly doesn't restrict your movements or impose any discipline on you."

"That's not it."

"Then tell me what it is."

"This isn't my home. It never has been my home."

"Why? Because you don't like John?"

"Please, please don't get angry with me, mother," Barbara begged her. "You said we could talk. It's not easy for me to explain what I feel. There's a teacher at school, Professor Carl Franklin, who conducts a seminar in sociology, and he said the Embarcadero was a slave market, different, but no better and no worse than the old Negro slave markets in the East, and I was so indignant I almost walked out of the class, because really, they don't think we're quite civilized out here."

"I don't see what that has to do with it," Jean said. "The Embarcadero is not a slave market. The longshoremen are well paid and their demands are utterly preposterous. And what on earth has this to do with your wanting an apartment of your own?"

"Like the ice cream at dinner," Barbara said hopelessly.

"What on earth! The ice cream at dinner?"

"Don't you see? There was that enormous brick of ice cream, and we just sat there and let it melt down while John lectured me about the strike. You can't do anything with ice cream once it melts. You throw it away, and it didn't mean a thing to any of us. It just doesn't. We can't think that way—I mean, we don't even understand what food is in a country where thousands of people are starving."

"But you do understand this," Jean said.

"Now you are angry with me."

"Barbara," Jean said calmly, "I am not angry. Not really. You're a very romantic child, you always have been. I'm well aware of the inequities of society, but we did not create them."

"I'm not a child, mother."

"I think you are. In many ways. You dislike John, and you compare him to your father. I don't think seeing your father has helped, and the romantic image of him that you have is far from the reality."

"Then I dislike John Whittier," Barbara said flatly. "I can't control who I like and who I dislike. Do you think it's pleasant for me to live under his roof?"

"It's my roof too. I happen to be married to John Whittier, and you are a part of a very wealthy family, like it or not. I have no intention of shedding crocodile tears or wallowing in guilt over what my father and his father created by their own sweat and wit. As for the apartment —well, we'll talk about that another time."

It had not been the best of days for Jean Whittier, and now, looking at her daughter, the strong, lovely face, the pale gray eyes, the honey-colored hair, so like her own— and thinking that this was probably the only person in the world she truly loved—it promised to end even more wretchedly than it had begun.

It had been Jean's last day as president of the Seldon Bank, a great, unshakable financial institution, which her grandfather had founded in a wagon at the placer mines just eighty-two years before, and which her father had continued and cherished and nourished. At his death, six years ago, Jean—then Jean Lavette and not yet divorced —had become trustee for three hundred and eighty-two

thousand shares of stock in the Seldon Bank, to be divided
equally between her two children, Thomas and Barbara,
twelve years later. With over seventy percent of the voting
stock of the Seldon Bank in her trust, with the right to
vote it, Jean had taken over the presidency of the bank,
becoming the first woman in California, if not in the entire
country, to sit as president of a major bank.

Now she was surrendering. No, as she saw it, not a surrender but an abdication. Willing or unwilling? She could
not be certain. Until today, she had felt that she was
certain, that she was taking a step out of her own free
will, doing what was best for her and for the bank. Walking into the bank that morning, passing through the great
marble-clad street section that fronted on Montgomery
Street, she had been shaken by a sudden and desperate
sense of loss. Which, she told herself immediately, was an
understandable and emotional reaction. Essentially, nothing had changed. She still, as trustee for her children,
voted the controlling interest in the stock; she would still
sit on the board of directors; and at long last she would be
able to return to the central interest of her life, her collection of paintings and sculptures, which she had so long
neglected. It would be said, as it was perhaps already
being said, that her husband, John Whittier, had persuaded
her to take this step; and she admitted to herself that it
was true in part—but only in part. It was her own decision.

Alvin Sommers, vice president of the Seldon Bank, had
been waiting and watching for her that morning, and as
he saw her enter, he hurried to meet her. He noticed that
she was wearing what to his way of thinking was civilian
dress, a bright flowered taffeta with pink velvet trimming,
both cheerful and youthful, he assured himself. Even at the
age of forty-four, Jean Lavette—he still thought of her as
Jean Lavette—was, as the news stories so often observed,
perhaps the most fashionable and attractive woman in San
Francisco social circles. He himself, a small, dry man in
his middle sixties with a small, pudgy wife, had long entertained his own fantasies about Jean Whittier; it was a
totally frustrated, totally concealed love, lust, hate fixation,
nourished on the one hand by her cold, distant beauty,
and on the other by his resentment at the manner in
which, after her father's death, she had taken over control
of the bank. The fact that the bank had flourished during
the first five bitter years of the Depression, when so

many banks were in crisis or closing their doors, only increased his resentment. Now that time had come to an end, but he was still not certain that his own temporary ascendancy to the presidency would be made permanent, and he was thus more deferential than ever, more effusive in his greeting.

"My dear Jean," he said to her, "I've never seen you look so radiant. But what will we do now? We'll become a drab and colorless place."

"You will manage, Alvin. In fact, you will manage very well indeed. By the way, I told Martin"—Martin Clancy was the second vice president—"that I shall empty my office. You'll be moving in, I presume, and I hardly think you'll be comfortable with an Aubusson carpet of pale blue, or with the Picassos and Monet's *Water Lilies,* which you and Martin have always regarded as being a slur on the entire tradition of banking."

"No, indeed. You have a beautiful office."

He had to quicken his pace to keep up with her as she swept through the bank into the main lobby of the Seldon Building.

"Alvin, how old are you?"

"Sixty-five," he answered, thinking, What an outrageous question, and the way she asked it, like making a remark about the weather. But no comment followed it, and his inner debate on whether to follow her into the elevator like an obedient puppy dog was decided by her own motion. They were alone with the operator in the elevator reserved for the top three floors, where the bank's offices were.

"We set the board meeting for three o'clock," he told her. "Tentatively, that is. If you are free then?"

"No, I'm not. I'm meeting Barbara at the station, and that's at two-thirty, I think. But you don't need me, Alvin. I've drawn up the agenda. Martin will propose you and the board will vote it that way. You do know that, don't you?"

"I had hoped so. Thank you, Jean."

Since she didn't invite him out, he remained in the elevator. Jean admitted to herself that she couldn't tolerate him. That was a plus for her decision; she would not have to face Alvin Sommers every time she came to the bank. Yes, there was a whole list of positive things. Six years was enough. She had taken the step originally because it was a challenge. Or was it because her life was coming apart at the seams? Or was it because she loathed everything about the bank and everyone connected with it? That, indeed, was an odd thought, and a new one, and it might very well be so.

Miss Pritchard, her secretary, regarded her sadly. "I was not sure of your time today—everything is so upset. Will you see anyone?"

"I don't think so. I have a luncheon engagement, and it's ten o'clock already. I won't be in at all this afternoon."

"And tomorrow?"

"No tomorrow, Lorna. You know that. Finis." She patted Miss Pritchard's thin shoulder. "It's all right, and you must not worry about your job. Just take your two weeks' vacation and enjoy yourself," she said, wondering just how skinny, spinsterish, fortyish Miss Pritchard would go about enjoying herself. "Did I have any appointments? I didn't think so."

"No. But Mr. Liu called again. The man from the Oriental Improvement Society. He said he would call back."

"Then you talk to him. What does he want, a contribution?"

"I don't imagine so. I think it's part of their campaign to place Chinese and Japanese in jobs in banks."

"We're not taking on anyone, you know that," Jean said with some irritation. "If he wants to see anyone, he can see Mr. Sommers next week."

Provoked, and annoyed with herself for allowing it to show, Jean went into her office, closed the door, and stood there, looking around. It was a large office, twenty by thirty feet. The walls, once covered by walnut panels, were now painted in soft tones of ivory. The pastel blue Aubusson measured eighteen by twenty-four, and Jean thought wistfully of how splendid it would have been on the floor of her bedroom in the house she had lived in on Russian Hill, when she had been Jean Lavette. In the Whittier mansion—well, a pastel blue rug in the Whittier house was as yet unthinkable. All in due time. She had already invaded her husband's house—which had once belonged to his father—with thirty-seven paintings, still only part of her collection, and now somehow she would have to find a place for the Picassos and the enormous Monet. It would mean a struggle, but she was determined that the

Monet would hang on a wall in the Whittier house, and there were few decisions of Jean's that did not come into being.

She sat down behind her desk, a graceful eighteenth-century French piece that she had picked up in Paris, and surveyed the room. Actually, there was nothing more for her to do here; she was simply going through motions, but she could recall with satisfaction that she had never been a figurehead. She had run the bank and not only the bank; there were huge land holdings that her former husband had acquired, the largest department store in San Francisco, and other odds and ends of a small empire that had become a very large empire since her marriage to John Whittier. She had nurtured it. She had been wealthy before; now, in this dismal year of 1934, she was a great deal wealthier.

"And totally miserable," she said aloud.

The telephone rang. It was her husband, John, explaining that something had come up and that he could not make lunch with her. "Can you go to the station alone?" he asked her. "The afternoon's just no good for me."

"I think I'm capable of getting to the station. Yes."

"You sound unhappy."

"Do I? I'm happy as a lark."

"Well, you'll be pleased to see Barbara again."

"Yes, of course." There was a long moment of silence, and then Jean said, "By the way, I've decided not to sell the house on Russian Hill. I shall keep it and turn it into a gallery."

"Oh. And when did you decide that?"

"Just this moment."

When she put down the telephone, she felt better. John hated the house on Russian Hill, just as he hated everything that related to Daniel Lavette.

As a matter of fact, John Whittier shared a sentiment held by his wife's former husband, Dan Lavette. It was less the house on Russian Hill that he disliked than the hill itself, the place, the ambience, the cluster of artists and writers who had given the hill a reputation almost as widely recognized then, in the 1930's, as that of Greenwich Village in New York. Those who knew John Whittier said that the only thing in the world that he loved, cherished, or respected was money—which was not entirely fair, for he

respected Jean, his second wife, and certainly he respected
the vast wealth that she represented. Whether or not he
loved her, or had ever been in love with her, is a question
which, if put to him, would have required for an answer
a degree of introspection of which he was by no means
capable. In his terms, she was a rewarding wife. She was
tall, beautiful, dressed elegantly and in the best of taste,
still youthful at forty-four, and in San Francisco terms at
the very apex of society, the only daughter of Thomas and
Mary Seldon; and Mary Seldon's mother had been an
Asquith from the Boston family that still resided on
Beacon Hill. All to the good. The various factors held
together like an analysis of an impeccable blue chip stock.
There were still other characteristics of his wife that John
Whittier regarded as assets, but her involvement with the
artists and writers of Russian Hill was not one of them.

He himself was a rather good-looking, tall, and somewhat overweight man of forty-six, with thinning blond
hair and pale blue eyes. His father, Grant Whittier, now
deceased, had been the largest shipowner on the West
Coast, and the combining of the Whittier and Lavette
interests had produced the largest single conglomeration of
wealth in California; still, it nettled him that he should
have to continue to pay taxes on a boarded-up mansion
that was certainly the best piece of property on Russian
Hill. Long ago, Robert Louis Stevenson had sailed out of
San Francisco on one of the Whittier ships, and had
afterward written a scathing little essay on how the ship
was run; and while Stevenson had never lived on Russian
Hill, his wife had, and Mrs. Stevenson's presence there
contributed to making the place an anathema to the
Whittiers. Even so small a matter as a piece in the
Chronicle mentioning how much Peter B. Kyne, another
resident of Russian Hill, was paid by the *Saturday Evening
Post* for his stories, elicited an angry denunciation by
Whittier against the large sums paid to writers in these
depressed times.

His own home was in Pacific Heights, a twenty-two-
room limestone mansion. It had been built by his father,
and when John Whittier and Jean Lavette were married,
they agreed that it would be their residence and that she
would rid herself of the house on Russian Hill as soon as
it was convenient for her to do so. Now it was to be a
gallery—whatever that meant.

Whittier's musing was interrupted by his secretary, who told him that there was a collect call for him from Thomas Lavette, from Lambertville, New Jersey.

"From where?"

"Lambertville. Will you accept it, Mr. Whittier?"

"Of course." He picked up his phone. The high-pitched voice on the other end was uneven, uncertain.

"John?"

"Tommy? Where the devil are you?"

"I'm in a frightful mess, John. Don't be angry with me, please. I didn't dare call mother. I don't want her to know—"

"To know what? Will you please tell me what happened."

"I'm in jail here."

"You are what?"

"Please," Tom begged him, "don't blow up at me. I'm miserable enough. I was drunk, and I smashed up the car."

"Are you all right?"

"I'm all right, but there was a girl with me, and they had to take her to the hospital. I don't think she's badly hurt. But they're holding me here for drunk driving, and I need five hundred for bail to get out—"

Whittier stared at the phone without replying. He had no children of his own from his first marriage—which had come late in life and lasted for only three years— and he had no attitudes at all toward children. They were not of his world. It grated when he heard Jean refer to the children. As far as he was concerned, they were adults, a woman of twenty and a man of twenty-two. Between him and Barbara, there was a fence of thorns. Her kisses were cold pecks on the cheek, and communication was almost nonexistent. His attitude toward Tom was more neutral; it consisted of tolerance without affection, but the tolerance was not too elastic.

"John, are you still there?" the voice pleaded.

"How the devil did you get into a scrape like that?"

"God, I don't know. I just don't know. I wish it had never happened, but it did. I hate to come begging to you, but I need the bail money, otherwise I'll just sit here. I'll pay you back."

"All right. I'll wire the money. What did you say that place is? Lambertville, New Jersey?" He scribbled the name on a pad. "You'll need a lawyer. I'll have my people

in New York find you someone in Princeton. I trust you'll
be in Princeton and stay there?" he finished sourly.

"I will, believe me. I don't know how to thank you,
John. It's very decent of you."

"Stupid young fool," he said as he put down the phone.
Then he called his secretary and instructed her to wire
the bail money and to call his New York attorneys and
have them find a lawyer in Princeton and have the lawyer
get in touch with Thomas Lavette at the college. "We'll pay
the costs," he added.

All of which he repeated to Jean, angrily and bitterly,
before they sat down to dinner with Barbara. It definitely
had not been one of Jean's good days.

Dressed in a woolen skirt, an old sweater, and the worn
loafers she had used at school, Barbara took the streetcar
down Market Street to the Embarcadero. On foot, she
drifted slowly south from the Ferry Building, studying the
striking longshoremen with curiosity and interest. Essentially, her mother was quite right about her romantic
nature, and her mind gave every incident in which she
participated a dramatic form and structure. She realized
that she had never actually looked at the faces of men
like those on the picket lines; the faces were worn, pinched,
lined without reference to age. "Longshoreman" had a
connotation in her mind of size, bulk, brute strength; but
most of these men were no taller than she was, many of
them shorter than she was, Mexicans and Orientals many
of them, hunched over, pulling their jackets tight against
the cold wind, holding their picket sings unaggressively,
signs that called for a dollar an hour and for a hiring hall
instead of the shapeup on the docks. Barbara had only a
fuzzy notion of what a shapeup was, thinking of an auction
system of some kind, which Dr. Franklin had referred to
when he called the Embarcadero a slave market. Barbara
went closer to read a sign covered with rough lettering,
and the man carrying it stepped out of line, facing the sign
to her and grinning a toothless, good-natured grin.

"Read it, sister," he said. "I'm in no hurry. I got all the
time in the world."

The sign read: "I want a dollar an hour. I got three kids
and a wife, and I average 15 hours a week. Can you
make it on that? When we struck, my pay was 75 cents an
hour when I worked."

He grinned again, stepped back into the picket line, and walked off. Barbara stared after him. She had thirty-five dollars in her purse, and her first impulse was to run after the toothless longshoreman and press all the money she had into his hands. No, that would be awful, perfectly awful, she decided. She walked along the Embarcadero, carrying the whole weight of poverty and suffering upon her shoulders. It made no difference to Barbara that every port on the West Coast was tied up, from Seattle down to San Diego; the entire guilt, in her mind, belonged to John Whittier and her mother, since they were the largest ship operator on the Coast—and thereby to her.

She came to a place where a truck was parked. The tail of the truck was down, and inside a sort of soup kitchen had been improvised; two men and a stout woman were serving coffee and doughnuts to the strikers. The lettering on the side of the truck read SCHOFIELD'S BAKERY, and under that a hand-painted card read BAKERY WORKERS, LOCAL 12. Barbara watched for a few minutes. Then she went to the woman and whispered uncertainly, "Do you take contributions?"

"We certainly do."

Barbara opened her purse, took out all the money she had, leaving herself only streetcar fare, and handed it to the stout woman.

"God bless you, honey," the woman said.

Barbara clenched her teeth and closed her eyes to keep back the tears.

"Are you all right, honey?"

Barbara nodded and walked away quickly.

At the age of sixty-six, Sam Goldberg was heavier than he had ever been. Six months before, at his doctor's office, he had tipped the scales at two hundred and twenty-five pounds, and since he was only five feet and eight inches, his physician told him flatly, "Keep this up, Sam, and you're inviting a coronary." Now, sitting in his office and munching gumdrops thoughtfully, he realized that the invitation still stood and that he was not terribly worried. His wife, who had always attempted to keep his weight in check, had died two years before. His partner, Adam Benchly—the firm was still Goldberg and Benchly—was a cadaverous Yankee who had died nine months ago at the age of seventy, and since then, Sam had been lonely

and depressed for the first time in his life. The two young
law clerks he had taken on to share the burden respected
him and agreed with him, which only served to depress
him further. Benchly had never agreed with him. They had
fought and snarled at each other for forty years; now life
without him was dull and uninteresting, and Sam Goldberg
saw no good reason to refrain from either the gumdrops
or the heavy, satisfying meals he ate each day at Gino's
restaurant on Jones Street.

In any case, this was a new, different, and discouraging
world, frayed at the seams and disintegrating. He and
Benchly were of the immigrants, a special breed. Goldberg's
father had come to California in 1852 to dig for gold and
had ended up with a fruit stand in Sacramento. Benchly's
father had jumped ship in San Francisco in 1850. He and
Benchly had lived through a time when all was possible,
and the possible was made real. Now the possible had been
honed down to size.

Brooding over this and other matters, he was interrupted
by his secretary's voice on the intercom, informing him that
a Miss Barbara Lavette would like to see him.

He had to adjust, put things in their place, establish a
perspective, and after a long moment of silence he said,
"Yes, of course. Send her in."

He rose and waited. Time plays tricks, and his first
thought as the tall, handsome young woman entered was
that his secretary had gotten the name wrong and that this
was Jean. The resemblance was striking. Of course it was
Jean's daughter. He had not seen Jean for years, but
certainly she was well past forty.

He came around his desk and shook the hand she
offered. Her manner was a curious mixture of shyness and
confidence, and the slight, uncertain smile on her lips was
very ingratiating.

"You're Danny's daughter," Goldberg said.

She nodded. "I should have called and asked you for an
appointment, Mr. Goldberg. But I don't have any legal
business. I want you to know that. I only wanted to talk to
you and ask you some questions, and I know how busy
lawyers are."

"My clerks are busy," he said. "I sit here and eat gum-
drops and brood about the past. I'm delighted—Barbara.
Can I call you Barbara? We shouldn't stand on formalities.
I was your father's lawyer for twenty years, but it was not

just being a lawyer, believe me. And you're Barbara. You have grown up to be a beautiful woman, my dear. The last time I saw you—well, you were six or seven. And now—"

"I'm twenty."

"That's a beautiful, beautiful age. And what about Danny? I know you saw him last year."

"I haven't been down to Los Angeles yet. I'll go soon. Am I intruding—on your time?"

"Intruding? My dear, this is such a fine, unexpected pleasure. It's almost twelve o'clock. Have you eaten yet? Or maybe you have a luncheon appointment?"

"Oh, no."

"Good. Then we'll go along to Gino's and we'll eat and talk."

"All right. I'd like that."

At the restaurnt, sitting opposite her at a small table with a checkered cloth, Goldberg ordered spaghetti, a veal cutlet, and coffee. "We'll eat light. That's the fashion now," he said. He introduced her to Gino, who fussed over her and insisted that they have a bottle of wine on the house. "Danny's daughter," Goldberg told him.

"I know this place," Barbara said when Gino had gone. "He used to come here with May Ling."

"Does that bother you?"

"No, not really. It's just part of the whole thing that I'm trying to understand. When I went to see him last year— you know, I drove down to Los Angeles—"

"I know."

"I was so happy to see him, and I didn't really know him. I still don't, and I guess I don't know myself, either, and I'm so confused."

"I can understand that." He pointed to the food. "You're not eating."

"I'm not very hungry. Please forgive me."

"Nothing to forgive. I'm a fat man, Barbara. The reason people are fat is because they like to eat. So I'll eat and you talk."

"I have questions. Does it annoy you when people ask you questions?"

"That's a lawyer's stock in trade, if he can answer them." He chewed thoughtfully for a few seconds while Barbara waited in silence. "Go ahead and ask."

"Why does he work as a fisherman down there in San Pedro? He was a rich man."

Goldberg ate his spaghetti and regarded her benignly. Finally, having consumed the last mouthful, he said, "He wants to be a fisherman."

Barbara shook her head.

"He doesn't want to be a rich man," Goldberg said.

"That's not an answer," Barbara said pleadingly. "You're laughing at me, Mr. Goldberg."

"No, I'm not. You're asking me why Danny Lavette did what he did. I can tell you what he did, but not why. Anyway, I'm sure you know."

"But I don't know."

"Didn't your mother tell you?"

"My mother doesn't tell me things."

"You know about May Ling, the Chinese lady?"

"Yes—I know she was his mistress for many years."

"No, that's the wrong word. Your father wanted a divorce, and your mother refused. Over a period of twenty years, your father built a small empire—ships, land, the L and L Department Store, a hotel in Hawaii, and the first commercial airline out here in California. When your grandfather died, he left the controlling stock of the Seldon Bank in trust for you and your brother. That was nineteen twenty-eight, and the trust was to extend over twelve years. In nineteen forty, when the trust expires, the control of the stock will come to you. You'll be a very wealthy woman then, but I'm sure you know that."

"Yes, I know that."

"Meanwhile, your mother was named sole trustee in the will, with the power to vote the stock as she saw fit. She then decided to take over as president of the bank, something no woman in this country ever did before, certainly not with an institution the size of the Seldon Bank. All right, your mother didn't know one damn thing about banking, but she learned. She was not a figurehead; she had her finger in every pie, and she didn't do badly, believe me. For the next five years, that bank became her life. But I suppose you know that too."

"Yes," Barbara whispered, "I know that. What about my father?"

"He had a partner, whose name was Mark Levy. The Levys had a chandler business down on the old wharf. Danny's father was killed in the earthquake. Danny had Joe Lavette's fishing boat and nothing else. He was just a kid then, but bright as hell, and soon he was operating three fishing boats, mortgaged to the hilt. He was always mortgaged to the hilt. Then he met your mother and fell in love with her, and nothing was going to stop him from having her and Nob Hill too. He and Mark Levy became partners—Danny was still a kid—and Levy mortgaged his business to finance the purchase of their first ship, a rusty old lumber carrier called the *Oregon Queen*. I still have a picture of it hanging in my office, and if you come back there with me, I'll show it to you."

"Do you know," Barbara said slowly, "I never met Mark Levy. All those years, and I never met him."

"Your mother didn't like him. He was a nice little feller, but your mother just didn't take to him. He's dead now, died in nineteen thirty. His son runs a winery up in Napa. Well, Danny and Mark stuck together to the end. They were like brothers. Way back in nineteen ten, they hired a little Chinese feller by the name of Feng Wo to be the bookkeeper. People didn't hire Chinese in those days for anything fancier than a houseboy, but Feng Wo was smart as a whip. There was no way they could have done what they did without him. May Ling was his daughter." He took a deep breath and began to eat his veal cutlet. "It's a shame to let it get cold," he apologized. "I think a lot of your mother, don't get me wrong."

"I do too," Barbara said. "What happened?"

"I could go into this in detail and spend the rest of the afternoon talking about it, but the long and short of it is that when the Crash came in nineteen twenty-nine, Danny and Mark were overextended and their empire began to crumble. They were into the Seldon Bank for about sixteen million, and they couldn't meet their interest payments. Your mother called the loan, and that was the end of it."

"My mother did that?"

Goldberg stopped eating. "Now hold on. It's not as simple as it appears. Your mother had no alternative, and in a manner of speaking, your father traded his edge for the divorce. He could have stayed on and run what the bank and the Whittiers took over, but Mark would have been out in the cold. Dan didn't want that. The truth is that he didn't want any of it. Something had happened to him. There's a community property in this state, and Dan could have come out of it with half a million, just in personal property, real estate, and such. He didn't want that, either, and he signed a release giving everything to your mother. No one forced his hand. There are no villains in the piece, not your mother and not Whittier."

"Yet you've just told me my mother destroyed my father."

"No one destroyed your father," Goldberg said with just a trace of annoyance. "I thought you knew all this. You saw your father last year. Did he look destroyed?"

"No."

"Well, that's it then. What Danny did, he did. Not your mother or Whittier."

"He was a rich man," Barbara insisted. "I know a little about community property. Whatever happened to his company, he could have remained a rich man. Why did he give it all to my mother?"

"I don't know." Goldberg sighed and shook his head. "Do you want dessert? You haven't eaten at all. Come on, have a piece of cheesecake." He motioned to the waiter.

"All right," Barbara agreed.

"Look, honey," he said, after he had taken his first bite of the cheesecake, "you're Danny's kid. He was like a son to me. But I don't know why he did what he did, and I don't want you to go home and throw this at your mother."

"I can't. She's not there."

"Oh? Do me a favor, eat the cake." She took a mouthful. "It's good, isn't it?"

"Yes, it is."

"Where's your mother?"

"She and John—her husband, Whittier—"

"I know."

"Well, they went east for my brother's graduation. John will be back next month. Tommy and my mother are going on to Boston for a while."

"You mean you're alone in that huge barn of a place?"

Barbara smiled for the first time since they had entered the restaurant. "Oh, no, Mr. Goldberg. You can't be alone in that place."

"Honey, suppose you call me Sam. I'm a little older than you, but we're practically *mishpocheh*. That's Yiddish for family. I know ten words of Yiddish, and that's one of my favorites. Now, why can't you be alone there?"

"Because John has six servants with nothing to do, and when we gave up the house on Russian Hill, mother took Wendy Jones with her. She was our nurse, and now she's old and nasty and nosy. Anyway, I'm hardly ever there."

"I'm nosy too. Why are you hardly ever there? What do you do with yourself? Run around, drink too much?"

"You're scolding me," she said in amazement.

"Yeah." He grinned at her. "I guess I am. Go on, eat the rest of your cake."

"I work at a soup kitchen," Barbara said. "I took today off. Most days I'm too tired to do much running around. I've been there two weeks, since my mother left."

"You work where?"

"The MWIU soup kitchen on Bryant Street."

"MWIU?"

"The Marine Workers, yes," Barbara said calmly.

"God Almighty! You mean Harry Bridges' outfit?"

"Yes."

"Does your mother know?"

Barbara smiled and shook her head.

"Well, she will, sooner or later, and sooner or later some wiseacre reporter will get on to you and spread it all over the front page of the *Examiner,* and that will certainly be a field day. My God, child, what has gotten into you? This isn't a lark. That's a brutal, dirty game they're playing down there on the docks."

"I only work at the soup kitchen. I'm not a communist. And they don't know my name. I call myself Bobby Winter. It's easier if I keep the first name the same, and that's what they called me at school, Bobby Winter, because I loved the cold winters there. So they won't find out who I am."

"Maybe not in the next ten minutes," Goldberg snorted. "Why? Because you think John Whittier did your father in? He didn't. I told you that."

"No. No, really."

"What do they pay you?"

"Nothing."

"What do you do there?"

"Mr. Goldberg, you're shouting at me and scolding me as if I were some stupid, senseless little girl. You have no right to. I came to you to talk about my father, not to sit here and be scolded by you."

"You're absolutely right. I'm sorry."

"I hurt your feelings," she said.

"Absolutely. I hurt your feelings, you hurt mine. Now look, honey, you're the daughter of a man who is like my son. That gives me certain privileges. I talk to you this way because nobody else is going to. It just happens that John Whittier is the largest ship operator on this coast, and it also happens that he's married to your mother. You got sympathy for the longshoremen; so have I. Now I asked you what you do down there."

"I told you what I do. I work in the kitchen. I help to cook the food and serve it. I have an allowance of forty dollars a week, Mr. Goldberg—"

"Call me Sam, I told you," he interrupted. "If I'm going to yell at you, at least make me comfortable."

"All right. Sam. Do you realize that my allowance is more than twice as much as most longshoremen earn in a week?"

"It's five times as much as the average weekly wage in India, maybe ten times. What does that prove?"

"I'm not trying to prove anything. I don't need the money. I spend most of it on food for the kitchen."

"Do they know that?"

"I'm not a fool. I tell them it's contributions. I help to cook the food. I peel potatoes. I clean vegetables. I help with the serving, and sometimes I wash dishes."

"And you like that? You enjoy that?"

"Yes, I do!"

"Who's shouting now?"

"Well, you keep at me as if I'm doing something wrong. I'm not doing anything wrong. In fact, it's the first time in my life I ever did anything right or useful. It's the first time I ever worked. And if you saw the faces of those men, if you knew how hungry and wretched and miserable they are, you would understand what I feel."

The waiter came, and Goldberg took out his wallet and paid the check. Still holding the wallet, he looked at Barbara and said, "You got a boyfriend, honey?"

"No, not really. There was a nice boy at school who came down from Yale on weekends. His name was Burt Kingman and he lives in Philadelphia. But that seems like a hundred years ago. I know some boys here, but I haven't seen them since I've come back. Why?"

Goldberg smiled. "Why? Why, indeed. You're a nice girl, Barbara. Don't get into trouble. Down there on the wharf, you are going to change nothing. Remember that."

"Not even myself?"

"Ah. That's where the trouble begins." He took three

twenty-dollar bills from his wallet and pushed them toward her.

"What's this?"

"Buy more groceries. And remember, the way you're going, it may be that you'll need a lawyer. I'm not a bad lawyer."

After Dan Lavette's partner, Mark Levy, died of a heart attack in 1930, his widow, Sarah, continued to live alone in their big Spanish Colonial house in Sausalito. Sam Goldberg and his wife were frequent visitors there, and when Goldberg became a widower, he fell into a pattern of seeing Sarah Levy on weekends. It was one of the few defenses he had against unbearable loneliness. The weekdays were endurable. He could remain in his office and work until seven or seven-thirty, and then dinner at Gino's or some other restaurant would kill the best part of the evening; but the weekend stretched out as an interminable period of nothing. So more and more frequently after his wife's death, he would invite himself to the Levy home on a Saturday or a Sunday. He had known the Levys for half a century, which, in the San Francisco of 1934, was an epoch that stretched back almost to the beginning. When Sam Goldberg had come to San Francisco from Sacramento, to read law at the offices of Colby and Jessup at the age of seventeen—as things were done in those days—he lived in a frame boarding house on the Embarcadero, opposite the Levys' chandler shop. As they were the only Jews in an overwhelmingly Italian neighborhood, he had come to know them well, and Mark's father had given him his first case, a salvage dispute that involved unpaid accounts at the store. He could remember, as if it were yesterday, the day in 1897 when Sarah arrived from New York, a lovely, slender, flaxen-haired girl, bethrothed to a man she had never seen through the correspondence of the mutual parents, tagged and addressed like a parcel.

Now Marcus had been dead these four years past, a quick death from a massive coronary, less to be pitied than his widow, whose daughter had been a suicide just two years before. Her single surviving child, Jacob, had married Clair Harvey, the daughter of Jack Harvey, who had been the first captain in the Lavette and Levy fleet of oceangoing vessels. In the early twenties, when the

Volstead Act wrecked the American wine industry, Jake
and Clair bought an old winery in the Napa Valley, and
they had managed to survive Prohibition through the manufacture of sacramental wine, first for a handful of
Orthodox synagogues in San Francisco, and subsequently
for most of the synagogues in California and for a good
many of the Catholic parishes. This had brought them to
a modest prosperity, yet even with the repeal of Prohibition there was no great demand for wine. While Prohibition appeared to increase the national consumption of
hard liquor, wine drinking became only a memory—and
those who remembered now preferred the imported wines.

The winery, called Higate, lay in the Napa Valley a few
miles north of Oakville, nine hundred acres on the eastern
slope of the hills, and now, driving to the Levy home in
Sausalito, Sam Goldberg wondered, as he had so often in
the past, why Sarah Levy did not accept Jake's invitation
to live there, where there were three children, winery
workers, life, and excitement, instead of in the huge
Spanish Colonial house where she was utterly alone. As
she so often told him, she would not inflict herself on her
children. But what else were children for, Goldberg wondered. He had no children of his own. If he only had, how
quickly he would accept such an invitation!

He decided that today he would raise this question with
her, pointing out that for a vital woman of fifty-four
years to bury herself here was both self-destructive and
wasteful; but it was Sarah who brought up the subject of
Higate. Clair had telephoned just this morning, asking her
mother-in-law to drive up to the Napa Valley—if Goldberg were willing—and for both to spend the afternoon
and stay for dinner.

"In which case, Sam," Sarah said to him after she had
greeted him and kissed him, "you will be my date."

"Nonsense. You are too young to be having dates with
a man of sixty-six. Visits, that's one thing. Dates, no.
Damnit, Sarah, you're a healthy, beautiful woman—too
beautiful to waste away here doing nothing."

She smiled and took his arm. When she smiled, there
was a reflection on her drawn face of the woman he had
known twenty years before. Her pale yellow hair had
turned white, but her eyes were the same bright blue and
her figure had not changed. "I would always tell Martha,"

she said, "never to contradict a man who said she was beautiful. Of course, Martha was, wasn't she, Sam?"

"Very beautiful, yes."

"And I don't do nothing. I read. I knit. I tend my roses. I cook, sometimes."

"And you weep for Martha."

"Yes."

"Which is precisely what living alone here does to you. The past is over. You must—"

"Sam." She stopped him. "We won't talk about where I live or why. Will you drive me to Higate?"

"Of course."

In the car, Goldberg said, rather casually, "Would you like to guess who walked into my office day before yesterday?"

"No. I don't like to guess things. But I would like to know."

"Barbara."

"Barbara? Barbara who?"

"Barbara Lavette. Danny's daughter."

"No!"

"Yes. Yes, my dear Sarah."

"She just walked in? Unannounced?"

"Yes."

"Why? If you want to tell me?"

"I'm not sure I know why. She asked questions about what happened when Jean took over, but I'm not at all sure that's what brought her. I think she was reaching out."

"What is she like?" Sarah asked curiously. "It's strange, isn't it, Dan's daughter, and Danny was like a brother to Mark, and I think I saw her only once, when she was a little child."

"Splendid woman—tall, like Jean, looks a little like Jean—not as beautiful, but then, who is?"

"Indeed. She's twenty, isn't she?"

"Yes. Finished her second year at Sarah Lawrence College in the East. Now she's working."

"Where?"

"No wages. She's a volunteer at the Marine Workers' soup kitchen on Bryant Street."

"Barbara Lavette!"

"I thought that would get you," Goldberg said, smiling. "The world turns, doesn't it, Sarah?"

"It surely does."

Long, straight, narrow, a gentle fold between low green hills that only now and then become mountains, the Napa Valley is unique, even in a place like California, where there are a hundred thousand valleys and canyons; for of all the places where grapevines grow in America, only the name of Napa is absolutely synonymous with the word "wine." It is an old place only in terms of California, where nothing of European vintage is really old, and the first vines were planted there in 1840, by a man named George Yount. Yet, in the European tradition, most of the early wineries, established for the most part by German and Italian immigrants, were built of stone rather than wood, substantial stone buildings that very soon were covered over with broadleaf ivy, and if not actually ancient, they certainly gave the impression of being so. It was such a cluster of stone buildings that Jake Levy and his wife bought when he returned from service in World War I, and when they bought the place, it was little better than an antique and useless ruin.

Now, fourteen years later, the aspect of the place was quite different. The old buildings had been repaired and refurbished. The hillsides, abandoned during the first years of Prohibition, were now planted in gently curving and contoured rows of vines. Hedges and plantings graced the shapeless stone houses, and half an acre of garden was given over to the growing of table vegetables.

Goldberg turned off Highway 29 onto a dirt road that twisted over the hills to the stone-pillared iron gates of the winery. As he got out of the car and helped Sarah out, Jake, Clair, and their three children and two dogs came to meet them. Jake was a tall, heavyset man of thirty-five, his wife, a year younger, long-limbed, freckled, with a great head of orange-colored hair, a sunburned, good-looking woman indifferent to her good looks. The two boys, Adam, twelve, and Joshua, ten, were small, grinning replicas of their mother, carrot-topped and freckled, and Sally, the youngest, eight years old, had the pale eyes and flaxen hair of her grandmother.

With a touch of sadness and not without envy, Goldberg observed the warmth and excitement of the family as they greeted Sarah. He stood apart from the scramble of embraces, chattering children, and barking dogs. It was mundane and sentimental to see himself in relation to this, but he was a sentimental man. Then Clair noticed

how woebegone and forgotten he appeared, and she went
to him and took his arm and told him how delighted they
all were to see him.

"It's been years," she said. "You and mother are all
that's left to us of the old times."

"I wouldn't recognize the place. It reeks with prosperity."

"An illusion," Jake said. "Are you tired, either of you?"

"Not at all," Sarah replied.

"Why an illusion?" Goldberg asked.

"Because Americans have forgotten how to drink wine.
If we were making whiskey, we'd be rolling in money. All
the decent wine during Prohibition was smuggled in from
France, and only the rich could afford it. Now they don't
want our domestic wine."

"Which is as good or better than what they make in
Europe," Clair added.

"Well, sometimes. Look, let me give you a tour of the
place, Sam. I'll practice on you. Clair has a notion that we
should open the winery to the public on weekends and let
people taste our product and build up demand that way.
It might just work if we could convince the big wineries to
do it, but we're too small to make much difference. We're
going to have a valley meeting next week and propose it,
but who knows? Anyway, I'll practice on you and mother."

"I've seen it," Sarah said. "Take Sam. I'll help Clair
inside."

Jake led Goldberg off toward the stone winery buildings, the children trailing curiously. He pointed up at
the sloping hillsides. "There are our newest plantings.
Pinot Noir. Of course you might say that Zinfandel is
endemic to this valley and it's what we're famous for. But
I tasted Pinot Noir in France that was like the wine of
the gods, and Clair and I decided that we'd produce a wine
as good or better, and by golly, I think we have. You'll
taste it later. We started with five hundred vines, and now
we've got the best stand of Pinot Noir in the valley.
Come back at the end of the summer when the grapes are
ripe, and you'll have a treat, Sam. We don't irrigate up
there. Some of the growers do, but for my money, you
get a better grape if you make the vines fight for moisture.
If you irrigate, the vines are loaded with grapes, and for
your greed there's a poorer quality." Jake paused. Gold-

berg was regarding him in amazement. "What is it, Sam?" he asked.

"Your passion, sonny. I'm astonished."

"Why? Wine is a passionate thing. God Almighty, Sam, do you remember how we scrimped and starved and worked to have this place? It's my whole life. It's like I know every vine up there on that hillside by name and number and character."

Trudging alongside them, young Adam said, "He does, Mr. Goldberg."

"You've inoculated them," Goldberg observed dryly.

"Higate has. I sometimes try to think of what it means to grow up in a place like this and have Clair for a mother."

"You have a pretty damn good mother of your own."

"I'm not selling her short, Sam, only making a point. It's too hot to climb the hill and look at the vines. Come in here," he said, indicating the entrance to the largest of the stone buildings.

As he stepped out of the hot sun, the cool darkness blinded Goldberg at first, and he paused to let his eyes adjust and to breathe deeply of the cold, sour-smelling air.

"That's the smell," Jake said. "At first it's strange. Then it becomes a kind of perfume. What do you drink, Sam?"

"Scotch whiskey."

"Of course. How long is it since you tasted a really fine wine?"

"I suppose the last time Jill and I were in France. Nineteen twelve. I'm not a wine drinker, Jake."

"You will be. Careful here." Followed by his three children, who were apparently fascinated by the very fat, bespectacled man who ambled after their father, Jake led the way down a set of stone steps into a cavernous cellar. There were rows and rows of wine—in bottles, in small kegs, and in large barrels. The air was cool and damp and heady with the musty smell of wine.

"The aging room. Over there"—pointing to the big barrels—"the sacramental wine. That's our bread and butter, Sam, if you can think of it that way. That's how we started and survived during Prohibition, first with old Rabbi Blum's synagogues and then with the churches. Now we produce about twenty thousand barrels of sacramental wine a year, port and Malaga, we call it, and not a bad imitation of the real thing. It's good, decent wine, if you like sweet wine. I don't. We don't grow the grapes for this stuff. We buy them down in Fresno. You'd think, with an assured market for twenty thousand gallons, we'd make money."

"Do you?"

"Not a nickel. Oh, we did make money back in twenty-eight and twenty-nine, but this Depression knocked the bottom out of prices. We break even. Come back at the end of the summer, and you'll find twenty men working here and in the fields. We meet the payroll and we're satisfied."

He pointed to the racks of bottled wine. "That's the Pinot Noir, the love of my life. That is wine," he said slowly, almost reverently, Goldberg thought. "We do about a thousand gallons a year, and we lager it, age it six months to a year in the bottle, laying it that way with the cork down. The cork stays wet and the wine breathes and lives."

"Good heavens, it's become a religion with you."

"It tends to. Religion and wine have never been too far apart. That's how we pay our bills. Let me show you the rest of it—this is only the end product."

Jake led Goldberg from room to room, past the crushers, the fermenting vats, the storage tanks, and into the bottling plant.

"All this to make a glass of wine," Goldberg said wearily.

"This and more. Instinct and luck. Without that, you're doomed. Maybe we don't have the instinct, but we've had a lot of luck. Over here, Sam."

He led the way to the end of the bottling room, where half a dozen uncorked, labeled bottles stood. "Our tasting room," he explained. "We don't have a real one yet. We will someday. These are all the Pinot Noir. We test them as they age. Open them, and then let them breathe for a few hours." He poured two glasses of the dark red wine. "Try it."

Goldberg drank the wine slowly. The last wine he had tasted was from the bottle Gino had brought to the table in the restaurant as his gift to the diners. He remembered the raw, flat taste of it. This wine was like liquid velvet, dry, slightly nutty, with a gentle, haunting fragrance.

"I don't know much about wine," Goldberg said.

"Do you like it?"

"If I knew anything about wine, I'd say it's pretty damn wonderful."

"You bet your sweet patooties. That wine, Sam, is going to conquer the world one day."

Willis Mackenzie, chief trainer at the Menlo Circle Club, at Menlo Park on the Peninsula, was something of an expert in the mores and ordinary habits of the rich and the children of the rich—in particular as they related to horses. Horses, as Mackenzie saw it, could be grouped with liquor, gambling, and desultory sex; they were less an indulgence than an addiction, less an interest than a demanding status symbol, to the rich of San Francisco and the Peninsula what the automobile was to the upper middle class—and even more specifically so since the onset of the Depression.

To this, however, there were a few exceptions, people who loved horses passionately. Mackenzie, a tall, hard-faced man of forty-five years, separated such people from the others with a reluctant smile. He was a bitter man, who hated the people he served, who hated and resented the rich, and who desired and resented their well-kept, carefully groomed women. He put Barbara Lavette in the special category of those who loved and understood horses, and on this day, when she informed him that she wished to sell Sandy, her seven-year-old chestnut mare, he looked at her thoughtfully and then suspiciously asked her why.

"I have my reasons, Mac."

"Well, she's a damn good horse, a good bloodline on both sides. You got the papers?" he asked, wondering meanwhile how much he could pick up on the deal. A local deal was a problem. If he sold her outside the county, he could possibly pick up a few hundred.

"Right here," Barbara replied, taking them out of her purse.

"I didn't mean right now. You know there's an auction in August."

"I don't want to wait. I want to sell her now."

"Well," he said slowly, "I got a lady at Flintridge in Pasadena. She's looking for a good gentle mare."

"That would take time, wouldn't it?"

"A week or so. She'd want to see the horse."

"No. I want to sell her today."

"Well—well, now there's something, Miss Lavette. You

don't just sell a horse like you sell a pair of pants. You got to find a buyer and you got to talk him around to it. You got to give him a run on the beast. No one buys a pig in the poke."

"Sandy's not a pig in the poke. I know you buy horses sometimes, Mac. What will you give me for Sandy?"

"You want to sell her to me?"

"I want to sell her today."

Mackenzie stared at her thoughtfully for a long moment. They were standing next to her car, a 1933 Ford station wagon, at the edge of the dirt road that led to the stables. Mackenzie looked at the car, ran a hand over the fender, and asked her, "What happened to your Buick?"

It was none of his damn business, Barbara thought. He was moving in. The careful wall of separation had collapsed. He had decided that she was in trouble, and he was breaking ground.

"Do you want to buy Sandy?" she said. She had no intention of talking about the car; there would be trouble enough with the car thing when her mother returned. The Buick convertible had been a gift from her mother on her eighteenth birthday, but it was nothing she could drive to the soup kitchen on Bryant Street, no way to explain a car like that, and anyway, the luggage compartment was too small for her purposes. She had sold it and bought the Ford station wagon.

"Let's go over to the barn and have a look at her."

"No. I don't want to see Sandy again. Will you buy her?"

"I'm just the trainer here, Miss Lavette. I ain't got the kind of money you find in the club. I suppose I could buy her." He rubbed his chin and thought about it. "I'll give you four hundred for her."

"Oh, no. You must be kidding. The saddle alone cost a hundred and fifty."

"Throwing the saddle in?"

"Sandy's worth a thousand. You know that."

He shook his head. "That's too rich for my blood. Throw in the saddle, and I'll give you five hundred."

"Why, Mac? You know what Sandy's worth."

"I told you, I'm just the trainer. You want to wait a week or two, this lady from Flintridge might give you seven hundred. Wait for the auction, maybe you'll get that much, maybe more."

"Will you pay me cash? Today?"

"I'll pay you cash," he said.

Barbara drove north from Menlo Park, tears running
down her cheeks and five hundred dollars in her purse. "I
will not weep over a horse," she told herself. "I will
not, I will not." Or was she weeping for herself and out
of her own fear? After all, she had been nine months without Sandy, and giving very little thought to the animal, if
the truth be told. It was the act of selling her, and selling
her to that miserable Mackenzie, that chilled her—even
more than the act of selling her car, her emerald pin, and
her gold bracelet. In time they would all return, her
mother, John Whittier, and her brother Tom. Her mother
noticed everything. She would come directly to the point.
"Why, Barbara, did you sell that beautiful Buick roadster
and buy that wretched Ford?" The fact that it was a very
special and splendid birthday gift made the surreptitious
sale even more heinous. "And where is your bracelet? And
what else have you sold? And what kind of trouble are
you in?" Barbara was a poor liar and badly versed in the
art. She would simply tell the truth, and then whatever
might happen would happen.

She told herself that she had done nothing wrong. She
had acted out of love and compassion. Or had she? Or was
the action taken out of loathing for her own way of life
and everything that had surrounded her? If so, it was a
very sudden loathing. A few months ago she had been a
reasonably content college student. Then she had returned
to a home that wasn't hers, yet now she wondered whether
even the house on Russian Hill had ever been hers in any
real sense. Or is any home of the parents the home of the
child? Now she was pitying herself, and that sort of thing
simply disgusted her. Her mother's friends pitied themselves; she could remember overhearing their conversa-
tions, recalling her own annoyance at the wives of
millionaires who pitied themselves in the America of the
nineteen thirties.

She hadn't gone to Bryant Street by accident. She loved
the waterfront, the Embarcadero, the docks, the fishing
boats, the big steamers, the freighters, the great luxury
liners. It was all part of the mythology of her strange
childhood, of the father she had never really known. This
had been his place, where he started as a hand on his own

father's fishing boat, out of which he built his empire of wealth and ships. And then he left it, abandoned it; and not comprehending that, Barbara made a quixotic act of nobility out of it. To have and surrender, to find something real, to sacrifice meaningfully—all this raced around inside her tinged with romantic dreams, novels she had read, discussions with her friends at college, and piled childishly into a confusion and despair at odds with her basically cheerful nature.

And then one day she stood outside the soup kitchen on Bryant Street, just stood there and watched as the striking longshoremen lined up to be fed. She had a vivid imagination, and her romantic notion of the working class had been shaped mainly by the novels of Jack London and Upton Sinclair. All of which led to her meeting Dominick Salone.

He had paused next to her and said, "Lady, is something wrong?"

He was her own height, skinny, the dark flesh of his face drawn tightly over the bones, deepset, dark intense eyes, a small nose, a head of black, unruly hair, and, curiously in one so young, a nest of wrinkles at either end of his wide mouth. He couldn't have been more than twenty-three or twenty-four. He wore blue jeans and a stained green woolen windbreaker over a T-shirt.

She just stared at him.

"Because you're crying, lady."

"I am not."

"Sure as hell you are. We got sympathizers, lady, but mostly they don't cry."

"I'm not crying."

"O.K., O.K." He shrugged and turned away.

Barbara touched her cheeks. They were wet. Then she called after him. "Mister!"

When he turned around, she was wiping her face with a handkerchief. He stood there, staring at her, and then she walked over to him.

"Could I ask you a question, mister?" she asked uneasily.

"My name's Nick. Nick Salone. Don't call me mister."

She was taken totally aback by his reply. She stood silent for a moment or two, and he said, "Well?"

"My name's Bobby."

"All right, Bobby, ask."

"What?"

"You said you wanted to ask me a question."

She nodded at the kitchen. "How do you run it? I mean, where does the food come from?"

"What's with you, sister? You work for a newspaper or something?"

"You're suspicious of me."

"You're damn right. I'm suspicious of anyone who looks like you."

"What do you mean? How do I look?"

"Oh, Christ," he said. "Let it go. You want to know where the food comes from? It used to come from the union funds, but that's gone. Washed out, used up. So it comes from wherever we can beg, borrow, or steal it."

"Oh." She said, almost primly, "Would it be all right if I brought you some food—as a contribution? I wouldn't be hurting anyone's feelings?"

"Hurting our feelings?"

"I don't know about these things," she said lamely.

"No, you wouldn't be hurting nobody's feelings."

"Where would I bring it?"

He pointed to an alley alongside the storefront. "That leads back to the kitchen. Just bring it to the kitchen."

That was how it began. Walking the few blocks to a grocery store, it occurred to Barbara that here she was, in the twenty-first year of her life, yet never before had she entered a food store to buy anything more than a bag of pretzels, or cookies, or sausage for one of their late-night feasts in the dormitory back at school. She had never gone out to buy food as food, food to feed people who were hungry. Now she had about twelve dollars in her purse, and she had not the faintest notion of how much food one could buy for twelve dollars.

The man behind the counter in the small grocery store had a walrus mustache and wet blue eyes. It was half an hour past noon, and there were no other customers in the store. The proprietor watched her, appraising her dubiously. Finally, when she continued to stand there without speaking, he said, "We don't sell no cigarettes, miss."

"I don't want cigarettes." She had read somewhere that beans possess a fine balance of nourishment, and in any case, beans and working people made some connection in her mind. "How much are beans?" she asked.

"Beans?"

"Yes, beans."

"What kind of beans? I got lima beans, navy beans, pea beans, kidney beans, Mexican beans—what kind?"

"I don't know," she said unhappily.

"You ever cooked beans?"

"No."

He was studying her suspiciously. They were all suspicious of her. She acted wrong, she looked wrong, she dressed wrong; and she was becoming acutely aware of this. Nevertheless, she pursued her course doggedly.

"If you were to cook beans, what would you cook?"

"I don't give cooking lessons."

"What are navy beans?" she asked desperately.

He reached down and held up a handful. "These."

"All right. Give me twelve dollars' worth."

He stared at her.

"What's wrong?" she asked.

"Lady, for twelve dollars you can buy a hundred-pound sack."

"I can?"

"That's right."

"Then give me ten pounds." Something recognizable caught her eyes. "How much is that salami?" she asked, pointing to where a row of them hung behind the counter.

"Twenty cents a pound. Each link is five pounds."

Loaded down with all the food she could carry, she made her way back to the soup kitchen on Bryant Street, went into the alley and through the open kitchen door, where she set down the food, and fled. After that, two days passed before she could gather sufficient courage to return. Meanwhile, she informed herself. She went down to the kitchen of the house on Pacific Heights and addressed herself to Mrs. Britsky, the Polish cook who presided over the place, asking her where most of the food money was spent—with the excuse that she was preparing a paper for her return to school.

"Meat, meat," Mrs. Britsky replied emphatically. "There's a Depression, but that don't mean they give it away. Always, your mama wants French style. Entrecote, fifty cents a pound; saddle of lamb, fifty-five cents; leg of lamb, forty-nine cents. You can die from such prices."

"But isn't there cheaper meat?"

"Cheaper meat for the Whittiers, go on!"

"Not for them. Just for my information. What would a poor family do? What would they buy?"

"You can buy beef heart for ten cents a pound, good meat if you cook it right, chuck for twenty-five cents, pork for thirty cents, breast of lamb for twelve cents."

"Where do you buy it?"

"Darling, in a butcher shop, where else?"

Afterward, Barbara wondered whether any of it would have happened had she not been alone in the big house, with her mother and John Whittier and Tom away in the East. Partly, it was a game that had possessed and intrigued her, and that she found so much more exciting than the parties she was invited to and the dates with boring, empty-headed young men; and in another part it was her own vendetta against John Whittier, who owned half the cargo ships that made San Francisco their home port; and in still another part it was her quick, romantic sense of compassion and pity.

For her return to the soup kitchen, she bought a cheap, imitation leather purse and wore an old sweater, a plaid skirt, and brown loafers. She brought twenty pounds of soup meat. She knew that she was playing a game and that it was a little girl game, that she had hidden herself behind a sort of Halloweeen mask, but that knowledge did not make the game less exciting. Dominick Salone was there that time, sitting on a fruit box and peeling potatoes, and after his initial surprise at seeing her, he grinned. The kitchen was a makeshift affair at the back of the store, and the cooking was done on an old coal stove. There was one other woman in the place, a stout Mexican woman whose name was Irma, and four men besides Salone, all of them longshoremen. They made a big fuss over the meat, and Salone introduced Barbara to the others. That was when she told them her name was Winter. She had also invented her own cover story, that she was a bookkeeper in the big L & L Department Store, and that she worked the four-to-twelve-midnight shift, closing the books for the day's sales. The L & L store on Market Street had been founded by her father, Dan Lavette, and his partner, Marcus Levy, and she had at least a vague knowledge of its operation. The job, as she invented it, accounted for her free time during the day, and she explained the money she spent for food as money collected from workers at the store.

That day she offered to help Dominick peel potatoes, and afterward she shared the beef stew that fed the striking longshoremen. That was the beginning.

It was a beginning threaded through with illusions. One illusion concerned the nobility of the longshoremen. She invested them with qualities that she felt she had found in her father, uprightness, quietude of suffering, morality. Another illusion concerned Dominick Salone, again as a variant of her father, who had started as a fisherman and had married a daughter of the Seldons of Nob Hill. Still another illusion concerned what she felt was a cloak of invisibility that she had thrown about herself, making the game of being another person with another life and background all the more enticing. The relationship with Salone had gone no further than their exchanges in the kitchen and then one day he walked with her down to the docks at the end of Townsend Street and pointed out Harry Bridges to her. Bridges, leading the strike, was Salone's hero, not a "phony," not "some lousy smart aleck" making a career out of the labor movement, but a plain longshoreman like himself. "The best goddamn man I ever knew in my life," Salone said. "There's nobody else like Limo, nobody."

"Why do you call him Limo?" Barbara asked.

"He's a limey, from Australia."

Looking at Bridges, Barbara realized how much like Dominick Salone he was, skinny, the same height, a narrow hatchet face, large pointed nose, dark hair that was combed flat over his head, held tight in the wind by Vaseline— contrasting both of them with the boys she knew in what was still called in the city the "Nob Hill set," the tall, well-fleshed, well-fed, athletic young men who kept horses at Menlo Park and sailed their boats on San Francisco Bay.

"You think a lot of Bridges, don't you?"

"I told you—the best man I ever knew."

They walked along in a world that was only a few miles from her home, yet another world entirely, looking at ships that her stepfather and her mother owned, ships tied to the docks and walled off by the lines of bitter-faced pickets. Salone talked slowly, throwing out the words in bits and pieces, sometimes glancing at her, but making no move toward her, no advances, not even taking her hand.

As for what she felt about him, if anything at all

beyond the curiosity his strangeness and difference aroused
in her, Barbara simply did not know. And now, weeks
later, driving north from Menlo Park after she had sold
her horse and wept for the horse and for herself, she still
knew no more of the reality of this thing into which she
had plunged. She remembered Oscar Wild's story "The
Happy Prince," about the gold- and jewel-encrusted prince
whose statue loomed high over some European city, and
the sparrow who brought the prince stories of poverty and
suffering. Each time, the prince surrendered a bit of gold or
a jewel to be sold to ease the misery of the poor—until
finally only the leaden core of the statue remained. She
made the comparison with herself, and then was wise
enough and sane enough to burst into laughter at her own
sentimentality.

"What a dreadful, impossible ass I am!" she said aloud.
"I don't blame mother for losing patience with me."

She was honest enough with herself to recognize that
in selling everything of value she owned—jewels, trinkets,
car, and now the horse—she had experienced more satisfaction and plain excitement than ever before in her life.
It was really a very easy game. She had never known
hunger, never wanted for money to exist, and each night
she went home to the great barn of a mansion on Pacific
Heights.

At the age of seventeen, Joseph Lavette was six feet and
one inch in height and weighed one hundred and eighty
pounds. The coach of the football team at University
High in Westwood in Los Angeles singled him out and
pressed him to try for the team. Joseph refused. He was
a gentle, soft-spoken boy, introverted and not very physical,
in spite of his large, heavily muscled frame. The coach,
loath to relinquish what he considered a prime physical
specimen, went into a lecture on the natural football
abilities of the American Indian. It was an understandable
error. With his black, slightly Oriental eyes, his straight
black hair, and his brown skin, Joe might well have been
taken for an Indian; and Lavette, a French-Italian name,
might well have been something out of the Northwest.

"I'm not an Indian," he said. "I'm Chinese. It doesn't
work the same way. We make rotten football players.
Anyway, I just haven't got the time."

"With a name like Lavette?" the coach snorted.

"My father is Italian. My mother is Chinese."

The time he hoarded so preciously was spent with books and with his grandfather, Feng Wo. He was a voracious reader, and he consumed everything he could get his hands on, almost without discrimination. As for his grandfather, two years before this, Feng Wo had decided that although he himself would live out his life on this land of the barbarian, it by no means meant that his grandson must of necessity grow up as a barbarian. Whereupon he raised the subject quite formally and very politely at the family dinner table, stating that if Mr. Lavette agreed, he would like to teach his grandson, Joseph, to read, write, and to speak that most ancient and commendable of all languages, called Mandarin. Being Chinese, Feng Wo did not ask for the opinion or consent of either May Ling, Joseph's mother, or Joseph himself.

"Chinese! Are you kidding?" Dan said. "In the twenty-five years since you first came to work for me, I never learned more than ten words of Chinese, and that includes being married to May Ling. Nobody can learn Chinese."

"Except five or six hundred million Chinese," May Ling said sweetly. "And that includes myself. Father taught me Mandarin, and I picked up enough Cantonese and Shanghainese to get along in that as well. So *sa qua trey bun.*"

"What the devil does that mean?"

"Best left unsaid," Feng Wo told him. "My daughter has many bad habits."

"Why don't we ask Joe how he feels about it?" Dan said.

"I like the idea," Joe said.

"Oh, not so quickly," May Ling put in. "You really don't know what you're getting into, Joe. If father's going to teach you to read and write, it means learning about five thousand ideographs—pictures, symbols. It's picture writing, you know. Not like our alphabet at all."

"Then that does it," Dan said. He had never completed high school himself. Most of what education he possessed had come from May Ling, out of books she had persuaded him to read and out of the gentle flow of her knowledge that he had absorbed almost without knowing it. Nevertheless, he was fanatically eager for his son to be educated, well educated. The drive to do what you do better than anyone else was still present in him. "Where's

his schoolwork? Where is anything else? And who is he
going to talk Chinese to?"

"To me," May Ling said gently. "To my mother and
father—and who knows who else? Why don't we let him
decide?"

"I could try it," Joe muttered uncertainly.

A year later, he was able to write a two-page letter to
Barbara at Sarah Lawrence, which she exhibited proudly
to her friends and which was translated for her, not by any
member of the faculty, but by a Chinese laundryman in
Yonkers.

Now, early in June of 1934, Joseph Lavette came home
and informed his mother and father that he had been
chosen to give the valedictory address at the commence-
ment exercises of his high school. Dan, who was still in his
work clothes, who had picked up May Ling at the library
only a few minutes before, listened to his son in silence,
nodded, and then went up the stairs to his room. Joseph
stared at his mother.

"Is he angry at me? Isn't he pleased?"

"Of course he's pleased." She threw her arms around
Joseph and kissed him. "He's as pleased and proud as I am.
It's a wonderful thing."

"Then why—?"

"Give it a little time, Joe. He's a strange man. I think
this is the most wonderful thing that ever happened to him,
but he can't cope with it."

"Why? I didn't ask for it, but God, I wanted to please
him. I thought he'd be excited—"

"Don't say any more. Not now. One day we'll talk about
your father. He was too long away from you. The Chinese
have an old saying that unless a man is to be doomed,
sooner or later he must turn to himself and ask the
question of why he exists. And find the answer. Your
father tries, desperately. He's not like any other man I ever
knew. Do you understand me?"

"I don't think so."

May Ling went upstairs to the bedroom. Dan was
standing in front of the window, looking out.

"Well, Danny?"

He turned to her. "I hurt him, didn't I?"

"He'll understand."

"Do you?"

"Perhaps."

"I didn't know what to say. There was nothing I could put into words."

"It's not so astonishing, Danny. He's a bright boy, and he worked hard. He's well liked. But whatever he does, he feels it falls short of what you expect from him."

"My God, does he feel that?"

"I think so."

"He's my whole world," Dan said.

"He shouldn't be," May Ling said, a note of asperity in her voice. "You're only forty-five years old. How can he be your whole world? He has his own life to live, and so have you. Did he ever tell you what he wants to do? Did you ever talk about it? Did you ever really sit down and talk to him?"

"What does he want to do?"

"He wants to be a doctor. He doesn't think we can afford it."

"We damn well can!"

"Then why not start by telling him that?"

Leona Asquith, Jean's aunt, was seventy-two years old. She was a widowed lady of moderate wealth—moderate if one excluded her house on Beacon Hill, where the eighteenth-century and nineteenth-century furniture and paintings were both authentic and priceless. Her living room held an unfinished Athenaeum Washington, which some experts held to be prior to the Stuart Washington in the Boston museum, and in her library there were two authenticated Vandykes. Jean, who had already gained a national reputation as a sponsor and patroness of the Ashcan School of American painting, and who was one of the first eager buyers of John Sloan, Kuniyoshi, Reginald Marsh, George Biddle, and so many others, had no real interest in acquiring early American paintings for herself, but she did dream of a coup whereby she could bring the Asquith collection to a San Francisco art museum. This was one of the reasons she would go out of her way to spend time in Boston with a woman who regarded California as only slightly less barbaric than a wilderness to the south known as Texas.

Her husband, John Whittier, on the other hand, loved Boston, at least the circle in Boston in which they moved, because its rigidity and folkways gave him a sense of comfort and belonging. At dinner in the Asquith house, the night before his departure for San Francisco, he expressed this and assured Mrs. Asquith that only the circumstances of the waterfront strike could make him cut short his visit. Jean and Tom were to stay for another week, much to Tom's annoyance.

"Oh, no," was his first reaction when she told him that she expected him to remain with her in Boston, to be her escort, and to be very charming to his Aunt Leona. "I am bored. I am fed up to the ears. Mother, I've done four years at Princeton. I've paid my dues. This is the dullest, dreariest place on earth."

Jean looked at him thoughtfully. He was tall, slender, blue eyes under straight brows, a shock of straight brown hair that he parted on one side, a wide mouth, and a long, thin nose—very good-looking in a lackadaisical manner, almost indolent. There was apparently nothing in him of Dan Lavette, nothing of many generations of Italian fishermen, and Jean couldn't decide whether that pleased or displeased her.

"This is the place of your ancestors. I should think you'd be curious. I've always loved Boston."

"I'm not curious."

"And you haven't paid your dues—not quite."

"Oh?"

"It cost us almost three thousand dollars—hospital bills, five hundred to the girl to keep her quiet, and bribing a district attorney. Altogether, quite disgusting, but otherwise you would not have graduated."

"My God, did John tell you?"

"Of course he did. I saw no reason why he should pay the costs."

"It was the one rotten scrape I got into. I admit I had too much to drink, and it happened. Thats all. Someday I'll pay back the money."

"I'm sure you will," Jean said gently. "Meanwhile, a few weeks in Boston is not too much penance. You'll still have most of the summer before you go into the bank."

"Then that's decided, that I go into the bank? God damn it, don't I have one thing to say about it?"

"Yes. Certainly. What would you like to do with your life?"

"Do I have to do something with it right this minute? Can't I have a few months to think about it? You and John may imagine that I just bummed away my years at

Princeton, and I know all the smart-alecky wisecracks
about the eating clubs, but if you look at my marks, you'll
see that I didn't do half bad. I didn't spend four years
getting drunk."

"I know that, and I did look at your marks. Many
times."

"I just don't see myself sitting in a bank eight hours a
day."

"Tommy," Jean said, "one day, not too many years
from now, you and your sister, Barbara, are going to be
very rich. The stock that my father left in trust for you
will amount to many millions. In effect, the two of you
own the Seldon Bank, one of the largest financial in-
stitutions in America. You know that. It's not just money.
Power goes with it, and some respect for the power and
some knowledge of how to use it. That's all I mean. Take
the rest of the summer to decide. I'm not pressing you.
But meanhile you can be very helpful."

"All right, I'll stick it out. And do what?"

"Aside from being my escort and enduring some dinner parties and a few visits to the Boston Museum of Fine
Arts, I would like you to be very charming and delightful
to your Aunt Leona. We're her closest relatives, and I
want her collection of paintings. I intend to turn the house
on Russian Hill into an art museum. I'm not sure that I
want her paintings there. My own taste runs to other
things. But they're invaluable, and having them would give
me tremendous leverage."

Tom shook his head. "I don't understand that. If you
don't like them—"

"I do like them. They're splendid. But I want to found
a museum of modern art. I could give these to some
established museum and trade off, and at the same time
there would be a Seldon Gallery of these paintings. There
are ways to do it. I'm tired of hearing about the Crockers.
The name of Seldon is just as important."

"Our name's Lavette, mother—except that yours is
Whittier now."

"And we're still Seldons. I'm not asking any great task
of you. Take Aunt Leona to lunch at the Copley Plaza.
Be pleasant. That's all I'm asking."

"I suppose I can do that."

"I suppose you can."

Aunt Leona Asquith was delighted with the invitation.

She came downstairs, where her great-nephew was waiting, wearing a dress of beige crêpe de Chine with white satin cording, a short cape of summer ermine draped over her arm against a possible chill, and a broad-brimmed, cream-colored Panama hat. Tom, like most men of his age, accepted older women without actually seeing them. Now, suddenly, he realized that his Aunt Leona had a very trim figure for her seventy-two years, and that once she must have been an exceptionally attractive woman.

"Dear boy," she said, once they were seated in the back of her chauffeur-driven Packard, "this is really very considerate of you. Oh, I know that your mother black-mailed you into it. Nevertheless, you are the most hand-some escort I have had in years. Your mother, like so many modern women, has found a substitute for sex. By the way, have you read Havelock Ellis?"

Bewildered, Tom shook his head. "No, I'm afraid not."

"A pity. You must. What was I saying? Yes, a substitute for sex. What do you think of John Whittier?"

"Mother seems to like him. She married him."

"He's a parody of what he appears to think Boston society is all about. Of course, he hasn't the faintest notion of what Boston is. Your great-great-grandfather, my grand-father, was in the rum trade with Jamaica. It was better than the slave trade, and it permitted his brother to be both wealthy and Abolitionist, and grandfather was a pillar of the Congregational church. Nevertheless, he had a black mistress in Jamaica, and according to the family mythol-ogy, he birthed five black children there—aside from his proper family here in Boston. By the way, do you ever see your father?"

Confused, taken aback, Tom replied that he had not seen Dan Lavette since the divorce.

"Why?" his aunt asked pointedly.

"I don't know," Tom said uncertainly. "He was never very close to me."

"Do you like him?"

"I don't know. Barbara does. She saw him last year. He's living in Los Angeles—"

"Yes, with his Chinese mistress, whom he married. Good heavens, you talk as if you were John Whittier's son. I met Dan Lavette once. Don't mumble."

At the Copley Plaza, in the dining room, the headwaiter greeted Leona Asquith by name and kissed her hand. At the table, she said to Tom, "Do the ordering, Thomas. I think it ought to be broiled lobster for both of us. Whatever elements of civilization have crept into that West Coast of yours, lobster is something they do not have. We'll have a Chardonnay to go with it." She was slightly deaf, and like so many slightly deaf people, tended to make her already high-pitched voice even more strident. It embarrassed Tom to have her conversation overheard by the tables around them.

"A substitute for sex, did I say that? Yes. She does it with those wretched pictures she collects, and being president of a bank. Thank heavens that's over. And now she wants my collection, and you are to be very charming to me."

"Oh, no, no. Not at all," Tom protested, dropping his voice as if pleading with her to drop hers.

"Don't mumble, Thomas. It's quite transparent, but then, people are transparent, all of us, although we all pretend to ourselves that we are well hidden. So you're trapped here and bored to tears."

"No. I'm not bored, Aunt Leona." Which was very much the truth. At the moment, he was nervous and bewildered, but not bored.

"You need a girl," she said flatly.

He stared at her.

"Well, you do like women, don't you?"

"Yes. Certainly."

"How long will you be here now?"

"Another week or so, I think."

"That's not time enough for anything. Do you want a drink?"

"I think so."

"You do mumble so. Order a martini for each of us. A week, you said. Well, I know a very respectable lady who runs a bawdy house. I think I'll send you there."

"Oh no," he said to himself. "I am not hearing this. It's not happening."

"Yes," she said. "That's decided. It's what you need, and you'll stop looking so wretchedly sour. Now I want you to tell me about this John Whittier your mother married. Tell me all about him."

Barbara carefully backed her Ford station wagon into the alley on Bryant Street, then went into the kitchen and asked for help to unload. It was eleven o'clock in the morning on the third day of July in 1934, and already the makeshift stove was smoking hot, piled with pots of stew to feed anywhere from two hundred to five hundred men. The kitchen was dirty, steaming, the garbage cans overflowing and spilling onto the floor, with two long-shoremen washing tin cups and bowls and arguing about a third man who was, according to their definition, either a fink or a pimp. Dominick and another longshoreman by the name of Franco Guzie were slicing stale, three-day-old bread. Volunteers from the bakery workers' union bought the unsold bread, paying for it out of union funds, and delivered it twice a week to the various soup kitchens the maritime strikers had set up. Sometimes it amounted to several hundred loaves, sometimes only a few dozen.

Salone looked up as Barbara came into the kitchen. Guzie shouted for a little quiet. "What have you got, Bobby?" Dominick asked her.

She was looking at the garbage. "Don't you ever clean this place?"

"It gets done," he said. "Is that what you come for—to tell us the place stinks?"

"No. I have a load outside."

"Come on, Franco," Dominick said.

She led the two of them out to the station wagon. "Jesus Christ," Guzie whispered. "What the hell have you got there?"

"I was down on the Peninsula, so I picked it up off the roadside stands," Barbara said proudly. "A lot cheaper there than here. Two hundred pounds of potatoes, two hundred pounds of onions, two bushels of cabbage, two crates of carrots, a hundred pounds of squash, and five hams. I got the hams at Tulip Farm in Belmont. They wanted twenty-five cents a pound, and I got them down to twenty. What do you think of that?" She was pleased with herself, as eager for praise as she had been as a child doing something noteworthy and deserving.

"What do we do with smoked ham?" Dominick said sourly. "You can't put it in stew."

"Who says you can't?" Guzie demanded. "Gives the stew a flavor. God damn it, Bobby, this is a bonanza. You're some lady, kid, you're some lady. I wish we had ten like you, ten like you. Don't pay no attention to this punk."

After they had carried the food inside, Barbara parked her car. Then she came back to the kitchen, put on an apron, and began to clean up. She hated this kind of work, yet she took a perverse satisfaction in forcing herself to do it. Dominick had finished slicing the bread. He stood watching her as she swept the garbage together and stuffed it into the cans. The smell made her gag.

"Take the cans out of here," she said to him. "This shouldn't be here with the cooking. You know that."

"Now you're running the joint."

"What? Oh, don't be an ass, Nick."

" 'Don't be an ass.' That's real classy talk. I'm sorry, duchess. I beg your pardon."

"Knock it off," Guzie said, and he picked up the can and carried it out.

Fat Irma Montessa, the acknowledged boss of the kitchen, shouted at Barbara, "Bobby, you forget about the cleaning, because with these pigs here, you can't keep nothing clean. The feeders are here, and we got to start serving. You want to help me?"

At the front of the store, standing behind the table next to Irma who was ladling the stew into tin bowls, passing out the bowls to the line of strikers and adding bread and chili pepper for those who wanted it, Barbara said to her,

"What's come over Dominick?"

"Men turn lousy, sweetie. Up and down. It's in their nature. Too much strike."

"It's not like him."

"Sure it is. What do you expect from a guinea longshoreman?"

Barbara had never heard the expression before. She finished serving the meal. She had been up at six that morning to drive down to Belmont for the food, and by now the sour smell of the stew filled her with nausea, so she went out into the alley for a breath of fresh air. Dominick was there, puffing on a cigarette.

"You're in a lovely mood today," she said to him.

"Yeah."

"I didn't mean to call you an ass. I lost my temper."

"Who the hell are you?" he asked angrily.

"Who are you?"

"I'm a guinea longshoreman, name of Dominick Salone."

"That's the second time today I heard that word," Barbara said. "What does it mean?"

"What word?"

"Guinea."

"Oh, Jesus Christ! You don't know what a guinea is, you don't know what a fink is, you don't know what a goon is. You give me a load of horseshit about working at L and L and collecting money, and you drive a car that nobody makes eighteen a week could afford, and you talk the way some pisspot society dame talks. You spend the day here and you tell me then you go out and put in an eight-hour shift at the store. That's bullshit, and you know it."

"What if it is?" Barbara said tiredly.

"I just don't like to be conned."

"What do you think I am? Some kind of labor spy?"

He threw away the cigarette and grinned. "If you are, they're scraping the bottom of the barrel."

"Thank you."

"I didn't mean it that way."

"I know you didn't. Look, Nick, nobody else here worries about who I am. Nobody else objects to my buying food, and nobody else cares where the money comes from. Nobody even objects to the way I speak."

"Yeah."

"So?"

"So I'm crazy. Since the first time I seen you, I can't think of nothing else. Ah, shit!"

"That's expressive."

"I'm sorry. God damn it, you're not like any dame I ever knew. I didn't need this. You come in here with your heart bleeding, and you do your lady bountiful act, and then back to wherever the hell you come from—"

"Come on, Nick."

"Don't patronize me!" He turned on his heel and stalked back into the kitchen.

She started to follow him, then stopped herself and shook her head, and she stood there staring at the cracked asphalt of the alleyway. He was not playing a game. No one there was playing a game. "And I'm not," she pleaded to herself; but then, had she nothing to do with the fact that he was in love with her? A skinny, undernourished, uneducated Italian longshoreman had fallen in love with her. A brief, romantic flow of imagery flashed into her mind—her father's conquest of her mother, the fishing boat captain from the wharf making his way up Nob Hill —and then she shivered and threw it off. The thought— which she had never actually entertained before—of being trapped down here in this bleak, dreary hopeless abyss of workingmen was not pleasant. She felt no more for Dominick Salone than she felt for Franco Guzie or any of the other longshoremen. He interested and intrigued her, and she had been direct and open with him. At first, the long-shoremen had frightened her; they were different, they spoke another language, they wore old clothes, and very often they were rank with body odor. But then, after only a few days of working around the kitchen, she discovered that they were amazingly correct in their behavior toward her. They always apologized for strong language used in her presence, they forbore any of the sexual in-nuendoes that were commonplace among the set of her own class, and all in all, they treated her with respect. It had simply not occurred to her that Dominick or any of the others might become emotionally involved with her.

She stood there in the alley for a few more minutes, trying to decide whether to go back into the kitchen and talk to Dominick again. Then she decided that it was best to leave it alone at this point, and she walked to where she had parked her car, got into it, and drove back to the Whittier house on Pacific Heights. She was tired; she would spend the afternoon curled up in a chair reading a book.

Knox, the butler, opening the door for her, said, "Mr. Whittier would like to see you, Miss Lavette."

"Oh? When did he get back?"

"Just about an hour ago."

Barbara went into the breakfast room. John Whittier was sitting at the table, dining on bacon and eggs and reading a newspaper. He rose as she entered and kissed her perfunctorily on the cheek.

"Sit down, Barbara. Will you have some lunch?"

"I'll have coffee," she said.

"Help yourself. There's a pot on the teacart there. I thought we'd have a chat, just the two of us. I never subscribed to the myth that servants don't have ears. They damn well do, and big mouths also."

"Did you have a good trip?" Barbara asked, bringing her coffee back to the table.

"Good enough. The wretched train takes forever."

"And Tom and mother—are they well?"

"Well enough when I left them. Your mother is determined to work your Aunt Leona for those dreary pictures that adorn her house. Did you know about her scheme to turn Russian Hill into a museum?"

"She mentioned something about it in a letter."

Her conversation was listless. Whittier looked at her thoughtfully. "Are you well, Barbara?"

"Perfectly well. Just a little tired. I thought I'd spend the afternoon with a book."

"Well, that will be a change."

She looked at him, wondering what was coming now.

"Apparently it's the first afternoon you decided to spend at home."

"What does that mean?"

"According to Knox, you've been out each morning and back each night since we've been gone."

"Really. Is it part of Knox's job to spy on me?"

"He's the butler. It's his job to know what goes on in this house."

"Then you have a faithful servant. That should please you, John."

"I don't think that tone is called for, Barbara."

"And I don't think I have to account for my time," she said coldly. "Thank you for the coffee." She rose and started to leave.

"One moment, Barbara." She turned to him, trying to control herself, trying to repress the loathing she felt for him. "What happened to your car?" he asked.

"Why don't you ask Knox?"

"I did. He says that your Buick disappeared, and that now you're driving an old Ford station wagon."

"Then you have your answer. Now I'm driving an old Ford station wagon." With that, she grabbed her purse and rushed out of the room, through the house, and out the front door. The station wagon was still parked in the driveway, where she had left it. She got into the car and suddenly burst into tears. She cried for a while. Then she felt better, relieved of what had been pent up inside her. She dried her eyes, turned the ignition key, and started the car. As she left the driveway, she saw in her rearview mirror that Knox was standing at the door, watching her.

She had no destination in mind, no thought except a

compelling desire never to return to John Whittier's home. She drove through the park, and she found herself on 19th Avenue, heading south.

Joe Lavette was curled up on his bed, reading, when Dan came into his room and sat down at the foot of the bed. He had rehearsed what he was going to say several times, and now he came directly to the point. "That day," he began, "when you came home and told us that you had been made valedictorian of your class—that day something happened inside me. I can't explain it, and I can't explain to you why I couldn't say anything. I can only say to you that I was so damn proud that if I had stayed there or tried to talk about it, I would have just gone to pieces, and that's nothing that I waned you or your mother to see. I couldn't explain that to you, and I couldn't explain it to your mother, either. I've led a strange life, Joe. You know about that. Did you ever wonder why I work as a hand on a fishing boat?"

Joe stared at him uncertainly. "Yes," he said at last.

"Why didn't you ever ask me?"

"I couldn't ask you something like that."

"You know," Dan said miserably, "I have to get up my courage to talk to you. Not just to talk to you. But to talk to you like this."

"Why? Why, pop?"

"I don't know. Jesus—" He stared at the bedspread and then looked up and met his son's eyes. "I love you so much. How many times I wanted to say that, and I couldn't say it. I loused up fourteen years of your life. All the time when you needed me, I wasn't there. And now I feel so damned empty, hopeless."

Joe reached out and put his hand on his father's. "Pop," he said softly, "all that stuff about college and medical school—it's not important."

"It's important."

"No. No, it really isn't. I see you come in after eighteen hours on that boat, so tired you can hardly stand up—it breaks my heart."

"Oh, no. No. Look, kid, I'm not an old man. You must not feel sorry for me. God damn it, no! I won't have that! Do you know when my life began to make sense, not much sense, but some sense?"

Joe shook his head.

"When I got enough guts to do what I wanted to do, what I had to do, when I was able to walk out of that house on Russian Hill in San Francisco and throw it away and want no part of it. Being a fishing hand—that's all right. I had to breathe a little. I could have dug ditches or cleaned toilets. It would still let me breathe a little. So if you want to go to college and medical school, you go. If you want to dig ditches, dig ditches. As long as you know what you have to do. It took me too long to find out."

After dinner that evening, after Joe had gone up to his room, leaving Dan and May Ling alone in the living room, May Ling asked Dan, "What did you say to Joe?"

"We talked."

"I'm glad. It changed you, both of you, I mean the way you are with each other."

"You noticed that?"

"Wouldn't I?" May Ling smiled.

"You're a damn smart Chinese lady."

"Thank you, Danny. Not for deciding that I'm smart, but for talking to him. Are you going down to San Pedro tonight? It's such a cold, wet night. I can't bear the thought of your going out on that boat."

"I'm not going."

"Oh?"

"I asked Pete Lomas for a week off, without pay." When she made no comment, Dan said, "We can afford it."

"Of course we can." Then she added, "We're not poor. It's time you had a vacation."

"I'm not taking a vacation."

"What is it, Danny?" she asked gently. "Do you want it again?"

"Do I want what?"

"The power and the glory."

"No. I want enough money to send the kid to medical school. Pete offered to sell me a half share in the boat. I don't want that, either. He's getting too old to fish. So am I."

"We have enough money. My father—"

"I won't take your father's money. It may not seem like it, but Joe is my son."

May Ling rose and walked over to him and kissed him. "Dear Danny," she said, "I love you very much. Do whatever you have to do."

"That's what I said to the kid."

"I suppose it's all you can say to anyone. Come to bed now."

They had started upstairs when they heard the car pull into the driveway. They paused, and then the doorbell rang.

"It's eleven o'clock," May Ling said. She waited on the staircase while Dan went down into the living room, turned on the lights, and opened the door. Barbara stood there, smiling wanly. Dan stared at her, trying to make a reference of time and place, and then she was in his arms. He held her tightly, wordlessly. May Ling came down and closed the door behind her.

Then Dan let go of her, and she turned to May Ling and took her hand in both of her own, and said, "Dear darlings, both of you. I can't believe I'm here. I drove all the way down here from San Francisco and never stopped for anything but gas, and I kept having the nightmare that you wouldn't be here and the house wouldn't be here, because nothing ever stays the way it is—and now I'm starved. I haven't eaten all day."

It was past midnight. They sat in the kitchen, Barbara and Dan and May Ling, and for an hour Barbara had eaten her fill and narrated the history of her life during the six weeks since she had left Sarah Lawrence College. "So here I am," she said, "and every day since I got back to California I told myself that I would come down here to see you, and that's simply the way it was. I sat in my car outside that hateful house, and then I began to drive, and I just kept on driving. I should have come before, but each day I worked in the soup kitchen, it became more and more the center of my existence, and now I won't go back to John Whittier's house. I'll never go back there. That's over."

"Do you have any money?" Dan asked her.

"That makes no difference," May Ling said quickly. "She doesn't need money to stay here with us."

"I have a hundred dollars or so in my purse. That's left over from what I got for Sandy. You do forgive me for that," she said to Dan. "It's rotten to sell a gift—she was so beautiful—but I had to. Anyway, I have an allowance of forty dollars a week. The bank takes care of that. They send it to me, or I can pick it up there."

"You're still under age," Dan said. "Jean could cut off the allowance."

"She wouldn't do that. Mother's not vindictive."

"To what end?" May Ling asked. "Barbara's old enough to live alone."

"It's not that simple. Jean is Whittier's wife, and sooner or later, someone's going to uncover Barbara at that soup kitchen. That will make one hell of a front-page story, and they'll both hit the ceiling. Are you going back there?" he asked his daughter.

"I have to," Barbara said. "I can't walk out of it now. As crazy as it sounds, my forty dollars a week and whatever else I add to it keeps that place going. Oh, they get other food, but not enough. You can't imagine how poor those men are, how hungry. I know the union has other kitchens, but this one is my own burden."

"Why?"

"I don't know. I keep asking myself that. I feel guilty, but why doesn't Tom feel guilty? No, it's not only guilt. It's because, because now everything is very real. I romanticize it, but believe me, daddy, I know where I am and I know what I'm doing. I don't look at it through rose-colored glasses. Those longshoremen are crude and ignorant and very often nasty, and I'm not even sure I like them or being around them. But they're right, and they're fighting for their lives, and that waterfront is a filthy slave market—and I am not talking out of hearsay. For almost six weeks, I've been there and watched it and listened to them. Do you know what the shapeup is?"

Dan nodded.

"Of course you do. Well, they're not nature's noblemen. A lot of them are just drifters and plain bums, but they're human, and they work on the docks because there's no work anywhere else. Well, they shape up on the docks at dawn, even before six o'clock in the morning, and they stand there shivering in the cold until the foreman comes to hire his gang. And he takes those who kick back to him out of the pitiful few dollars they earn, and sometimes they don't pay in money but with a brass check, which the longshoreman has to cash in some wretched bar. And every bartender is a nickel man—"

"What's that?" May Ling asked.

"It means that the bartender takes a nickel out of every dollar's worth of the brass check he cashes, and he won't take the brass check unless the longshoreman buys a drink first, and the trick is to get them drinking. When it's over, they have nothing, and their wives and kids can starve. And each day it's the same, shape up and pray to God you'll be lucky enough to find a day of work, even for a brass check. And if they're lucky enough to be paid in real money, they can work nine or ten hours for four dollars. They talk to me. They tell me about men who have dropped dead from exhaustion. There's the loading hook, and they have to keep up with that hook, without even the time off to empty their bladders. You know, the people from the bakery union bring us their stale bread. I've seen longshoremen empty the tin bowls of stew we cook for them into tin cans they bring with them. All they eat is the two slices of bread each man gets. The rest goes home to feed their kids. So I'm not being romantic, am I? When I think of the Embarcadero now, I always think of it as they do, in one single phrase: the shithole of creation. And the ships tied up there belong to John Whittier and my mother."

"Suppose they belonged to me," Dan said. "Some of them did once. How would you feel then?"

Barbara thought about it for a while. "They were your ships once?"

"Some of them. I didn't use the shapeup. I used steady gangs. They worked better that way."

"If they were your ships," Barbara said, "I don't think I'd feel much different."

"The point is that you're Jean's daughter and Jean is Whittier's wife. It has to explode. Do you want that?"

"I don't care."

"What about college?"

"I don't know whether I want to go back. I really don't know."

"I want you to go back," Dan said.

"Daddy, listen to me. I'm not the same, and I don't think I'll ever be the same again. I don't truly know who I am or what I want, but I can't imagine myself back there at Sarah Lawrence."

"I think," May Ling said, "that we're all too tired to imagine anything properly. I think, Danny, you should call Whittier and tell him that Barbara is here, and then we should go to bed. We'll open a cot for you in the living room, Barbara. Is that all right?"

"I'm so tired I could sleep on the floor."

"Did you know," Joe said to Barbara, "that to read and write Mandarin properly, one must know at least five thousand ideographs?"

"Well, that letter you sent me at college—"

"Full of errors."

"Yes, that's what Mr. Ming said."

"Who's Mr. Ming?"

"A laundryman in Yonkers."

"Oh, no."

"But he was the only one who could translate it, Joe." She burst out laughing while he stared at her tragically. "Oh, I'm sorry, Joe." She threw her arms around him and held him as he tried to pull away from her. "No, I won't let go until you say you forgive me."

"O.K. But don't laugh."

"Only because you're trying so hard to impress me, and the fact is that I am enormously impressed. Valedictorian. Chinese. Mandarin. Medical school. You're so smart it terrifies me, and you're one of the few boys I know who is at least five inches taller than I am."

"You're laughing at me again."

"I am not."

They were in his grandfather's rose garden. There, in a space of a few hundred square feet, Feng Wo had created a controlled wilderness of more than thirty varieties of roses—hybrid teas, Chinese tea-scented roses, evergreen and Polyantha, and manicured hedges of rugosa backed by frames of burning red ramblers. Now, in the early morning, the wet blooms gave off a powerful, heady fragrance that made Barbara feel that she had indeed awakened into a kind of a dream world.

"Do you know," Joe said, "I saw you once long ago. I guess I was only ten years old. That would have made you thirteen. We were still living in San Francisco, and I walked all the way to the house on Russian Hill and stood there, across the street."

"Then you knew where we lived?"

"A kid knows everything. They don't understand that. I must have stood there for almost an hour, and then you came out and got into the car. A big Rolls. You had a chauffeur who wore a gray uniform. You were wearing a white fur coat, and you had long hair then. I thought you were the most beautiful thing I ever saw in my life. I think I fell in love with you, and I was very disturbed by the notion of being in love with my own sister."

"That's the nicest thing I ever heard."

"It's all crazy, Barbara. I can't get used to the idea. This is the third time in my life that I've seen you. It makes no sense. And now, if you don't go back to the Whittier place, what will you do?"

"How do you know I won't go back?"

"I sat on the stairs last night and heard the whole thing."

"Why didn't you come down?"

"I don't know. I was in my pajamas. I don't know. I suppose it was none of my business, but I heard it all. I think you're great. I wish you'd stay here—at least for a while, at least long enough for us to get to know each other a little."

"I'll come back. I promise you."

"Don't get hurt. Please. Don't let anything happen to you."

She kissed him impulsively. "You are absolutely darling, and I'm just glad that you're the way you are. Nothing will happen to me, Joe—except that I may grow up a little."

A few minutes later, May Ling called them into the house for breakfast. They were all at the kitchen table together, except for So-toy, who was very old-fashioned and would not sit down until after the men were fed. Feng Wo surrendered his Oriental inscrutability and responded with unconcealed delight to this tall, lovely, rosy-cheeked woman who was his beloved Dan Lavette's daughter, and Dan himself sat there, entranced with joy that these two children of his were together in the same house at the same table, chatting so easily with each other. In May Ling's mind, Jean had always been the "snow lady," her own somewhat malicious definition. May Ling was a very wise and compassionate woman, and now she fought down any impulse to resent Barbara or to see in her anything more than a physical resemblance to her mother. It was not easy. She forced herself to be very gentle, very concerned, begging Barbara to remain with them for at least a few days.

"I have a small study," Feng Wo said, "which I really do not need. My daughter considers me a scholar because

I have published some translations from the Chinese. Let us turn it into a bedroom. You will be very comfortable."

"That's so kind. Thank you," Barbara said. "But I must go back. I've taken on a job that may make no sense to any of you, but I must finish it."

"It makes a lot of sense to me," Joe said. "Only I wish you'd stay. Please stay, Barbara."

She left at ten o'clock that day, Wednesday, the fourth day of July. Dan walked out to the car with her. "I'm here," he said, "whenever you need me. I'm not much good at saying these things, but I love you very much. *Vaya con Dios*. And come back—soon."

Barbara drove north without hurrying. She was still wrapped in a dreamy, delightful sense of well-being, encased in the warmth of the family she had just left. Never in her own home had she experienced this same sense of family, of support, of plain, uncritical approval and admiration; and the excitement of finding a brother who was both a stranger and a blood relation was quite wonderful. She tried not to compare him to Tom, telling herself that it was unfair, yet the comparison inevitably entered her mind again and again.

She stopped for gas and for lunch at a roadside stand, and then she drove on. It was late afternoon when she reached the peninsula and began to compare prices at the roadside vegetable stands. She bought sacks of potatoes, onions, and carrots and four bushels of oranges. The kitchen workers had reacted with annoyance the first time she brought oranges. "What the hell good are they in stew?" But she persisted in her own campaign to get the longshoremen to take them home for the children, holding forth again and again on the virtues of vitamin C.

It was almost seven o'clock when she turned into the alley on Bryant Street, only to find that the soup kitchen was closed for the day. She parked her car near the St. Francis Hotel, locked the doors, and hoped that no one would break into it. Then she checked into the hotel, and having no luggage, she paid for her room in advance.

She called the Whittier house from her hotel room. Knox answered the phone, and when she asked for Mr. Whittier, she was informed that he was out for the evening. Knox added that Mr. Whittier had been quite disturbed by her absence the night before, despite Mr. Lavette's call.

"I want you to assure him that I am perfectly all right.

I spent last night at my father's house in Los Angeles, and if my mother telephones, she is not to be alarmed. I will stop by the house sometime tomorrow."

Then she went downstairs to the coffee shop and ate two ham sandwiches, a glass of milk, and a piece of pie. She brought a newspaper back to her room, hoping to catch up with the progress of the strike, but once in bed, she found that the words blurred and that she couldn't keep her eyes open. By nine-thirty, she was sound asleep.

Barbara awakened with the first light of dawn in the hotel room, at about five o'clock in the morning. She felt wonderfully rested and refreshed, and at first she just lay in bed languidly, enjoying the adventure of being naked between the sheets in this strange hotel room, away from her home, free at least for the moment to do as she pleased when she pleased. Then she remembered her car, filled with food and parked on the street. She leaped out of bed, considered taking a shower, wavered, then darted into the shower, dried herself and her hair as best she could, swished soapsuds in her mouth in lieu of toothpaste, and then pulled on her clothes, shrugging away the fact that she had not changed in three days. She should have washed her underthings and stockings the night before. Well, she had forgotten. So much for that. The dark blouse, the cardigan sweater, and the plaid skirt were durable and quite clean. The saddle shoes she was wearing did not matter. She grabbed her purse and dashed out of the room.

The lobby of the hotel was empty except for a clerk, who dozed behind the desk. The restaurants had not yet opened. It didn't matter. She wasn't hungry, and there would be time enough to eat after she had unloaded her car at the kitchen. Usually it did not open until seven o'clock, but Barbara decided that she would drive her car into the alley and then sit there, guarding her load of food, until someone arrived to open the doors. She walked down Stockton to Market, and as she was crossing the street, a file of a dozen mounted police trotted by, their horses' hoofs making a strangely loud tattoo on the empty street. They looked at her strangely. A block away, there were two men. Otherwise, no one.

Her car was parked on 4th Street, and she breathed a sigh of relief to find it was untouched. It was a quarter

after six. She got into the car and drove to Bryant Street
and into the alley. There, to her surprise, the kitchen door
was open, and the sound of men's voices came from inside. As she cut her motor, Guzie and Salone came out of
the kitchen, and Salone called out to her, "God damn it,
Bobby, where the hell have you been?" But there was no
rancor in his voice, and evidently the squabble of the
day before yesterday had been forgotten.

"I drove down to Los Angeles to see my father."

"You sure picked the day."

"Everyone gets a day off," she said testily, "even longshoremen."

"Sure. Sure. Maybe it's good you weren't here. All hell
broke loose on Tuesday."

Barbara got out of the car and started to let down the
tailgate. Salone helped her. Guzie began to unload the
sacks of food.

"What happened?" Barbara asked.

"That sonofabitch Joe Ryan sold us out. That lousy
bastard, calls himself a labor leader, comes here from
New York and sells us out."

"That was two weeks ago," Barbara said.

"All right. They were only waiting for Whittier to come
back from wherever the hell he was. Tuesday, they decide
to bust the pier on Townsend Street. Seven hundred cops
and goons, riot guns, tear gas—the works. We had maybe
six, seven hundred guys there, and they roll through us
with a line of trucks like tanks."

"Did they break the strike?"

"Like hell they did!" Guzie said. "The trucks got
through onto Pier Thirty-eight, but then we held the
lousy goons for four hours, and then they broke it up.
All right, they got one lousy pier open, and now the
papers are screaming that the strike's busted. It ain't—
not by a long shot."

"Bobby, today's the day," Dominick said. "They laid
us off for the Fourth. They're so stinking patriotic, they
don't want to break nobody's head on the Fourth of
July, but the scuttlebutt is that today they gonna open
the whole waterfront. We got every member of the union
out for today, and the seamen too. That's the way Limo
laid it out when Ryan tried to sell us—the seamen and
the longshoremen together or nothing. So today we gonna
have a thousand seamen and a thousand longshoremen on

the docks, and let them try to bust that up. The point is, Bobby, we want to borrow your car. We need cars. All hell is gonna break loose. We need the cars for command posts, first aid stations, maybe ambulances, food. This picket line ain't gonna stop. Nobody goes off, nobody gets relieved. So we figure to load sandwiches and coffee, and we got some bandages and iodine. We been cleaning up the room in front here, and we're supposed to have two doctor-volunteers—they'll cover the place. So you can stay here and help them when the trouble starts. Honest to God, you can trust us with the car—"

"It sounds like a war."

"That's right. Maybe. So what do you say, kid?"

"You can have the car," Barbara said, "but I go with it. I don't want anyone else to drive it."

"Kid, that's crazy. You don't know what can happen down there."

"You can have the car for whatever you need," Barbara said firmly. "But I drive. I know the car. The clutch is ragged. You put someone else in here, and in a pinch he'll stall it."

"I can drive anything," Guzie said. "Anything."

"That may be. But if you want the car, I drive it."

Dominick nodded. "O.K., O.K. We ain't got time to argue. Let's load and get rolling."

They loaded the station wagon—a milk can of hot coffee, a bushel basket of tin cups, another of wrapped sandwiches, a box of rolled bandages and adhesive tape, two bottles of peroxide, and a quart bottle of iodine. By now, dozens of longshoremen and seamen were pouring into the alley. Barbara went into the kitchen, gulped hot coffee, and munched on a piece of stale bread. The longshoremen crowded in, and she found herself pouring coffee and hacking pieces from a salami. The bread was gone now, used up in the making of sandwiches, and with wonder Barbara watched the half-awake men making a breakfast of salami and black coffee. It did not matter. They were victims of a pervasive and consuming hunger.

Irma Montessa arrived, and she shouted for someone to take a basket of oranges and put it in the station wagon. "Stupid bastards," she said to Barbara. "All they know is meat and potatoes."

From outside, Dominick yelled, "Bobby, Bobby! Let's get it on the road!"

She pushed through to the door. Out in the alley, forty or fifty strikers, some of them with picket signs, were crowded around the station wagon. They were rubbing their hands, hopping up and down to keep warm, grinning at her as she came out. Many of them knew her, and they shouted things like, "Hey, Bobby! Here's our girl!" and "You'll tell 'em, Bobby!" as they opened up for her to get through to the car.

She heard one of the men say to Dominick, "The goons are forming up across Fourth Street. They say they're going to make a cordon from the depot to Market Street."

"Listen, you guys," Dominick shouted. "We go down Bryant, slow. So stay around the car. If the cops try to stop us at Fourth, we push through. We get the car inside the police line and as close to the docks as possible."

Dominick climbed into the car next to her, and Barbara started the motor, easing it into low gear and moving slowly out of the alley, the longshoremen walking in a group around the car. It was eight o'clock, and already the city appeared to be converging on the waterfront. Empty of cars, Bryant Street was spotted with clusters of strikers, sympathizers, kids, curious citizens. On the other side of the street, a solid knot of a dozen men moved toward the docks.

"Goons," Dominick said.

Moving at a walking pace, the Ford's motor whining in low gear, they were approaching 4th Street. Barbara saw the line of police stretching across the street, almost shoulder to shoulder. The kids and the curious were being barred, a crowd of people beginning to fill the street. She was also able to see herself in perspective: Jean Whittier's daughter, driving a car loaded with food and medical supplies into a police barricade. She was frightened and excited at the same time.

"Are you O.K., kid?" Dominick asked.

"O.K.," she said. "I'm fine," with just the slightest quaver in her voice.

"Don't stop unless I tell you to. Just keep it going at the same speed."

They were now about fifty feet from the police line, and the crowd of strikers around the station wagon had increased to several hundred. The tight group of men that Dominick had specified as "goons" now moved into the street on a diagonal toward the strikers. A police officer moved to meet them. Another police officer began to make his way through the strikers to the station wagon. A young man with a press card in his hat pushed in among the strikers and yelled at Barbara,

"Hey, lady, what's your name?"

"Roll down your window," Dominick said. "Keep it down."

"Not closed?"

"Down. Down."

The strikers were at the police line now. "Move it, move it!" Dominick yelled.

"That wagon don't go through!" an officer shouted.

Barbara kept the car moving, and the police line gave. Several of the policemen drew their sidearms, and then an officer who appeared to be in charge waved his arms, and the policemen dropped back, opening the way for the strikers and the station wagon to move through.

Barbara's heart had stopped beating. "Thank God," she whispered. Dominick grinned at her. The man with the press card in his hat swung onto the running board.

"Lady, you got guts. What's your name?"

"Buzz off!" Dominick yelled. The strikers pulled him away. Then he said to Barbara, "Just right on down as close to the Embarcadero as we can get." They passed 3rd Street. In her rearview mirror, Barbara could see the police re-forming their line and holding back the increasing crowd of spectators. "We're in," she said to herself, "but how do we get out?"

"Turn left here," Dominick said, "and pull over to the curb."

Longshoremen and seamen were filling the street. Barbara eased the car through them up to the curb, and then she kept her hands on the wheel for fear that if she lifted them they'd shake violently. Dominick reached over and cut the ignition. "Good kid," he said. "You got lots of stuff."

Now she saw the crowd open up to let Harry Bridges through. His hair was slicked back, his blue eyes alive and darting from face to face. Two other men, heavyset, moved on either side of and behind him. He came over to the car and said,

"Hello, Nicky. Got some boodle?"

"Coffee, sandwiches, and medical stuff."

"Good. Who's the kid?" he asked, nodding at Barbara.

"It's her car. She's a good kid."

"Yeah." He stared at Barbara thoughtfully for a moment, then he said, "What's your name, miss?"

"Bobby Winter."

He called over his shoulder, "Hey, Fargo!" Fargo pushed through the crowds, a big, slope-shouldered, heavy-bellied man in his forties. "Fargo was a medic during the war. Fargo, that's Bobby behind the wheel. Bobby, you show him where the stuff is, and maybe if you want to, lend a hand."

Suddenly, their attention was diverted by a roar of men shouting and swearing, a gush of anger and profanity such as Barbara had never heard before. An apparently endless line of red trucks was moving down Harrison Street. The men swarmed toward the trucks, and at the same time a group of a dozen mounted police, backed by a hundred more on foot, moved in to bar their way. Barbara glanced at the little fox-faced man. He didn't stir. The longshoremen rushed the trucks, climbing onto the motors and trying to get into the cabs, and the foot patrolmen rushed the strikers, swinging their long nightsticks wildly and viciously. The mounted police spurred their horses into the strikers, lashing from side to side with their clubs, and now police reenforcements came running from across Harrison Street, darting between the slow-moving trucks. More seamen and longshoremen poured into 2nd Street, running toward the trucks, but by now the police were able to form a solid line across the street while others dragged the strikers from the trucks and clubbed those caught between the police line and the trucks.

"Lousy, bloody bastards," the fox-faced man said, and he walked toward the mass of strikers who were falling back before the police. The cops were shooting over the heads of the strikers now and flinging tear gas bombs, and for the first time Barbara experienced the acrid taste of tear gas. Dominick jumped out of the car to follow Bridges, leaving Barbara sitting behind the wheel, too paralyzed with fear and horror even to attempt what her common sense told her was the thing to do, to start the motor and get out of there before it was too late. Instead, she remained at the wheel, staring at the battle raging only a hundred feet from her—the surging mass of longshoremen and seamen, the line of police, the gunfire, and the windblown cloud of tear gas.

It ended. The last truck passed down Harrison Street, and the line of police gave back toward Harrison Street, leaving a neutral space between them and the strikers. Now Barbara could hear gunfire and shouting from the direction of the Embarcadero. It was all a dream, an insane, impossible dream.

"Lady, for Christ's sake, where the hell are those bandages?" It was Fargo, prodding her arm, shaking her back to reality, and she realized that the bloodied, hurt men being helped toward the car were part of no dream.

She forced herself into action, clenching her shaking hands, climbing out of the car and fumbling with the tailgate. "Let me do that," Fargo said. Then she crawled into the car and found the corrugated vegetable box that was packed with bandages and peroxide and iodine. Her hands were steadier now. She glanced up. A man stood in front of her, his face covered with blood. "Where the hell are the gauze pads?" Fargo shouted at her.

"None. We don't have any," she said, fighting back her tears and her desire to be sick.

"Shit! Don't none of you have an ounce of brains? O.K., cut up the wide bandage and make me pads. Where's the water?"

She was struggling with the bandage now, realizing that no one had thought to provide a pair of scissors. "Water?"

"Water! How the hell do you expect to wash wounds without water?"

"We don't have any water. Just peroxide and iodine."

"Oh, Jesus God!"

Barbara was trying to tear the heavy cotton bandage with her shaking hands and her teeth.

"Here, use this," Fargo said, taking a knife out of his pocket, opening the blade and handing it to her. "You got court plaster?"

She nodded.

"O.K. Make the pads and then have strips of court plaster ready to hold them in place." He turned to two of the longshoremen. "You two—take that can"—pointing to the milk can of coffee, and saying to Barbara, "What's in it?"

"Coffee."

"Dump the coffee, and fill it with warm water."

"Where?"

"Shit! Don't ask me questions. Get the fuckin' water!"

Glancing up from the pads she was making, Barbara had a vision of the particular hell that she had been plunged into. Kneeling in the station wagon, she was looking at a mass of bleeding, battered men gathered around the tailgate, their faces covered with blood, gashed, eyes swollen and closed, one man with a bullethole in the palm of his hand, groaning with pain, another holding an obviously broken arm.

"Line up, mates," Fargo said, his voice suddenly gentle. "Worst injured first. Let me see that hand. Peroxide, Bobby."

She handed him the peroxide. She was getting the knack of stripping the bandage, piling the pads neatly in the box. "Please, don't shake so," she whispered to her hands. She began to strip the court plaster into different lengths, sticking the end of each piece onto one of the ceiling struts of the station wagon. "That's the girl," Fargo said. "You're doing fine."

"There's supposed to be two doctors in the soup kitchen on Bryant Street," Barbara said.

"That's just fine. We need them in the soup kitchen. Hand me a pad. Now plaster."

"The man with the bullet wound—he ought to go there."

He had bandaged the hand. Now he was putting a pad on a head cut. "You're O.K., buddy. Take him over to Bryant Street, and if the goddamn doctors won't come back with you, get more plaster and bandages. And gauze pads. And more peroxide. And get them back here."

Now the street had almost emptied of everyone but the hurt men, yet they came, more and more of them. The battle had moved down to the Embarcadero, and Barbara could hear the shouting and the screaming and the gunfire in the distance.

"We're going to close the belt line," Fargo said.

"You mean the railroad?"

"That's right. They got their scabs and they're shipping goods. Either we stop the railroad or it's over."

The two men who had taken the milk can returned. One of them had a cut over his eye. Fargo was occupied. "Let me help you," Barbara said.

Without looking at her, Fargo said, "Get the can open. Wash it with the water. Then use iodine, carefully. We'll save the peroxide. It's half gone already."

She had stopped thinking about what she was doing,

simply doing it. She washed the cut, touched it with iodine, pressed a pad on it as she had seen Fargo do, and then secured it with strips of plaster. Another man took his place. Head cuts, cheekbones laid open, a broken mouth with half the teeth gone. She recoiled from this, fighting back the tears again. "Fargo, please, I don't know what to do with this." As with a broken arm. "Hold it like this," Fargo said to her. He broke up a picket sign to make splints. Then, "More pads, Bobby. We're running out."

As she began to fold pads, she realized that these were not just the men who had fought the police when the trucks came through Harrison Street. These were the wounded from another battle, raging down on the Embarcadero. "Buckshot wounds," Fargo said. "Where the hell are those lousy doctors?"

A longshoreman appeared with a box of gauze pads and bandages. "These are from Bryant Street."

"Where the hell are the doctors?"

"They got their hands full, Fargo. All hell has broken loose down on Steuart Street. It's like a goddamn battlefield all the way over to the Ferry Building. Maybe fifty, a hundred men lying on the streets with their heads broken. Half the city is there, every cop, and they say they're calling out the National Guard. They got these fuckin' gas guns, and we're not giving ground. Jesus, I never seen anything like it."

Barbara's eyes were burning, and she had had only a taste of it, a whiff of it. The men coming up to the station wagon now were stumbling, falling, half-blinded, their hands pressed to their faces.

"Fargo, what can we do?" she asked desperately.

"Wet gauze pads on their eyes. That's all we can do, kid. Dip the pad in water, don't wring it out. Put it on their eyes wet and let them sit on the ground and hold it there until the pain eases."

Gauze pads for the eyes, clean the head wounds, pads, bandages. A police plane circled overhead. The sun was shining, the morning chill gone, and the day had turned as gently warm and fine as only a San Francisco day can be. An apparently endless stream of the curious moved down Harrison Street, many of them filtering into 2nd Street to stand and watch. And still, in the distance, the sound of hundreds of men shouting in rage, the sound of gunfire. Time had no end. Once Barbara thought she saw a film camera directed at them, but when she looked again it was gone.

"Fargo," she said, "no more bandages, no more pads." She was very tired, but the nausea and the fear had gone away. She looked at her hands. Hadn't she seen them before? They were covered with caked blood, blood on her arms up to her elbows, blood on her blouse. The gunfire had stopped. The shouting had stopped.

"We'll send the rest to Bryant Street. No real bad ones anymore." He spread his arms. "Sorry, guys. Go up to Bryant Street. They got doctors there. We're out of everything."

Barbara was staring at what was left of the milk can of water. Blood had colored the remaining water pink. She hadn't noticed that before either. Fargo sat down on the tailgate, clasping his hands across his huge stomach. "Christ, I'm tired. What time is it, Bobby?"

She looked at her watch. "Four o'clock." She shook her head in amazement. Where had the day gone? "It's four o'clock. It's so quiet suddenly. I guess everything's over." She took a crumpled handkerchief from her purse, dipped it into the pink water in the milk can, and began to wash the blood off her hands and arms. Fargo watched her.

"You're a funny kid, Bobby," he said at last. "But you're all right. You're all right."

In the photo lab at the *Examiner*, a man called Blakely fished a wet print out of the developing solution and clipped it to the board. He stared at it for a while, and then he called over two other men in the room to have a look.

"It's all right. It's not great."

"Who's the fat guy?"

"Never mind him. Look at the girl. I seen that girl somewhere. I swear I have."

He took it to the photo editor, who glanced at it and pushed it aside. "We got too much already."

"Look at the girl. She's a beauty."

"So she's a beauty. Who is she?"

"I don't know, but I seen her somewhere."

He stared at the picture. The numbers on the license plate of the car were barely discernible. He copied them off and picked up the telephone on his desk.

A few minutes later, he dropped the photograph on the city editor's desk. "This is a lulu. Look at that girl."

"What about the girl?"

"If the car belongs to her, her name is Barbara Lavette."

"Look, this is Thursday. 'Bloody Thursday'—that name's going to stick. We got the worst war in the history of this city, two dead and God knows how many injured."

"Barbara Lavette. Her mother is Jean Lavette. Jean Lavette divorced Dan Lavette about five years ago and married John Whittier. This picture was taken on Second Street at about one o'clock today."

The city editor picked up the photo again and stared at it.

Alone in the car, Barbara drove back to Bryant Street. Fargo had taken off. She had no desire to return to the soup kitchen, no desire to do anything but get away from all this, to be by herself, to be quiet for a while; but in the car were the uneaten sandwiches, the tin cups, and the emptied milk can that Fargo had upended, a pink stream of blood and water pouring into the street.

The street in front of the soup kitchen and the alley too were crowded with men—longshore, seamen, reporters. Two ambulances were in the street, backed up to the storefront. Barbara's first impulse when she saw the crowd was to keep on going; but she pushed it away and eased the station wagon into the alley, the men giving way in front of her. As she cut her motor, she saw Franco Guzie come out of the kitchen. He made his way through and stood at the car door, staring at her.

"I brought back the stuff," Barbara said. "I'm very tired. Could you have someone unload."

"Sure, kid." Still he stood there.

"What's wrong, Franco?"

"You ever get together with Dominick?" he asked unhappily. "I don't know what was with you and Dominick."

"What difference does that make?" She was tired, annoyed, every nerve in her body taut and strained.

"Dominick's dead."

"Oh, no," she whispered. "Oh, no. No." The pent-up flood of emotion released itself, and she laid her head down on the wheel and wept. A reporter worked his way down the alley and wanted to know what went on with the woman.

"Fuck off!" Guzie snarled at him. Then he opened the car door and helped Barbara out. The longshoremen in the alley pushed the reporter away and then stood there watching, grim-faced. "Come inside," Guzie said gently. "You sit down and have some coffee. You rest a little."

Irma was in the kitchen. Wet-eyed, she folded Barbara into her massive bosom. "Poor baby, poor baby."

They found a chair for her. "She needs a drink," Irma said. "One of you find her a drink." "Where?" "Jerks," Irma snapped. She took a half bottle of gin from behind the stove and poured some into a tin cup. "Drink this, baby."

Barbara swallowed the gin, choking on it. Guzie stood in front of her, watching anxiously.

"I'm all right," she managed to say. "I don't have a handkerchief."

Guzie took a dirty, bloodstained rag out of his pocket. She wiped her face with it and handed it back to him. "I'm all right, Franco. What happened?"

"A bullet in the head. Two guys killed, and one of them has to be Nicky."

"Has he any family? Do they know?"

"Not here. He got a mother up in Seattle."

"What happens to him? Who takes care of him?"

"The union takes care of that."

"Where is his body?" She had to ask. She had never encountered death before. She had no knowledge of the way of death.

"At the hospital. Look, kid, when the time comes, we'll tell you. You don't want to stay here. There's nothing but grief in this lousy place. You got a place to go?"

She nodded.

"Can you drive? Are you O.K.?"

"I can drive."

"All right. Just rest up a little, and then I'll clear the way and you can back out of the alley. You don't have to talk to none of them lousy reporters. We'll take care of that."

She sat there for another ten or fifteen minutes. The longshoremen who came in and out of the kitchen looked at her curiously, but no one spoke to her. They were filled with the horror of the day, and distantly, as if she were in another world, she listened to their talk of the pitched battles fought with the police and the company goons on the Embarcadero, of what had happened on Pier 20 and Pier 22 and Pier 38, of who had been clubbed and who had been gassed. Irma was cooking stew. Most of them had not eaten at all during the day, and vaguely Barbara felt she should remain and help. But she couldn't; she had to get out of there. Finally, she got up and went to the door. Guzie helped her to back out of the still-crowded alley, and then she began to drive. She just drove, with no destination in mind.

It was still early evening, a beautiful, golden California evening, the city sitting over the bay like a shining jewel, the rust-colored tower of the unfinished Bay Bridge glowing in the slanting light of the sun. Beauty and misery always go together, Barbara thought. It was all a part of the chaotic senselessness that had replaced the well-ordered serenity of her life.

She was on Franklin Street when she realized that she had no place to go, and she pulled over to the curb and sat behind the wheel, staring glumly at the shining waters of the bay. She couldn't face another night alone at the St. Francis Hotel, not the way she felt now, and to go to the Whittier house was simply out of the question. As for another trip to Los Angeles, the very thought of the long drive turned her weariness into a nightmare. For a few minutes, she just sat there, and then, noticing a drugstore down the street, she locked the ignition and got out.

She found Sam Goldberg's number in the directory, but when she called the office, there was no answer. She should have known that; it was past six o'clock already. There were three residence numbers for three Samuel Goldbergs. The man at the counter changed a dollar for her, and she said a silent prayer. She had already ruled out her friends and her mother's friends. To face any one of them now and try to explain was patently impossible. The first number did not answer. The second number brought a familiar voice.

"Is this Sam Goldberg the attorney?" she asked.

"Yes?"

"This is Barbara Lavette. You do remember me?"

"Of course. Are you in trouble, Barbara?"

"Yes—no. Oh, I don't know. Could I see you, now?"

"Certainly. Where are you?"

"I'm at Franklin, near Clay Street. I have my car."

"I'm not far away, Barbara, at Green on the corner of Polk. A white house with yellow trim. You can park right in front."

A middle-aged black woman opened the door for her. "You're Miss Lavette? Mr. Goldberg's expecting you—right inside, dear."

It was an old Victorian house, the outside scalloped and bracketed, the inside full of framed plush pieces upholstered in olive-tinted velour. Barbara walked into a library: three walls of books and on the fourth wall an oil portrait of a pretty, delicate-featured woman. Goldberg got up out of a leather armchair and greeted her warmly.

"This is a wonderful surprise, Barbara—" He broke off, staring at her. "Is that blood on your blouse? On your neck too. Are you hurt?"

"No, I'm not hurt. I'm all right. I'm just so tired, and I had no other place to go. And please forgive me, Mr. Goldberg, but I'm so hungry. I haven't eaten all day. Could I have something, anything? A sandwich?"

Sam Goldberg sat at the dining room table with her, watching admiringly as she consumed roast chicken and mashed potatoes and string beans. "I'm eating your dinner," she protested at one point.

"Enough for both of us, dear. And for me to have company at dinner is a very special treat." He was less admiring and more dubious as he listened to her story of what had happened that day. She choked up as she told him of Dominick Salone's death.

"All right, Barbara. A man died, tragically, wastefully. It's your first encounter. You're part of the living. You accept it. Death goes with life. Sooner or later, you face that."

"But he was so young, so alive, so cocky. I never met anyone like him before. He had no education to speak of, but he knew so much."

"Were you in love with him?"

"No. But that only makes it worse, because he was in love with me and I didn't care about him at all, not that way. And don't you see, it's my fault?"

"No, I don't see that at all. How could it possibly be your fault? You did what you could. God knows, you did more than anyone else I know."

"I sit here stuffing myself with food, and Nick is dead somewhere in some hospital, and Jean's my mother, and Jean's married to John Whittier."

"And John Whittier's a monster?"

"Yes!" she snapped.

"But suppose Whittier were a shipowner you loved instead of a shipowner you dislike intensely. As I told you, your father was also a shipowner once."

"Daddy would never have done this!"

"I don't know." Goldberg sighed. "You know, Barbara, I saw some of it. I was on Rincon Hill at eleven o'clock, watching. That's when they were fighting on Harrison Street. I wasn't alone there on Rincon Hill. There were a thousand others, and we just stood there and watched, the way they watched the gladiators in the old days. All over the place, thousands of people watched, and they saw men clubbed and shot, the way I did, and none of us lifted a hand. You did something. You cared for people who were injured and bleeding. Now I am going to be presumptuous and didactic, so forgive me, but I must tell you something about guilt. Guilt is shared, because we belong to the human race. It is convenient to have villains like John Whittier, because it absolves the rest of us; but there's no absolution from what happens, and until we learn that, we just blunder about in the dark. Now enough of this, and certainly you have been through enough today. The question now is, where do you go from here?"

"I don't know."

"The place was swarming with newspaper men. Did any of them get your name? Or photograph?"

"Not my name. Maybe my picture. I just don't know."

"Will you go home?"

"To Whittier's place?"

"It's your home."

"No," Barbara said quietly. "I'll never go back there. I'll never set foot in that house again."

"Well, 'never' is an uneasy word. Have you seen Dan yet?"

"I was in Los Angeles yesterday. I could go back there, but I don't want to. Not now."

" 'Never,' Barbara, leaves your mother in a very difficult position. Would you like to stay here for a while? I have a comfortable guest room, and you're welcome to stay."

"For a few days? Could I?"

"Yes. Of course. Will you go back to the soup kitchen?"

"I don't know. I feel that I should, but I don't know whether I can. It's as if I did something, and now it's finished."

"The strike isn't finished. It's only begun."

"I know that. But I don't think I can go back there. It's not that I'm afraid. I was, but I got over that, and it's not that I don't feel for them. It's as if something inside of me is broken, and I have to put it together again. I know that makes no sense—"

"Perhaps it does. Now, will you let me call Whittier? Is your mother home yet?"

"No, she's still in Boston—I think. I don't want you to call John."

"Barbara, someone has to know where you are. You can't disappear. They may have already reported you missing—"

"No. I spoke to the butler. I told him mother must not be alarmed."

"But she will be. And you need clothes. I must call him. Tomorrow, I can send my secretary over to pick up some things for you to wear. Now, you must let me call him."

"You will anyway, won't you?"

"I'm afraid I must, Barbara. I'm your father's friend, and I am also an attorney."

The following day, John Whittier telephoned Jean in Boston. The conversation was unsatisfactory to both parties. Since the Boston newspapers—like the newspapers all over the country—carried accounts of what had happened in San Francisco on what was already known nationally as "Bloody Thursday," she knew more or less what had taken place. She received the news that a picture on page two of the *Examiner* had depicted her daughter in the midst of a group of injured strikers in the act of rendering first aid to one of them without comment, and when her husband angrily pressed the point, she said,

"It appears to me, John, that what she did may have been foolish and romantic, but hardly earthshaking. I'll talk to her when I return."

"When you return? I want you to start back here now, today."

"That's out of the question. I can't leave Boston today. We have things planned—"

"Jean, you don't hear one damn word I'm saying. This city is in a state of civil war. We're expecting a general strike, and that bastard Bridges and his commie pals are ready to take over. And I'm in the center of it. I'm already late for a meeting with Mayor Rossi and Governor Merriam. Can't I get through to you what's happening? There are troops on the Embarcadero, and God only knows when Bridges will decide to move against the ships. I have no time to track down your daughter and discipline her."

"What do you mean, track her down? Isn't she at home?"

"She is not. She's apparently decided to stay with a Jew lawyer called Goldberg. I spoke to him this morning, and he sent his secretary over here for her clothes."

"You mean Sam Goldberg?"

"I suppose so."

"All right. I suggest you forget about Barbara for the time being. You have sufficient troubles of your own. Tom and I will be back in San Francisco within a week."

"And I suggest you leave immediately. I may be able to handle this strike, but your children are more than I can cope with."

"Thank you."

"What does that mean?"

"John, this discussion is pointless. We will be home within the week. Meanwhile, try to relax and get some perspective. I don't think there is civil war in San Francisco. This will all be settled in due time."

On Sunday, two days later, Dan Lavette took the bus from Los Angeles to San Mateo. Long ago, some thirty-six years chronologically but reckoned as an eternity in California, where the land and the people still retain a sense of newness and incompleteness, a man named Anthony Cassala had lent Joseph Lavette, Dan's father, the money to buy a fishing boat. At that time, Anthony Cassala was a laborer who lent small sums of carefully hoarded money to the Italian workingmen. After the earthquake, during the few days when the city's banks were entirely inoperative, Cassala's tiny hoard of money became immensely valuable, and a few years later he obtained a license to establish the Bank of Sonoma. Together with his son, Stephan, he nurtured the bank, moved it onto Montgomery Street, and it might well have become an institution comparable to the Bank of Italy, later the Bank of America. But circumstances intervened, and after the crash of 1929, a run started that left the Cassala enterprise crippled and eventually bankrupt. Anthony Cassala died the following year, and Stephan went to work at Wells Fargo.

In their days of prosperity, the Cassalas had built a large, rambling house in San Mateo, on the Peninsula, south of San Francisco. There Cassala's widow, Maria, his son, his son's wife, Joanna, and their one child, a boy of seven named Ralph, still lived. After Dan Lavette's father and mother died in the earthquake of 1906, the Cassalas became a sort of surrogate family to him. Anthony Cassala financed his early ventures into the shipping business, and when the run on Cassala's bank took place, Dan and his partner, Mark Levy, depleted themselves of every dollar of cash they could lay their hands on in an effort to halt it. Four years had passed since Dan had seen Stephan Cassala, but he did not think that time would change anything that had existed between them. There were too many ties, too many threads that bound their lives together.

"Still," May Ling had said to him, "you must be careful what you ask. It lays a burden on them."

"I don't know that I'm going to ask for anything. I just want to see Steve and talk to him."

Then he had telephoned Stephan Cassala and asked if he might stop by and spend a few hours with him. Stephan had persuaded him to come on Sunday and stay overnight. The Sunday edition of the Los Angeles *Times* dealt in great detail with the events of "Bloody Thursday," and on page four of the main section, they reprinted the photograph of Barbara. Riding north on the bus, Dan read the story:

A curious sidelight to the events of "Bloody Thursday" still remains unexplained. The car in the above picture is registered to one Barbara Lavette, and the owner is listed as residing in a house on Pacific Heights in San Francisco. The address in Pacific Heights is the same as that of John Whittier, a prominent member of San Francisco society and the president of California Shipping, the largest operator of oceangoing vessels on the West Coast. According to a number of people who are friends or acquaintances of Miss Lavette, the woman in the photograph is Miss Lavette.

Barbara Lavette, twenty years old, is the daughter of Daniel Lavette, one-time partner in the firm of

Levy and Lavette, and Jean Seldon Lavette, daughter
of Thomas Seldon, and for some years after her
father's death president of the Seldon Bank. The Lavettes were divorced in 1931, after which Jean Lavette married John Whittier. The car in the
photograph was parked on 2nd Street in San Francisco and allegedly served as a first aid station and
supply depot for the strikers. Miss Lavette could not
be reached for comment.

Stephan met Dan at the bus station in San Mateo and
embraced him. The four years had not wrought any great
change in Cassala. Thirty-nine years old now, tall, slender,
with dark moist eyes, his skin still had the pallid, yellowish
tinge it had taken on after his stomach was cut to pieces
by shrapnel in World War I. The same overwhelming
almost unendurable warmth and emotion greeted Dan
when they reached the Cassala home. Maria, Anthony's
widow, fat, shapeless, permanently encased in the black
of mourning, wept over Dan and babbled away in Italian.
Joanna stared and smiled at him, and then, at the table,
Maria ushered in an unending river of food, pressing him
to eat and eat, and still eat more.

It was almost eleven o'clock before Stephan and Dan
were able to sit down alone, in Anthony's old study, and
talk about what had brought him there. Stephan poured
brandy. A wood fire burned in the grate.

"Like old times," Stephen said. "God, it's good to see
you again, Danny. I know you been through a lot, but I
swear you look ten years younger than the last time I saw
you. Hard, too—no more paunch."

"Living right, and a good wife. How about you?"

"Day to day. I manage one of the branches for Crocker,
but you know what banks pay. It's all right. Pop had in-
surance, and we keep this big barn of a place going. When
I'll get a chance to pay you back what you dumped into
the run—well, I just don't know—"

"Forget it."

"I haven't forgotten, Danny. But I just don't know how.
I haven't the heart for the game anymore. You have to
want it."

"I know." He tasted the brandy. "This is good."

"Still the old stuff, from during Prohibition. Montavitti

used to make it on his place in San Martin. Pop bought twenty gallons."

"How's it going with Joanna?"

"What should I say, Danny? I live with damn guilts. I'm a lousy husband. You know what I keep thinking? I keep thinking that if I could find a way to pay the bills, I'd enter the priesthood."

"Hell, no. God damn it, Steve, we're alive, both of us."

"In a world I can't make head or tail of. You know what happened in San Francisco. How? Why? Are we all going crazy? In Italy, that stupid bastard Mussolini. In Germany, Hitler. In Russia, Stalin. What's happening to the world?"

"Like always. Give it a chance, and the shit floats to the top."

"And what about Barbara? You read the papers."

Dan smiled. "I know what I read, that's all. She's quite a lady, Steve. A lot like Jean in some ways, but maybe with a little of me. I thought I'd drive up to San Francisco tomorrow—you do drive, don't you?"

"I leave at seven. Sure, come with me. But what about you, Danny? What brings you up here?"

"Money."

"God, I wish I had it to give to you. I got a few thousand. If it will help—"

"No. I don't want any money from you, Steve. Some leads, some advice. You know I've been fishing—on Pete Lomas' mackerel boat out of San Pedro. You remember Pete. He used to be my boatmaster before I teamed up with Mark. Well, in a good week, a damn good week, I bring home forty dollars. Mostly less. May Ling works in the library—thirty dollars a week. We make out, but not much more. Now Joe wants college and medical school. He's a good boy and a smart boy. May Ling's mother and father live with us, so it's tight. Well, I've been looking around. Christ, I can't go on fishing forever. There are a couple of things I know, and one of them is boats. With this rotten Depression on, there hasn't been a boat built down there in years. And they're going to need them, because the market for fish only grows. Well, there it is. I thought I'd set up a small boatyard. I might just pull it off."

"Wooden boats?"

"To start, yes. Plenty of shipwrights pleading for work,

and wood is cheap. I can rent space for peanuts. And one
business that isn't suffering in this Depression is films.
The film people have money and they buy boats. The way
I calculate, Steve, I can put together a beautiful little yawl
for five hundred dollars—and undersell anything good on
the market."

"How much do you need?"

"About ten thousand to start. With less than that I'd be
scrounging, and it would be pointless. Do you suppose
Crocker would let me have it?"

"With what collateral, Dan?"

"We have the house—that's all."

Stephan shook his head. "No, I wouldn't want that.
There's got to be another way. Why don't you see Sam
Goldberg tomorrow. He still pulls a lot of weight around
town. And he's got money."

"I'm not going to trade on Sam's friendship."

"Talk to him. Please. As a favor to me. We can always
go to the banks."

On the morning of the next day, Barbara awakened early
and dressed herself in a plain navy blue skirt, a white
blouse, and a black cardigan. Goldberg's secretary had
succeeded in retrieving a suitcase of sweaters, skirts, shirts,
and underthings from the house on Pacific Heights. Now
Barbara slipped out of the house quietly, without awakening Goldberg. She left her car parked where it had been
and set out on foot for the International Longshoreman's
Association's headquarters on Steuart Street. She had no
desire to attract additional newspaper stories with her license plates, and anyway, it was a clear, cool, lovely
morning. The blanket of fog on the bay was breaking up
into rivers of creamy, golden mist, and as Barbara walked
down California Street toward the Embarcadero, she felt
so totally alive that she had to fix her mind willfully on
the misery of the occasion. Yet that did little good, and
she thought to herself that there was some deep flaw in
her personality. If I had a shred of human sensibility, she
reflected, I would be utterly downcast, and instead I am
behaving like a perfect pig and feeling like a person going
to a picnic. The thought worried her, and she sought in
her mind for the source of this streak of what she could
only consider as a basic lack of humanity; she finally
decided that it was because she had slept well the night

before and because of the weather, which was beautiful
indeed.

By now, the streets were filling up with men and women
on their way to work, the clanging cable cars stuffed
with more crowded, clinging people than seemed possible,
considering how tiny the cars were, the sidewalks bustling
with properly dressed men, carrying their briefcases, as
much the mark of this place as the umbrella was the mark
of London's City. The stream of commuters pouring out
of the Ferry Building was no different than on any other
day. It shocked and startled Barbara; she was only beginning to realize how easily life and death go together.

Once on Steuart Street, it was a different matter. Here,
the funeral procession would assemble. A delegation of
longshoremen had visited Chief of Police Quinn on Saturday and had stated in no uncertain terms that whether he
agreed or not, the funeral of the two men killed on
"Bloody Thursday" would proceed along Market Street
and not on some quiet side street. He agreed. Now, as
she turned the corner into Steuart, Barbara became part of
another San Francisco. Men, women, and children, not
in their work clothes but dressed in their best, the men in
old, ill-fitting suits, wearing black ties, black armbands,
black hats, the women in black too, their faces grim
and tired, a look that even the children shared—here they
were coming by the thousands, all of Steuart Street in a
slow movement that converged on the union hall. As she
became a part of them, Barbara's mood changed, as if the
anger and grief and hopelessness these people felt was a
palpable substance that penetrated to the core of her
being.

The movement slowed and stopped, and the thousands
of men and women and children who packed the street
stood there motionless. Slowly, the people making way
for them, four flatbed trucks moved into the street and
lined up in front of the union hall. An odd assortment
of musicians, violins as well as horns, and two bass drum-
mers took their place behind the trucks, and now people
came out of the union hall, carrying wreaths and baskets
of flowers and hundreds of bouquets, all of which they
piled onto the trucks. Many of the women and children
had brought flowers, most of them home-grown, roses and
zinnias and marigolds picked out of gardens, which they
put on the trucks; and Barbara wondered with a sudden

pang why she had not thought to bring flowers. But she had not imagined that it could be anything like this. The people were still coming along the Embarcadero, and down Mission Street and Harrison Street and Bryant Street, waiting for the crush in Steuart Street to ease so that they might join the procession.

Then the pallbearers came out of the union hall, carrying the two coffins, many of them, as with so many of the crowd, still wearing head bandages and patches of gauze. Barbara recognized some of them. There was Guzie and Fargo and some others whom she had come to know at the soup kitchen. She saw Bridges among them. As they came out of the hall, the musicians began to play Beethoven's funeral dirge. The pallbearers slid the two coffins onto the flatbed truck, and then the crowd gave way for them to take their place in front of the trucks. Slowly, almost imperceptibly, the procession began to move. No one gave orders; no voice was raised other than whispered requests by a group of longshoremen that the march be ten abreast—and so the grim river of silent people turned into Market Street and began to march southwest across the city. The same group of strikers who had whispered the marching orders now spread ahead of the funeral procession, shunting the traffic off Market Street into the side streets.

Barbara fell into one of the lines and walked slowly with the procession out into Market Street. Looking back at the apparently endless stream of people coming out of Steuart Street, she realized that the procession could not consist of longshoremen and seamen alone, not even with their families. Thousands more had joined the march, and thousands of others lined Market Street to watch in silence as the procession passed. Indeed, the silence was uncanny and incredible. The little group of musicians had stopped playing. No traffic moved on Market Street, and nowhere was there a policeman to be seen. There was no other sound than the tread of thousands of slow-moving feet.

Dan Lavette, standing at California and Market, was one of the thousands who watched the procession, watched it come out of Steuart Street. He suspected that Barbara would be somewhere in that great throng, but though he looked for her, he was unable to spot her. He tried as best he could to understand what forces motivated her and what this experience meant to her, but for all their closeness now, his daughter was very much a stranger to him. He himself had never been very political. Most of his adult life had been spent climbing the path to Nob Hill, to success and wealth and power. Even as a fishing hand, he could not think of himself as a workingman. A workingman was a victim by his lights, and to his own way of thinking he had never been a victim but always the manipulator, always the man who controlled his own destiny. The only time he had ever thought and acted in political terms was when he had supported Al Smith for the presidency. If Smith had won, Dan Lavette's life might have been very different, but Smith had not won.

Now, watching the mass of people passing slowly by, he could only think of the strike and of "Bloody Thursday" in terms of stupidity, stupidity on both sides, but specifically the stupidity of men like John Whittier. He didn't hate John Whittier; he simply despised him, as he had once despised Grant Whittier, the man's father. For perhaps half an hour, Dan stood and watched the funeral procession; then he turned away and walked to Sam Goldberg's office on Montgomery Street.

Goldberg received him warmly and immediately put to rest his fears about Barbara. "She's staying with me," he said, "and I hope you will too, Danny. There's plenty of room in the old house."

"Have you talked to Whittier?"

"I have. It was not pleasant. He regards her as some kind of crazed kid out to destroy him. I agree with Barbara. She can't go back there."

"Did she say what she wanted to do?"

"Only that she won't go back to college. She said something about going abroad for a few years, but who knows? She's been through a profound emotional experience, and it's going to take her time to get her balance back. By the way, Jean called me from Boston. First time I've spoken to her in years. She'll be back in San Francisco on Wednesday. I think you ought to stay over and talk to her."

"Why?"

"Because your daughter's a part of both of you. And what about Tom? He's coming back with her. Don't you want to see him?"

"I'm not sure that I do."

Goldberg shook his head. "All right. We won't talk about that. We'll talk about you and May Ling and Joe."

They talked for almost an hour. For Dan, it was a process of reliving a life he had literally wiped out of existence. Sam Goldberg had drawn up the papers when he bought his first ship, the *Oregon Queen*, and then Goldberg had walked with him every step of the way through twenty incredible years, the building of an empire and the destruction of an empire—through the divorce proceedings that put an end to that section of Dan's life. It was a long time since they had seen each other, and there was a great deal to put together. When Dan finally went into his notion of starting a small boatbuilding business in San Pedro or Wilmington, Goldberg simply spread his hands and said,

"No problem. I'll give you the money."

Dan shook his head. "That won't work. You're in a position where you have to say that. I don't want your money."

"Then whose money? I'm sixty-six years old, overweight, a rotten heart—as my doctor so cheerfully informs me every time I see him—no wife, no children, and rich. Principally as the result of having you and Mark as clients for twenty years. Do you know what you paid me over that time?"

"I never thought much about it," Dan said.

"Did you ever collect a nickel of money you put out—as personal loans?"

"Not that I can remember. But what the hell difference does that make?"

"Look, Danny, either you go to a bank and mortgage your soul, or what is worse, May Ling's house, or you find investors. All right. I'm an investor. I'll put up twenty thousand, and we'll be partners in the deal."

"You're crazy."

"Like a fox, Danny. You're no businessman, but you're something else. There's no word that fits it, and the time for it is over, anyway—except maybe for a few men like you. God damn, you opened Hawaii and made it a competitor of Florida. You and Mark established the first great department store on this coast. You opened the first commercial airline in California, and starting with nothing, you built one of the biggest steamship lines in the country. Now you spend your days fishing for mackerel. Why, I don't know. What in the name of God are you afraid of?"

"Myself."

"That's great. That's really beautiful. You sound like one of those psychoanalysts that this city is being plagued with."

"Nevertheless, it's true."

"True or not, I don't buy it. Now look, I'm a lot more hardheaded than you are. I'm offering you a partnership. You do the work, and we split the profits. There's only one condition."

"I'm listening."

"You stay away from the books. You create it. You manage it. Build your boats, ships—any damn thing you want to build. But leave the financial end of it to Feng Wo."

"My father-in-law? You're out of your mind."

"Why? For years, he was the best damn comptroller you ever had."

"No, no, Sam, it wouldn't work. He's an old man. He translates from the Chinese and he grows roses. I can't involve him in this."

"How old is he?"

"Almost sixty."

"Then you damn well can ask him. I swear, I just don't understand you, not one bit."

Dan sighed. "All right, Sam. If I ever understand myself, I'll lay it all out for you."

"Are we in business?"

"Let me think about it."

At dinner that night at Sam Goldberg's house on Green Street, a thoughtful, subdued Barbara asked her father quietly, "What do you think I am, daddy? Am I a fraud? Is that all I am—a fraud?"

Goldberg watched both of them with interest, this huge, dark-eyed man and the slender, bright-eyed young woman, with her clear skin and honey-colored hair, who by the wonders of genetics was his daughter. The combination of their alikeness and their unalikeness fascinated him. Both were incurable romantics; both lived their lives with zest and endless curiosity, and both of them were filled with doubts and guilts and quixotic passions. Like Dan, Goldberg had been born in California, a place he was fervently dedicated to and that he often felt was the only place on earth where a Jew was not a Jew but simply another immigrant in a world of immigrants. And these two, Dan Lavette and his daughter, were unique products of California.

The three of them sat at a round, club-legged Victorian table in a fussy little Victorian dining room, untouched and unchanged since his wife had died. Dan had agreed to remain with him overnight, and Barbara had returned from the funeral late that afternoon, still in the mood of what she had experienced.

Dan took a while before he answered. "Well," he said at last, "we all are, you know. Frauds. I don't suppose we want it to be that way, but who the devil are we? If there's no way to find out, you invent your own answer." He looked at Goldberg, who shrugged.

"I'm an aging, overweight lawyer, Danny."

"I'm very rich," Barbara said suddenly. "I mean, someday I will be."

"I suppose so," her father agreed.

"How rich?"

"Don't you know?"

"Not really. I've never thought much about it."

"Well, it depends on a lot of things. According to the terms of your grandfather's will, you and Tom were left three hundred and eighty-two thousand shares in the Seldon Bank, to be divided equally between you in nineteen forty. That will give you a hundred and ninety-one thousand shares. The stock is privately held, so there is no market price. What would you guess, Sam?"

"Hard to say. Twenty-five, thirty dollars a share. It's hard to say."

"About five million dollars. Of course, what the price will be six years from now, no one can say."

"Most likely higher."

"Then I am very rich," Barbara said.

"Comfortably so," Goldberg agreed.

"Do I have to accept it?"

"What?"

"The money, daddy."

Dan laughed. "Well, I'll be damned!" He turned to Goldberg. "There's one for you, Sam."

"Right now, Barbara," Sam Goldberg said, "you have no rights in the matter. For one thing, you're still a minor. The stock is held in trust for you. Your mother's the trustee, and she has the right to dispose of the income as she sees fit. In nineteen forty, according to the terms of the will, as I understand it, you accept the bequest. What you do with the stock after that is up to you."

"Then like it or not, I am very rich and I remain so."

"Do you find it uncomfortable?" Dan asked her.

"Yes, I do."

"Poverty can be more uncomfortable," Goldberg assured her.

"I think I know that. But I can earn my own living. No one gave anything to daddy."

"That's not really to the point," Dan said. "You've got six years to think about it. Meanwhile, I think you should go back to school."

Barbara didn't have to think about that. "No, I won't go back. That's over."

"Don't close all the doors," Goldberg said.

"I'm trying to open some."

"What will you do?" Dan asked.

"I don't know. I don't know what mother will say. I can't stay here with Mr. Goldberg. I have to think about it."

"Come back to Los Angeles with me," Dan said slowly. "We'll both sit down with Jean tomorrow or the next day. I'll talk to her. Then come back with me—if you want to."

"I think—I'd like that," Barbara said.

But it was not until three days later that Jean returned to San Francisco and Dan was able to reach her. It was the first time in almost five years that he had spoken to her, and when he heard her voice the space of time became meaningless. He found himself thinking, Only yesterday. Everything is like that, only yesterday.

"This is Dan," he said, almost casually. "I'm in San Francisco, and Barbara is with me."

"Yes, Dan. I thought you might call."

"Could we sit down together, you, myself, Barbara, and Tom, and hash some things out?"

"I'd like to talk to you alone," she countered.

"No, that wouldn't be a good idea."

"Why not?"

"Because I want to talk about Barbara, and I want her there when we do."

"And if you will forgive me, I don't think that's the

best idea in the world. Let's not pick up where we left off, Dan. I think we're both older and wiser."

"All right. Where shall I meet you?"

"Tomorrow? Lunch at the Fairmont?"

"At twelve-thirty," Dan agreed.

Dan was already at the table when Jean walked into the dining room, and he rose and stared at her unbashedly. She wore a Chanel suit of pale pink wool over a rose silk blouse, a shell pink felt cloche, and around her neck a double strand of pearls. His were not the only eyes that turned toward her; he could remember only too well this shift toward her that made her the center of attraction in any room she entered. It was not simply that she was a beautiful woman; she carried her beauty without self-consciousness, with an easy, erect certainty; and now, as always, Dan could not look at her without desire, without feeling that familiar longing for something that once was his yet never his.

She saw him, walked to his table, and gave him her hand, looking at him, measuring him, a slight smile and the slightest twinkle in her fine blue eyes. "Danny," she said, "you look splendid, ten years younger, thirty pounds lighter, healthy, happy—oh, I envy you." She always made the rules, specified the ground for any conversation.

"Shall I return the compliment?" he asked, moving the chair for her to be seated.

"Please."

"I have never seen you look more beautiful."

"Thank you." Her eyes took in his brown tweed suit, the white shirt and the cheap tie, without appearing to do so; but he was sensitive to her every gesture, and he said pointedly,

"The suit is eighteen dollars, Jean. I'm hard to fit, but then, I had no notion that we'd be lunching at the Fairmont."

"The suit is fine," she said with a touch of annoyance, "and I also happen to know that you don't give a damn what it cost. You never did. What have you been doing, Danny? You look as if you've been taking a miraculous health cure at some European spa, but that's hardly likely." She pulled off her white kid gloves, reached across the table, and took his hand in both of hers, smiling as she ran her fingers over his palm. "No, hardly a European spa. I do love your hands, always have. I do not like soft hands on a man."

"I'm a fisherman, Jean. I work for Pete Lomas, down in San Pedro. You remember Pete Lomas. He was fleet captain on my crabbing boats. I think you met him that first day on the wharf—back in nineteen ten. I average thirty dollars a week."

"Stop it, Danny," she said, laughing. "It's bad taste to be so damned ostentatious about your poverty."

"Then I'm right back in form."

"No, you're not, and it's much too late to play the hardboiled kid from the Tenderloin. Anyway, you look splendid, very healthy, very content with yourself, and I have no intention of feeling sorry for you."

"Good. We're on even ground. I have no intention of feeling sorry for you."

"I'm not sure I like that," she said slowly.

He had not intended to mention it, to speak of it at all, and then it came out. "Jesus Christ, Jean, why the hell did you marry him?"

Her face tightened. "Shall I ask why you married your Chinese mistress?"

"That wasn't called for," he said unhappily. "It's the same damn thing, Jean. Why does it always happen as soon as we start to talk? Why does it always go to pieces? When I saw you come into the room over there, I looked at you and I said to myself, Danny boy, you are wrong about most things, but not about women. This is one hell of a woman. Do you know why I married May Ling, why I love her? Because from the first moment I saw her, she made me feel that I was a man, that I was human, that I was something of value and not misplaced dirt from the Embarcadero."

For a long moment, Jean stared at him, then she shook her head. "I'm sorry, Danny, very sorry. It's always too late, isn't it. I want a drink. Will you order a martini for me? And then we'll talk about Barbara and Tom."

He ordered the drinks. They sat in silence for a while, Jean watching him thoughtfully.

"You've changed."

"Both of us," he said.

The drinks came. "To the kids?" she asked.

"Yes."

"Tell me, Danny, what do you think of your daughter?"

"I like her. She's the best of both of us."

"Then I'm not the worst mother in the world?"

"Hell, no. I'm a rotten father, but you did something. Was John burned up about that newspaper story?"

"A perfect rage, yes. He takes it as a personal affront, something she did out of hatred for him. And of course it doesn't help his own position."

"It doesn't help hers. She can't go back there. She's John Whittier's daughter—at least in their eyes."

"I don't see why she should want to."

"For the same reason she went there in the first place."

"And what was that?"

"Guilt. Compassion. A desperate need to find out something about herself and the world she lives in."

"Not John?"

"I don't think she gives a damn about John Whittier. She doesn't like him. Does Tom like him?"

"I think so. What's more important is how Tom feels about you."

"He hates my guts."

"No, Danny, no. He doesn't know you."

"I lost him somewhere on the way. Like you said, Jean, it's always too late."

"You could try."

"Could I explain to him why I work as a boathand for thirty dollars a week?"

"I don't think you could explain that to me, Danny. How did you explain it to Barbara?"

"I never had to."

"You know, Dan, she adores you. She'll listen to you. She won't listen to me. She doesn't want to go back to college. I spoke to her this morning."

"I know."

"I think she should. I think she should heal the breach with John. This is a terrible time for John; whether you like him or not, he's facing his own moment of truth. Everyone says there'll be a general strike tomorrow."

"It looks like it."

"I can't imagine it. Everything stops—the whole world. John hasn't slept in three days; there have been endless meetings with the mayor, the governor, and heaven knows who else. If Barbara could be made to understand—"

"I think she does understand, from her point of view."

"Dan, she's not a communist. Or is she?"

"No." He grinned. "I hardly think so."

"What does she want?"

"I think she wants to get away from all of us for a while. She wants to go to Europe, to Paris. Study and work."

"And you encourage that?"

"Jean," he said gently, "I encourage nothing. I want her here as much as you do. But I won't impose anything on her. I won't even try to persuade her. You and me, my dear, we have one hell of a kid. She survived being born in a golden crib, and if she survives that, she'll survive anything. On the other hand, you're the trustee of her estate. If you cut off her money, she'll have a hard time of it."

"That's what John wants me to do."

"Will you?"

"That's a hell of a comment, Dan. I love her as much as you do. It's her money."

Dan looked at her and nodded. They ordered lunch, but hardly touched the food. They talked around things, awkwardly—Barbara's sale of her car, her horse—but the matter of their daughter was decided already. When Dan said that she would be coming to Los Angeles to stay with him until she left for Europe, Jean said almost hopelessly, "I suppose that's best. She won't come back to John's house. I'll spend the next few days with her. Don't worry about the money." Then she talked about Tom, and her tone became almost plaintive. "I never turned him against you, Danny."

"I know."

"So strange, Danny, to sit here like this, the two of us. You feel that, don't you?"

"I feel it."

"Danny, if I said to you, take a room and go upstairs and wait for me—?"

"Are you saying it?"

"Danny, I could endure anything except to have you reject me again. So I'm not saying it, really."

He reached over and took her hand. "Jeany—" He had not called her that in years. "Jeany, I have twenty-two dollars in my pocket and a return ticket on the bus, and that won't buy us a bed at the Fairmont. But thank you. I'll remember that."

"John is sure you hate me. He begged me not to see you. He actually was afraid you'd commit mayhem."

"I guess John knows as little about men as he does about women."

She made no effort to take the check, and inwardly he thanked her for that.

A few days later, the day Dan left San Francisco to return to Los Angeles, one hundred and fifteen San Francisco trade unions met in delegation and voted to call a general strike. The next day, the most feared, the almost mythical weapon of the working people came into being as the San Francisco trade unionists walked off their jobs and left the city paralyzed. Among the various devices that the employers and the so-called nabobs resorted to was the resurrection of the vigilantes, so notorious in San Francisco's past. Rumors were circulated that a communist army was already marching on San Francisco, although its point of origin was never revealed. There were other carefully circulated rumors of bomb plots and planned attacks on police headquarters and the general post office. None of the rumors was founded in any basis of reality; nevertheless, the vigilante gangs went into action, carrying out raids against the headquarters of the Marine Workers International Union, the Communist Party headquarters, the headquarters of Upton Sinclair's Epic Plan movement, and a number of other places, among them the soup kitchen on Bryant Street.

Barbara went there the day after she read the account of the raids in the *Chronicle*. She walked through a city that teemed with police, National Guardsmen, and unofficially deputized American Legionnaires. She came to Bryant Street and stood there looking at the wreckage of what had been the storefront soup kitchen. The windows had been smashed, the tables and chairs inside broken, the dishes shattered and scattered about. The destruction was maniacal, childish, and thorough.

The following day, she left for Los Angeles.

Dan did not make up his mind about Sam Goldberg's offer until after he had spoken to May Ling. He had an almost mystical regard for her good sense and wisdom. He told her all that had been discussed in Goldberg's office and then let the question hang.

"What do you really want, Danny?" she asked him.

"The money to put Joe through medical school."

"We can manage that. It's four years away. He'll go to UCLA, where the tuition's free. I have some money saved, and pop has his savings."

"I won't touch that."

"Joe will be working this summer. He'll save that money."

"Where?"

"While you were gone, I phoned Jake Levy at Higate. He offered Joe a job at the winery. Joe wants to go. So we'd manage the money."

"All right. I've had it with fishing. I'm not young anymore." He was sitting opposite her in the living room of their little house in Westwood. It was on toward eleven o'clock, the hour that was theirs alone. She sat with her hands in her lap, a small, slender ivory-skinned woman whose hair was turning gray, and he thought to himself. She's all of it—everything. Love was something he could never adequately put into words.

"You don't enjoy being poor, do you, Danny?"

"I don't give a damn about that. Only, the good years —Christ, we couldn't even walk into a decent restaurant together."

"They weren't such good years, Danny. These are the good years."

"I can't go on in that damn mackerel boat."

"Then tell Sam you accept."

"You won't mind?"

"Come to bed, Danny. You'll call Sam tomorrow."

Lying in bed with May Ling's head cradled in his arm, her naked body pressed close to him, both of them easy in the afterglow of their lovemaking, he said, "There is one thing more I should tell you about the trip."

"Oh?"

"I had lunch with Jean at the Fairmont."

"The snow lady. Yes?"

"Eleven dollars with the tip. That's half a week's wages when the fish aren't running."

"She didn't offer to take the check?"

"Come on, baby. We talked about Barbara. That's all."

"She didn't ask you to go to bed with her?"

"You know, my darling May Ling, under that satiny Oriental skin of yours lurks traces of a bitch."

"Then you've found me out. What did you say?"

"What do you mean, what did I say?"

"When she asked you to go to bed with her?"

"I said that with twenty-two dollars in my pocket, there was no way I could afford a room at the Fairmont."

"You did?"

"Yes."

"I hate you."

"I've suspected that."

She pressed closer to him, running her hand over the hair on his body. "I like it when two bodies become one. That's the way it should be. Only, Occidental men are so hairy, apelike."

"How the hell would you know? You've never been to bed with anyone else. Or so you tell me."

"So I tell you. Would you?"

"Would I what?"

"Would you have gone to bed with the snow lady if you had had the price of a room at the Fairmont?"

"I don't know—"

"You're not very nice, Danny. But I love you."

Part Two

THE LEAVE-TAKING

Barbara met Marcel Duboise on the Champs-Élysées. It was on an afternoon in April of 1937, a cool, lovely, sun-drenched day, the kind of a day that people who love Paris will insist occurs only in Paris and only in April, although Barbara remembered many days like it in San Francisco, when the wind blew gently from the Pacific and when the sunlight danced on the water of the bay. Indeed, this kind of a day filled her with nostalgia and homesickness and led her to think that she had lived enough away, and that it was time to go home.

She had lunched out of a bag in the garden of the Tuileries, and that was when Marcel Duboise saw her. She was unaware of this until he followed her across the Place de la Concorde and up the Champs-Élysées. He quickened his pace until he was alongside her, and then he said, speaking very quickly,

"My name is Marcel Duboise. I am honest, decent, fairly intelligent, of good character, and not a criminal or a depraved type, and I do not make a habit of speaking to strange women on the street. But what else can I do? If I don't speak to you now, you will disappear and I will never see you again. I never saw you before, so it is quite logical that I will never see you again, and then my life will be desolate and meaningless until the end of time."

The words poured out of him with such speed that Barbara retained only a vague impression of what he had said. By now her French was adequate, but she still had some difficulty following when it was spoken very quickly, and her instinct was to ignore the man and quicken her pace. She glanced sideways at him. He was slender, tall, brown tweed jacket, gray flannel trousers, white shirt, striped tie, wide mouth bent in a pleading smile, wide jaw, brown, humorous eyes, a large, narrow nose, and a mop of unruly brown hair.

"Please, please do not ignore me."

"What on earth do you want?" she asked him, shocked into English without thinking. "What do you want?" she repeated in French.

"Ah, you are English."

"I'm an American, if it's any affair of yours."

"So much better. Please, may I talk to you?"

She stopped, turned to face him, and stared. "Monsieur what-ever-your-name-is, you *are* talking to me. I don't know why, but you are. A mile a minute," she added in English.

"Of course. My name is Marcel Duboise. What did you say, a mile a meeneete?"

"Too fast. My French is not that good."

"Yes. Of course. Forgive me." More slowly, he asked, "Is this better?"

"Much better. Now I am sure you have mistaken me for someone else."

"Oh, no. No. Impossible. I could not."

She sighed and began to turn away.

"Please, one moment. I could not mistake you for anyone else because I have never seen you before."

"Then what on earth—?"

"I am trying to make your acquaintance," he said desperately. "Believe me, I do not make a habit of this kind of thing. I have never done it before. For ten minutes I stood there watching you eat your lunch. Then I took the plunge."

"I still don't know what you're talking about," Barbara said.

"If I try to explain, I will only sound more insane, and I'm not insane. I mean, no more than the next man. One dreams for years about a woman, and then one sees her? Well, what is one to do?"

In spite of herself, Barbara began to laugh. He appeared to be so absolutely ingenuous that for the life of her she could not be rude or coldly unapproachable.

"Only one terrible thing occurs to me," he added.

"Oh? Yes, what terrible thing?"

"That you are happily married."

She hesitated and then replied, "Neither happily nor unhappily. I'm not married."

"God be praised. Now, please, please, I introduced

myself before. But now more formally. My name is Marcel
Duboise. I am unmarried, twenty-nine years old. I was
born in Toulouse, which accounts for my accent. I work
for the newspaper *Le Monde* in a most shameful way. You
see, I hold nothing back. I write a daily column about food
and restaurants, and the only redemption in my work is
that I am the substitute play critic. Once, twice a week, if
I am lucky, I am allowed to review a play. Also films,
but again as a substitute. One time, the film critic was sick
for a month. That was glorious."

"That's very interesting," Barbara said, for want of
anything else to say.

"Then you find me interesting. Good. Please tell me your
name."

She thought about it for a while. He stood there,
hopeful, earnest, not a very good-looking man, but with an
undeniable charm and with a boyish openness and
vulnerability that she simply did not believe could be
assumed.

"My name is Barbara Lavette," she said at last.

"But that is a French name. You are not French?"

"My grandfather came from Marseille. He was part
French and part Italian."

"Of course. The wonderful thing about Americans—they
are always from somewhere else."

She was laughing again. Common sense said to her,
You do not let yourself get picked up on the street in Paris
by a strange man. On the other hand, strange men do
not bother to pick up a woman who wears no make-up, a
brown woolen suit over a beige cashmere sweater, not to
mention scuffed ghillies with heels only three quarters of an
inch high. She was also lonely and homesick, and fancied
the smell of the April air to be like the salty scent of the
sea on a breezy day on Russian Hill.

Sensing her mood and hesitation, Marcel Duboise said,
"Mademoiselle, what harm will it do if I walk with you
and we talk? If you tire of me, I will go. Surely, on the
Champs-Élysées, on an April afternoon, nothing unpleasant can happen?"

"But you don't even know where I am going."

"That's where I am going. There is nothing in the world
more important." A half-hour later, he was telling her the
story of his grandmother, who had written her first novel

—and had it published—at the age of seventy-two. "Very risqué, very risqué indeed."

Barbara realized how little she had laughed in the past three years.

"But of course, you are serious," he said. "There is your charm. Myself, I am a fool. So my family regards me. So the world regards me."

"You are certainly not a fool, and as for myself, you know nothing about me. Oh, I wish my French were not so wretched."

"Your French is very correct, and your accent is absolutely delightful."

"Thank you. But I really must go."

"Where? You see, you are in flight because we were not properly introduced. If an aunt of yours said, 'This is Marcel Duboise, a proper gentlemen,' then the whole thing would be so simple."

"But my aunt is three thousand miles away, so it is impossible."

"Miles, yes. What is that in kilometers? Oh, devil take it!" They were at the corner of the Avenue Victor-Hugo now, and Duboise pointed to a sidewalk café. "We sit down there for one moment. I buy you a small drink. Vichy water, tea. I accept the fact that I must be neutral and harmless."

The proprietor greeted him by name. "You see, I am not a nameless thug," he reassured her.

"All right." She dropped into a chair. "You are Marcel Duboise. I am Barbara Lavette. We have met. It is absolutely formal now. For a half-hour, you have been introducing yourself to me."

"And you have not driven me off."

"True. Could I have a beer?"

He ordered two beers and stared at her in delight.

"Monsieur, you must not stare at me like that."

"But certainly. Forgive me. I have told you who I am, what I do, what my father did, what my grandfather did. You have told me nothing."

"How could I? Do you always talk nonstop?"

"Oh, no. Certainly not. I was fighting time and tradition. I was talking for my life—really, truly. Now tell me about yourself, Barbara Lavette."

"You are rather nice—"

"Thank you. Bless you."

"And I am entirely able to take care of myself. But when a stranger tries to pick you up in Paris—"

"Not to pick you up. Only to keep you from walking out of his life."

"That's just it. Would I select a man and accost him on the street because I was attracted by his face? It stinks a bit, doesn't it? That's an American expression," she explained. "It doesn't work when I put it in French."

"I get it. My face? Never. But it wasn't only your face, but yourself, all of you."

"And still you know nothing about me."

"Not so. It's true, you have told me nothing. But just wait. The suit is Molyneux? Am I right?"

"Heavens, no. I bought it in San Francisco."

"Well, so much for clothes. I know this: you are kind, gentle, sure of yourself, intelligent and—all right, I say it. I think you are one of the most attractive women I have ever seen. So I have sinned. And your French is excellent, so you have lived here for some time."

"I wish that were true." Barbara sighed. "I had four years of French at secondary school, two years at college. Six years. So I would be a perfect donkey if I couldn't get along with it. I've been here for almost three years."

"With your family?"

"No, alone. I came first to study at the Sorbonne, which is the rationalization of so many Americans who come here, but I just don't have the character of a student. I stuck it out for a year and a half. I was almost ready to give up and go home when I ran into a piece of luck. I met Frank Bradley, who is editor of *Manhattan Magazine*. Do you know it?"

"Yes, of course. My English isn't good enough for me to enjoy reading it, but I love the cartoons."

"So do I. Well, you know it's a weekly, and every other week they publish a 'Letter from Paris,' a sort of grab bag—some politics, fashion, the arts and letters, and whatever gossip might strike a chord back in the states. Well, Bradley and I got to talking, and then I showed him some pieces I had written. He liked them, and he let me try the 'Letter from Paris.' They liked what I did and I got the job—I guess for want of anyone else at the moment —and I've been doing it ever since."

"Then we're both writers. Do you see how sound my instinct is?"

She nodded, smiling, and he ordered another round of beer.

Ten years after the turn of the century, the leading citizens of Los Angeles, already suffering from a sense of inferiority imposed by San Francisco, which was arising like a phoenix out of its ashes, realized that they needed a harbor. History had bequeathed them a city twenty miles from the sea, and they felt that as an inland city in a semidesert, their future was far from bright. Long, long ago, ancient Athens had faced the same problem, and the Athenians, a vigorous and intelligent people, decided to build a pair of walls, each four miles long, to connect their city with Piraeus, their seaport. On the Pacific coast, in the vicinity of Los Angeles, there was unfortunately no harbor worthy of the name, but there was an ocean; and, never daunted, Los Angeles incorporated into itself a strip of land a mile wide and sixteen miles long, stretching from the westernmost edge of the city to two coastal fishing villages, San Pedro and Wilmington, two sleepy villages that fronted on a great mud flat called Terminal Island. The citizens of San Pedro and Wilmington, facing sudden absorption, were of mixed feelings, but the city of Los Angeles undertook a public relations campaign calculated to convince these people that their destiny and future were much brighter within Los Angeles than outside of it. In August of 1909, elections were held in San Pedro and in Wilmington, and when the results had been counted, Los Angeles was at long last a seaport. Eventually a stone breakwater, miles long, threw a great circle around San Pedro, Wilmington, and the neighboring port of Long Beach, providing Los Angeles not only with a seaport but with a large, safe harbor.

Within this enormous breakwater were enclosed the mud flats of Terminal Island, which was transformed into a busy hive of shipbuilding during the years of World War I and in the early nineteen twenties, employing literally thousands of men. With the onset of the Depression, the shipyards of Terminal Island closed down, succumbing one by one to the economic malaise that gripped America, until only a hardy handful were left to try to survive and dream of better times.

One of the companies that failed to survive and ended up in the hands of the local banks was Occidental Marine, a medium-size shipbuilder that had specialized in the construction of wooden minesweepers during the war. It had twenty acres of land, shops, cradles, groundways—even a small drydock that had fallen into disuse and disrepair. The whole enterprise was offered to Dan Lavette for a hundred thousand dollars, but, hoarding his tiny store of capital, he delayed, bargained, and finally took over the place for a total price of sixty-five thousand dollars, the bank taking back a mortgage of sixty thousand dollars at four percent interest, and considering itself fortunate in the deal. Dan was less fortunate in his plan to make enough money to send Joe through medical school. During the next three years, he built seven boats, only managing to keep his head above water, to pay his bills, and to meet the payroll for the five men he had hired—and to make them understand the situation when he had to lay them off. The first boat was ordered by Pete Lomas, whose converted mine sweeper-turned-mackerel boat was beginning to come apart at the seams. There were two other fishing boats, one of which saw its owner go out of business. The remaining four vessels were small sailing craft, pleasure boats. The bank, which dreaded the possibility of another bankruptcy and the possession of worthless property, forgave him a year of interest payment, and somehow or other Dan forced his enterprise to survive.

One day in the early spring of 1937, Pete Lomas walked into Dan's office on Terminal Island and offered him a pure Havana cigar. The office, where Dan was the only occupant—the little bookkeeping he required was done by Feng Wo at home—consisted of six rooms in the main shop building, all but one deserted. The room that Dan occupied had a desk, a swivel chair, a row of empty filing cabinets, and a splendid walnut architect's chest, whose many shallow drawers were filled with old Occidental blueprints of boats Dan would never build. There was also a table and five captain's chairs, obviously for meetings to discuss the plans.

Pete Lomas dropped into one of the chairs while Dan examined the cigar and admired it.

"Courtesy of Alex Hargasey."

"Thank him. Who the hell is he?"

"Oh, nobody. Nobody. Only the most important director in Hollywood."

"Yeah. And that's why you're sitting here in white ducks

and a white shirt and that silly captain's hat of yours instead of being out fishing."

"Exactly."

Dan bit off the end of the cigar, and Lomas leaned over to light it for him.

"Go on," Dan said.

"You be nice to me, Danny," Lomas said. "You be very goddamn nice to me because I am going to blow your ass sky high. You want to know why I'm not out fishing? Because Paramount Pictures—you heard me, Paramount Pictures—is paying me fifty dollars a day, seven days a week, and all expenses and the crew's wages for the use of my boat. They're making a film about a fisherman, and they're using my boat. Only today they're not shooting on location, which is my boat, so I'm a gentleman of leisure. You got anything to say about that?"

"It couldn't happen to a nicer guy. But it doesn't blow my ass sky high."

"Be patient." He reached into his pocket, took out his wallet, and extracted a folded check. "Five hundred." He handed it to Dan. "Last payment on my boat. Took two years, but it's done."

"It helps. Believe me, it helps."

"Now, listen to me, Danny. This Hargasey, he's a Hungarian, very emotional, blows up, yells, screams, but he's a nice guy. Since they start this film, he becomes absolutely crazy over the sea. He says it's because there's no ocean anywhere near Hungary. Well, he wants a yacht. He's got this girl, Lorna Belle—you heard of her?"

"I heard of her."

"She's the star in the film, and I guess they're shacked up, not married or anything, but that ain't too important with them, it seems. Well, she's just as nuts as he is on this business of a yacht. Hargasey is in love with my boat, and when I tell him that you built it, nothing else but you got to build him a yacht."

"What?"

"Hold on, Danny. Not just a yacht. He wants a hundred-foot Diesel with eight bedroom suites."

"Is he crazy?"

"Have I blown your ass sky high or not?"

"Pete," Dan said, "You can pick up yachts all up and down this coast—and for a damn sight less than it costs to build one. You know that. He must know it. And who has enough money for a hundred-foot Diesel? It could run to a quarter of a million—more."

"Danny, they got nothing but money. There's no Depression in the movies. Anyway, he wants to meet you, and I said I'd arrange it. One deal like this could turn this white elephant of yours into a paying proposition. You phone him at Paramount Pictures and arrange to meet him. And bring some stuff with you—plans, blueprints, photographs."

"I can do that," Dan agreed. "I got a beautiful set of Sparkman and Stephens blueprints and drawings that I inherited with the place. But, god damn it, how much does a movie director earn?"

"The hell with that! Go out there and sell him the job. Let him worry about paying for it."

Three days later, Dan drove his 1930 Ford from Westwood to Hollywood, turned off Melrose Avenue into Marathon Street, and faced the imposing gates of the Paramount studio. The guard at the gate regarded his car dubiously, checked his name, then passed him through and directed him where to park and how to find Alex Hargasey. It was the first time he had ever been inside a film studio, and after he had parked his car, he walked past the huge sound stages and the bungalow-like office buildings and dressing rooms with the gawking curiosity of any tourist, thinking that this was certainly an intriguing, childlike world, the great factories of make-believe drenched in the morning sun, men and women hurrying past in the colorful costumes of cowboys and Indians and maidens and knights of the Middle Ages. He found the half-timbered building that housed Hargasey's office, fake English between fake modern and fake Spanish, and was directed upstairs to a suite of offices. There he sat for fifteen minutes, leafing through a copy of the Hollywood *Reporter,* an object of interest to the peroxide-blond receptionist who sat behind her desk and studied him unabashedly.

Finally Hargasey emerged, an enormous, fat, bald man with a bulletlike head, his stomach pressed tightly behind a broad leather belt that encircled whipcord riding breeches. "Ah, boatbuilder!" he boomed. "You are this Lavette. I am Hargasey. Come on in." He studied Dan as they entered his office: a white rug that Dan felt was enveloping him like quicksand, white overstuffed chairs, a great black desk. "Son of bitch!" Hargasey exclaimed. "You are damn sight more photogenic than stupid star I got to work with. Maybe I forget about boat and I make you star? What do you say, Lavette? No. Joke. I got idiot sense of humor. Sit down. I got half-hour to tell you what I want. Then you make it for me."

That night at dinner in the cottage in Westwood, May Ling, her son, her mother and father, listened fascinated as Dan described his experience at the studio. "It makes no sense," he said. "The country's going down the drain, starving, dying, and this man tells me to spare no expense. Mahogany woodwork, silver-plated fixtures, teak decks. I told him it might run to three hundred thousand. He just grinned at me and said, 'Good, good.' "

"Then you'll build it," May Ling said calmly, "if you can."

"I can build it. I can build anything he wants."

Watching his father thoughtfully, Joe finally said, "You don't want to build it, do you, pop?"

"I guess I don't."

"I know," May Ling agreed. "But what difference does it make, Danny? It means work for a lot of men. If you don't build it, someone else will."

"If I don't build it," Dan said, "then I close down. It's the end of the road. So I guess I'll build it."

When Marcel Duboise came into Barbara's apartment on the Quai de Passy for the first time, he looked slowly around him and then shook his head and sighed hopelessly. "You lied to me," he told her. "You said you were a journalist. No journalist lives like this. No journalist lives on the Quai de Passy."

"What on earth are you talking about?"

He prowled through the place. "Bedroom, sitting room, kitchen, bathroom, shower, tub, bidet—you're an heiress."

"All right. Then you've found me out. I am. You thought I was a plain *fleur de l'asphalt*, since you did pick me up, and here I am an heiress."

"Don't be silly." Still, he kept turning and staring. "A place like this—at least a thousand francs a month."

"Eight hundred." She smiled at him. "Do you like it? I adore it myself. It's my first real home, can you imagine? And you never have to meet the man who pays the rent. He comes only one evening a week—"

"Don't talk like that!" he snapped at her. "I've known you for two weeks and you've never talked like that before. I don't like it."

"There you are, my dear Marcel. Every Frenchman is a moralist. They pretend otherwise. Oh, stop being so pompous and sit down." He sank into the chair, fingering the upholstery. In her mind, Barbara could see him calculating the price. It irritated her. So much that was French irritated her, and yet so much enchanted her. "I'm an heiress," she said deliberately. "I should have told you that at the beginning, but at the beginning I was sure I'd never see you again, and anyway, it's a cliché for an American girl in Paris to be an heiress. I'm very rich— oh, not at this moment. Don't be alarmed. I don't come into the money for another three years, and anyway, how do you think I feel about it with my country in the middle of this rotten Depression?"

He just sat there and stared at her. Then he asked, "Why did you never let me take you home before?"

"Oh, you ass!" she exclaimed. "You think I'm a *putain*. You do, don't you? A classy whore. You don't believe a word I said."

"Should I? After all the lies?"

"What lies? I told you I'm a correspondent. I am!" She walked over to a pile of magazines, picked up a handful, and flung them at him. "Read it, if you can read English. That's the work I do, and I'm damn proud of it." She stared at him, shaking her head. "Oh, what's the use! You'd better go."

"No!"

"Then stay there and let your thoughts rot in that stupid bourgeois mind of yours."

"So I'm bourgeois? Me?" he cried indignantly.

"Yes. And now, excuse me." She went into the bathroom, washed her face with cold water, stared at the angry face in the mirror, and then began to laugh. Her lips were still twitching with a smile she fought to control as she returned to the sitting room. Marcel stood facing her.

"I love you," he said desperately.

She burst out laughing.

"And you laugh at me, you heartless bitch!"

"Who do you love, Marcel, the *putain* or the heiress?"

"Stop that!" He grabbed her, started to shake her, and

then embraced her. She stopped laughing. She met his lips and closed her eyes and felt the tears start. Then she pulled back and stared into his dark eyes.

"Why are you crying?" he whispered. "Did I hurt you?"

"You're such a strange Frenchman. I've seen you eight times and you never made a pass. I could have been your sister. Oh, I know you were being careful. And now, when you decide that I am a kept woman—"

"No!"

"That's not why I'm crying. Don't you see? I love you so much."

In a way, she told herself, she had never been made love to before—remembering the clumsy pawing on college dates, remembering the argumentation and pleading of those who did it vocally, remembering what was almost a knock-down, drag-out fight on a Princeton football weekend, remembering and then remembering nothing, only lying naked and alive with a man whose hands and lips worshipped her body, and who told her over and over again, in a language so well made for it, how very beautiful she was.

"Marcel," she said.

"Yes, my love?"

"When it happens, don't be alarmed."

"Alarmed? My God, alarmed?"

"Oh, I hate to have to tell you this, but I'm a virgin."

He raised himself from where he lay beside her, stared at her, reached out, and touched her cheek. "Oh, no."

"God's truth," she said in English.

"You're twenty-three years old. You've been in Paris almost three years."

"I know. I don't know what else to say. I'm so ashamed." She was giggling.

"Darling, lovely Barbara," he begged her. "Don't laugh. You cannot make love and laugh at the same time."

Later, hours later, lying side by side, smoking, watching the tendrils of smoke drift and twist, too languorously surfeited even to dress, Marcel said, "Being an heiress makes it difficult. It would have been easier the other way."

"What other way?"

"A kept woman. We could have worked that out. But an heiress—I don't have two francs. What I earn, I spend."

"Then we'll both be poor."

"And what about the fortune?"

"I'll probably give it away," Barbara said indifferently.

Late at night, on the twenty-seventh of May, 1937, Thomas Lavette knocked at the door of his mother's room. There was no response, and he opened the door gently. Jean sat at her dressing table, and as he opened the door, she turned to face him.

"It's me, mother. Is it all right?"

She picked up a handkerchief and wiped her eyes.

"You've been crying?" He had never seen his mother in tears before.

"Not really. Tears, but not really crying, Tom. Just a long day and too much emotion."

"May I come in?"

"Please."

"It's past midnight."

"Come in, come in."

"John's asleep?"

Jean nodded. She pointed to a chair and then dropped into a chaise longue. "Sit there, Tommy. Let me look at you. I haven't seen you for days."

"Not my fault, mother. You've been so wrapped up in the bridge. How did it go today?"

"You don't want to know about the tears?"

It embarrassed him. "I don't want to pry."

"I wish you would pry. I wish we both could pry at each other enough to break through. Well, I was crying. Today, just before the ceremonies began, Mr. Strauss came to me—"

"Mr. Strauss?"

"You don't know, do you, Tom. The name doesn't even ring a bell."

"That's not fair, mother. He had something to do with the bridge."

"A little. He and Clifford Paine built the bridge, the Golden Gate Bridge that we dedicated today. I first met him six years ago—"

Tom half-rose. "Mother," he said, "it's very late."

"No. I'm in a very singular mood, Thomas. I wish you would just sit there and listen to me. I intend to talk to my son, perhaps because I have no one else to talk to. So if you will—please."

"If you wish."

"I do. It's very late, but I am not a bit tired. I want to talk about Joe Strauss, a small, not terribly impressive, Jewish man. A least I think he's Jewish. Perhaps not. When I was your age, I had all the normal—no, not entirely normal—prejudices against Jews. Your father's partner, Mark Levy, was Jewish, and I could barely tolerate him. So you see, I have a very clear understanding of what growing up rich on Nob Hill does to one. It happens quickly. My grandfather panned gold. My father was Thomas Seldon—"

"You're going to lecture me again," Tom said.

"Again? No. I think this is the first time."

"Have it your way."

"I intend to, this once. You see, there never would have been a bridge without Joe Strauss. It was his demonic compulsion. Everyone said that it was impossible—oh, mostly the geologists. They knew it was impossible. But Joe decided to build the bridge or die in the attempt, and I think he did both."

"He died?"

"No, my dear. Please don't ask me to explain. But, you see, once he had fought it all through—the legalities, the politics, the plans, the concepts—once he did all of that, he still required the money, and there all the wise and practical people decided that they had him stopped cold. He needed twenty-seven million dollars. Six years ago, he walked into my office at the bank and introduced himself. Oh, I knew who he was, but we had never met. He told me that he was putting out a bond issue. The banks had laughed him out of their offices until he went to Giannini. Giannini didn't laugh. He told Joe that his bank, the Bank of America, would take the bonds. But there was still an overage, some six million. So Joe Strauss came to me. I asked him why, and he said, 'You're a woman, Mrs. Lavette. You know about men, the kind of men who remain children and dream the dreams the kids dream.' Or something like that. I don't remember exactly."

"That was a damn strange thing for him to say."

"Not really. He knew about your father, and I did something to your father once that he never hated me for, so perhaps I knew less about men than Mr. Strauss thought. Anyway, I took the bonds, and I bullied my board of directors into accepting my position. That was how I came to know Joe, and today the bridge was finished and opened and dedicated, all nine thousand feet of it, all twenty-seven thousand strands of wire—and that's why I was crying. Now, please go to bed."

Tom started to say something, to tell her that he had come into her room to talk about his job and money. Then he shook his head and sighed. "All right. Good-night, mother." He walked over to her and kissed her dutifully, then he left the room, and Jean sat there, staring at the door, disliking herself for being obtuse and unreasonable with him.

Lately, it was getting to be a habit for her to dislike herself. Tom was no worse, perhaps a little better, than most of the young men in his set. He tended to his work at the bank as an assistant vice president in charge of loans, and in view of her own obsession with the building of the bridge, it was quite natural that he should block out Strauss's name, natural even if it were simply a pretense to irritate her. She irritated him, and she certainly irritated her husband, John Whittier. Why on earth she should have started out, a few minutes before, to tell Tom of all people what Joe Strauss had said to her before the ceremony, she simply did not know. Of course, Strauss was in an unusual condition, keyed up, filled with the wonder of the miracle that they had wrought there in San Francisco, yet depressed too. He took her hand in both of his and said, "Dear Jean, I will tell you what it's like today, the way it must feel to a man who knows you and loves you—when the love is returned. So the bridge is built and done. There's no other way I can say it."

Her husband overheard this, and Whittier said to her afterward, "Now what the devil did he mean by that? Is the silly ass in love with you? Or have you—"

He stopped short. She was staring at the bridge, at the great, incredible red-orange monster of steel and wire, as delicate and graceful as a glowing spider's web in the sunshine, so proper and immediate a signature for this strange people who had settled the Pacific edge and, oblivious to desert and earthquake, build there the one American city that was like a dream. She was staring at it, a part of it, until Whittier spoke; and then she turned and glanced at him as if she had never seen him before.

And now she wept. Her tears were her own. She had never shared them before, and it provoked her to have to share them with her son. She felt very strongly that if you are alone in the world, utterly, totally alone, you use that loneliness as your comfort and your strength.

Barbara gave a party for Marcel's friends. She felt that since neither of them had any family available, friends were the next best thing, and the occasion, though unannounced, would be to celebrate the fact that someday, in the distant or not too distant future, they would be married. Two of her own friends, the only close friends she had in Paris, were included: Susan Clark, a Philadelphia girl who was a student at the Sorbonne, and Betty Greenberg, a junior correspondent for the New York *Times*. Marcel invited his three best friends, Jean Brissard and Maurice Jouvelle, both of them staff writers on *Le Monde*, and Claude Limoget and his wife, Camille. Limoget, Marcel explained, was a reporter for *Humanité*, the Communist Party daily, which meant that sooner or later the evening would explode into a wild argument, but then, as he said, "What else makes a good evening?"

"Food, for one thing, and I'm a rotten cook. But this Claude Limoget, he's a real, live communist, in the flesh?"

"Why not?"

"Because I've never met one."

"After all you told me about the strike in San Francisco? What about that man who was killed, Dominick Salone?"

"I never asked him. You don't ask anyone in the States."

"Why? It's not Germany."

"We'll go into that another time. Meanwhile, what ever am I to cook? I can't cook for Frenchmen. It would be grotesque."

"We'll do it together."

"Marcel," she exclaimed in delight, "can you cook?"

"This and that. Not really. But I do know how to prepare a *cassoulet*, a huge pot of beans and sausage and pork. That's all we need—and good bread and good wine."

The *cassoulet* turned out to be delicious. The fresh, golden spears of bread were like no other bread in the world, and the inexpensive table wine was as good as any Barbara had ever tasted. Marcel's friends were charming, full of praise for everything—the apartment, the food, and the three "absolutely delightful" American girls. They were all in their late twenties: Brissard stout, jolly, a sort of French G. K. Chesterton in appearance, at least to

Barbara; Marcel had described him as Balzacian. Jouvelle and Limoget were small and slender and filled with energy, and Camille Limoget was petite and pretty, causing Barbara to feel oversized and gross. Thank heavens, she told herself, that Marcel was taller than she. The two American girls were both in the five-foot-two or -three range, attractive and unconcerned over their execrable French. Barbara rarely gave much thought to her height —she had grown up in a city where tall women were not uncommon—but now she whispered to Marcel that she felt utterly grotesque. He in turn assured her that she was the loveliest and most desirable grotesque in the City of Paris.

They ate the food and drank the wine and talked at first about America, San Francisco, Roosevelt, the New Deal, the sit-down strike in Flint, Michigan, the CIO, and the ravings of Father Coughlin. Barbara answered questions when they were put to her, but otherwise she listened in silence. She was amazed at their knowledge of what went on in her own country. They were all newspapermen, but still and all, they were far better informed than she was. Also, it was the first time in her life that she had ever been at a dinner party where the discussion was totally political. Not even at college had anything like this ever taken place, and she found herself concentrating fiercely to follow their rapid French.

Then the conversation turned to Spain and the Spanish Civil War, which had been going on for almost a year now. Camille Limoget had a brother in the French Battalion of the Internationals, fighting on the Republican side and against Franco, and she spoke bitterly of the embargo of munitions.

"I put Roosevelt with Hitler," she said. "One is no worse than the other."

"Why not with Hitler and Stalin?" Brissard said lightly.

"Of course, of course," Claude Limoget said sarcastically. "What is the difference? Only that Hitler fights on the side of Franco and Stalin for the Republic. But how can that make any difference?"

"They are both practicing, testing arms, testing airplanes. You are going to tell me that Stalin gives two damns for the Republic? Each has theories. They work them out in Spain."

Until now, Barbara had sat in silence. She started to

say something, but Limoget broke in with, "Ah, that is
splendid! How I love a cynic. He is absolved from responsibility. A plague on both your houses. Isn't that Mr.
Roosevelt's phrase?"

"If you mean—" Barbara began.

"What I love," said Jouvelle, "is the way you cannot be
wrong. You cannot be open to argument. No discussion.
When Zinoviev and Kamenev were beaten and tortured
into submission and forced to confess and then executed
like dogs, you knew. Oh, yes, you knew they were guilty.
Of what? But you knew they were guilty, even before they
knew it themselves."

"Who were Zinoviev and Kamenev?" Barbara whispered
to Marcel.

"Two loyal old Bolsheviks. Stalin accused them of trea-
son and executed them."

"Tell her the whole story," Camille snapped.

"That would take all evening. How many were there—
sixteen in the first trial, seventeen this past January, Mar-
shal Tukhachevski and his whole general staff—it is simply
too dismal."

"Absolutely," Limoget agreed. "Dismal. You see," he
said to Barbara, "this never angers me. I don't hear Marcel.
I hear *Le Monde.* Who speaks? The whore or the pimp?
The driver or the horse?"

Barbara expected Marcel and his two friends to react
in rage, but instead they exploded with laughter. Evidently
they had been through all this before.

"You were trying to say something before," Marcel said
to her. "Talk quickly, or you'll never get a word in here."

"I can't in French, truly," she told them. "Only you were
blaming Roosevelt for the embargo. It was an act of Congress, you know."

To her amazement, all four of them turned on her. Only
Marcel forbore to attack.

"Your Congress!"

"Running dogs of the bourgeoisie!"

"Running dogs of Roosevelt!"

"Who is the lead dog of the bourgeoisie!"

"You abuse the child. The child is innocent."

Through all this, Betty Greenburg and Susan Clark had
sat as silent as Barbara. Now, Betty came to her defense,
saying, "You really don't know all that much about the
States. It was a joint resolution of Congress on January

sixth. I am sure that if Mr. Roosevelt had made the decision—"

"He did!" Limoget snapped. "You Americans are children when it comes to politics. He leads your Congress by the nose."

"It hurts me to agree with Claude," Jouvelle said placatingly. "But, mademoiselle, it is a fact. Roosevelt could have blocked that resolution. He did not. Thereby, he practically condemns the Spanish Republic to death. Where will they find arms? Franco gets all he needs from Hitler and Mussolini."

"Then why not from Russia?" Susan Clark demanded.

"Because Stalin is very careful about offending Hitler," Marcel said.

"Nonsense! Everything the Republic gets is from Russia."

"But your own Léon Blum is a socialist," Barbara protested. "It's easy to blame Roosevelt three thousand miles away, but why does Blum do nothing?"

"Why indeed?"

"Because a French socialist," snapped Camille Limoget, "is a French pig. No difference. Frauds, cheats, liars—"

"Oh, come on, come on," Jouvelle said.

It continued. It went on and on until midnight. They consumed every drop of wine, and never paused from talking, shouting, waving their arms, and insulting each other. After the first exchange, Barbara and the two other American women retreated into silence; at last, when everyone had left, Barbara sighed in relief and said, "Thank heavens. No blood spilled."

"But they are dear friends," Marcel protested.

"And they always do that?"

"When you have communists, a socialist government, a war in Spain, Hitler, Mussolini—oh, yes, they argue. I suppose it might be thought of as a sort of intellectual exercise."

"I've never heard anything like it before."

"Then, my darling Barbara, you've been in the company of dullards."

"Perhaps. But the things you say to each other—"

"Better said than unsaid. You know, you Yankees pretend to be so different from the British, but you share their fear of passion. It is the same word in English as in French, no?"

Barbara nodded.

"Only I think it goes further in our language. Did it ever occur to you, my dear Barbara, that our whole world is coming to an end?"

"You are being very serious, and I have to think about that. Mostly, you are only serious when you make love to me."

"And you refuse to be serious."

"It's so late. And do you know, Marcel, in spite of all the sound and fury of your friends, I had a wonderful evening, and since Jouvelle and Brissard took the girls home—well, who knows, I may have done my good deed for the day. And it's impossible for me to consider that the world is coming to an end. I'm much too pleased with you."

"Not the world. That goes on. Our world. I cannot understand communists, I cannot agree with them, but damnit, they see what is happening in Spain, and if the lights go out in Spain, as in Germany and Italy—"

"But not tonight. Tonight, only the lights in this apartment. After which—"

"For a good, innocent American heiress, you have the strangest single-track mind."

"One of these days," Barbara decided, "we will examine that entire question. Probably we will discover that the white Protestant American schoolgirl has the most explosively repressed sexual urge of anyone on earh. And in French, that is a mouthful for me. But not tonight. Tonight, let's just curl up in bed and let the world take care of iself."

Alex Hargasey was fascinated with Dan Lavette and with the yacht that Dan was building for him. On Dan's part, he had never before come in contact with this particular type of man-child-idiot-artist, all of which described Hargasey and none of which described him adequately. He appeared to know his business of making films, but emotionally he was infantile. At the age of fifty years, he was alternately enraged, gentle, wild, or demonic. He was paid enormous fees, tolerated, kowtowed to; and he in turn abased himself before the stars in his film. He would not be crossed. When he demanded Dan's presence, Dan had to appear or endure his threats to break his contract for the yacht; and he in turn spent hours at the shipyard, watching the work in progress, asking endless questions.

At first indignant, angry, ready to tell him to go to the devil and take his damn contract with him, Dan came to realize that Hargasey and the people around him lived in a world totally separated from reality. Their work was the substance of dreams. They admitted no other responsibility than that to the film they were making, and like overindulged children of over indulgent parents, they simply accepted the fact that rules contrived for others did not apply to them.

When Hargasey informed Dan that he was giving a party at his home to celebrate the completion of his sea film—a wrap party, he called it—the information included a royal summons. Dan was to appear, with his wife, if he had a wife and desired to bring her, without her if he so desired—there would be single girls in plenty—or with anyone else he cared to bring. Informed of this, May Ling's immediate reaction was, "No, I can't go, Danny. You go without me."

"Why, can't you go? My word, honey, I would think that just out of curiosity you'd want to. He tells me that Garbo will be there, and Joan Crawford and Spencer Tracy and Marlene Dietrich and a lot of other names that I can't even remember—and it's the kind of thing we'd never get to see if not for that crazy yacht of his. Come on, come with me."

"Danny, darling, how can I go? I'm a middle-aged librarian, a very plain Chinese lady."

"Like hell you are!"

"I have nothing to wear. Danny, we haven't been to a party in years."

"Then it's high time, isn't it? Whatever you say about Hargasey, he's ended our condition of being broke. He's spending money on that yacht like it's going out of style. So just you go out and buy any dress you think is right for it."

"What about you?" she asked forlornly.

"I'll rent a tux. I got no choice. This is a crazy man. If I don't show up there, he'll go out of his mind."

Many years before, when Dan Lavette was still married to Jean, he had made a trip to Hawaii to open negotiations for building a hotel on Waikiki Beach. He had taken May Ling with him, and at a party given by their hosts, she had worn a dress of thick black silk decorated with dragons in gold thread. The dress had been a gift from her father, and she had worn it only once, on that single occasion. Now she took it out of the chest where it had been all these years, carefully wrapped in layers of tissue, and tried it on. It still fit perfectly, a very simple dress, ankle length, split on the sides to above the knee. Anyway, her figure had not changed.

The night of the Hargasey party, she remained in the bathroom, making up her face, until after Dan had dressed and gone downstairs. She felt like a silly young girl and giggled at her reflection in the mirror—it was so long since she had used make-up. Her skin was still smooth and unflawed. She sighed when powder failed to conceal the tiny wrinkles about her eyes. How awful it was to feel that the perfectly natural process of aging was your enemy! She had never cut her hair, but since she was a Chinese lady they would make allowances for that, just as they would for her curious dress. But what if Dan were to be disappointed? After all, he had urged her to buy a new dress; but a new dress for one single occasion made no sense whatsoever, and anyway, it was too late. She drew her hair into a heavy bun at the back of her neck, pinning it in place with two gold combs that Dan had given her. When? She tried to remember. It was the first anniversary of the night he had taken her to bed with him. And the evening slippers had come with the dress, of the same black silk and the same gold thread. Dressed, her hair finally set, she stood there lost in thought, remembering how Feng Wo, after five years of working for Lavette, had finally gathered up the courage to ask Dan whether he and his wife would come to partake of a Chinese dinner at their home. Jean, as Dan told her afterward, had reacted in horror. Dan came alone, and that was the beginning, the first time he had seen her. But she was already in love with him before he ever set foot in her father's house, in love with the image of this strange, huge, unruly man who had defied all mores of San Francisco prejudice to hire a Chinese to run his business. And then, the second time, he had turned up at the library where she worked, the temporary library that had been put together after the earthquake, fumbling, uneasy, like a small boy avowedly doing wrong, asking her whether he, a married man, could take her to dinner.

His booming voice broke in on her reverie. "May Ling, we're going to be the last ones there!"

She came downstairs slowly, very tentatively. They were all waiting there to review her—Dan in his rented tuxedo, Joe, Feng Wo, and So-toy. No one said anything as she appeared. They just stared at her speechlessly, and Dan's thoughts, like hers, leaped back to that evening in Hawaii, when, with her hand on his arm, they had come out onto the lawn, under the light of the Japanese lanterns, and every face in the great crowd of people at the luau had turned toward her. It seemed to him that nothing had changed, and now he said, almost reverently, "My word, you are one hell of a woman!"

Marcel's English left more to be desired than Barbara's French; but then, she had been living in France for almost three years, while his English was simply the product of school and two weeks in London. The letter she proposed to read to him would, she insisted, help him practice.

"But I don't need practice," he said. "I live in France."

"Now. Conceivably, someday, you might desire to live somewhere else."

"Why? You know what the Frenchman said when asked why his was a nation of nontravelers?"

"I don't. Tell me."

"He said, 'Monsieur, why should I travel? I am already in Paris.'"

"That's not arrogant, it's only modest and reassuring. This letter is from Dan's wife. She's Chinese."

"The letter is in Chinese?"

"You know it isn't. She's a lovely, cultured woman, a librarian, and her name is May Ling. It's a very romantic thing, although when I was a kid I thought it quite horrible. He met her a few years after he married my mother, and then for years she was his mistress and lived in a little house on Willow Street in San Francisco, which he bought for her—"

"It sounds very French."

"I suppose so. She had a child, who is my half brother, Joe, but that was before they were married, and it wasn't very romantic, I guess, but pretty terrible, and then she couldn't stand it anymore, and she and Joe and her mother and father left San Francisco and went to Los Angeles, and

then finally my father divorced my mother and followed
her there."

"If you hadn't told me this before, there's no way in
the world I could follow what you're saying. Must you
read me the letter in English?"

"Yes. You'll meet her someday. She's dear and sweet
and very clever, and she looks like one of those porcelain
ladies out of an old Chinese print."

"Porcelain ladies out of a print?" Marcel asked dubiously.

"You know what I mean."

"Then read slowly, please." He kicked off his shoes, sat
crosslegged on her couch, lit a cigarette, and prepared himself to listen. Barbara stared at him thoughtfully until finally he said, "Well, go on. Begin."

"I was just thinking—I love you. You're very kind and
very gentle and very patient, nothing like my notion of a
Frenchman. No, that's not exactly what I mean."

"Of course it is. Don't go on with this. Just read your
Chinese letter, very slowly."

"Dear Barbara," she read, "I have allowed too much to
accumulate, which is the punishment of a very bad letter
writer, so this will have to go on and on. I have the whole
evening, because Dan drank too much last night, and he's
not a good drinker, so here it is nine o'clock, and he's
sound asleep. And the reason he drank so much is that
we went to one of those Hollywood glamour parties that
you read about in the newspapers, except that it was in
Beverly Hills and not in Hollywood—"

"I don't understand that," Marcel interrupted.

"They live in Los Angeles, and it's very confusing. If
you are in the movie business, they call it Hollywood, but
there are lots of small towns in Los Angeles, and Beverly
Hills is in Los Angeles. It's kind of a city inside of a city,
and very posh—"

"That's enough," Marcel protested. "Just read the letter,
but slowly."

"—not in Hollywood," she read, "but in one of those
fantastic pink stucco palaces that these people live in, and
it all happened because Dan is building a yacht for a Hungarian film director by the name of Alex Hargasey. You
know about the old boatyard that Dan and Sam Goldberg
took over on Terminal Island. The whole venture wasn't
going well at all until Hargasey hired Pete Lomas's mack-

erel boat for a film he was making, and then Pete brought
Hargasey to Dan, and now Dan is building him this huge,
expensive yacht that will cost enough money to keep the
boatyard going another year.

"Well, Hargasey is absolutely intrigued by your father,
and he insisted that we come to this party, which was
held to celebrate the completion of the film, which will be
called *The Angry Sea*. Can you imagine, a middle-aged
Chinese lady among all those movie stars and glamorous
people! At first I absolutely refused to go, but then Dan
and Joe insisted that I must, and I put together a sort of
Chinese costume, and Dan rented a tuxedo, and there
we were. Barbara, your father was wonderful. Not only was
he the most impressive and handsome man there, but all
these beautiful, celluloid women were practically climbing
all over him. But Hargasey, who is about fifty and paunchy
and has the most incredible accent, attached himself to me,
and presently informed me that he had conceived a great
passion for me and that we must have what he called a
'liaison.' Isn't that a wonderful word? They are absolutely
the strangest people I have ever known. When I told
Dan about it, I expected him to be furious and prepared
myself to calm him down, but he laughed himself silly. I
think he's becoming much too sure of himself. We were
introduced to Greta Garbo and Bette Davis and Spencer
Tracy, only I think it was not Spencer Tracy but his twin
brother, who goes places instead, and it was all absolutely
unbelievable. And the strangest part of it is that my
father, who is such a serious old Chinese gentleman,
insisted that I go into every detail of who I saw and met—
such is the power of the movie industry."

"Your grandfather is Chinese?" Marcel said in awe.

"No, no, no. How many times must I explain to you?
Feng Wo is Joe's grandfather, a very scholarly and dignified
gentleman who translates Chinese philosophy and who has
had a book published by the University of California Press.
He also managed my father's business for years and
years."

"No, please, don't explain anymore. Is the letter over?"

"Not quite. I'll read slowly. Joe—I'm reading now—"

"I can see that. Your brother, Joe."

"Joe is starting his second year at college. He spent the
summer in the Napa Valley, at Higate, working for Jake
and Clair Levy. You never met the Levys, but you will

soon. They're taking a trip to Europe and they'll be in Paris, and I took the liberty of giving them your address and telephone number. They'll arrive, I think, about three weeks after you get this letter. I know that it was a liberty, but they're dear, good people. Jake's father, Mark, was Dan's partner for twenty years, from nineteen ten to nineteen thirty. Clair's father was Dan's first captain. He died when the *Oceanic* was torpedoed in nineteen seventeen, and after that Clair lived with the Levys until she and Jake were married. Jake had some bad experience overseas during the war, and he wanted no part of his father's money. Very idealistic. He felt the money was tainted, since Dan and Mark built their empire out of war shipping, and he and Clair took whatever savings they had and bought an old winery for a song during Prohibition. It's quite a place now, and part of the reason for their trip to Europe is Jake's plan to put their wine on the French market. Can you imagine Frenchmen buying California wine?

"And if it were not sufficiently complicated with Joe being half Chinese and one quarter French and one quarter Italian, Sally, Jake Levy's youngest child, has fallen madly in love with him. Since she's not yet thirteen, no one is taking it very seriously, but the combination, at some future date, would be absolutely fascinating, since Jake is Jewish and Clair is a mixture of Irish, English, and German. Sally is a strange and lovely child, wild as a hare and smart as a whip and as unlike Joe as anything you could imagine, skinny, long legs, and the same pale blue eyes and straw-colored hair that her grandmother, Sarah, once had. She is convinced that she is ugly and undesirable, and she confessed to me in utter misery that her breasts were too small, her legs too long and skinny, her skin too freckled, and her hair no better than straw. Can you imagine? From a thirteen-year-old. She is much too liberated for her age, and she told Joe that if he ever looked at another girl, she would kill him. I think he is flattered.

"Anyway, there is a little of our life back here. Please, do be kind to the Levys. But I know you will. I don't think you could be unkind to anyone. Dan sends all his love, and I do keep after him to write, but to him a letter is a monumental task. Joe misses you, as we all do. When will you come home?"

"Zat, dear one, is zi question," Marcel said in English.

"Very good."

"The question or my English?"

"Your English."

"Thank you. But if we were married, it would make for problems."

"Are you asking me? It's an odd way to propose."

"I'm afraid to ask."

Barbara, staring at him thoughtfully, said nothing.

Joe Lavette could not get her out of his mind. The University of California campus did not lack beautiful girls There was a long-limbed, tawny-skinned breed that California seemed to produce, robust, good-looking women whose eyes followed and admired the young student. With good reason. Twenty-one years old, Joe Lavette stood six-foot-two, slightly taller than his father; he had Dan's broad shoulders without the thickness, without the heavy overlay of muscle; his features were more delicate, the nose smaller, the dark eyes with a slight Oriental cast, the black hair straight and cropped short. He was not simply a handsome young man, but different, unusual, race and breed titillating the curiosity of everyone who noticed him. Warm, emotional, perhaps overly sentimental, he found that he fell in and out of love all too easily. His problem, which he recognized, was to remain unattached until he finished medical school and his subsequent internship. It had been a miracle to him that he had been accepted at all, and to resist making a permanent alliance with one of the number of blond, blue-eyed women who welcomed his affection required all his will power.

Sally Levy helped. At least to the extent that once the summer at Higate was over, he found himself thinking about her constantly. "I am not in love with her," he assured himself. "I am not stupid or romantic enough to be in love with a demented thirteen-year-old kid." He had had affairs with four girls, successively, and had convinced himself that he was sincerely in love with all four of them, also successively. But when he fixed any one of them in his mind as candidates for marriage, the image was always blocked by the memory of Sally Levy, her oversized hands scratched from the grape picking, her fingers stained with grape juice, her face covered with freckles, her straw-colored hair an unwashed tangle, and her eyes filled with a foolish, cowlike worship. She followed him everywhere, made an ultimate nuisance of herself, and then finally said to him, one evening,

"You might as well know about it. I love you."

"You're crazy," he told her.

"Sure, that's a fine thing to say."

"Jesus, you're thirteen years old."

"I didn't have anything to do with that. Anyway, it's no reason why you can't be nice to me."

"I am nice to you."

"You are like hell. You don't even know that I exist. You pay more attention to the damn dogs."

"Why don't you stop trying to talk tough?" he asked her gently.

"Maybe it's just the way I am."

"Maybe."

"How do you feel about me?" she demanded.

"What do you mean, how do I feel about you. I like you all right. We're sort of related, aren't we?"

"No. How could we be related? You're Chinese. But that doesn't bother me."

"Thank you."

"Because I'm in love with you."

"Yes, you said that before."

"In a few weeks you'll be going back to Los Angeles. You'll forget all about me."

"Not very likely."

"You don't even say that nice. You think I'm just a crazy kid, don't you?"

Joe shook his head hopelessly.

"Well, I'm not. I started to menstruate."

He stared at her, unable to think of an appropriate comment.

"Well, if you're going to medical school, that shouldn't shock you."

"It doesn't shock me. It's just a funny thing for a kid to say."

"Why don't you stop calling me a kid? Why can't you take me seriously? If you did, you'd at least come up here sometime to see me. I can't go down to Los Angeles. What do you think my mother would say if I told her that I was in love with you and I have all kinds of crazy dreams about you making love to me?"

"I can imagine what she'd say."

"So you won't come to see me, not even once?"

"How can I, Sally? I'll be in medical school. Do you know what medical school is like? They work you twenty-four hours a day."

"And in between, you sleep with the nurses."

"God Almighty, where do you get your ideas?"

"I read a lot."

"I bet you do."

"Anyway, you can be sure of one thing. If you marry anyone else, I'll just kill you."

"Just like that?"

"You bet."

"Well," he said, "you don't have to kill me, because I don't intend to marry anyone."

Thinking about it now, months later, her image remained with him, vivid, alive. Whoever he was with paled into dullness against that memory.

It was a year since Barbara had met Marcel Duboise, and to celebrate the occasion, she prepared dinner for the two of them in her apartment on the Quai de Passy. She had been reading French cookbooks, practicing assiduously, and for the occasion she decided on a *boeuf en croûte*. She had to finish her piece for the magazine, and that took the morning. Then she skipped lunch, contenting herself with a cup of coffee and a cigarette, and went to work on the *boeuf*, wondering meanwhile, as she had so often before, how it was that a nation of superb cooks built apartments with such wretched kitchens. Hers was no better than a large closet. The dish was a challenge; for herself, she considered *haute cuisine* to be an utter waste of time and rather silly in the bargain, but since she happened to be in love with a Frenchman, she was determined to conquer it. She had done her shopping in the early morning, in the best local tradition. Beef fillet. She trimmed it carefully, tied it up, giggling at her careful effort, rubbed it with pepper, and then browned it in fresh sweet butter, all the while feeling that she was working out a puzzle rather than preparing food. Ten minutes in a hot oven. While it was cooling, she read over her piece for the magazine: the new spring fashions, a scattering of politics that she had picked up from *Le Monde*—she was still on uneasy ground with politics—the three new best-selling novels, particularly Aragon's new book, and the opening of a new loan exhibit of the Impressionists. She was on firm ground there; at least that much her mother had given her, and after reading it, she decided that Jean would like it. Jean read every piece she wrote, and discussed her pieces in the letters they exchanged. It was in her last letter that Jean had observed that her daughter was becoming a "damned competent and professional writer." It was high praise.

The meat had cooled by now. Slice the mushrooms, sauté in butter, chop the mixed herbs with the parsley, add that, cool again. Now to make the puff pastry, so absolutely foolish and so absolutely complex. She had pinned up the recipe on the wall in front of her. Roll out the pastry and divide in two. Mixture of mushrooms and spices on the larger piece. Place the beef on top of it, fold pastry up and around, second piece of pastry over the top. The egg glaze. She had forgotten that entirely. Then into a hot oven for forty minutes. It left her only enough time to shower and dress. When she took the dish out of the oven, brown and beautiful, filling the house with its good smell, Marcel was at the door.

He brought a bottle of champagne and another of red wine, and under his arm was a long loaf of fresh bread. "A double celebration," he announced, after Barbara had taken the packages and kissed him.

"Double?"

"Our anniversary and my promotion. I am no longer a contemptible critic."

"Oh, wonderful! But you were never a contemptible critic, never a contemptible anything."

"All critics are contemptible. Who was it, Shaw or some other very wise man, who said the critic is like the eunuch in the harem? He watches the trick turned every night, but knows he could never do it himself."

"Yes, very clever. Now please tell me what happened," Barbara begged him.

"Ah. So you wish to know?"

"Yes, I wish to know."

"Very well. My estimable editor, I hear he is looking for someone on special assignment in Spain. True, we have three men there already, but this is very special. So I go to him, I plead, I threaten, I entreat, I become a veritable Cyrano of persuasion—and finally he melts, he agrees. Whereby, I am going to Spain."

"What kind of special assignment?" Barbara asked slowly, quietly.

"Ah, come, come." He started to kiss her again, but she pushed him away.

"What kind of special assignment?"

"What is that marvelous, enchanting smell?"

"Stop it! Don't be cute now. I want to know what you are going to do in Spain."

"All right. You have heard of the Fifteenth Brigade, the Internationals. It includes an American Brigade of volunteers, which they call the Abraham Lincoln Brigade. My editor wants a series of pieces on them. They are very brave, very gallant, and we have printed very little about them. You see, I speak English, thanks to you."

"You told him you speak English?" she asked coldly.

"But I do, Barbara."

"I suppose you do, in a manner of speaking, if you call it English. I think the whole thing stinks."

"Just like that?"

"How else? Shall I tie it up in a rose-colored ribbon? You know how I feel about war, about this insanity of men killing each other for their filthy causes, for their noble aims."

"We never talked about it."

"You've been living with me and sleeping with me for almost a year. You don't know me? Must I spell everything out—this is how Barbara feels about this and this is how Barbara feels about that?"

"You're right. There's a lot I don't know about you. I've never seen you in such a royal rage before."

"Then it's time."

"Baby, baby," he said, "we can't have a fight. We never had a fight. Please, please try to understand what this means to me, a by-line assignment as a special foreign correspondent. I don't have to argue the cause of the Spanish Republic. You know it as well as I do, and you know what that butcher Franco has done. I'm not enlisting. I'm not a volunteer. I am simply going as a writer, as a journalist, to put down what I see and hear."

"So you can say, thank God for a war."

"No, that's not fair."

"What is fair? For me to fall in love with a man who goes off to get shot at in this stupid game? I told you about the kid in San Francisco, his poor wasted life. He was in love with me. I was selfishly spared, because there was no way I could love him. But I do love you, and I will not have this happen to me again. I will not. I know I live in a world of maniacs, but I thought that you and I—"

"Would be spared?" he asked gently. "No one is spared, Barbara, dear love, no one. And this is something I have to do, believe me. It's not forever. Only six weeks, and then I'll be back, whole and safe and sound, I promise you."

She dropped into a chair and began to weep.

"No, no tears, please." He knelt beside her, kissing her hand, first on the back and then on the palm, a gesture so French, so unexpected, that she began to giggle through her tears.

"May I open the champagne?" he asked her.

"Yes."

"And will you tell me what the marvelous smell is?"

"Boeuf en croûte."

"Am I not the most fortunate of all men? Am I not?"

Later that evening, her emotions under control, Barbara tried to be both practical and helpful. "Remember," she said to Marcel, "you are an observer. You have no obligation to put yourself in a dangerous situation. That would be stupid and wasteful. Your job is to see things and write about them."

"Yes, my dear," he agreed.

"You're not listening."

"But I am. Every word."

"By the way, I do know someone in that unit. Well, no. I don't really know him, but the Levys do. You remember? I told you about them."

"Yes. Of course."

"It seems that this boy worked for them at the winery. His name is Bernie Cohen. Can you remember that?"

"I will try. What is he doing in Spain?"

"Well, he's Jewish and he's a Zionist or something of that sort, and he intends to go to Palestine. From what my brother wrote to me, he enlisted in the Lincoln Brigade to get experience in fighting—which is perfectly insane, but I don't know what part of this is not insane. But Joe met him at Higate, and he says he is competent and reliable, so at least that would be one person you would know."

"Barbara, I don't really have to know anyone. I'll be

with the press. You simply must not worry about me. I'll be all right."

"You don't have to go. You can still tell them that you don't want this wretched assignment."

"I can't. You know that."

"All right. I won't speak of it again. You know how I feel. Just think about it."

"Not only that, but I'll do the dishes."

"To hell with the dishes. Take me to bed, and we'll pretend there are only two of us in a very beautiful, uncomplicated world."

Marcel left for Spain the day before the Levys arrived in Paris, and the evening of the day they arrived, they telephoned Barbara and asked her to dine with them the following day. On her father's side, Barbara had no blood relations. Daniel Lavette, the child of two immigrant parents, had been left an orphan at the age of seventeen. Since she was a child, Barbara had known of his close attachment to the Cassala family in San Mateo and the Levy family in Sausalito, and she had also known of her mother's distaste for both families. They were a part of her father's life. She had never met any of them, but through the years she had heard a great deal about them. For most Californians, the wine business wears a halo of romance, and Barbara was intrigued with the notion of two young people buying an abandoned winery during Prohibition and turning it into a prosperous enterprise—and now the thought of selling California wine in France delighted her. In any case, they would fill some of the empty hours that faced her during Marcel's absence. Until he left, she had not realized how totally she had come to depend on him, and when she looked back now at her years in Paris before she had met him, they appeared to be lonely and barren beyond belief.

There were no tears after her initial outburst. She had gone with Marcel to the Gare de Lyon, and while waiting for his train, they lunched at one of the stands in the station, agreeing that the ham, sandwiched in small loaves of fresh bread, and the mugs of cold beer were as good as anything they had ever tasted. They laughed a good deal, and she expunged the scene that had taken place in her apartment by assuring him that she would steal from his pieces in *Le Monde* without conscience, incorporating what she stole into her own "Letter from Paris." They were self-consciously gay and young and delighted with themselves until it was train time, and then she clung to him, whispering, "You bastard, I'll never forgive you for going away." But then, when the train began to move and he had poked his head out of his compartment, she ran alongside and shouted, "I've forgiven you, but only for six weeks. One day more and I'll cut your heart out."

Two days later, getting out of a cab at the Hôtel de la Trémoille, where the Levys were staying, she felt that she had worked out her period of being alone and that six weeks was by no means the eternity she had imagined. Jake and Clair Levy were waiting for her in the lobby. Barbara recognized them; she knew that Clair Levy was a redhead, but she was unprepared for the striking, unusual look of the woman, almost as tall as her husband, who was well over six feet, long-limbed, almost raw-boned, a high, full bust, and a strong-featured freckled face under a mop of flaming red hair. She was quite beautiful, yet Barbara felt that to think of her simply as a beautiful woman diminished her. Jake Levy was a burly heavyset man, with dark hair turning gray, a prominent nose, pale blue eyes, his heavy shoulders tight in his clothes, like a farmer in city dress.

Barbara walked over to them and said, "I know you because daddy told me so much. I'm Barbara Lavette."

Their greeting waited on a moment of amazement and delight; then Clair Levy folded Barbara in her arms, kissed her, and then stepped back to look at her. "Oh, great! You're just what you should be!"

Barbara kissed Jake. He stood there grinning at her. "We're such old friends," Barbara said. "We mustn't pretend that we've just met. I knew you both the moment I came into the hotel. Daddy always spoke of the green eyes and the red hair."

"You see," Clair told her husband, "being a bit freakish has its advantages."

"Oh, no!" Barbara cried. "I think you're the most stunning woman I've ever seen."

"So do I," Jake said comfortably. "We're so glad to finally meet you, Barbara. I saw you once, when you were two or three years old. Danny sneaked you out to Sausalito. You remember, Clair?"

"I certainly do. You've changed, darling."

"I'm sure I have."

"We didn't make any dinner arrangements," Jake explained. "This is my first time back since the war, and the first for Clair, and I've forgotten what little French I picked up then. I thought you'd know where the food is good, since you're practically a native."

"One of the delicious things about Paris is that the food is good practically everywhere. There's a little restaurant on the Left Bank called Lapérouse where I know the proprietor. We're sure to get a table, and the food is good. We can take a cab."

They listened with the awe that Americans hold toward anyone fluent in a foreign language as she gave directions to the cab driver and then to her conversation with the owner of the restaurant, to whom she introduced them as members of her family.

"Your French is amazing," Jake said as they were seated.

"It should be. My goodness, I had four years of it in private school and then two more years at college, and I've been living here almost four years. I even think in French now, and do you know, I dream in French."

"Don't go on." Clair sighed. "I don't have two words."

"She speaks Spanish like a native," Jake said.

"Oh, come on, Jake. Don't be defensive. We have Chicanos working at the winery, and I can tell them what to do. That's about it."

At Jake's urging, Barbara ordered dinner while he pored over the wine list. He selected three chateau Burgundies, each a different label and a different year.

"Are you sure?" Barbara asked him. "We'll never finish three bottles."

"We don't have to. We've been tasting Burgundies at every meal on the ship coming over."

"It's a practically demonic compulsion with Jake," Clair explained. "They talk of carrying coals to Newcastle. We come carrying wine to France. Every grower we know says we are totally out of our minds—even for dreaming that America could sell wine to France. But I guess Jake and I have been out of our minds ever since we got into wine, and do you know, Barbara, I do think that all wine makers are a little crazy. It comes from breathing the fumes day and night."

"That's nonsense," Jake said. "If we're crazy, we're

crazy like foxes. I'm the kind of jingoistic American who thinks we can do anything better than anyone else, and that includes wine. Are we boring you with all this talk of wine?"

"No, no, please. I'm fascinated," Barbara assured him.

"All right. I'll try to explain. Up in the Napa Valley and the Sonoma Valley, where wine is like a religion, the growers with very few exceptions have decided that our Cabernet Sauvignon is the great red wine of California and thereby of America. Oh, it's good all right, and when it's well made, really well made, it can compare with some of the fine French Médocs. Essentially, it's a claret. Also, it's a wine that can stand aging, and if you can afford to lay it away and let it sit for ten years, you have a wine as good as anything in the world. But we can't put away our wine for ten years; we just don't have the money or the reserves, and as for a young Cabernet—well, it has a little too much tannin for my taste."

"That's the stuff in wine that makes the cheeks pucker," Clair said. "It's also rather sharp."

"So we broke with the crowd," Jake said, "and decided to experiment with Pinot Noir. That's a Burgundy. The first of our vines came from France, but California soil and California sunshine change it—improve the grape to my taste. Pinot Noir is a beautiful wine, soft and smooth as velvet when it's well made, and with much less of the tannic taste. But the decisive fact is that while it is also a red that needs aging, two years of laying it away will produce as fine an aged wine as eight or ten years with the claret. Now ours is a varietal, which means wine made out of a single type of grape. The French tend to blend their Burgundies. By now, Clair and I have tasted at least forty Pinots and Burgundies, and we still think we're sitting on top of the lot."

"That's to *our* taste," Clair said. "We're by no means great wine tasters. We know a little, much less than Jake likes to think we know, and the wine is as much an excuse for this trip as a business venture. We shipped ten cases over here, not so much for France as for Holland and Denmark, where we think there might be a market. Just for tasting. Not for selling. Germany would be ideal, but we wouldn't set foot in that hateful place. Anyway, American wine might just be a novelty. What do you think of the notion?"

"I think it's great," Barbara said. "Just great. And I think I could be of some help. I know people on *Le Monde*, which is one of the most prestigious papers in Paris, and I think I could arrange for an interview. They're Marcel's dear friends, and I do think it's newsworthy. I'll write about your visit myself, but I'm afraid publicity in New York won't help you much."

"Marcel?" Clair asked.

Barbara smiled. "There goes the cat out of the bag. You're the first to know. I haven't told mother or daddy, but I simply must tell someone. Marcel Duboise is a French journalist whom I love very much. Someday, I suppose, we'll be married. He's thirty years old, dark, skinny, kind of funny-looking, and very kind and very smart."

"I'm so glad. He sounds wonderful," Clair said. "Will we meet him?"

"Only if you can stay six weeks. He left two days ago for Spain." Then she went on to tell them about Marcel —who he was, what he did, and how they had met. She found herself talking to Jake and Clair as if she had known them all her life, in part because she was so hungry for some part of home, of California, and in part because they were warm and open and easy to talk to.

The food came and the wine came. The wine was tasted, judged, discussed. Barbara knew very little about wine. She and Marcel were quite content with *vin ordinaire*, a liter of which could be bought for a franc, and she was quite in awe of the manner in which Clair and Jake discussed the virtues of the three Burgundies. Then they told her how they had gotten into making wine, with old Rabbi Blum coming to them with the proposal that they make the sacramental wine for the Orthodox synagogues of San Francisco. "He's been dead these past five years, rest his soul," Clair said. "But would you believe it, we just about built Higate on sacramental wine. We sold to the Jews, the Catholics, the Episcopalians—sweet, horrible stuff. Yes, we still make a good deal of it."

A whole past came alive for Barbara that evening. They told her the story of how Dan Lavette and Mark Levy bought their first iron ship, the *Oregon Queen*, from an old Swede called Swenson. Clair's father, Jack Harvey, was the captain of the *Oregon Queen*, and Clair, then ten years old, had her first mad crush on Dan.

"He was always my hero," Clair said. "That never changed. Martha—poor child, she's dead. She was Jake's sister—Martha and I both worshipped the ground Dan walked on—"

Jake, uncomfortable, changed the subject. They had scheduled ten days in Paris and then would be off to Amsterdam. Would it be possible for Barbara to spend some time with them, perhaps show them some of the sights? She said she would love it, and with Marcel away, it was the best thing that could have happened to her. They talked on and on, and suddenly they discovered that it was midnight, and that they were the last ones in the restaurant.

Before she left them, Barbara said, "By the way, Joe wrote to me that there was a man named Cohen who had once worked at Higate and who's now with the Lincoln Battalion."

"Bernie. Of course," Clair said.

"He's quite a guy," Jake added. "A little mad, but then, who isn't?"

"A little mad?"

"He has this obsession about a Jewish homeland in Palestine. He learned farming, and now it's fighting. That's a hell of a reason to enlist in a war, but it takes all kinds."

Barbara waited—for a by-line dispatch in *Le Monde* or for a letter. With the Levys, she wore an air of relaxed gaiety. Her anxieties were none of theirs; they had planned this trip and looked forward to it for years, and she felt a proprietary responsibility for their time in a city she knew so well and loved so much. Jake and Clair were almost childlike in their delight with what they saw. They put themselves wholly in her hands, and when she told them that they must have an entire day for the Ile de la Cité, they accepted the assignment willingly. Barbara's first hour in Westminster in London had left her in tears; her first hour in Notre-Dame had left her in a state of exultation, and when she came there now with Jake and Clair, she tried to recapture the feeling, to feel that in the Europe of 1938, God was in His heaven and all was right with the world. It was not there, and she slipped away to be by herself and let her tears wash out her eyes. When she joined them again, Clair said, "You've been crying. Why? What's wrong?" And Barbara assured her that she was simply an overemotional person. "I cry at the drop of a hat. This place is haunted, you know. Let's go to the flower market. This little island has the most marvelous flower market in the world." But then she changed her mind, as if she had betrayed her new friends, and insisted that they climb to the top and see the breathtaking view. They stood there entranced, all the hazy, misty beauty of Paris spread out beneath them.

It was almost midnight when they dropped Barbara at her apartment, and in spite of her vow to be both patient and calm, she telephoned Marcel's friend Jean Brissard, awakened him, and then begged him to forgive her. "But there's been nothing," she said, "nothing in the paper and no letter."

"Barbara, he's only been gone five days."

"But the paper must be in touch with him."

"Barbara, don't you understand about Spain? He had to go over the Pyrenees. The lines are very fluid. He might have to hole up for days. Also, he's not there as a regular correspondent. He's not required to file a dispatch every day. He's doing a background piece on the Americans. He might not file it for two weeks. As for the mail, it goes by sea. It could take a week for a letter to reach Paris. So just be patient and don't worry."

It was reassuring, and Barbara, exhausted after her day as a tour guide, slept well. The Levys had a wine-tasting appointment the following afternoon at the offices of Lebouche & Dume, one of the largest wine wholesalers in Paris, and Barbara had agreed to go along as interpreter. The Levys had been assured that English would be spoken, but Barbara explained to them that such assurance meant very little in France. She assigned the morning to the regular American tourist routine, up the funicular to the heights of Montmartre, or the Butte, as she called it, apologizing for the cheap, touristy gimmicks that had invaded it, but also repeating Marcel's story of the bloody battle that had raged there during the time of the Paris Commune. They lunched at a little restaurant in the shadow of the Sacré-Coeur, where they were plagued by the vendors of so-called Paris postcards.

"But this is a part of it," Barbara explained. "How could you go home and tell them you were not at Montmartre?"

"I love it," Jake said. "Don't apologize."

"Tomorrow we will begin with the Medicis fountain in

the Luxembourg Gardens, and that will take the taste of
this away."

With Clair carefully cradling two bottles of Pinot Noir
in a canvas bag, they made their way to the Faubourg-
St.-Honoré, where Lebouche & Dume had their offices in
an old town house that rented space to an antique dealer
on the main floor. They passed through an archway and
went up a lift and then into a splendidly furnished set of
rooms. An ancient, gilded wine press was the only indication of the business conducted there. The waiting room
contained an assortment of lovely pieces from the time of
Louis XIV and XV that caused Barbara to exclaim in
delight. A door opening momentarily revealed another
room where half a dozen clerks labored at desks, but no
sign or sound of commerce was permitted in the waiting
room or in the office of Monsieur Lebouche, into which
a stout, middle-aged receptionist conducted them and
where they were received by Lebouche himself, a bearded
gentleman in his seventies, dressed in striped trousers and
a morning coat, pink-cheeked and white-haired. He greeted
them graciously, obviously amused at the notion of American wine being sold in France.

"Monsieur Dume is indisposed," he explained. "Otherwise, we would both be here, no? He is only sixty-two, a
young man, but he abuses his body. You are Mr. and
Mrs. Levy, of California. But this enchanting young
lady?"

Barbara explained her position and the Levys' lack of
ease with the French language.

"They do not speak French?" Monsieur Lebouche asked
in amazement. "They make wine and they do not speak
French?"

Barbara apologized profusely. California was very far
away. It occurred to her to mention that they both spoke
Spanish.

"Excellent. We will converse in Spanish."

Jake sighed and resigned himself to silence. Clair unpacked the two bottles of wine, explaining that it was a
varietal out of an ancestry of Burgundian vines. Lebouche
could not keep his eyes off Clair. She was at least four
inches taller than the wine merchant, and the interesting
combination of green eyes and red hair obviously fascinated him. "Ah, what a splendid woman!" he said to
Barbara in French. "If Monsieur Dume were here, he

would be quite out of his mind. An extraordinary woman."

Clair was holding forth in Spanish about California soil and sunshine. Barbara whispered to Jake in English that Monsieur Lebouche considered Clair to be an extraordinary woman.

"So do I," Jake said. "This is a damn peculiar way they do business here."

Lebouche found a corkscrew and opened the bottles. Then he took two beautiful crystal decanters out of a cabinet. "We decant it now," he explained to Clair. The others no longer mattered. "We let it breathe a little. Then we taste." He selected two wine goblets. Obviously, he and Clair were to be the tasters. "Madame," he said to her, "you ennoble the art of wine-making."

"You haven't tasted it yet," Clair replied, smiling.

"I refer to you, not to the wine. Now we taste."

He poured two glasses of wine. "You must drink with me," he said to Clair. The others watched and waited, Barbara utterly entranced by the old man, his manner and ritual, Jake trying to maintain a calm face and repress a desire to burst out laughing. Clair accepted the ritual gravely and calmly. No toast. She followed the old man's motion as he raised the glass to his lips and tasted. He rolled his head, rolling the wine around in his mouth, and she did likewise. Then he swallowed. Then he held the glass to his nostrils, sniffing the aroma.

"Pinot Noir?"

Clair nodded.

"How long is it aged?"

"Two years."

"In what wood?"

"Our cooperage is German oak."

"How long in the bottle?"

"Four months."

"We'll taste again." He lifted the glass to his lips. Again the ritual. "You've tasted our Burgundies?"

"A good many of them," Clair replied.

"This is quite different. Is it warm in your Napa Valley?"

"The summers are hot, yes."

"Very strange. Hot weather spoils the Pinot Noir, but this—very excellent. And different. A most unusual wine, befitting a most unusual woman. If I were ten years younger, I'd challenge that great ox of a husband of yours,

I would, the woman and the wine. He doesn't know what I'm saying, does he?"

"I'm afraid his Spanish is not up to it," Clair said sweetly. "I am sure that if you were ten years younger, Monsieur Lebouche, we would welcome the challenge. Will you take the wine?"

"Can I refuse you so small a thing? But only as a novelty. France is France. What will you charge me for two hundred cases?"

"What the devil's going on?" Jake demanded.

"But you speak Spanish, dear."

"Plain Spanish, not this."

"He says he'll take two hundred cases to start. He feels it will be simply a novelty, but he's interested. He wants to know the price. Oh, yes, he approves of the wine."

Outside again, Clair asked Barbara whether she had followed the conversation inside.

"No, I don't have two words of Spanish. But you were wonderful, I could see that."

"Enlighten me," Jake said.

"He liked the wine. He said that if he were ten years younger, he would have both, myself and the wine. Isn't that perfectly wonderful, Jake? I'm almost forty years old. France is one hell of a place, don't you think?"

"That old goat. I'll be damned."

Six days later, the Levys departed for Holland, and on the same day, Barbara received a letter from Marcel, the first letter. He told her how much he loved her, assured her that all was going well, explained that since he did not care to have the letter censored he would go into no details, and promised to write again very soon. It was not, to Barbara's way of thinking, a very satisfactory letter, but it relieved her anxiety. He also mentioned that he had met her fellow Californian, Bernie Cohen, and that he liked him immensely.

Dr. Kaplan had never treated a Chinese before—there were few Chinese families in Westwood—and now he appeared troubled and uncertain as the frail Chinese gentleman dressed himself. Feng Wo sensed this, and directed the conversation very matter-of-factly. "It is cancer, isn't it?"

Kaplan was a young man, in his early thirties, and he had come to Los Angeles from New York and set himself up in practice only a short time before. Feng Wo had chosen him almost at random, looking for a physician who would have no possible connection with his family. He suspected that it might well be Dr. Kaplan's first terminal case.

"It's not operable, is it?"

"Both lungs," Dr. Kaplan said miserably.

"You're quite sure?"

Strange, a small Oriental gentleman who spoke perfect English, who appeared to be undisturbed by a sentence of death. Dr. Kaplan nodded. "I mean, there's no reason why you shouldn't have another opinion, but it's not something that is easily mistaken. If you'd like me to recommend an internist?"

"No, that won't be necessary. How long do I have?"

"A few months, perhaps a little more."

"I understand."

"I'd like you to see me again, perhaps in a week or two."

"Yes, most likely."

It was almost noon when Feng Wo arrived at the boatyard in San Pedro, and during the trip down there, he examined himself, his being, and the fact of his impending death. He was only sixty-three years old; he had not yet begun to think of himself as an old man; and once again he was managing the affairs of Dan Lavette. From the moment his son-in-law had asked him to come in and take charge of the books and finances of the new enterprise, he had felt youthful and renewed. Years before, when Dan Lavette's great empire had washed out in the debris of the Depression, his daughter, May Ling, had arranged for him to make a translation of the writings of the Chinese philosopher Lao Tzu. At that time, he had paid tribute to her skill in putting together a situation where he was commissioned to do the work for the University of California Press. His scholarship left something to be desired, yet somehow he had managed the translation, plodding through the work more as an effort to please his daughter than himself. It was only a temporary stopgap in the process of dying from lack of purpose and a feeling of utter uselessness. Now he was dying in fact, from a malignant disease for which there was no cure.

He went into the office that he now occupied at the shipyard and sat down at his desk, just sitting there and staring through the window at the mud flats and the still water of the bay. Then the door swung open and Dan Lavette entered, his voice booming with energy and excitement.

"Feng Wo, where the hell have you been? It's starting again, and I don't know whether to start climbing that lousy shitpile of success or to kick the whole thing into the mud."

Feng Wo turned to face him, his wrinkled face as impassive as ever. "What happened, Mr. Lavette?" he asked calmly.

"You won't believe this. Hargasey comes down this morning to look at his yacht. He's like a kid. He can't stay away from it, and this time he brings Samuel Carlwin with him. Carlwin's the owner of the studio where Hargasey's slated to make his next picture, and I suppose he has more money than God. I lead them around the boat and explain things, and Carlwin never says a word. Then, when we climb down from the cribbing, Carlwin takes me aside. Lavette, he says to me, I want you to build me a yacht. Just like that. I say, sure, I'll be happy to build him a yacht. Then he says to me, I want it to be twice as big as the one you're building for that sonofabitch Hungarian gypsy.

"Can you imagine? I try to calm him down. I try to explain to him that a ship that size would be damn near an ocean liner, that it would cost him over a million dollars. But he doesn't want to listen. All he wants to know is what I need to get the job started. I tell him I need fifty thousand dollars to draw up the plans and start ordering the material, and so help me God if he doesn't take out his checkbook and write out a check on the spot. Here it is." He took the check out of his pocket and handed it to Feng Wo, who looked at it, smiling slightly.

"Well, what about it, old man? What do we do?"

"We build the ship," Feng Wo said calmly. "In this strange and unreasonable world, nothing should surprise you, Mr. Lavette."

"I'll draw up a letter agreement, and I'll telephone Sam Goldberg to put together a contract. Meanwhile, get the check to the bank before he changes his mind, and then we'll get to work on costs. I don't know any more about what he wants than he does, but we'll figure something out. Twice the size of the one out there. Can you imagine?"

A week later, on his way home from San Pedro, Dan

stopped to pick up May Ling at the library. She was waiting for him at the entrance. She took his arm and said,
"Leave your car parked for a while, Danny, and we'll walk
on the campus. I want to talk—here, not at home."

"You sound damn serious."

"I am, Danny. Very damn serious."

They began to walk. He didn't press the point. May Ling
would tell him what she had to tell him in her own good
time. Anyway, it was a good walk, the sun dropping into
a lacework of clouds, the air sharp and cool.

"It's about my father, Danny," she said at last.

"He's not feeling too well, is he?"

"Then you noticed."

"Do you know what's wrong with him?"

"He's dying, Danny."

"No! Good God, what are you saying?"

She nodded miserably.

"How do you know? That's crazy. He was down at the
shop today. All right, he's tired. He doesn't have to work
that hard. I don't push him."

"Danny, Danny, listen to me. Joe noticed that something was wrong, and he asked me if I could get papa to
go down to USC with him, where they could do some tests.
Papa got very annoyed at me. Joe insisted that I try to
find out something, so I called five local doctors. The
fifth was a Dr. Kaplan, and when I told him who I was,
he admitted that papa had seen him twice. I went to see
Dr. Kaplan. Papa has cancer of the lung. It's inoperable.
He hasn't very long to live."

"My God," Dan whispered. "Are you sure? Who is
this Kaplan? We don't have to let it rest there. We'll get
the best doctors in California. There must be something we
can do."

"Danny, dear, there's nothing we can do. Joe spoke
to Dr. Kaplan. He took the X rays down to the medical
school at USC. It's too late. Nothing can be done."

"Oh, Christ, what a lousy, rotten deal." They walked
on. After a few minutes of silence, he asked her, "Does
your mother know?"

"I'm sure she doesn't. I can't tell her. It has to come
from papa. Danny, I want you to do this for me. Don't
treat him differently, please, and don't let on that you
know. Just let him work on as before. Dr. Kaplan said

that in a few more weeks, he won't be able to work, but until then, he must decide."

It was an empty evening. Barbara had tried all day to begin her "Letter from Paris," but the words wouldn't come. Her contributions to *Manhattan Magazine* had achieved a reputation for their air of gaiety, for their lightness and gossipy quality, but all this day her heart had been heavy as lead. The single letter from Marcel had been her only word from him; then, day after day with nothing, no word in *Le Monde,* and nothing in the mail. She had gone to the newspaper and had been assured that they knew no more than she did. Then she waited, while all the joy and exuberance drained out of her life and the wonder-city of Paris became a bleak and lonely and strange place. She had never experienced anything like this before—days utterly empty, time moving like thick, reluctant oil. April became May. Susan Clark returned to America. Betty Greenburg went to London to cover an economic conference. And Barbara felt utterly abandoned and forsaken.

Then, a little after six o'clock, her doorbell rang. It was Jean Brissard, and before she could even ask what he was doing there, he said to her, "He's alive. He's all right, and I have a fat letter for you right here in my pocket. So may I come in?"

She threw her arms around him and burst into tears. "You darling, sweet man!"

"Actually, I had hoped he would never show up. Then I could have you for myself."

"I don't believe that. Come in. Come on in." She ran into the bathroom to throw cold water on her face and wipe away the tears. Then, a moment later, she said, "I must get over crying about everything. I never do it when I'm alone."

"We were worried," Brissard admitted.

"Where is he? When will he come back?"

"First question. He's in Toulouse, in a hospital."

"Oh, no!"

"He's all right. I told you that. He was wounded in two places, a shell fragment in his right arm and a bullet wound in the leg. But he's all right."

"Are you sure?"

"Decide for yourself. Here's a letter to you." He handed her a thick envelope. "It's dictated. He found someone down there to take his dictation, and he's charged the paper the two hundred and eighty franks he paid her. But he sent us one hell of a story, believe me. It's on the front page tomorrow."

"What hospital?"

"The Sacred Heart."

"Could I get a train to Toulouse tonight?"

"I doubt it. Look, Barbara, he's all right. You can telephone the hospital, if you wish. You can't speak to him because there's no telephone in his room. Go down there by all means, if you wish. But wait until tomorrow——"

She was tearing open the letter, her hands shaking.

"I'm going to run along," Brissard said. "I'll be at the paper if you want to talk to me."

She hardly realized that he had gone. She began to read:

"My darling Barbara, I am dictating this letter because my right arm is unfortunately not functioning. The lady taking the dictation, Madame Clouet, is, we think, some sort of a distant relative. She has five children, and she is an excellent stenographer and typist. You know that my father and mother still live in Toulouse, so in a way I have finally come home to them, a bit battered, but otherwise in fine fettle. As for the story, I think it's good. As for my English, no more snide remarks from you and no more innuendos. I have been communicating in English——or American, if you will——believe it or not. My God, how I love you! How I adore you! Now Madame Clouet is regarding me very strangely. She is very proper. She says that for a writer, I am diffuse. She reads Balzac. I tell her to read Proust. She says she has no time for Proust, and that he bores her."

Laughing and crying all at once, Barbara paused to dry her eyes with the towel she had brought from the bathroom. "Not at all true that I don't cry when I'm alone," she whispered to herself. "Not at all true." She turned back to the letter.

"Very well, where have I been? You will read my story in the paper, but it's a newspaper story. I have to tell it to you differently. To get here, they had to carry me part of the way over the passes in a litter, and in my rational moments I debated with myself whether to tell you what happened. Then I decided that I must, since neither of us had ever held anything back. So I begin with the group I joined, the 58th Lincoln Battalion, Americans. It is, or was, part of the 15th International Brigade, and when I joined them they had about three hundred men. Very young, most of them younger than we are. I wore my old service uniform, with a correspondent's patch and a tricolor. Not much of anything, but most of the kids in the 58th wore old pants and what you Americans call sweat shirts. They were volunteers from every part of the States, lots of them from New York City, and a good many from your place, California, and I felt that those were particularly wonderful, since they shared a place of origin with someone I love so much. Have you predisposed me toward America? I think I fell in love with those kids. They didn't look like soldiers. They carried bolt-action Springfield rifles, most of them, and they didn't even have cartridge belts. They stuffed their pockets full of cartridges and hand grenades. But my God, they are something.

"I heard rumors when I joined them that the Republican front was breaking up and that soon there might be a general retreat across the Ebro, but they didn't know anything about this. I was with them two days, mostly experimenting with my English and trying to get some backgrounds stories, when orders came for the 58th Battalion to advance and to keep advancing until the orders were countermanded. There were six other correspondents there at their bivouac, three of them Americans. We had a meeting, and the correspondents decided that, in the light of the rumors they all had heard, the best thing would be to head back toward Barcelona for the time being. But I had just arrived. My lovely darling, I am not a brave man, and I know how you feel about 'heroes,' which is why I put it in quotation marks, but I had just arrived, and where was my story? Believe me, I had a vision of a lifetime of cursing out bad restaurants in print and reviewing second-rate plays, and I could not face it. So I decided to move along with the 58th and see what happened. I had made some slight acquaintance with the two officers in command, one by the name of Dave Doran and the other by the name of Bob Merryman. Merryman was from California. Poor boys, they both died. I also met your Bernie Cohen, but more of that later.

"At first, they said flatly that I couldn't go along, but when I explained that I would be doing a special feature for *Le Monde* and that, since I was French, I had done my army service and that if it came to the worst, I could take care of myself, they relented and agreed I could move with them.

"The 58th began to advance. No opposition. It was hot and dry and bleak. Our water gave out, and we lost our liaison. We didn't know it then, but the Republican army had already broken, and the whole line was in retreat. The 58th had simply cut loose, and there we were, three hundred men advancing against the whole fascist army. About noontime, we spotted a fascist water truck. The men guarding it gave up without a fight, and everyone's mood changed. We had plenty of water, and the little victory over the truck gave us confidence. We tied up the three rebel soldiers, left them there, and continued our advance. But Merryman was nervous about the silence all around us, and he cut out on our flank to try to effect some kind of liaison.

"It was very hot. About three o'clock in the afternoon, we decided to rest, and we sprawled in the shade under a grove of olive trees. We waited there for Merryman to return. It was very strange, just the American battalion, all alone, a few goats in the distance, not a living soul otherwise, the hot Spanish sun sinking slowly toward the west, and silence. Where were the armies? Where was the war? Then Merryman returned and told us that the 58th had advanced deep into fascist territory, while behind us the whole Republican army was in retreat. Also, he had met a Republican soldier who told him that the way back behind us was closed.

"Doran gave the orders to march, and we headed back, not quite the way we had come but through some rough country. We marched very quickly, and it was quite exhausting. Then we came to an elevation where we could look down into a little Spanish town—I think it was called Gondese or something of the sort. That's where the line of battle was, behind us now. We were behind the fascists, and we could see them driving their attack through the streets of the town, while the Spanish soldiers were trying to hold the little clay houses. Merryman and Doran decided that the only thing to do was to break through and join up with the Spaniards. It was getting on to twilight now. They detached a patrol of twenty-five men, and ordered them to fight their way through the fascist lines, join up with the Spaniards, and then we would mount an attack and drive the fascists out of the town. I thought it was very poor tactics to send out twenty-five men with no support, but I was in no position to comment. Well, we watched it happen. The whole patrol was wiped out. My God, those boys were so brave and so senseless! They were caught in a crossfire, attacking against machine guns with their old Springfields, and we watched it happen. There was nothing we could do.

"Then the Spaniards gave up the town and retreated to a hill beyond it, and there we were, holding our hill with the Republican soldiers on the other hill, and the fascists between us. We tried to dig in, but there weren't enough trenching tools. Then, in the last light of day, the fascists sent a regiment of cavalry charging up the hill against us. Would you believe it, men in shining cuirasses waving their swords? I guess that with the Republican army retreating everywhere, the fascists felt that any show of force would carry the day. We stopped that charge and took a heavy toll of the cavalry. Night came, and we were joined by a few hundred Spanish soldiers who had been cut off. But by then the fascists had brought up their artillery. For two hours they shelled us. It wasn't good. Eight more Americans died there, and that was where I got the piece of shrapnel in my arm. It wasn't too bad at first. But we knew that if we stayed there, it would be the end.

"We set out in the dark, and we walked all the rest of the night. By some miracle, we were not intercepted by the fascists who had been shelling us. Then, toward dawn, we ran smack into what may have been a German Nazi outfit. It was as if all the devils in hell had broken loose, as if their machine guns were set up and waiting for us. The Americans, instead of turning and getting out of there, attacked, and they were just cut to pieces. Afterward I heard that Merryman and Doran were both killed there, and I don't think that even a hundred of the Americans survived that battle. Anyway, it was the end of the 58th Battalion. I was shot in the leg, and the same Bernie Cohen I spoke of before dragged me out of it, and then it was over, with only the crying and moaning of the wounded, and I got out of it somehow, hanging on to Cohen, and we found a little shed, which we crawled into. We couldn't see what was happening from where we were, but we heard German voices all around us, and we were sure that sooner or later they would find us, and Cohen said that if they did, they'd shoot us on the spot, that the Germans didn't take prisoners. Whether or not this is true, I don't know, but I heard the same thing from others. Cohen was very strong and competent. He made splints out of some old wood in the shed and bound up my leg. I was in great pain, and after that, the events are somewhat vague.

"We stayed in the shed all day, and when night came, we left the shed, Cohen carrying me on his back. We were close to the Ebro. He asked me if I could swim, and I said I thought I could, and somehow or other we got across the river. It's all like a sort of nightmare. Then, to compound it, an Italian division of Black Shirts was encamped on the other side. With Cohen dragging me, on our hands and knees, we crawled through a whole sleeping Italian division, believe it or not. They didn't even have a single guard posted. Then Cohen carried me on his back, and toward morning we were picked up by an English ambulance that was searching for wounded in the area between the fascists and the retreating Republican army.

"So there is the whole story, my dear love, a confused, tragic little bit of an obscene and heartbreaking war. I wait now and count the hours before I see you again."

The nature of the immigrant is the state of being alone. Even if he goes to where he goes with a wife and family, he leaves behind him the whole intricate structure of the extended family that is hundreds of years in the making. So it was that when Feng Wo was laid away in the ground in the bleak, interdenominational cemetery in Los Angeles, six thousand miles from the land of his ancestors, in another land that designated him an outsider, a yellow man, a Chinese man, there were only six people present to hear the dirt fall on his coffin, Dan and May Ling, Joseph, So-toy, bent, withered, drying up from her tears, and Sam Goldberg and Sarah Levy, both of them down from San Francisco for the funeral.

They all returned to the little house in Westwood after the burial. It was the first time since she had been married, in the year 1895, that So-toy had not prepared the evening meal—with the exception of those days when there was no food at all to put on the table. She sat in a corner in the kitchen, a tiny, withered woman, as if the death that had claimed her husband had mistakenly passed her by, waiting now to be taken.

Sarah and May Ling prepared food, and May Ling explained to Sarah, "You see, she never learned English. She speaks a dialect called Shanghainese. So who will talk to her? That's the most terrible part of it."

Joe had returned to school. Dan sat in the living room with Sam Goldberg, who was recalling the day they bought the *Oregon Queen,* that first almost mythical, iron ship on which the empire of Levy and Lavette was built. Feng Wo had brought his abacus with him then, and when Swenson, the owner of the *Oregon Queen,* proposed that they buy his two garbage scows along with the iron lumber freighter, the abacus became as active as a modern computer. Goldberg remembered how the kids had gathered around to watch with awe as Feng Wo added, subtracted, and multiplied on what Dan had called his "Chinee harp."

"They were all there, weren't they," Goldberg said, "Steve Cassala and his kid sister—what was her name?"

"Rosa."

"Right, and Clair Harvey and Jake Levy and Martha Levy, all the kids."

"I remember," Dan said.

"Well, it's gone. God Almighty, the world changes. Only thirty-two years since the big earthquake, and the whole world's different. Do you think we'll have a war, Danny?"

"I've thought of it. You know, it was the last war that made us millionaires. Christ, when I think of it, it sours my gut. Still and all, that Nazi bastard won't be satisfied. Sooner or later, he'll want the whole hog."

"You don't want any part of it, do you, Danny?"

"None."

"Still, if we couldn't stay out of it, where would they find the ships?"

"That's not my worry."

"What do you hear from Barbara?"

"We got a long letter. Jake and Clair were over there, and that let the cat out of the bag." He smiled ruefully. "She's in love, or so she writes, with a French journalist. She says she intends to marry him."

"And live in France?"

"God knows. I hope not. I miss her. On a day like this—Christ, it eats my heart out the way I miss her."

May Ling came into the room, leaned over Dan, and kissed him gently. "I've been meaning to say this since papa died. I'm in your debt for a great deal, my husband."

"For what, May Ling? For all the years of grief?"

"For all the years of love. But something else—for what you gave papa. You gave him his manhood. Without that, life is wasted, the way thousands of Chinese here live wasted lives. His life wasn't wasted. And I thank you for that."

She went back into the kitchen. Dan said slowly, "You know, Sam, she's Chinese. She's the second generation in this country, and she's still Chinese."

"She's also a very remarkable woman."

"She is. She certainly is."

The earliest train to Toulouse was a sleeper, which arrived there the following morning. Barbara was thankful to have had the compartment to herself, with no one to intrude on her thoughts except a solicitous wagon-lits conductor, a London cockney who assumed that every American or British girl traveling alone on the Continent was in constant and mortal danger. She read Marcel's letter again and again. The end of it troubled her. An ambulance had picked him up, and then he was in the hospital in Toulouse. Even with a bullet wound in the leg, he should have been able to limp—unless it struck the bone. She had read somewhere that a bullet striking the bone in the leg makes the most devastating type of wound. What had happened at the end of the letter? Was he simply tired of reliving the experience?

She compared his letter with the story in *Le Monde*. The headline read: LE MONDE CORRESPONDENT WITNESSES THE GALLANT FORAY OF AN AMERICAN BATTALION The story was longer than the letter and it went into more detail, and *Le Monde* provided background material on both Doran and Merryman. The facts of the battle with the German detachment were more explicit, as was the story of their progress through the Italian division. And there it ended. She read and reread both pieces until she could repeat most of it by heart. She had telephoned the hospital last night, but only a night nurse was on duty, and she could give out no sensible information. Now she regretted that she hadn't called again before she rushed off to catch the train. The train was impossible, slow, tortuous, stopping again and again. How much of her life had been spent on trains! They were lonely places that trapped her and forced her to examine the innermost recesses of her being. And she had brought nothing to read, nothing but the letter and the copy of *Le Monde*. Anyway, she did not want to read or divert herself. She wanted to be with the man she loved, and she wanted to recreate him lovingly in her mind, each part of him—the way he thought, the way he smiled, the way he touched her, the thin wrinkles that curled around either side of his mouth, the way he spoke English, mangling words and sentences, the time he bought a straw boater to do an imitation of Maurice Chevalier, their endless walks through the streets of Paris, the time they charmed a barge captain on the St.-Martin Canal and then drifted through an afternoon on that incredible, dreamily improbable waterway—all the days and weeks that they had been with each other, examining each other, finding each other. They were both so far from home, so free, so uninhibited in their giving.

She fell asleep. The wagon-lits man awakened her to make up her bed. Didn't she care for dinner? The thought of food was impossible. "I am certainly the most over-emotional, neurotic woman in the world," she told herself. Then she forced herself to go into the dining car and order dinner. A diaper salesman sat opposite her, a fat, jolly man as pink as a baby himself. What an extraordinary way to earn a living, she thought, listening to him pour out the tales of his trade. He chattered through the whole meal, and she was relieved to have something to divert her thoughts.

She slept poorly that night, awakening each time the train stopped, and then lying awake, listening to the sound of the wheels. She was up and dressed with the first light of dawn, waiting eagerly with her single small suitcase as the train pulled into Toulouse. A taxi took her to the Hospital of the Sacred Heart, a cream-colored stucco building on the edge of the city, and, still carrying her suitcase, she told the nurse at the admissions desk that she wished to see Marcel Duboise. The woman regarded Barbara dubiously and then stared at the suitcase.

"I've just come from the Paris train. I didn't want to stop at a hotel. Can I put this somewhere?"

"It will be safe enough right here. Are you Monsieur Duboise's wife?"

"I will be—when we marry."

Again the woman stared at her. In sympathy or annoyance? "What is your name?" she asked.

"Barbara Lavette."

"Mademoiselle Lavette, the visits are restricted to members of Monsieur Duboise's family. He's a very sick man. Those are the doctor's orders."

"I am as close as any member of his family," Barbara said, her voice hardening. "I want to see him now."

The woman regarded her thoughtfully, then nodded. "Very well. Try not to tire him. The sister will take you there." She motioned to another nurse who stood nearby. "Take her to Monsieur Duboise."

Barbara followed the nurse down a corridor, up a staircase, and along another corridor. She had never been in a French hospital before. This place was cloisterlike in its stark white severity.

'His father and mother are here," the sister told Barbara.

"Oh? Where are they? With him?"

"There is a sitting room at the end of this corridor. I saw them there before. Shall I tell them you're here?"

"I suppose so."

"What is your name, Mademoiselle?"

"Barbara Lavette."

"Here." She opened the door for her.

Barbara went into the room, white, white counterpane on the bed, an arched window with sunlight trickling through the slats of the blind, making a pattern on the bed; and Marcel lying there, very still, his eyes closed, his face drawn, his skin white.

She walked softly to the bed. Could such a change take place in a matter of weeks? His hands lay on the counterpane, thin, fleshless.

Then he opened his eyes and saw her, closed his eyes again, opened them, and whispered, "I have been feverish. This is a hallucination?"

"No, my dear darling." She bent and kissed his lips.

"Barbara?"

"Yes, Barbara."

He reached up to touch her face. "You're real. I am not delirious."

"Very real, my darling."

"You never were before."

"Always. Always real."

"Thank God. Everything is proper now."

"Everything."

"You won't go away?"

"From you? Never." She laid her hand on his cheek. It was hot to her touch.

"When did you get here?"

"This morning, on the train from Paris."

"We'll go to Hermés and I'll pick out a purse for you. You never let me buy you things."

"Yes."

"After lunch. First, lunch. Then we take the afternoon off and cheat the monsters of *Le Monde*. That's good, isn't it? The monsters of the world."

"Marcel," she whispered, "Marcel."

"We'll find a new place and charge the paper. I'll review them. The soufflé is noble but the traffic, the traffic—" He closed his eyes, and his voice dropped to a mumble of meaningless sound. The door opened. A small, bald man with a pince-nez entered the room, tapped Barbara on the shoulder, and nodded toward the door. She followed him out into the corridor, her heart sinking.

"I am Dr. Lazaire," he said to her. "And you are Barbara Lavette."

"Yes."

"I hope you are not a hysterical young woman."

"Not when it matters."

"This matters. I know all about you. He has told me, and his mother and father have told me. Now listen to what I have to say. Your young man had the bone in his leg, the femur, splintered by a bullet. A very serious wound, and not properly attended to before he arrived here. He is suffering from what we call 'spreading gangrene.' Under the best conditions, such a wound is very serious, but in that ghastly situation in Spain, their medical services are primitive. Now, understand me. His leg must be amputated. It should have been done five days ago, immediately when he came here, but he refused permission. Now you must understand clearly. This is not an amputation at the knee but at the thigh. It may already be too late. I am not the surgeon but the Duboise family doctor. I brought this young man into the world, so it means something to me. If another night passes without the operation, he will almost certainly die, and even if we operate immediately, I can guarantee nothing. He is very weak, and he may not survive the amputation. He says he will not live in that condition, and we cannot amputate without his consent. His mother and father have pleaded with him, but to no avail. Now you are his beloved and pledged to him. I must ask you this. If the amputation takes place, will you still marry him?"

Moments went by before Barbara could reply. She felt a hollow sickness, a hopelessness such as she had never known before. Curiously, she did not weep. She tried to make an image in her mind of the man without the leg.

"That's not the question," she blurted out. "The operation must take place. You must not let him die."

"That is the question. You must know the answer and he must know it."

"I love him. The answer is yes. Yes!"

"Good. Now go back into the room. Don't be tender with him. Part of the delirium is a matter of will. He can slide into it as a retreat from reality. I want you to shock him. Don't be afraid to shout, to become angry, to make him angry. You will be fighting for his life. Can you do that?"

"Yes."

"Go ahead then. His mother and father want to meet you, but that can wait. This is more important."

Barbara went back into the room. Marcel lay there with his eyes closed. "Marcel!" she said. He opened his eyes and stared at her. "Marcel, we must talk."

He shook his head and closed his eyes.

"Marcel!" She sat on the edge of the bed and laid her hand on his hot cheek. "Marcel, listen to me! When I say I love you, I am repeating an old cliché. But those are the only words I have. You are my flesh and my blood. You are the first man I ever loved, the only man. We know each other. You knew me before you ever spoke to me. Now if you die, a part of me dies. I don't give a damn about your leg. I don't love your leg. I love you."

"Who told you?"

"Well, who do you think told me? Dr. Lazaire told me. And I want you to do it, now!"

"No."

"Don't say no to me. What gives you the right to say no?"

He closed his eyes and shook his head tiredly.

"No! Don't go away from me! Damnit, we are going to talk about this. You've wasted enough time dreaming."

"All right. We'll talk. Do you know what they want to do? They want to take my leg off at the thigh. Is that what you want—a monster with half a body?"

"Yes, that's what I want."

He was alive now, aware of her. "Then think about it! Reach down for my penis to fondle me and think about what you'll find there. Think of what it will look like. You'll look at it every day of your life. You'll watch me crawl around, like some rotten beetle."

"Is that it?" she snapped. "Is that your whole case?"

"Don't you understand that I love you?"

"No. Such love is worthless, because you're putting yourself in my place, and you can't stand the thought of looking at me with one of my legs gone."

"No, no," he whimpered. "No."

"Yes. Don't deny it. It's not my love that frightens you. It's yours. And because your love can't stand the test, you're ready to die. What a rotten, lousy thing that is!"

"Oh, God, no. You don't understand."

"I understand only too well."

"It's because I love you. Barbara, believe me. How can I come to you with half of me gone? How can I ask you to give your life to a worthless, helpless cripple?"

"You don't have to ask me. Nothing you can do would stop me. I intend to marry you, and I intend to marry a man who is alive, not a corpse."

"No."

"Stop saying no like a broken record. What do you expect me to do, to agree with you, to kneel down and weep with you and say that you're better off dead? We're not living some stupid, romantic story. We're two people of flesh and blood who love each other and who are tied together with that love. What have I ever asked of you? Now I'm asking for your life. How can you refuse me?"

"Because I love you," he said weakly.

"Damnit, I will not accept that. We are beyond words. Words are for those who have nothing to give and nothing to lose. You have a life to give me, and I have a life to lose—and I will not accept no for an answer!"

His face slowly breaking into a smile, he raised himself

on one elbow, stared at her for a long moment, and then said, "You are splendid. I am so proud, so proud."

"Then you'll do it?"

"No."

Her control collapsed. She stood up, moved back from the bed, sat down in a chair, and began to cry.

"Barbara."

"Leave me alone, damn you!" She leaped to her feet suddenly and shouted at him, "You're killing the only thing I love, you bastard!"

"Barbara, please, please—"

"No!" she shouted. "No, damn you. If you say you love me again—"

He began to laugh, shaking with laughter and wincing with the pain of it.

"What are you laughing at?"

"You. My God, I adore you. You are quite magnificent. I love you so, I'm not afraid of anything, even of death."

"Bullshit!" she snapped, using the English word. "You're not afraid of death. Only of life."

He stopped laughing and stared at her. Then he sighed, closed his eyes, and fell back onto his pillow. Used up, Barbara sat and waited. Two, three minutes passed. Then Marcel said softly, "Over there, dear love, on the chest of drawers, is the form they want me to sign. There is a pen there too. Give it to me and help me sit up, and I'll sign it, and then you can give it to Dr. Lazaire, who, I'm sure, is waiting outside the door. You win, God help us both."

It was an hour and a half since the operation had begun. Barbara sat in the little waiting room with Monsieur and Madame Duboise. As with so many French parents of that generation, their single child was born in their later years. Duboise was well past sixty, his wife in her mid-fifties. Duboise, a pharmacist, was very much like his son, slender and tall, but stooped and bald, with a fringe of gray hair around his head. His wife was a tiny, pretty woman with prematurely white hair, very neatly and correctly dressed, very prissy, even in her grief, out of a lifetime habit. Evidently Marcel had written to them in detail over the past year, for they knew a good deal about Barbara. Under other circumstances, they might have been distant and difficult, regarding her with the peculiar suspicion the French reserve for all foreigners and for Amer-

icans in particular. But in this case, she came to them as
a sort of savior. What chance their son had for life was
due to Barbara's intercession. They embraced her and
poured out their hearts to her. That their son should
return to them this way, after so long; that he should have
to endure this mutilation—that was almost too much. Yet
at least they would have him for a while, and with him
this lovely young American.

Thus they sat for an hour and a half, while the day outside turned bleak and dark, the rain beginning, sometimes
in silence, again with Barbara as the object of their
attention and solicitude, Madame Duboise recalling some
incident of Marcel's childhood, clinging to his childhood
now, or with Monsieur Duboise gravely questioning Barbara about life and family in that half-mythical place
called San Francisco. It came out that Marcel had written
to them of the possibility of himself and Barbara making
their life in the United States, testing himself as well as
his parents; and they questioned Barbara about America.
Was there any place on earth as beautiful, as civilized, as
France? Of course they could not expect Marcel to live in
Toulouse; it was much too provincial a place. But was
there anything that could not be found in Paris?

It was all a dream, all of it—all the fears, all the hopes:
Barbara knew this the moment Dr. Lazaire entered the
waiting room. His face spelled it out.

"I'm so sorry," he said. "But it was too late. The infection had taken over his body. Gangrene is a monster.
Even yesterday it would have been too late."

"What is he saying?" Madame Duboise whispered.

Her husband put his arm around her. "He is telling us
that Marcel is dead."

"Is that what he's telling us? That can't be what he's
telling us."

Barbara rose and walked out, past the doctor, down the
long white corridor, down the stairs, and out into the rain.

Part Three

INTO EGYPT

In April of 1939, late in the afternoon, the doorbell rang in Barbara's apartment in Paris. She had been expecting no one, and she opened the door to find the hall filled with an enormous hulk of a man, at least six feet two inches in height, broad, sloping shoulders, thick hair, a round, moonlike face, large nose, and pale blue eyes. He wore a leather jacket over a turtleneck sweater and shapeless corduroy trousers. He smiled at her tentatively and wanted to know whether she was Miss Barbara Lavette.

"Yes?"

"Good. I'm glad to meet you finally, miss. My name is Bernie Cohen."

"You?" She was astonished, speechless, dislocated in time and space. A year that had begun in misery and hopelessness backed up and jarred her mind, and then she grasped one of his oversized hands and pulled him into the apartment. "Forgive me, please, but my mind wouldn't work. It's yesterday and it's also an eternity ago. But you're blessed in my memory, believe me. Come in, please."

"Yes, ma'am, I can understand the way you feel. It's been one hell of a year, hasn't it? It's all over in Spain, all done and finished. I'm just passing through, and I thought I owed it to Marcel to just stop by and at least have a word with you."

"More than a word. Oh, I'm so glad to see you. Sit down, please. I'll get some wine."

He eased his bulk into a chair while Barbara brought wine and glasses.

"You know about Marcel?" she asked him.

"I stopped in at *Le Monde*. They told me. They gave me your address. I'm sorry, believe me. I liked him."

"You saved his life."

"I wish I could have saved his life. It was a lousy, rotten bloodbath. So many good boys died there, and for what?

To be sold down the river by those bastards in England and here."

"Still, you saved his life. You sent him back to me—at least for the little time I had with him. I'm so grateful. How many times I said to myself, I'll meet you one day and tell you how truly grateful I am."

Obviously embarrassed, he raised his glass. "What shall we drink to, Miss Lavette?"

"We'll drink to peace, and a little human decency. And call me Barbara. We're old friends."

"O.K., Barbara. A little human decency. Only, I don't look for it in my time."

"When did you leave Spain?"

"Two weeks ago, after Madrid fell to the fascists. It was all over then. Most of the Internationals had left already. I walked over the Pyrenees, same way I came in. Funny thing, I'm pretty big, but I was never hit, never even scratched. Ah, it was a nightmare, first to last. But I don't know why I'm talking to you about Spain—"

"Please, do, yes."

"Well, what's to say? Now the Nazis have it their own way. France will be next. I hope to God you get out of here."

"The magazine wants me to stay, but I don't think I can. I'm homesick and lonely, and without Marcel, Paris is empty. Suddenly, I look at it and it's a city without a soul. And my mother and father give me no peace. They're very upset at what is happening in Europe."

"They should be."

"Then you think there'll be war?"

"There'll be war, no doubt about it. Spain, Czechoslovakia, Poland next—and then England and France, maybe America."

"I hope not. I hope you're wrong," Barbara said earnestly. "It's such madness, such insanity, a whole world gone insane and thinking of nothing else but to kill."

"Or be killed."

"That's such an ancient excuse, isn't it? Thank God I'm a woman."

"I can say amen to that."

They sat and drank and talked and finished a bottle of wine between them. Cohen was an easy man to talk to. He was from San Francisco; they had common ground. Barbara was overcome with nostalgia. How good it was

to talk in her own tongue! Cohen told her how he had
worked at Higate when the Levys were filling their first
order for sacramental wine. The federal agents had staged
a raid, and he, Cohen, had faced them with an old, rusty
shotgun.

"Real stupid," he said. "They could have shot me. Life
was so damn simple then. No Hitler, no Nazis, no war,
just the feds to cuss out and hate. I was just a kid then.
First time I ever held a gun in my hands. And now—"

"What now, Bernie?" Barbara was a little drunk, warm,
almost content, her eyes wet with the memory of a lost
love, not with tears, only moist with the remembering.

"Marcel said you were beautiful—but damnit, I think
you're the most beautiful woman I've ever seen."

"You're a little tight, Bernie. So am I. Let's go out and
eat."

"Well, I don't know."

"If you have a dinner date?"

"Date?" He began to laugh. "Funny thing is, I was
going to tell you that. Hell, look at me. I haven't had a
bath in two weeks. I just can't imagine what I smell like.
I came out of Spain without a dime. When I got to Ceret
in France, I sold my rifle and a German Lüger to a
Rumanian who had an arrangement with the border
guards, a small-time munitions dealer. He gave me two
hundred francs. I have four francs left. That won't buy us
dinner."

"Then let me buy you dinner."

"No!"

"Oh, great! I just love men who are proud. The whole
world is bleeding and ready to die from the pride and
stupidity of men, and now you're too proud to let me buy
us dinner."

"Hey, don't get angry at me!"

"Why not?" Barbara demanded. "You won't accept repayment. You're too proud for that. You saved the life of
a man I loved more than anything on earth, but I can't
buy you dinner."

"All right. O.K. I'm half-starved. If you're not ashamed
to be seen with me, buy me dinner. But I warn you—I eat
a lot."

"I'm not ashamed," she said.

They went to Allard's; it was the first time she had
been there since Marcel died, her first evening out with a

man. It seemed incredible to her that she could have been
alone so long. Her mourning had been like a death of her
own. Her American friends had left Paris. There had been
days and weeks when she had sat in her apartment, did
nothing and saw no one. Then one day she left her apartment and walked for hours in the rain, "As if the rain had
never stopped after that day in Toulouse," she told Bernie
Cohen. "And then the rain stopped and the sun came out.
Suddenly, it was all right for me to be alive. As if I had
paid a debt. Do you understand?"

"I know the feeling, after they die," he agreed. "I felt
that way. Like I'm the murderer, not the fascists."

"I'm all right now. I'll never let go of Marcel, but I'm
all right now."

"I know."

"Good. Dessert?"

"Sure. Why not. I've eaten like a pig. I might as well
finish like a pig."

"You're a big man. You need food. You remind me of
my father."

"I don't want to remind you of your father."

"O.K. You remind me of Jake Levy. How does that
sit with you?"

"Better. I like him. It's a damn small world, isn't it?
Here we are, you and me, and we got a link that goes
way back. I used to hear a lot about your father. Everyone
in San Francisco knew about him. There was a kid in the
Battalion from Palo Alto, and it turns out that his father
worked on one of Dan Lavette's ships during the World
War, he was a mate or something. So who knows, maybe
there are only a hundred people in the world and they're
all connected."

"And what about you?" Barbara asked. "Where are
you connected? Where are your mother and father and
sisters and brothers?"

"I draw a blank. I grew up in the Hebrew orphanage—
no mother, no father, nothing. Old Rabbi Blum sort of
adopted me, and I did odd jobs for him, and then after I
got out of high school I worked for the Levys for two
years, and then I got into school at Berkeley, where I
majored in agriculture. I worked all over the place—
Sonoma, Napa, Fresno—a strong back and not too much
brains to bother me. I'm a kind of crackpot Jew, and ever
since I was a kid I had one goal, to settle in Palestine.

There were two things I had to learn about, agriculture and guns. I got the first in California and I joined the Lincoln Brigade for the second. At first, they wouldn't have me. They claimed I had no ideological commitment. I had none to communism, but I hated the Nazis with the best of them. I got on a ship to France as a deck hand, and then I got to Spain and joined up with the Fifty-eighth Battalion there. Their casualties were heavy, so they didn't bother about commitment. Well, I lived through it, and I learned what I had to learn."

Barbara shook her head. "I don't understand that. You're warm and kind and gentle, and you join an army to learn the trade of killing. If you believed fervently in the Spanish cause, if you felt that the Republic had to survive, that might make some sense, but just to learn how to kill——"

"I killed fascists and Nazis. You know what's happening in Germany."

"I do know, and still I don't understand it. A bullet makes no judgment. Marcel died because men play a lunatic game, but it was meaningless and senseless."

"You don't hate, do you?"

"No, I find it too hard," Barbara said.

"You're a strange, sweet woman. Can I ask how old you are?"

"Twenty-five."

"I guess Marcel was the luckiest man on earth."

"To die the way he did?"

"I didn't mean that. I meant to have your love, to be loved by you."

She shook her head, tears welling into her eyes. "No, Marcel was not lucky."

"I'm sorry I said that."

"It's all right. Only, it reminds me of myself. At least you have a goal and a drive. I don't. I'll go home, but not because it makes any great sense. What will you do, Bernie?"

"I was thinking I'd head south tomorrow. Hitch my way down to Marseille. Get a job as a deck hand there on something heading east. That's not hard, I'm told. Then I'll jump ship at Suez or Beirut, and then to Palestine. That's all the plans I have."

"And it doesn't worry you—being broke? Eating? Sleeping?"

"I've always been broke. It's normal for me."

"What about tonight? Where will you stay?"

He shrugged. "I'll make out, kid. Believe me."

"Come home with me. Sleep on the couch. No, you won't fit. We'll pile some cushions on the floor."

"You're sure you want me to?"

"I'm sure."

"I'm rank. The place will smell like a barracks."

"I have a real shower, a real, North American shower. Oh, come on, don't be silly about it."

She didn't want him to leave, to walk off into the night. The taste of home was on her lips, the salty smell of the fog as it rolled into the bay, the remembrance of the treeless, rolling hills, the singing hum of the cable cars. Suddenly, she was alone and dreadfully lonely in this strange place. Her time of mourning had been virgin and aseptic; she had clutched death in a dying place, and by now she had had enough of the taste of death. There had been no men in her life since Marcel died, and now here she was, mellow with wine and food and with the open ingenuousness of the man who sat with her, a huge, heavy, round-faced man—she could understand how he had lifted Marcel to his back and carried him for miles—with a boyish, diffident smile and pale, baby blue eyes that worshipped her unequivocally. He was right about his smell, a strong male body odor that Barbara did not find particularly unpleasant; but where does one bathe in France when one is penniless? His attitude was full of respect and diffidence and admiration, but he had not even reached out to touch her hand. He had crossed the Ebro River, bearing with him the broken body of the man she loved, and again her eyes filled with tears, remembering a childhood picture of Saint Christopher wading through a rushing stream with the Christ child on his back.

"Don't cry, please," he said to her.

They walked back to her apartment. It was a calm, lovely evening, just two years from the time Marcel had intercepted her on the Champs-Élysées, pouring out his plea that she not disappear from his life. Was that always to be her fate, to step in and out of the lives of others?

At the apartment, she gave Bernie Cohen a robe that Marcel had kept there, and while he showered, she scrubbed his shirt and underthings, wrung them out, and hung them to dry. He came out of the bathroom grinning, the robe, so small on him, pulled tightly around him. He looked at the couch and shook his head. "The floor's better. I can sleep anywhere."

"Come to bed with me," Barbara said simply. Her whole body ached with desire. She could not face the thought of seducing or of being seduced.

His smile went away and he stared at her thoughtfully. "You're sure you want that?"

"Yes, I'm sure."

"You're not in love with me?"

"No."

"I think I love you. Not that it can mean anything to you. I know who I am. I know who you are. So maybe it would be better if—"

"I asked you to come to bed with me. Don't you want to?"

"My god, Barbara, what do you think?"

"Then come to bed and don't talk about it anymore."

After they had made love, she fell asleep in his arms, easily and trustingly. For hours he lay awake, afraid to move for fear he would disturb her. Then he slept. It was just dawn when he opened his eyes. She was asleep next to him, and for a while he lay there quietly, wondering whether he should wake her. He knew he had to go, and he knew she would not let him go without pressing money on him, and because he was quite sure of that, he slipped out of bed silently, moving with ease and grace for so large a man. He found his clothes in the kitchen, not quite dry but clean. He dressed, found pen and paper on her desk, wrote a note, and then left, closing the door gently behind him.

An hour later, Barbara saw the note and read it: "My darling, lovely woman: I am leaving like this because there is no way I can say goodby. If things were otherwise, if I had anything to offer you, I might stay and fight it through. I don't think I fell in love with you yesterday; I think I fell in love with you just listening to Marcel talk about you. Well, there it is. I don't know what else to say. Half of being a proper guest is knowing when to leave. This is the time."

Jean telephoned Dan at his home in Los Angeles. May Ling answered the phone, turned to her husband, and said uncertainly, "It's Jean. She wants to talk to you." She handed him the phone gingerly, as if it were something unsavory, and then walked out of the room.

"Dan," Jean said, "I want to talk to you about Barbara."

"Sure. Go ahead."

"Not on the telephone. I want to see you. I want you to come up here."

"That's impossible. Not for the next ten days, I couldn't. Why can't we talk about it now?"

"Because I won't discuss this on the phone. If you can't come to San Francisco, I'll fly down to Los Angeles."

"If you wish."

"Can you lunch with me tomorrow at the Biltmore?"

"All right. I'll see you at twelve-thirty."

He walked into the kitchen, where May Ling sat with her mother, the old woman silent, obscure, still living with her grief. "I behave so badly," May Ling said. "I was never that way. I'm getting old and ugly."

"I think you're very young and very beautiful, and the hell with it! Do I stop loving you because we pass forty?"

"I'm forty-three, Danny."

"She wants to talk to me about Barbara."

"Oh, no. Nothing happened?"

"No. She wants the kid back. So do I."

"Are you going to San Francisco?"

"No, she's coming here. I'm having lunch with her at the Biltmore tomorrow."

"Why at the Biltmore?" May Ling asked. "Why doesn't she come here?"

"Do you really want her to come here?"

"No! But she's so damn beautiful—"

"You never used to swear."

"Damn isn't swearing. The way you talk, that's swearing."

"How do you know she's still beautiful?"

"Because you told me so."

So-Toy said something to May Ling in Chinese.

"What's that?" Dan asked.

"She said I must not challenge the opinion of a man so good and wise as my husband."

"She's right."

"Danny?"

"Yes?"

She rose, took him by the arm, and led him into the

living room. "My mother understands more than she admits to. I want to talk very seriously."

He pulled her down on the couch next to him, curled an arm around her, and drew her to him. "Go on. Talk seriously."

"I used to be very strong, Danny. No, I can't talk when you do this to me." She pulled away and faced him. "I knew how to be alone. Now I've had you for eight years. I don't know how to be alone anymore. What if you fall in love with her all over again?"

"What if I do?"

"I couldn't stand that, Danny."

"Well, I'd have to stop loving you first, wouldn't I?"

"That's just talk, Danny. You never got Jean out of your blood."

"I was never in love with Jean, not the way I love you. You know that."

"You wanted her and you never really had her, and that's worse."

"Chinese thinking."

"What?"

"That's Chinese thinking. Jean's married."

"Oh, sometimes, Danny—Chinese thinking! What a dumb thing to say. You told me who Jean married. You despise him."

"But she doesn't."

"How do you know she doesn't?"

He didn't know, and he didn't want want to talk about it. They went to bed, May Ling pleading softly, "Make love to me, Danny, make love to me. Make me feel that I am not drying up, withering away. Make me alive." But he was asleep almost immediately, and she lay there with her eyes open, looking into the darkness and remembering the single time she had seen Jean Lavette. How strange it was, knowing Dan Lavette, knowing about him at least since she had been fourteen, falling in love with him when she was eighteen, and never really being apart from him, at least in her heart, in all the twenty-five years since then, yet seeing his first wife only once. It was before she actually met Dan. She was seventeen at the time, applying for a job in the Oriental section of the San Francisco Public Library, and there were some papers her father had to sign. She met him on the Embarcadero, in front of the Levy and Lavette warehouse, and as she stood there, the

"snow lady" swept by, in a white silk dress under a
white woolen coat, a piled mass of honey-colored hair, and
the bright blue eyes that were for May Ling so much a
symbol of the Caucasian. She had caught just that single
glimpse of her, yet the image was printed on her mind
and remained there, clear, beautiful, untouched by time,
of a translucent, enviable creature that had haunted her
all through the years. If she herself, May Ling, had aged
and changed through the years, the illusion persisted that
Jean had remained untouched by time.

The following day, in the dining room of the Biltmore
in downtown Los Angeles, the same notion occurred to
Dan. Five years had passed since had had met Jean in San
Francisco. Time was kind to her. A little more make-up,
more careful grooming, perhaps a few tiny wrinkles
around the eyes, but the totality of her beauty remained
untouched. Perhaps she dyed her hair. He himself was
almost entirely gray, but not a gray hair showed on
Jean's head. He tried to remember how old she was. He
had just passed fifty; she would be forty-nine then. More
than she had been five years ago, she was now a stranger,
a woman he had known once and only in fragments—or
had he ever known her at all?

Yet there was a difference, and he sensed it almost
immediately. The certainty was lacking, the almost uncon-
scious arrogance, the built-in, magnificent confidence of
the very rich and the very beautiful, as a gift of birth and
never requiring cultivation. There was both fear and uncertainty—in the way she greeted him, in her petulant
criticism of the place, the unlikely pretentiousness of the
Biltmore.

"It's ridiculous in this wretched city. How can you live
here, Dan?"

"You get used to it. Los Angeles has its points."

"I haven't noticed. I heard you're doing very well."

"Well enough. I build yachts for millionaire movie
moguls."

"And what happened to all your vows of poverty?"

He looked at her thoughtfully. "That's a damn funny
thing for you to say. Anyway, how did you know that I
was doing well?"

"I had lunch with Sam Goldberg. You know, he's
Barbara's lawyer, so we talk occasionally."

"You don't approve of him."

"He's old, Dan. He's past seventy."

"And he's also Jewish."

"That's not fair. You never forget, do you? You never forgive, either."

"I told you once that there was nothing to forgive." He grinned at her. "No fights, Jean. I'm glad to see you, I swear I am."

"When you smile like that—well, it's like long, long ago. All right, Danny. I'm worried about Barbara. I want her to come home. Europe is boiling and it's going to explode."

"Have you asked her to come back?"

"Pleaded with her in my letters."

"Well, she's coming back. We had a letter from her yesterday."

"When?"

"Soon. She said she had one more thing to do, and then she comes back."

"What thing?"

"She didn't say. You know, she's had a bad time of it. She was in love with a French boy. They were going to be married. He was wounded in the Spanish war, and he died. That was about a year ago."

"Oh, no. I never knew a thing about that. Why didn't she tell me?"

"Maybe she didn't want to upset you. Barbara's not the kind who likes to share grief. She locks it inside herself."

"Danny, I've lost her," Jean said, her voice full of anguish. "I love her so much, and I've lost her."

"We've neither of us lost her, Jean. Give it time. She'll be back."

"I've run out of time, Danny. How much time does anyone have? I lost you—and now my daughter."

"No, you never wanted me. Don't make a world of illusions now. It doesn't help."

"You're a damn fool, Danny."

"Thank you."

"Did it ever occur to you to wonder why I wouldn't give you a divorce all those years?"

"It occurred to me. You told me once that Seldons didn't divorce."

"What's the use?" Jean sighed. "I'm making a fool of myself, and I don't enjoy that. I came here to talk about Barbara. What shall we do?"

"She's a grown woman."

"I thought of going over there and talking to her."

"That's not smart. She has to make her own decisions.
And Europe's no place to visit now. Jean," he said gently,
"I think she'll be back soon. She had to get over what
happened to her, and she chose to stay there until she got
over it. I think she's over it now, and I think she'll come
back."

"Who was the boy? She told you, not me. Do you know
how that hurts?"

"A writer. He worked on the newspaper *Le Monde*."

"What was he like?"

"She sent us a picture. I thought you'd like to see it."
He took the picture out of his pocket and handed it to her,
and he watched her as she stared at the smiling face in
the photograph.

"It's a nice face," she said wanly. "Poor Barbara, how
she must have suffered."

Dan reached across the table and took her hand. It was
a new sensation for him. He had never pitied Jean before.

The following day's edition of the San Francisco *Examiner*
carried the titillating tidbit that Jean Whittier had "flown
to Los Angeles for a rendezvous with her ex-husband,
Daniel Lavette, where they were seen lunching at the
Hotel Biltmore." It said no more than that, but it was
suggestive and sufficiently embarrassing to John Whittier
for him to bring it up the first time he saw Jean, which was
at dinner that day. Tom was at the table with them.

"I think we should discuss this at another time," Jean
said coolly.

"This is a very appropriate time. At least you're here. I
see little enough of you these days."

"I prefer our squabbles to be private."

"If Tom wants to leave, he can leave."

"I'm having my dinner," Tom said. "I'll take it elsewhere if you wish."

"No, you might as well remain," Jean said. And then to
Whittier, "You want to know how it got into the papers?
I can't tell you that. Someone must have recognized us at
the Biltmore. Certainly I had nothing to do with that."

"This is the second time you've seen him—as far as I
know."

"In five years! You're tiresome." Jean sighed. "I don't enjoy this. I see whom I please when I please."

"Yes, you can do as you damn well please, but don't involve me in any scandal."

"Do you ever listen to yourself?" Jean asked gently, and when Whittier stared at her, she added, "You tend to be pompous and quite boring. I saw Dan to discuss my daughter, Barbara. That's it. We'll drop the subject."

Flushed, Whittier rose, his cheeks puffed out, his face red. He swallowed, contained himself, and then said coldly, "I'll have my dinner elsewhere." He turned on his heel and left the room.

Jean and Tom sat in silence. The butler entered with the roast and looked at Whittier's place. "He won't be dining with us," Jean said. "He was called away." Tom remained silent. The butler served them and left.

Tom took a few bites of his food, then bit his lower lip and shook his head. "It gets worse."

"Yes, my dear," Jean said. "But it's my problem, not yours."

"If you felt this way, why the devil did you marry him?"

"Because, Thomas, I did not feel this way at the time."

Now in his twenty-seventh year, Thomas Lavette was tall, slender, and still unmarried. His face had fixed into a rather controlled, handsome mask. He had the refined, almost plastic good looks of a film star or a men's clothes model, light brown hair that he parted on the side and that fell gracefully over his brow, blue eyes, and a wide, slightly petulant mouth. As the years passed, he had retreated behind his face and figure, rarely permitting himself to exhibit either pleasure or disappointment. Women found him attractive, clever within limitations, and coldly closed to any specific designs on their part. He had remained as part of the Whittier household, showing no desire to move out or to establish a place of his own. He had joined Whittier's city club through the sponsorship of Whittier, he was a member of the San Francisco Golf Club, and he kept a small boat at the wharf, although he rarely sailed. He had moderated his drinking, and he smoked an occasional cigarette. He lit one now and said to his mother. "What do you intend to do?"

"Nothing. Anyway, I don't see that it concerns you, Tom."

"It does."

"Might I ask how?"

"I like John."

"That's very nice."

"Do you intend to divorce him?"

"What is your sudden interest in my intentions?"

"I simply think that another divorce would do you no good. I think it would be a mistake."

Jean smiled coldly. "So now you advise me on my conduct."

"Someone has to."

"You're insolent and rather nasty. I have no desire to discuss this with you."

"I'm sorry. I didn't mean to be insolent. I just don't want you to leave John."

"Why?"

"Can I talk to you, mother?"

"You've been talking to me. Quite outrageously, I think."

"I apologized for that. Can I talk to you, straight off the cuff?"

"Go ahead."

"All right. In a few months, your trusteeship will expire. At that time, Barbara and I will have not only the ownership but the voting rights to our Seldon Bank stock, which will amount to about twenty million dollars apiece. John and I have discussed this at some length. I will control the bank. A combination with the Whittier interests would constitute the largest and most powerful financial block on the West Coast. John has been to Washington, and he has it from the best authority there that the arms embargo will be repealed before the year is out. You can see what that would mean to the Whittier shipping interests. I must say that the idea of a combine of interest came from John, and I think it's very decent of him. He doesn't need us as much as we need him."

For a long moment, Jean just stared at her son. "You amaze me," she said at last.

"Why?"

"Never mind why. That can wait. Tell me, why do we, as you put it, need John Whittier?"

"Because without him we are just a bank, a large bank, but still just a bank. With him—well, damnit, mother, you must see the power in such a combination."

"And that's what you want? The power?"

"Frankly, yes."

"You're a strange boy, Tom," she said, thinking to herself that "stranger" would be a better word, a stranger who was her son and whom she knew so little.

"What else should I want?" he demanded. "Money? I've always had enough money. My job at the bank? It's piddling nonsense. I have my own dreams, mother. Is that so strange?"

"And if I were to divorce John, it would endanger all this?"

"It would make it very awkward."

"And what about Barbara? You've left her out of your plans. She gets half the stock."

"I think I can handle Barbara."

"Do you? That's interesting."

"I mean, why shouldn't she do what's best for the family?"

"Are you sure you know what's best for the family? Barbara might have other ideas—or she might decide to do what she feels is best for Barbara."

"I still think I can convince her. The first problem is to get her out of the hands of that Jew lawyer of hers."

"God help us both," Jean whispered.

"Just what do you mean by that?"

Jean did not reply, only looked at her son, feeling that she was going to scream, to burst out in rage, yet realizing that she was entitled to neither reaction.

"Don't tell me you're shocked, and don't accuse me of anti-Semitism," Tom said. "I had dinner last night at the club with Arthur Schwartz, and he's about as Jewish as you can get. It's just that Sam Goldberg is Dan's partner. You know that."

"I'm sure that some of your best friends are Jewish," Jean said.

"You're right."

"And Dan happens to be your father."

"He happens to be."

Jean sighed hopelessly.

"I'm sorry, mother," Tom said. "If I offended you in any way, I'm sorry."

"I don't deserve sympathy, my dear. I have a son who is enormously rich and has no sense of humor, and I deserve both. It took me half a century to grow up, and it's too late to weep over that."

"I think I have as much of a sense of humor as the next person. But damned if I see what's so funny about all this."

"No, I don't suppose you do," Jean said.

In mid-May of 1939, two weeks before Barbara planned to leave Paris for Cherbourg, where she would board the *Queen Mary* for the journey back to America, Marcel's old friend Claude Limoget telephoned her and asked whether he and his wife could drop by to see her. Barbara was working on her last "Letter from Paris," and she hoped that by late afternoon most of it would be out of the way. She was not particularly eager to see Claude and Camille, but they were friends of Marcel, and even didactic company was better than no company at all. And they were didactic. They were well-meaning enough; they had come by half a dozen times in the year since Marcel's death, and she had been to their home for dinner on two occasions, but one always paid a price of instruction. They lectured her on Spain, on fascism, on Nazism, on the new world that was being wrought in the Soviet Union, on the weakness of Chamberlain, on the wickedness of Deladier, on the spinelessness of the Czechs, on the betrayals—of Spain and Czechoslovakia—by Roosevelt, and on other kindred subjects.

Since Barbara disliked argument and had a deep-seated conviction that little was gained and no one really convinced by it, she was more inclined to listen and swallow her various disagreements than to attempt to prove her point. In her own way, very slowly and thoughtfully over a period of years, she was crystallizing her own point of view. She had possessed an almost instinctive repugnance for suffering inflicted on anyone, for cruelty, for the act of inflicting pain and for the ultimate act of killing. Five years ago, she had left Sarah Lawrence College possessed of a gentle and comprehensive innocence, which, as a very sophisticated student in a very sophisticated college, she would have denied completely. Since then, she had learned a great deal, coped with the situation of a young woman alone in a foreign country, found a job as a correspondent, and proved to herself and others that she could do her work in a professional manner. In a sense, she had formed herself in terms of ideas and beliefs, and she saw no need for inflicting these ideas and beliefs on others.

She had listened to the arguments and persuasions of the Limogets as she had listened to the arguments and persuasions of others. If at times she was bored, boredom was something she had learned to cope with. This time, however, she was not bored.

Claude and Camille Limoget arrived at precisely five o'clock, which they had learned was the proper American cocktail hour. They brought a bottle of wine, downed a glass apiece, munched on Barbara's crackers and cheese, made the proper inquiries about her health and state of mind, and then came directly to the point.

"We understand," Claude said, "that you plan to return to America in two weeks."

"Yes. I've overstayed my leave."

"Of course. Yet Paris has been a happy as well as an unhappy experience."

"That's true, Claude. Some of each."

"Barbara," he said very seriously, "we are coming to you to ask you to change your plans. We would like you to put off your departure to America and go to Berlin instead."

She smiled. "You can't be serious."

"Very serious. Let me explain the reasons for this request."

"No," Barbara said firmly. "Whatever you have in mind, I don't want to hear about it. I regard what is happening in Germany, in Berlin, with loathing and with horror and disgust. Nothing you have to say could persuade me to go there, now or ever."

"Will you only listen?"

"No. I am going home. I have been away almost five years. I am totally heartsick for home. You're French. You ought to understand that."

"We do understand it," Camille said. "But isn't it unreasonable to refuse to listen? You're not a person of weak character. We've spent too many hours trying to convince you of things you absolutely refuse to accept, and I'm sure we haven't convinced you. But at least you listened."

Barbara sighed. "Very well, I'll listen."

"That's all we're asking," Camille said. "I insisted on that with Claude. We would simply put the facts to you, and then you could say yes or no."

"You know we're communists," Claude said. "We've made no secret of that."

"Indeed you haven't." Barbara was forced to smile. There were times when she almost liked the Limogets.

"All right. Now, over the past few years, there have been many discussions in Party circles concerning the question of Nazi Germany. In the beginning, German comrades participated in these discussions—comrades who had escaped from Germany, a few others who moved back and forth. These few became fewer, and finally all our contacts with Germany were broken. At this moment, we don't even know whether the Party exists in Germany, and the way events are moving, it is desperately necessary that we know, not only for ourselves but for the whole world—"

"Oh, no," Barbara interrupted. "You can stop right there. I am not a communist. I don't think I am even a communist sympathizer."

"You said you'd hear us out," Camille reminded her.

"All right. Go on."

"I want to say right here that we have no intention of placing you in a position of danger. Other measures are being undertaken to make contact in Germany. This is a singular case, for which you are ideally suited. No, please wait"—as Barbara began to stop him—"please, listen to me. There is a Professor Wolfgang Schmidt, who teaches philosophy at Friedrich Wilhelm University in Berlin. He is one of those who espoused the Nazi theories of the master race. He has published two books on the subject, and his writing has been warmly received by the Hitler gang. Nevertheless, we have reason to believe that this man, who was once secretly a Party member, still remains a communist and uses his present role as a cover. If that is the case, he may have contacts, there may be some sort of organization that can be reached and helped."

Barbara shook her head hopelessly. "You are quite mad."

"I don't think we are. Barbara, we are not asking you to try to establish that contact; others will do that. We only ask that you see this Professor Schmidt, that you talk to him as what you are, an American correspondent, that you get a sense of the man and of what his deepest beliefs are. This is something you can do quite legitimately —and if you are able to give us a sound estimate, then the next man we send will not be going to his death. He won't be walking into a trap."

"You mean I am to spring the trap for him."

Camille Limoget's round, pretty little face took on an expression of pain, as if Barbara's remark had cut to her soul. Her wide blue eyes became moist, and Barbara reflected that she was indeed the most unlikely communist.

"We loved Marcel," she whispered. "We love you. What a thing to say!"

"I'm sorry," Barbara apologized. "I shouldn't have said that. But I am not going to Berlin. You know, you and Claude and your friends—you've told me a dozen times how you feel about everything that's happening today. But you never asked me how I feel. Of course, I understand that American women are not supposed to have much sense—"

"That's not fair," Camille protested. "We never stopped you from speaking. You were always quiet, listening."

"True," she responded, not feeling that this was the best moment to remind Camille that to get a word in during one of their discussions was virtually impossible. "Then it's my fault. Let me tell you what I feel, in just a few words. I feel that men who fight wars share a common insanity, and that men who kill, for whatever reason, for whatever justification, are also insane. I have listened to the theories and rationalizations and accusations for hours, but I still feel just that way. I loved a man who was like a part of me, and he died senselessly, for no reason and no cause." She sought for more words, and then felt that what she had said encompassed the whole matter. "That's the way I feel," she said.

Camille bit her lower lip and pouted. Claude studied Barbara thoughtfully, and for a little while the three of them sat there in silence.

Finally, Claude said, "Marcel was my friend. I don't like to parade my emotions, but I sat down and cried when I heard that he was dead."

Barbara nodded.

"It wasn't an accident. The Nazis killed him. They have killed thousands, and they will kill thousands more."

"And Stalin?" Barbara asked tiredly. "He kills no one?"

"It doesn't change what happened in Spain and what is happening in Germany."

"And will I change that if I go to Germany? Can anyone change it?"

"I don't know," Claude said quietly. "We try. If we don't try, there's not much worth living for, is there?"

Again they sat in silence, and at last Claude said, "I don't blame you if you're afraid. I'd be afraid."

Barbara didn't deny it. There was a cold knot in the pit of her stomach when mentally she placed herself in Germany. Her strength and independence did not come from a lack of sensitivity. For years now, day after day, she had read the newspaper reports of life in Nazi Germany, not to mention the books on the subject that filled the French bookstalls. In her mind, it had become the place of ultimate horror, a gigantic and grotesque nightmare that had grown like a fetid mushroom out of the heart of Europe.

"But, you see," Claude went on softly, "there is really no one but yourself we could turn to. You are not political. You never have been. You have no organizational connections, yet we trust you. When I told you Professor Schmidt's name, I put his life in your hands. We know you."

"And you know a hundred others," Barbara said unhappily.

"Not really. Consider. You're an American, and the Nazis are cultivating America with every bit of sleazy propaganda they can contrive. You are a correspondent, so you have a legitimate reason to go there and to interview. There is nothing on you in the Gestapo files. You are also the daughter of one of the great, wealthy families of America. You can't imagine what kind of clout that will give you there. Barbara, I would die before I would ask you to step into a dangerous game. This isn't dangerous. Nasty, perhaps. Any sewer is nasty and stinks to hell. On the other hand, you're a writer, and this can be an experience well worth having. There's profit along with the loss. And you might just be saving the lives of a good many decent people."

"I think I'd like a cup of coffee," Barbara said. "Will you join me?"

They shook their heads and sat in silence while she brewed the coffee. She had stopped thinking, stopped building protests within herself. She felt a dead, heavy weight inside of her, a kind of hopelessness. She was like a boat without a rudder, without an anchor. Everything and everyone went in and out of her life—her father, her mother, her brother, Dominick Salone, Marcel Duboise, Bernie Cohen. She suddenly felt an intense longing for the big, slow-moving, slow-speaking man, for his judgment, for his advice.

She drank the coffee strong and black. "It's American coffee," she explained. "I'm an addict. It comes of living alone. You turn either to drink or coffee."

"I grew up with chicory," Camille said, smiling. "You lose your taste for the real thing." She was relaxed, gentle. The argument was over. Barbara had never particularly liked her before. She liked her now.

"If I were to go," Barbara said, "and I am not committing myself to anything—but if I were crazy enough to do this, what makes you think that I could find out anything worth finding out about this Professor Schmidt? I'm no great judge of character. I can't ask him outright."

Claude shrugged. "I have faith in you."

"I wish I did."

"Can we take you to dinner?" Camille asked.

"No. No, I want to think about this whole thing. I have to think it through, and it's better if I'm by myself."

There were no more arguments, no more persuasion, and awhile later, Camille and Claude left. Barbara took the wineglasses and her cup and saucer into the kitchen, washed them, and then decided that the floor of the kitchen was quite dirty. Why hadn't she noticed that before? She got a pail of suds and a brush and scrubbed the kitchen floor, obtaining a good deal of satisfaction out of the physical act of doing something. Then she took a bath, luxuriating in the steaming hot water. It was nine o'clock by the time she dried herself, combed her hair, and slipped into a robe, and now she felt ravenously hungry. She had a piece of *chèvre* and some bread that she warmed in the oven, and she sat in the kitchen, stuffing herself with cheese and hot, golden-crusted bread and drinking what was left of the coffee. Afterward, she would recall that there were no interior discussions with herself during this time, no profound thoughts to weigh, one against the other. At half past nine, with the last crust of bread in her hand, she picked up the telephone and asked for the overseas operator. She then put through a person-to-person call to Frank Bradley, the editor of *Manhattan Magazine*.

It was well after ten when the telephone rang and the operator informed her that she had her party in New York.

It was a good connection. Bradley's voice boomed out at her.

"I hear you quite well, Frank. You don't have to shout."

"Girl, you've become famous and you're deserting us. When are you arriving? Why didn't you call me collect?"

"Because I'm rich, and I'm not arriving. I've decided to look the beast in the eyes. What would you say to a few 'Letters from Berlin'?"

"I love you."

"You know they censor everything. I'm no great political commentator."

"Just write about the weather, the women, the food—anything you want. Or make notes and write the stuff in Paris."

"How many words?"

"As many as you want. I love you."

"I know that. You said it before."

"How long will you stay?"

"I have no idea, Frank."

"Now don't get into trouble. Three publishers have been bugging me about doing your letters in a book. But I'm holding off until you get back. So just don't get mixed up in anything and write me something immortal."

"What publishers?"

"That can wait. Now look, Barbara, I don't want you to stick your neck out, and I know how you feel about those bastards, but if you could get an interview with Hitler or Ribbentrop or Himmler, or any one of those lice, it would be worth its weight in gold."

"Frank, you're crazy."

"Like a fox, I am. You're a beautiful woman, and that counts. Look, if it comes your way, grab it. If it doesn't, I still love you."

Dan observed his son Joseph occasionally with awe, frequently with admiration, and always with wonder that this tall, long-limbed creature, with the strange mixture of the Occident and the Orient written on his snub-nosed, serious face, could be a product of his loins. A few months past, a chain lift had snapped at the boatyard, and the raw link had gashed Dan's arm from elbow to shoulder, not deeply, but nevertheless leaving a long, painful cut. They had bandaged it crudely out of a first aid kit, but when Dan got home, Joe—there on a day off—regarded it with disgust, removed the bandage, cleaned the wound, put it together with what he called plaster butterflies, and then rebandaged it. Half a year in medical school had not made him a doctor, but in Dan's mind he was a repository of medical knowledge.

So-toy's sight was failing, and Joe with the aid of a medical flashlight diagnosed the condition as cataracts, which was later confirmed by the opthalmologist to whom May Ling brought her mother. Joe explained the required operation in great detail to his mother and father, thereby increasing Dan's awe, and to the amazement of May Ling, he spelled out some of the facts to So-toy in Shanghainese.

"Where on earth did you learn to speak Shanghainese?" his mother asked him.

"I picked it up from granny."

"You picked it up? I've been around her all my life and I don't know much more than a hundred words."

"Well, that's the way it goes. Anyway, mom, you know more than a hundred words. I like her. You can't like someone and not want to talk. You know," he added, "it's funny, but I'm picking up some Cantonese. Whenever they get a Chinese patient in the ward and they can't get through, they send for me. Mostly, it's Cantonese."

When May Ling told Dan about this, he said, "You know, it puts me in a hell of a spot. His school will wind up in a couple of weeks, and he's got to earn some money this summer. I can put him on as a laborer and justify paying him twenty-five a week, but hell, I can't."

"Why can't you?"

"He's a doctor. How the hell can I ask him to work in a boatyard as a laborer?"

"Just ask him. That's all."

"Ah, no. I can't."

"Well, you won't have to. He wrote to Jake Levy up at Higate, and Jake offered him a job for the time between semesters."

"What? What kind of a job?"

"The same thing you're afraid to offer him, digging irrigation ditches, picking, pruning—goodness, I don't know. Whatever a hand does at a winery."

"What is Jake willing to pay him?"

"You know," May Ling said gently, touching Dan's hand and smiling at him, "your son isn't a doctor. He's just a medical student. And if he appears to be very bright to you, it's perfectly natural, because he has a very intelligent father."

"Come on, I'm a boob and a roughneck. That's all I've ever been."

"I suppose so, but you're an unusual boob and a remarkable roughneck, and that's what counts."

"Thank you. What's Jake paying him?"

"Forty a month and keep. That's what Jake pays, and Joe wouldn't have him shown any favoritism because he's your son. Anyway, Joe says it's ten dollars a month more than most of the growers pay."

"He's got to be crazy!" Danny exploded. "I can pay him twice that!"

"Calm down, Danny. He wants to go to Higate."

"Why?"

"You don't notice things. Sally Levy's been writing to him every week through the winter. I think he wants to be around her, that's all."

"Sally Levy? Jake's kid? God Almighty, she can't be more than ten years old!"

"Will you calm down. She's almost fourteen."

"Joe's twenty-two. What in hell does he want with a kid of fourteen?"

"When you were twenty-five, I was only eighteen."

"That's different."

"Why? You're seven years older than I. Joe's eight years older than Sally."

"You were eighteen. Fourteen! God Almighty, that's jailbait, and with Jake's kid it stinks."

"You are a hoodlum," she said, smiling sadly. "You'll never be civilized."

"You call that civilized? A fourteen-year-old kid."

"I just don't want you to talk to Joe about this. His head is on right. Leave him alone. You remember what you said about Barbara. She had to be left alone. That goes for Joe too."

"All right. All right. But I still don't see it."

He was not the only one. His son was almost equally confused about his own motives for going to Higate. He was not in love with Sally Levy, who was not yet fourteen years old. He was confident that he knew all about love, having found time during his first year in medical school to conceive a passion for two more girls, both of them as blond and blue-eyed as his college infatuations. But both

passions were short-lived, coming to earth in two frantic
bouts of lovemaking: once at night on the beach at Santa
Monica, when it was so cold and wet that his true love
shivered and shook all through it, begging him to get it
over with so that she could put on her clothes and not
freeze to death; and with the second girl, unconsummated
when her parents came home early and informed her, in
his presence, in very high decibels, that if they found this
"Chink" in their house again, they'd call the cops. He took
the insult philosophically, deciding that it was a question
of time. Romance required time. As a college student, he
had had all the time in the world, whereby his success.
As a medical student, regardless of the depth of his passion, there simply was no time to make love properly. As
a college student, he had been content to be mistaken for
an American Indian, although their lot in Los Angeles was
little better than the lot of the Chinese; in medical school,
he affirmed his identity as a Chinese. For some reason, the
eighteen-hour day of a medical student, instead of stultify-
ing his sexual drive, increased it to a fever pitch. There
were three middle-aged, cooperative nurses at the teaching
hospital, but like a good many medical students, Joe had
fallen prey to what was called "first-year hypochondria,"
and having learned all the symptoms and details of vene-
real disease, he avoided promiscuous women like the
plague.

All this went through his mind as he drove his father's
ancient Ford north from Los Angeles to the Napa Valley.
Dan had given the Ford to Joe—the very first Model A
1929 vintage—and had replaced it with a secondhand 1935
Buick. Joe treasured the tiny car and its apparent ability
to run forever, the odometer having given up at a hundred and ten thousand miles. He drove it without haste,
and the long trip gave him time to ask himself just why he
was going back to Higate and exactly what he felt for Sally
Levy. It was not an easy question for him to answer; he
only knew that he wanted to see her again, an admission
that he modified with the arguments that he loved Northern California and that he wanted desperately to get away
from home for a time.

Sally had written to him as regular as clockwork, every
week, apologizing for the wretched scrawl of her hand-
writing with the excuse that she had been born left-
handed and then forced in school to write with her right

hand—a situation that her mother had attempted to reverse recently, but too late, since the scrawl from her left hand was even worse than that from the right.

Joe had discussed the matter with one of his professors, who admitted that so little was known about the alteration of a left-handed person into a right-handed person that no firm conclusion could be drawn, and then he asked whether the child in question was strange?

"Pretty strange," Joe confessed, and the professor said, "Well, there you are."

"Strange" was a rather generic term. Some of the letters Sally had written were very detailed, sensitive, and often quite beautiful. Once she had written two lines: "It's all over, and I think you stink for not writing to me." Another time she sent him two beautiful sonnets, which she claimed she had written, one of which began, "Unlike are we, unlike, o princely heart! Unlike our uses and our destinies." Joe was so impressed with the language and the flight of fancy that he showed them to his mother. May Ling read them through, sighed, and studied her son thoughtfully.

"They're great, don't you think?" Joe asked her.

"Oh, indeed they are. I could never interest you in poetry. If I had, you would know that both these lovely poems were written a hundred years ago by Elizabeth Barrett Browning. They were copied faithfully from her *Sonnets from the Portuguese*. That's an unusual little girl, your Sally."

"No. Why would she lie?"

"To impress you."

"That dumb kid!"

"Not at all. At least she read the poems. That's more than you can say."

He wrote back to her, annoyed and accusing, and she replied, "So what! I could write poems just as good if I was her age."

He came to wait for her letters, to read them eagerly. For his part, he replied about once a month, generally when she had become angry and threatened to stop writing.

Now, driving north, he decided to dismiss her from his thoughts. She was an interesting kid, a little crazy. He had no intention of allowing her to tag around after him as she had done the summer before. But when finally, late in the evening, almost at sundown, he arrived at Higate, having driven with just a few stops for fourteen hours, there she was, standing, watching, waiting, and the moment he got out of his car she ran toward him, stopped, and stood staring at him.

And he stared back. It was not entirely the physical change in Sally. She was still very slender, but the once-tangled flaxen hair was combed straight and fell only to her shoulders, bobbed straight across the front of her brow; she had developed breasts; instead of old, torn jeans she wore a cotton dress; and she had grown at least two inches. Yet more than these changes, it was the expression in the wide blue eyes, frightened, hopeful, wary.

"Hello, kid," Joe said to her.

"I wish I could have got rid of the stinking freckles, because then I might look all right, but there's just no way. How do you think I look?"

"You look fine."

"You don't look like a doctor. You look just the same as last year. Do you want to kiss me?"

Joe walked over to her and kissed her lightly on the cheek.

"That's some kiss," she said.

He shook his head despairingly.

"Well, what do you think? You think I don't know why you came back? Only you won't go near me because I'm jailbait. That's right. I know a lot more than you think."

"My word, Sally," he said desperately, "what do your mother and father think about all this?"

"They think I'm crazy, but they trust you. They know how stupid you are."

"Yeah, stupid."

"They said I could walk you around and show you the place just by myself."

"But I have to go inside," Joe said. "I have to say hello to your folks and your brothers."

"You can do that later. There's only about ten minutes of light left. We got a new truck and two new wells and a big new stainless steel aging tank. Don't you want to see that?"

"I guess so." Joe sighed. "I've been driving since six o'clock this morning."

"You talk like an old man."

"That's what I am. I'm an old man." He surrendered himself, and they began to walk along the dirt road that led up the slope. Now the sun had dropped behind the mountains to the west, and the hills had turned jet black, topped by a burning red fringe; but over to the east, on the other side of the Napa Valley, the setting sun still caught the hilltops, bathing them in a golden glow. Sally paused, and they both turned to look. They stood there in silence for a little while, and then Sally said, "I guess we'd better go back, because if I stay up here with you I'm going to cry or something the way I feel, which you couldn't understand in a million years, even if you're older than me, and I just finished reading *Sister Carrie*, by Theodore Dreiser, so I know how stinking men are, and I don't even care if you don't look at me again, because you'll be here all summer, and I can tell you this: men don't really know how to love anyone because all they're interested in is the flesh, and I'll eat a lot and stuff myself and get fat and sexy, and then you'll look at me all right."

"I'll be damned," Joe said.

"Oh, come on down," Sally said lightly. "I'll help you carry your stuff into the house, because you might just strain yourself. Anyway, it's getting dark."

"You are something," Joe said slowly. "You really are something."

Barbara had purchased a compartment for herself on the Paris-Berlin express, determined to make productive use of the hours on the train. She had armed herself with a French-German dictionary, an English-German dictionary, a Berlin guidebook, a French translation of Scherber's *Rambles in Berlin*, and a French translation of *Mein Kampf*. Since she had embarked on her journey without being possessed of a single phrase in the German language, she had little hope of any great progress, but since the French-German dictionary had an appendix that gave the modern equivalents of the confusing German Gothic letters, she hoped that she might at least progress to an easy reading of street and shop signs.

Actually, during the first two hours of the journey she did not even touch her books. Now that she had overcome her initial repugnance toward the idea of Germany and managed to put her trepidation in its proper place, fairly well convinced that she would face no real danger, the notion of a sort of secret mission into what she could only think of as "the lair of the beast" excited and fascinated her. Also, since she had been earning her living as a writer during the past several years, it was quite natural for her to think as a writer. Apparently, three publishers had asked to put her "Letters from Paris" into book form. How exciting it was to think of her name on the jacket of a book! And why hadn't she insisted on knowing the names of the publishers? Why did she always think of the proper thing to do hours after the time for doing it? That, she decided, was a character defect that she would have to remedy. In any case, now that she had taken the bit in her teeth and was actually on the way to Germany, she could appreciate the value it would have to her as a writer. On the other hand, Hitler had already taken over Austria; Czechoslovakia had been handed to him through the infamous betrayal at Munich, and when she left Paris, the papers had been full of the possibility of a Nazi invasion of Poland—and speculation on whether this would mean another full-fledged European war. For the first time, Barbara decided, she would have to pay some attention to politics, more, much more, than the cursory attention she had given it in the past, and she would have to try to do what her left-wing friends in Paris called "thinking politically." She didn't have a very clear notion of what thinking politically meant exactly, but certainly she must read carefully whatever French or English newspaper would be available in Berlin.

She was so filled with ideas and plans that she failed to notice a man who had stopped in front of the corridor door of her compartment, even though she was staring out of the train window, in which his image was faintly reflected. Then she turned and saw him and realized that he had been standing there for at least a minute or two. He was a tall man in his mid-fifties, impeccably dressed in an English tweed jacket, blue worsted vest with brass buttons, white shirt, and striped tie—thus on his upper half, which Barbara could see through the door. He had a long, narrow face, iron gray hair, a thin, long nose, and dark, curious eyes. The door window was down about eight inches, and once he caught her attention, he spoke to Barbara in German.

"I'm afraid I don't speak German," Barbara replied in French.

"Ah, then you are French," he said, speaking French easily, with only a slight accent.

"No, I'm an American."

"But your French is faultless."

"So is yours," Barbara said, smiling.

"Ah, no. I have a clumsy accent, about which I can do absolutely nothing. Am I intruding? Do you have a bias against speaking to strangers on trains?"

"That depends on the strangers."

"Ah, so. Of course. Yes, you are American. It becomes more noticeable when you smile. Europeans smile differently. May I come in, for a few minutes?"

Barbara said nothing, watching him thoughtfully.

"I am quite harmless. Let me introduce myself—Baron Franz Von Harbin. I am a refugee in the corridor. This wretched train has no club car, and my compartment is impossible. So until the dining car opens for dinner, I am exiled to the corridor, which is not only uncomfortable but boring."

"Why not?" Barbara asked herself. "On a train, nothing can happen, and while he does not look harmless by any means, he is certainly elegant, and a German who speaks French, which is a beginning." She was completely confident of her ability to discourage unwanted advances, and she did not mind the fact that he styled himself a baron. He might or might not be one. Titles were plentiful and fluid in Europe in the thirties.

He opened the door, and as if he read her mind, he reached into his pocket and handed her his card. Then he waited until she had read it before he seated himself facing her.

Staring at his card, Barbara said, "Your name appears very familiar, and I feel that I should recognize it, and I feel foolish that I don't."

"Why should you? I am not terribly important. I have served my government here and there, in an advisory capacity, but nothing of great importance. And you, Madame?"

"Mademoiselle. My name is Barbara Lavette. I live in San Francisco."

"How charming—that wonderful, beautiful city! But your French accent and your French name?"

"No connection. My grandfather came from France, and as for my French, well, I've been living in Paris for almost five years." She paused, wondering how much information to impart, and decided that her best defense from here on was no defense at all, but simply to be herself, which she felt was the only role she was fit to play. "You've been to San Francisco?" she asked him.

"I certainly have. I was consul general there for two years, twenty-seven and twenty-eight. Of course, Lavette. He was the man who married the lovely Jean Seldon." He clapped his hands together with pleasure. "What a small, delightful world! I entertained them. They are your father and mother?"

Barbara nodded.

"Yes. You do look like her. I entertained them at the consulate, and once I was at their home. Where was it— Russian Hill?"

"That's right. Russian Hill." Barbara was reassured, relaxed.

He switched to English. "Why don't we talk in English. My accent is not great, but better in your own tongue, yes? Do you know, your father was planning a New York-Bremerhaven run for one of his ships. It never came about, but we discussed things like docking facilities at great length. And now you, here; what a pleasant occurrence!" He smiled at her. His smile made his otherwise stern and fixed face almost warm. "Don't you think so?"

"I certainly do," Barbara agreed. "But tell me, why was your own compartment impossible?"

"A sudden change in plans and I booked too late to have a compartment for myself. I found myself sharing one with two Bavarian pigs."

"Bavarian pigs? I don't understand."

"Shopkeepers. Munich shopkeepers, a very loathsome and crude form of humanity."

"Oh? But," Barbara said gently, "that doesn't sound at all like a description of the master race."

"Yes. Touché." He appeared not at all disturbed. "The master race, as you put it, is by no means a homogeneous mass. I profess no disloyalty to the Führer by maintaining my own sense of discrimination and preference." He pointed to the books on the seat beside her. "I see you have been reading *Mein Kampf*."

"I bought it. I bought the whole pile to ease my way into Germany, but I haven't cracked one yet."

"You come as a tourist, if I may ask?"

"Oh, no," Barbara said bluntly. "I would hardly choose Germany as a place for a holiday. I do a weekly story for a New York City magazine, and my editor decided that I should do a few from Berlin."

"May I ask what magazine?"

"*Manhattan Magazine.*"

"Ah, a very fine magazine, perhaps the best in the States. But of course, B.L., Barbara Lavette—you sign with only your initials."

"Then you read *Manhattan?*"

"When I have the opportunity, certainly. It is witty, iconoclastic, and I enjoy the cartoons."

"Careful," Barbara said to herself, "careful, my girl. He knows too much about too many things."

"It's also anti-Nazi," Barbara said.

"Ah, so it is. Yes. But that is an affliction common to most American publications these days. However, if I remember your own writing, you don't dwell on that."

"The woman's touch," Barbara agreed. "I would be the world's worst political commentator, so I confine myself to the civilized aspects of life."

He looked at her keenly, smiling again, but thinly. "You interest me, Miss Lavette. One would take you, on the face of it, for a very average, very beautiful, American college girl. One would be mistaken, I think."

"Yes. I left college five years ago."

"Of course. And tell me, if you will, what will you write in your 'Letters from Berlin'?"

"I haven't the vaguest notion."

"Then you must let me help you. I am prejudiced, being a Prussian, yet I regard Berlin as one of the most interesting cities in Europe, certainly the best organized and the most modern. Of course, much depends on how you approach it. You can approach it as a city of great avenues, of parks, gardens, lovely canals, splendid public buildings, theaters, libraries, museums, as the place of the Friedrich Wilhelm University, with its lineage of great teachers, such as Hegel, Schelling, Richter, the brothers Grimm, Helmholtz, Lipsius—the place where Schinkel created some of the noblest buildings in all of Europe. Or again, you can approach it with a closed mind and only distrust and hatred for people who attempt to right an old injustice."

"Baron Von Harbin," Barbara said, "I approach it

only as an American traveling in Europe. If I knew what I was going to see, I would not have to go there, would I?"

"Excellent. Now tell me, where are you staying?"

"I have a reservation at the Esplanade."

Harbin frowned and shook his head.

"I heard it was an excellent hotel."

"So—yes and no. You must stay at the Adlon, on Unter den Linden. That's the only place. Believe me."

"But I have no reservation there."

"Leave that to me."

Barbara's impulse was to tell him that she had no intention of changing her hotel at his insistence. She had never allowed herself to be dominated or directed by either the desires or directions of men, and she found this man repellent and in a strange way somewhat terrifying. It was not that she feared him, nor did she experience the slightest unease at being alone in the compartment with him. His manners were impeccable, even courtly, and his admiration for her was obvious. An American male, traveling alone, would have been playing every card of the game; Harbin gave her the impression that he valued her company and that any gesture beyond that would be obscene. At the same time, she had a sense of something totally alien, totally different, from anything she had ever encountered. A Frenchman would have been praising her looks, identifying her perfume, commenting on the cut of her dress, pulling his every trick out of the bag to charm her. Harbin made no attempt to charm her or to be charming; he was simply himself, and it was his self that she found terrifying without being able to define or identify the source of the terror. Still, she felt that the meeting was invaluable, that there was more to Harbin than he displayed, and that he was a key that could open many doors. What a coup it would be to step into the inner circles of the Nazis, to do an interview with Hitler, or even with Göring or Ribbentrop! She could see Frank Bradley reading her copy and whooping with delight.

So instead of telling Harbin that she had no intention of changing her hotel, she simply nodded and asked him why it had to be the Adlon.

"Because I think you should have the very best door into my city. You have never been to Berlin, but you will see that I am correct. Yes? And now, since I find you so delightful as a traveling companion, will you dine with me?"

Barbara said that she would.

John Whittier had been spending more and more time with Tom Lavette, pleased that now the once rather irresponsible young man had become a very serious and dependable banker. They lunched together at least once a week, and Whittier invited Tom to accompany him on a trip to Washington.

"If you're not afraid to fly," Whittier said. "I can't spare the time for the train."

Tom was very much afraid to fly. On the other hand, there was no one in his circle of acquaintances who had ever flown crosscountry, and if he made the trip it would do wonders for his status as well as his self-esteem. And once the big, lumbering DC-3 was off the ground and into the air, circling over San Francisco Bay and then climbing to cross the coastal range, Tom's nervousness disappeared. He felt a sense of validity, as if this were his proper inheritance. He did not often think of his father these days, nor had he seen him in years, yet he could not help recalling that it was Dan Lavette who had established the first passenger airline in California, Dan Lavette whose Ford Trimotors had given Californians their first taste of air travel.

"Look down from here, Thomas," John Whittier said, inspired to what was for him almost a poetic flight of the imagination. "Take a good look at this California of ours." It was in deference to Tom that he used the plural; he would have been more inclined to say this California of mine, which was the way he often thought of it. "There's no other place like it on earth, and someday it's going to be the center of the country, not geographically, but in every other way. This is where the power is—food, oil, lumber, and land, and the men who run California will damn well run the country. That's something to think about, young fellow. We'll be talking to Harry L. Hopkins tomorrow, and I'm going to bring you with me. God, I hate the ground Roosevelt walks on—or rides on. That crippled bastard doesn't walk. You know, they hold him up when he speaks. He can't even stand erect, and that's where the malignancy of his nature comes from, but the fact remains that he is President, and now he needs us. That's why

Hopkins made this appointment. When we were fighting that bastard Harry Bridges five years ago, Roosevelt didn't lift a finger to help, but he needs me now. He needs the ships, because there's going to be a war, and we have the ships. I can remember the last war, Thomas. Do you know what happened to shipping rates?"

"I imagine they went up."

"Doubled, tripled, quadrupled—no end to it. And it will happen again. Roosevelt thinks he can control it, but power is a slippery thing. There is no separation of money and power. Now this man Hitler—he's not all bad, not by any means. Lindbergh found positive things in him and Göring, but the trouble is, he doesn't know where to stop, and Roosevelt does nothing to calm him down. The point is, Thomas, that come what may, we function; the family functions and the enterprise functions. Right now, in the eyes of the Rockefellers, the Morgans, the Lamonts, the Vanderbilts, and the rest of them, we are Johnny-come-latelies. They still look upon the West Coast as a sort of colony. But they've had their day. If there's going to be a war, we'll come out of it a damn sight better than the eastern establishment. Now just when do you come into your control? When does your mother's trust expire?"

"January 1940."

"Half a year. That will give us time to plan and consolidate. What do you think of Martin Clancy?"

The question came unexpectedly. When Jean Lavette had given up the chairmanship of the board of the Seldon Bank, Alvin Sommers, the first vice president, had moved into her place. Martin Clancy, the second vice president, had moved into Sommers' position. Sommers had been sixty-five then; he was now seventy. Clancy, six years younger, was a tight-mouthed, icy-eyed little man who had never displayed to Tom any trace of emotion, sentiment, or attachment to any living thing. His total attachment was to the bank.

"How do you mean that?" Tom asked Whittier.

"The way I put it. What do you think of him. Do you like him?"

"No one likes Clancy. But he does know banking."

"Al Sommers is going to retire in September. Clancy wants to be chairman of the board. That's been his dream all his life."

"What do you think?" Tom asked diplomatically.

"I think no. I don't like him. He started out as a little mick in the Tenderloin, and essentially this is what he remains. You will control the stock. I want you to assert yourself. Can you do it?"

"I think I can," Tom replied, pleased and not a little amazed at his own self-assurance. Whittier's frankness with him had helped build this assurance. He had never opened up quite in this manner before, never taken Tom so wholly into his confidence.

"I've been thinking about this consolidation for years," Whittier told him. "There's no doubt in my mind that once our interests are joined, we'll hold the balance of power on the Coast. From there on, we'll call the plays. I don't know yet exactly how we'll do it. That has to be worked out. But I want no slip-ups with Clancy. If he remains, it means only trouble. We want him out. Do you agree?"

"He's been with the bank forty years," Tom said slowly. "He's sixty-eight or sixty-nine. We could put through a sixty-five-year-old retirement rule, which would make it a little less personal. I think I could manage that."

"Only as chairman of the board. Do you think you can manage that?"

"If I have the votes, yes."

"So it's a question of Barbara. Between you, you'll have three hundred and eighty-two-thousand shares, seventy per-cent of the stock. What about Barbara?"

"I haven't seen her for years."

"Do you correspond?"

"Occasionally. She's supposed to return next week—at least that was her plan the last time I heard from her."

"I never asked about the split between you, never felt it was my affair. Truth is, I never quite got over that business of the strike. Was it over your father?"

"In part. Oh, we're not enemies. I can talk to Barbara. I can't think of any reason why she should stand in my way."

"You might plan to spend some time with her when she returns, win her confidence. It's important, Tom. I don't want to upset you, but Clancy and Sommers hold enough stock between them to tip the balance if we were to have Barbara turn against us."

"I don't think she would."

"On the other hand, your mother holds enough stock to tempt Barbara. She must not be tempted."

"I think you must let me handle it," Tom said.

"I have faith in your abilities," Whittier agreed.

The following day, as they stood at the gates to the White House, he spelled out that faith. "The trick, Thomas," he said, "for a man who intends to take up residence there someday, is to plan in advance. Not a month or a year in advance, but a lifetime. You have some of the qualifications, but it's a damn sight more than that. You have to establish a record. You have to calculate every move in your life, and one thing you damn well cannot afford is sentiment. Whether you're going to a toilet, a cathouse, or a dinner party on Nob Hill, you think of how it will look on the record. That benighted, crippled man in there will not live forever, and sooner or later our party will have its day. So take a good look at it."

"You're being very kind, John. But you're overrating me."

"I certainly am, Thomas," Whittier admitted. "At this moment, I don't think you have the qualifications for the state assembly, and that's pretty much the doghouse of it all. You've spent your twenty-seven years sitting back and waiting for the Seldon trust to fall into your lap. If you think you can do something else with the next twenty-seven, I'll back you to the hilt." He paused and faced Tom. "When we go in there and sit down with Harry Hopkins, it can begin an association that can change some history. Do you like the idea?"

"I do. Thank you, John," Tom said, not humbly, but as a confirmation between equals.

"Good. Now let's get to work."

The enormous, ornate, two-room suite in the Adlon dismayed Barbara. "I don't want this," she informed the manager flatly, staring at the baroque furniture, the thick gold and blue rug, the gilted drapes, the huge vase of fresh flowers. A black Mercedes limousine, waiting at the station for Harbin, had taken her there—Harbin still the proper, reserved, avuncular tour guide and protector— where Harbin had whispered a few words to the manager. Already Barbara was beginning to regret the fact that she had committed herself to Harbin's cloying courtesy. To be on her own, to do as she pleased and go where she pleased, had become second nature to her. She told herself that she was perhaps the most poorly equipped candidate in the world for the act of dissembling. This whole venture, she felt, was both romantic and stupid.

"I don't want this," she said, "and furthermore, I can't afford it."

The manager's English was not the best. *"Bitte, sprechen Sie langsamer.* Slow, yes? I understand, but slow."

"It is too expensive."

"So? No. I agree with ze baron, price is the same as Esplanade. *Bitte.* You are important guest."

Her luggage was in the room, and she was too tired to carry on the argument. The manager left, and Barbara kicked off her shoes and sprawled out on the vast bed. What on earth was she doing here in Nazi Germany, in Berlin? "If I had an ounce of intelligence," she told herself, "I'd be on the next train back to Paris and then to Cherbourg and home." Suddenly, she felt so wretched and lonely and aimless that she began to cry, and, still crying, she got up and walked to the huge mirror that took up most of one wall of the bedroom. Staring at the woeful, weeping face in the mirror, she burst into laughter, weeping and laughing at the same time. "Oh, I am a card," she told herself. "What a great undercover agent I have turned out to be!"

Enough of that, she decided. She stripped off her clothes and showered. It was still early, not yet midday. She dressed herself in a pleated plaid skirt, white blouse and light cardigan, and a good, solid pair of walking shoes; then she paced around her suite, studying it, and beginning, in her mind, the composition of her first "Letter from Berlin": "One discovers, immediately, a German gift for tastelessness. This is no inconsiderable talent. One would have to haunt the bazaars for weeks to discover a rug so garish and vulgar as that which covers the floor of my hotel living room."

She rejected it, annoyed with herself. She had hardly looked at the city, and she had no right to judge. She also realized that she would have to change the manner of her writing. There was something almost obscene about commenting on taste and manners and hotel furnishings in Berlin of 1939. "No preconceived notions," she said to herself, "not even in this cesspool. You go out and you see, and you make no judgments until the facts are presented before your own eyes."

It was just past noon when she came out on the street to a pleasant, sunny day, a cool breeze, and stretching before her, the magnificent reach of Unter den Linden. She knew from her guidebook that the university was on the same avenue, but she had carefully avoided mentioning it or asking about it. Now she decided to set out to find it on her own, after which she would find a restaurant and have some lunch. She strolled down Unter den Linden, studying the faces of the people who passed by. In all truth, she had to admit to herself that here on this lovely avenue there was no indication of what she had read about Germany. The people were well-dressed, cheerful, very ordinary human beings. Men looked at her, but then, she was sufficiently aware of her own face and figure to accept the fact that men looked at her, even though she herself could not accept a picture of herself as a beautiful woman. It was all so normal, so very matter-of-fact a picture of life in a busy, prosperous city, that she had to keep reminding herself where she was.

When she reached the university, opposite the Zeughauess Musum, she had the eerie feeling that the unseen eyes of the Gestapo were fixed upon her, and she made sure not to slow her pace or give the university buildings more than a passing glance, which she felt was all their unattractive architecture deserved. Certainly, her reaction was based on nothing more than her own excited imagination, yet for all that, she felt naked and alone. She would not go near the university on her first day in Berlin, nor on her second; she had to have, in her own mind, a valid excuse, some pages in her writing that would deal with higher education. She wandered along and found herself in Leipzigerstrasse; she ate a sausage and drank a glass of dark beer at a food bar and then walked back to the Adlon. First things first. Bits and pieces of reading surfaced in her mind. If one went in for this sort of thing, one had to cover every movement. She picked up her copy of *Mein Kampf*, regarded it distastefully, and then began to read, thumbing the pages, picking up passages here and there:

"All the human culture, all the results of art, science and technology that we see before us today, are almost exclusively the creative product of the Aryan. This very fact admits of the not unfounded inference that he alone was the founder of all higher humanity, therefore representing the prototype of all that we understand by the word man—"

A knocking at her door gave her an excuse to throw the book from her in disgust. "Oh, no," she whispered. "There are people with a penchant for wandering in sewers. I am not one of them." Then she went to the door and opened it.

A tall, slender, thinly handsome woman stood there, black hair in a close bob, high-bridged nose, and cynical gray eyes. She wore a flowered dress of red silk with a fur piece thrown across her shoulders. "My dear," she said, without formalities, "you are beyond question the beautiful, enchanting Barbara Lavette. Dutzi is quite right. You, my dear, are a knockout. In your own way, mind you." The accent was British, the voice high-pitched, confident, and touched with arrogance.

"Who are you, if I may ask? And who on earth is Dutzi?"

"Ah, so much for the famous—or for the infamous, should I say? I am the notorious Pleasance Rittford. Does it shock you, my dear?"

"Should it?" Barbara wondered, trying desperately to place the name. Certainly she had heard it—something British upper class and reasonably scandalous.

"My dear child, must I stand in your doorway? Even if you bloody well don't approve of me, you can invite me in."

"Please come in," Barbara agreed. "How do you know I disapprove of you?"

"Plaid skirt, walking shoes, cardigan—all of it eminently sensible. Eminently sensible people do not approve of me. You see, I do not hate Nazis. I quite adore them, and I make no secret of it."

It fell into place, Lady Pleasance Rittford, wife of Lord Nigel Rittford, both of them eager and articulate supporters of Hitler's new order and very vocal propagandists against Britain taking up arms against Germany. Barbara's first inner reaction was cold shock, a kind of sick disgust and an impulse to burst out in a storm of righteous anger. This she controlled, even managing to maintain her expression of naive bewilderment. After all, she was not a tourist. She was a writer who had stupidly agreed to do a job for a cause she neither understood nor approved of; but she was also a writer whose editor would turn handsprings after reading the kind of story she could do on Lady Pleasance Rittford.

"I don't shock you?"

"Perhaps a bit," Barbara admitted, forcing a smile, studying Lady Pleasance carefully. "At least forty," Barbara said to herself, "neurotic, terribly thin, hardly a sex object, and absolutely obsessed," trying to remember what she had read of Freud on the subject of obsession and compulsion. How wasted her two years of college had been; but again, how is anyone at age eighteen to know what educational necessities will arise a decade later?

"Poor dear, to come blasting in on you like this." She pointed to the great mass of yellow roses on the coffee table. "Dutzi's trademark. He is quite taken with you. You must thank him profusely. He's very sensitive and sentimental under that fishface Prussian mask of his."

"Who is Dutzi?"

"The Baron—Harbin, your traveling companion. His close friends call him Dutzi." She wet her lips with her tongue and leaned back, assessing Barbara. "Not you. It wouldn't sound right from you at all. It's that English schoolgirl look that has his heart dancing. Keep it. It's worth its weight in gold—or in yellow roses."

"What on earth are you trying to tell me? I barely know this man."

"Oh, he's not in love with you, my dear, if that's what you're thinking. Men like Dutzi don't fall in love. But Dutzi has his Aryan image and ideal. He's quite nutty on the subject, and you fulfill it."

"Good heavens! Would you please tell him that I am a mongrel."

"That won't make a bit of difference. Aryan is as Aryan decides. They get rid of only the truly loathsome types. You wouldn't have a drink, would you, dear? I'm positively parched."

"I haven't had time. I only arrived this morning, and I've been wandering around Berlin. I'll have them send up something."

"I'll do it." She sighed. "Unless your German is good?"

"Nonexistent."

"I thought so. What will you have?"

"A white wine cooler?"

Lady Pleasance made a face, then went to the phone and

ordered. Then she stalked around the living room, grimacing disapproval. "You know, my dear, Germans have even less taste than the British. Dutzi says you're a writer. What do you write?"

"I do a weekly piece for *Manhattan Magazine*. Gossip, people, and fashion. Books and theater. My editor wants a few pieces from Berlin. But now that I'm here, I'm up against the language. I never had that problem in Paris."

"Gossip, people, and fashion," Lady Pleasance repeated, clapping her hands with pleasure. "Forget fashion. They don't have it. But gossip—dear one, we must talk and talk and talk. You're not political, are you? I mean, you're not going to pal around with that stupid group of American and British correspondents who pin virtue all over themselves by sitting around and hating the Nazis. But of course not. They write the dullest, dreariest things imaginable, and whatever Dutzi may appear to be, he has a nose like a bloodhound. You're very lucky that he approves of you. It's an open sesame."

"To what?" Barbara wondered.

"You name it, love. You could even get to the Führer himself, and he's not such a bad chap at that. No gentleman, like Dutzi and Papen and some of the others, but power is a heady drink, and one forgives. And speaking of drink, where is it?"

The drinks came then. Lady Pleasance had ordered two double whiskeys, and she drank the first one neat, as if it were water. She mixed some soda into the second, and then launched into a rambling discourse on the character of the Führer.

By now, Barbara had had her fill of Lady Pleasance, and it occurred to her that perhaps she had also had her fill of Berlin. How had she ever gotten herself mixed up with this crew, and why didn't she put a stop to it? She knew the answer. Professor Schmidt and the university had dropped to the background of her mind, and like a child offered candy, she was composing, witty, cynical pieces for *Manhattan*, close-ups of these "creatures," as she thought of them, journalistic scoops that might never have come her way under different circumstances. A door had been opened, and it needed only one angry, disapproving remark from her to close it; whereupon, she sipped her wine cooler and forced herself to make polite, leading remarks to a Lady Pleasance, who was rapidly becoming quite drunk.

"The Führer will like you," Lady Pleasance confided. "I wouldn't dwell on that mongrel business. What is it, a French father? Dutzi says your French is simply divine. Goebbels is somewhat confused about the French, whether to give them Aryan status or not, but with a woman who looks like you, it's nothing to worry about, not one bit. You don't have a few drops of Jew blood anywhere? No, of course not. Now, you're just about the Führer's height, love, if you don't go in for high heels. But don't be too chummy. I think Dutzi has his own plans. He had a wife once who died or something—"

"Died or something?" Barbara asked.

"Or sleeping pills. Who knows? Not that I blame her. Dutzi's great fun—but to be married to him? Heaven forbid. He's jolly good for an evening or two, a trifle kinky, but darling, they all are, and it's all good fun, you know, if you don't take it too seriously, and don't look at me like that. I don't kiss and tell, but I do draw the line. I drew it with Göring. He's a disgusting fat pig, and I told him so to his face. Anyway, his *Lüger*—good name for it, don't you think—anyway, it's so buried in fat that he can't do anything much, or so I've heard, and anyway, he's a bit of a dope fiend. Papen, now that's something else. There's a gentleman, only he's a bit stupid, and Dutzi thinks the Führer will find him a bit of too much. You don't want to chum up with anyone who's on the way out. It can get quite nasty. Well, Pleasance will mother you through the sticky places. I do hope you're here for a long stay, and don't be put off by this war talk. There won't be any war. Winston, Neville, Tony—the whole lot of them are a pack of sniveling idiots, and as for your Deladier, he's the toadiest of the lot. What Adolf wants, Adolf will get, and he'll get it his way—the whole bloody continent—"

And on and on. She returned to the phone, and the waiter reappeared with two more double whiskeys. Finally, at long last, she rose unsteadily, told Barbara, "I must toddle, dear one. We'll have another darling chat very soon," and made her way to the door.

Alone, Barbara sat and shivered, and then, moving like an automaton, she went into the bathroom and began to brush her teeth. Then she paused, thinking, What on earth am I doing here, brushing my teeth? Really, Barbara, you are behaving like a child.

She returned to the sitting room, which was now quite

dark in the gathering twilight. She put on the lights, called
room service, and in a mixture of French and English
managed to order some dinner. She took out her notebook,
and then she paused. She sat for at least ten minutes, pen in
hand, staring at the empty page, and then sighed and confessed to herself that she was afraid. She realized that
there would be no "Letter from Berlin." She could not remain here, and she could not write from here. She would
do what she had to do, and then she would leave. Suddenly, it was not just Berlin, not just Germany; in her
mind, the whole of Europe was turning into a miasmal
nightmare, and somewhere inside her a voice was screaming to be let out of it.

That night she lay awake for hours. "I want to go
home," she told herself. "I want to go home. I'm so afraid
and so lonely. I can't go through with this. I want my
mother and I want my father, and I want to be able to see
plain, ordinary people, who are not sick and not insane."

She turned on the light, picked up the telephone, and
asked for the overseas operator. It was one o'clock in the
morning, and it took an hour more to get through to Dan's
office on Terminal Island.

"Daddy," she said at last, "is that you? Is that truly
you?"

"Barbara? Where on earth are you? We've been trying to
reach the ship."

"I didn't sail, daddy. I'm in Berlin."

"Berlin? No, you're kidding."

"It's the truth."

"God Almighty, what the devil are you doing in that
filthy place? Are you all right?"

"I'm fine, daddy. Just a little homesick. Don't scold me.
I'm here on a story. I wrote to mother. I know I should
have written to you, but I knew how troubled you'd be."

"Well, I am troubled. I can't tell you how troubled I
am. That's no place for you. All hell is going to break
loose. Baby, please get out of there."

"How's Joey and May Ling?"

"Fine, fine. Joe's up at Higate. Where are you staying?"

"At a very posh hotel called the Adlon. I'm all right.
And I'll be home soon, I promise you."

"It's been too long, Barbara."

"I know, daddy."

"When will you be coming back?"

"Soon, I promise. Very soon. Daddy, do me a favor."

"Anything you say."

"Call mother. Tell her I'm all right." Barbara paused. "Be kind to her, daddy. She's so unhappy."

Barbara felt better after that. A few minutes later, she was asleep.

She slept until ten the following morning, awakened slowly, and lay for a while in the luxury of her bed, lazy, comfortable in the thought that she had finally made a decision and admitted to herself that the whole enterprise was a mistake. In her mind, she worked out the steps: return to Paris, go to her apartment, pack her things, write a letter to the Limogets, confessing her cowardice and horror and her total ineptitude as an undercover agent, call the travel agency, get a room on any ship leaving for America, train to Cherbourg, and then be out of it forever. Dreaming this way, she heard the telephone ring.

There was a flow of German, in which she recognized her name, then a few words in English.

"Yes, this is Barbara Lavette," she said.

Frank Bradley's voice: "Barbara, for God's sake, is that you? Can you hear me?"

"Of course I can hear you, Frank."

"Do you know, we've been calling every hotel in Berlin. I finally reached your father in Los Angeles. From here on, will you please, please let me know where you are."

"Frank, there's no need to get excited. I'm perfectly all right. Now I want to tell you what I've decided—"

"Hold on and listen to me. There's a great picture of you on page four of the New York *Times*. Tomorrow's paper. I got a proof. Headline—beauty and the beast. The point is, I want you to get to one of them—Hitler, Göring—and do an interview. I know it's not an easy assignment, but I got faith in you. And listen, just take notes. You don't have to do your piece until you get back to Paris. Then you can let go. We're ballyhooing this to the sky, so, baby, do your thing."

"Frank—"

"Whatever you need—money, whatever—just let us know. And listen, there's a feller by the name of Buck Crombie at the American Embassy. An old classmate of mine. I sent him a wire, so if you require a friend in need, he's there."

"Frank, what makes you think I can get an interview with one of them?"

"I told you. Faith. And take notes. You can do three pieces for us, and believe me, the publishers are licking their chops. So carry on."

"Frank," she pleaded, "I don't know. This is a strange place. I think I shouldn't have come here at all."

"Angel, don't go soft on me. You're there. You don't have to stay forever. Just get what you need."

She put down the phone, despising her own lack of fortitude, her weakness and indecision, admitting to herself that when the lines were drawn, she came off as a person of absolutely no character. "And no resolve," she said to herself. "Anyone can change what you so euphemistically call your mind."

While she was dressing, there was a knock at the door: two dozen fresh yellow roses, to replace the ones already in the sitting room. There was a note with them: "I've been up to my ears in the tedious business of politics. Forgive me for ignoring my most charming traveling companion. Will you lunch with me? I'll be in the lobby at one. If you do not appear, I shall be devastated." It was signed, Baron Franz Von Harbin.

There was no return address or telephone number. She could refuse by not appearing. It was only half past eleven. There was still time to pack and take a taxi to the railroad station. She was under no compulsion to obey the imperious demand of Frank Bradley, nor did she need to continue her association with *Manhattan Magazine*—both of which she presented to herself as reasonable arguments and then rejected them. Her earlier mood was gone, and she told herself that she would be a fool not to take advantage of the situation she had fallen into. She also told herself that living with herself would be difficult indeed if she simply forgot about Professor Schmidt and wormed out of her commitment to the Limogets with a letter confessing ineptitude and cowardice.

She got out her notebook and proceeded to put down as much of her conversation with Lady Pleasance as she could remember, pleased that she was able to capture the Englishwoman's tone and inflection. At precisely one o'clock, she went down to the lobby, defiantly dressed in a pleated gray wool skirt, a white cotton blouse, a gray cardigan, and her

English walking shoes. If Dutzi wished to take her to lunch, he would take her as she was.

He greeted her with great formality, with only a slight, quizzical smile as a reaction to her costume. "We will eat here, yes? The food is French, but very good." In the dining room, the headwaiter almost collapsed in a fit of obsequiousness. It was a new experience for Barbara. The waiters behaved as if they belonged totally to the Baron, as if they were offering their lives and not just food. She had to restrain a desire to giggle.

She thanked him for the flowers. "But it seems wasteful," she said. "The ones already there would have been lovely for days."

"Possibly. But then I would be robbed of an opportunity to pay tribute to a beautiful American woman, no?"

"I don't think there's any need to pay tribute, as you put it. You've been more than kind to me."

"My pleasure and my indebtedness. Americans appear to harbor a—what shall I call it?—a native distaste for our system. Perhaps I can show you the more pleasant side of Berlin, of Germany. That's why I sent Lady Pleasance. I felt that a touch of your own tongue on your first day might be comforting. What did you think of her?"

"She was very informative," Barbara replied without enthusiasm.

"Yes." He smiled and shrugged. "She has been very useful to us. Her husband is a good friend. We need friends in England, just as we need friends in America. My dear, I hesitate to force myself on you, but you are alone, and the day after tomorrow there is to be a large reception—food, dancing—at Kunstler Halle. The Führer will be there, and others too. If I cannot entice you to allow me to bring you by, let us say, my own credentials, then perhaps I can lure you as a journalist. It will be an opportunity to meet some of the ogres, as you think of them."

Barbara considered it for a while. He waited, smiling. "How do you know I think of them as ogres?" she asked.

"Ah. But I am not entirely insensitive. You offer no opinions. You simply listen. Even Lady Pleasance was unable to squeeze an opinion from you."

"I didn't know she tried." Barbara smiled. "Yes, I would like to go. I am very curious to meet your leaders. Will you interpret for me?"

"Delighted."

"Will I be able to ask questions? To have more than a few minutes of conversation?"

"Alas, it is not my charm that draws you."

"I am afraid not entirely," Barbara said bluntly. "As you remarked, I am a journalist."

"I shall make your opportunities." He studied her thoughtfully. "May I call you Barbara?"

"Yes."

"Then you will call me Franz, never by that ridiculous name that Lady Pleasance must have informed you of. Barbara, I will call for you then, day after tomorrow, seven o'clock—" He was looking at her blouse and sweater.

"I will not wear my walking shoes," she said, smiling.

He took his leave after lunch, apologizing for the pressing demands his work made on him. It was a fine afternoon, with a cool breeze taking the edge off the summer's heat, and Barbara decided to explore the city further. She drifted along without plan or purpose, down Unter den Linden to the Tiergarten, where she watched children playing and listened to the music of a barrel organ, forgetting for a little while where she was and what she was there for. Back at the hotel, she finished a meticulous description of her experience up to this point, had a sandwich and coffee in her room, and then spent the evening working out a series of questions that she would put to whatever leader of the Third Reich Harbin arranged for her to question. At the same time, her thoughts wandered to what she felt was an inevitable moment in the future when Harbin would attempt to make love to her. She was neither innocent enough nor sufficiently unaware of her own attractiveness to doubt that this would happen, and the very thought of it sent cold shivers up and down her spine. Nor could she analyze this response on her part as other than a total response to the existence of Nazi Germany. She had spent two days in a clean, well-run, and in parts very beautiful city. No one had been ungracious to her, and Baron Von Harbin had on every occasion been the soul of courtesy, concern, and impeccable behavior. Barbara was a very independent and self-confident young woman; she knew and accepted this quality in herself; and she also knew that she was very different today from the wide-eyed college student who five years ago had embarked on the Twentieth Century Limited for the journey back to California. But she also knew that since she had arrived in Berlin, there had been an undercurrent of fear in her that she simply could not shake off.

She went to bed without contriving any solution to the Harbin problem, telling herself that when it surfaced, she would deal with it. She awakened early the next morning, discovered that she was ravenously hungry, and ate an enormous breakfast of sausage, eggs, fried potatoes, rolls, and coffee in the hotel dining room. Well, she had eaten almost nothing the day before, bereft of her appetite by the presence of the Baron and then content with a sandwich in her room. She felt more normal now, and, filled with purpose, telling herself, "Devil take the consequences. I said I would do it and I will," she strode along Unter den Linden to Friedrich Wilhelm University. There was nothing wrong, nothing curious, nothing suspicious, in what she was doing. Professor Schmidt had published two books, *Race and Religion* in 1936 and *Aryan Philosophy* in 1937. Neither book was obtainable in Paris, but she knew that *Aryan Philosophy* had been translated and published in New York, and she had read a scathing review of it in the files of the Paris *Tribune*. The reviewer had found Schmidt's attempts to connect the Bhagavad-Gita with Hitler's theories of the master race and with the half-baked theology of Bormann, Rosenberg, and Himmler both childish and tasteless. Barbara's own impression was of a man undertaking an exercise in self-preservation, but this was only a guess, since she had not read the book. However, the book had created sufficient furor for her to be justified, she felt, in interviewing him.

At the office of the university, hidden in a Gothic maw, she found, happily, a young woman who spoke French well enough to explain that Professor Schmidt was not teaching the first summer semester. The young woman thought he could possibly be found in his apartment, which was on a street called Kurfürstendamm. If Barbara desired to walk, it was about three kilometers, off Unter den Linden onto Hermann Göring Strasse, then onto Potsdamer Strasse, and then it would be on her right. But the Fraülein, she was told, would be better advised to find a taxicab.

Barbara decided to walk. It was the only way to really see a city, to get the feel of it, and the day was still young. Past the looming bulk of the Kaiser Schloss, past the gardens and public buildings on Göring Street, past the chancellery, it was like walking through a dream or into

the pages of a horror tale, yet it was all perfectly ordinary.
Then she was in a street of shops, and there was a shop
boarded over, and scrawled on the wooden boarding, JUDE;
and how very strange and chilling that was, the first indication of the things she had read! She thought to herself,
They are so competent and clean. They keep things out of
sight.

Kurfürstendamm was a street of apartment houses. She
had an odd sense of familiarity; there were streets exactly
like it in Paris. She began to read the numbers, looking for
the professor's building.

Then Barbara saw a small crowd on the street in front of
her, and a barrier that diverted traffic into a single, narrow
line. There were two men in the white uniforms of sanitation workers. They were standing by the barrier. On the
sidewalk, a dozen onlookers watched in silence. Out in the
street, a group of men and women were sweeping what
appeared to be the remains of sewage, the overflow of what
Barbara guessed might have been a broken or malfunc-
tioning sewer line. As she approached the group, the strong
smell of the sewage increased, and she could see on the
street the damp residue of what appeared to be human
feces, dark clumps and streaks of unidentifiable refuse that
had apparently backed up out of the sewer. About fourteen or fifteen men and women were sweeping the offal
into several piles. The men and women were not young.
Most of them appeared to be in their fifties and sixties,
some older; one woman was white-haired, very old, apparently feeble. They were decently dressed in suits and
dresses, and several of the men wore spectacles. If she had
met these people in the ordinary course of things, Barbara's impression would have been of a group of profes-
sionals and their wives—doctors, lawyers, storekeepers,
teachers. Their work was being directed by four men,
heavyset men who wore belted raincoats and hats in spite
of the early summer weather. These four men shouted
commands at the sweepers, pushed them, and snarled at
them when their pace slackened. The two sanitation workers stood in silence, as did the onlookers on the sidewalk.
Beyond the group, a sanitation truck and two black sedans
were parked.

Barbara reached the group and stopped and watched,
resisting the urge to avert her eyes and walk past quickly.
She was trembling; she felt sickened; yet she could not

tear herself away. She had read numerous accounts in the
Paris newspapers of Jews summarily pulled out of their
homes to clean streets, yet the fact was hideously different
from the written account. It was not what they were
doing that filled her with a kind of numb horror, but the
blank-faced silence of the onlookers and the two sanitation
men; and this, together with her inability to understand
anything of the shouts and imprecations hurled at the
sweepers by the burly men in raincoats, increased her sense
of having stepped into a nightmare.

Now most of the offal had been swept into piles. The
elderly men and women paused in their work, and one of
the men in raincoats said something to the sanitation
workers. In response, they walked over to the truck and
returned with two empty metal cans, which they set down
close to the mounds of garbage. They started back to the
truck and were stopped by an order from the man in the
raincoat. Then an exchange of dialogue. It appeared to
Barbara that they were arguing with the man in the raincoat. Suddenly he raised his voice and shouted. The two
sanitation men shrugged and walked to one side.

Now some of the onlookers turned and walked away.
Other pedestrians walked past without pausing, without
even glancing at what was going on. Some instinct told
Barbara to go, to leave it alone, to get away before whatever was going to happen happened; a stronger force held
her there. She had forgotten for the moment that she was
on her way to find Professor Schmidt; she had forgotten
everything except the drama that was being played out in
front of her.

Now the same man in the raincoat who had argued with
the sanitation workers turned to one of the sweepers. This
was a man who appeared to be close to seventy; he was
stoop-shouldered, scholarly in appearance, with a fringe
of white hair around his bald head, and neatly dressed in
a brown suit, a white shirt, and a dark tie.

The man in the raincoat pointed to one of the piles of refuse and gave an order. The old man looked at him without moving or replying. Raising his voice, the man in the
raincoat gave the order again, pointing at the same time to
one of the metal cans. His meaning was obvious. The old
man was to pick up the filth in his barehands and put it
in the can, and now Barbara realized that the sanitation

men had probably been going to the truck for shovels when they were stopped.

All sound, all movement on the street, stopped. Onlookers, sanitation men, sweepers—all of them stood frozen, watching the man in the raincoat and the old man. Now the three other men in raincoats moved toward the old man.

Again the order, this time quietly and coldly. The old man shook his head and sighed. The man in the raincoat took a step and swung his open hand across the old man's face, and the old man went down on the pile of filth. As he tried to pull himself away, the man in the raincoat kicked him so that he sprawled in the filth again, then he bent, dragged him to his feet by his collar, and drew back his hand to strike him again.

Barbara could stand no more. "Stop it!" she cried. "Stop it, you animal!"

The man in the raincoat paused with his arm drawn back for the blow, still clutching the trembling old man by the collar. He looked at Barbara. Everyone else stared at Barbara. The man in the raincoat grinned, disposed of the grin, and snapped at her in German. Then he struck the old man.

Afterward, Barbara had no clear memory of what happened in the next few seconds. She had never before in her life engaged in an act of violence, never been in a fight, never struck a blow or had a blow struck at her; so what she did was totally a response, without thought or premeditation. She flung herself at the man in the raincoat, swinging the leather handbag she carried at his head. The old man, whom he still clutched by the collar, was between him and Barbara, and the man in the raincoat was unable to ward off the blow. It caught him on the side of the head and staggered him. The three other men in raincoats leaped at Barbara and grabbed her; and then all reason departed, and she fought like a wildcat, biting at their hands where they held her, scratching, kicking. The fourth man in the raincoat let go of the old man, swearing and pressing his hand to his eyes. Then he joined the other three and managed to slap Barbara across the face, a heavy stinging blow, yet one that she hardly felt at the moment.

Then the fit passed, the rage drained out of her, and she stopped struggling and stood trembling and sobbing in the grasp of the three men; yet even in that moment of anguish and indignity, she noticed that no one moved a step to help her. No one but the men in the raincoats moved or spoke, not the two sanitation workers, not the onlookers, not the old people with the brooms. They watched in silence as the man she had hit with her purse raised his hand to strike her again. One of the men who held her barked at him, let go of Barbara, and pushed the fourth man away. He then turned to Barbara, speaking quickly and angrily.

"I don't speak German," she managed to say.

The fourth man in the raincoat, the one who had been beating the old man—who now had collapsed on the pavement, blood running from his nose—the fourth man walked up to Barbara until his face was only a few inches from hers. One of the men holding her said something to him. He shook his head and smiled. Then he spat in Barbara's face.

The act had an electrifying effect upon her. She stopped trembling, stopped sobbing. She felt that something deep inside of her had turned into ice, and she said, slowly and precisely, "You filthy Nazi pig. I am not afraid of you. Not afraid of you at all. Do you understand me?"

His companion pushed him back and spoke to the other two. Then he turned to the sweepers and barked at them. The two men who held Barbara began to lead her off toward where the black sedans were parked. At first she held back. Then, rather than submit to the further indignity of being dragged across the filthy street, she walked with them to the cars. They opened the back door of one of them and motioned for her to get in. She felt cold, tired, weak, used up, but no longer half-hysterical, no longer afraid. One of the men got in next to her. The other went back to where her purse had fallen on the street, picked it up, and, returning, gave it to her. Then he got into the car and they drove off.

She took a handkerchief from her purse and wiped her face, then she looked at herself in her hand mirror. There was a red welt on her cheek where she had been struck, but her eye just above it was not bruised or swollen. Both the man beside her and the driver were silent. It was no use asking them where they were taking her. They either did not speak English or refused to. She leaned back in her seat, bereft of emotion. There was nothing she could do but wait.

They drove for only a few minutes, no more than a kilometer, she decided, then entered a narrow street and pulled up in front of a gray stone building. Over the door, brass letters spelled out: POLIZEIAMT. Barbara breathed a sigh of relief. At least they were taking her to a police station, not to some dreaded Gestapo house.

The man next to her got out and motioned for her to follow him; then, with a raincoat on either side of her, she was ushered into the building. Barbara had never been inside a police station, in America or elsewhere, so she had no measure of comparison. There was a wide entranceway painted dark green, with a cement floor, benches on either side, a staircase going up to a second floor, a wooden railing with a gate in the middle, and behind it a man in uniform at a desk. They went through the gate, and then she was standing in front of the desk, the men in raincoats on either side of her. One of them spoke to the man at the desk; Barbara stood there while the conversation went on, the man at the desk making notes on a pad in front of him. Then the two men in raincoats turned and walked out, leaving Barbara standing there while the officer behind the desk continued to write on his pad.

He finally stopped writing and looked up at her thoughtfully. He was a stout man, with a round face, tiny blue eyes, and a very small mouth, which he pursed constantly.

"Englisch?" he asked her.

"I'm an American."

"Ah, *Amerikanerin.*" It was evidently the extent of his conversation in English. He pointed to one of the benches. *"Sitzen!"* Barbara walked to the bench and sat down. A clock on the wall facing her said one o'clock. Where had the morning gone? It seemed to be a gap in her existence, as if what had happened out there on Kurfürstendamm had happened an eternity ago. The man at the desk picked up a telephone and talked into it. Then again silence. It was strangely quiet for a police station. Then a man in ordinary clothes came down the stairway. Barbara was looking at a large photograph of Adolf Hitler hanging on the wall alongside the staircase, thinking, as she had in the past, of how ridiculous the tiny Chaplinesque mustache was—and then she noticed the man on the staircase: no mustache, but nevertheless a striking resemblance. Did he realize it, she wondered? And then it struck her that, for some reason, she could not focus clearly on her present situation, in a police station in a foreign country, apparently under arrest, unable to speak the language—and sliding into some sort of daydream. Yet it was like a dream, vicious, stupid, impossible.

The man who looked like Hitler without the mustache walked to the desk and said something to the officer sitting there, who pointed to Barbara. He came over to Barbara and said, in English, "My name is Schlemer, Inspector Schlemer. What is your name, Fräulein?"

"Barbara Lavette."

"Yes. Good. Come with me, please." He had a heavy accent, but otherwise his English was fluent and grammatical. He led Barbara up the stairs and down a hallway, where he opened the door to a small room that contained a desk, several wooden chairs, a bookshelf, a filing cabinet, and on the wall facing the door another picture of the Führer.

"Please, sit down, Fräulein," he said, indicating a chair. There was a window in the room. Schlemer switched on his desk lamp, evidently to increase the light, and he peered at Barbara's face. "How did you get that bruise?"

"One of your men enjoys striking women—and old men."

Schlemer walked around his desk and sat down behind it, facing Barbara. "They are not my men. My men don't enjoy striking women or old men."

"They arrested me—if I am under arrest. They tore my clothes and dragged me through the street," Barbara said coldly, angrily.

"Do you wish a doctor to look at you, Fräulein?"

"No, I'm quite all right. I just wish to know why I was thrown into a car and brought here."

"You are an American?"

"Yes."

"What is your business in Germany?"

"I'm a journalist. I'm here on assignment for my magazine. And you haven't answered my question."

"In time, in time. Where do you live, Fräulein?"

"I'm staying at the Adlon."

The expression on his otherwise impassive face changed ever so slightly. Barbara noticed this. "Am I under arrest?" she insisted.

"Please tell me what happened."

"I was walking down the street—"

"On Kurfürstendamm? Do you have friends there?"

"I was taking a walk."

"I see. Strolling."

"Yes. And then I saw these old people sweeping filth on the street. Four men in raincoats were supervising them. Then one of these men in raincoats insisted that an old man pick up the filth with his hands and put it into a metal can. The old man refused. The thug in the raincoat then began to beat the old man. I tried to make him stop. That's when he struck me. Then the other three grabbed me, dragged me into a car, and here I am."

"So. You should not have interfered, Fräulein. The sweepers were Jews, put to useful work for the common health of the city. They should be grateful that they are allowed to contribute in whatever way they can for the good of the Reich. When they become stubborn and willful, they must be disciplined."

"By beating an old man? By flinging him face down in that filth?"

"There are things you do not understand, Fräulein."

"Thank God!"

"Your own position is difficult. Are you under arrest?" He shrugged. "I have no alternative. You interfered with security officers in the performance of their duties. You attacked them. You struck one of them."

"I don't believe this!" Barbara exclaimed.

"You say you are a journalist. It's very odd for a journalist to be living at the Adlon."

"I assure you, Inspector, that I did not choose the Adlon. But what if I did? Have I no right to stay at the hotel I choose?"

"Every right, Fräulein. But if you did not choose the Adlon, who did?"

"Baron Von Harbin insisted that I stay there."

The inspector stared at her thoughtfully, a long moment passing before he said, "Is the Baron a friend of yours?"

"Yes."

Again, moments of silence. Then Schlemer rose. "If you will excuse me for a few minutes, Fräulein——" He left the room, closing the door behind him. Barbara sat there, ill at ease, dissatisfied with herself, angry at herself for having mentioned Harbin's name, telling herself that she would rather rot in a cell than turn to Harbin for help. Right at this moment, Harbin symbolized everything that had happened to her this day, and she realized that she lacked the courage to say, "No, he's no friend of mine. I have only contempt for him."

"Well," she admitted to herself, "there it is, Barbara. You are not the stuff of which heroes or heroines are made. You are scared." And then she whispered, "Oh, God, I *am* scared, terrified. What if they put me in one of their jails, or a concentration camp. I never thought of that."

She sat there, pleading inwardly for Schlemer to return and tell her what her fate was to be. Would they allow her to communicate with the American Embassy? Would they allow her to reach her parents, to speak to anyone?

And then the inspector returned. She rose to face him.

"I am sorry for what has occurred, Fraülein," he said to her. "You must understand that those men were not my men, not Berlin policemen. I have arranged for a car to take you back to your hotel. I trust that you will understand that this is not the normal order of things in Berlin."

"Do you mean that I'm free to go?" Barbara asked uncertainly.

"Please. I will take you downstairs."

Back at the Adlon, Barbara went up to her suite and dropped tiredly into a chair. What a mess she had made of things! And what now? Did she dare go again to Kurfürstendamm and seek out Professor Schmidt? Could she stay in Berlin? Could she sleep at night?

She looked down and noticed that her stockings and shoes were covered with filth. Why hadn't she noticed that before? Disgusted, she kicked off the shoes, pulled off her stockings, and then threw both into the trash basket. Again she sat down, closing her eyes, stretching out her bare feet. At least she was free, not in a police station, not in a Gestapo house, but free. That was something. No, that was everything. She had always been free; she had never realized the sweet taste of it. Even here in Berlin, even with all the problems facing her, the taste of freedom was as sweet as honey. And then her sense of relief gave way to the picture of the old Jew lying with his bleeding face in the sewage. She felt suddenly nauseated and ran into the bathroom, where she vomited. She hung over the toilet bowl, vomiting convulsively until her stomach was empty. The vomiting relieved her. She felt clean and empty for the first time since the incident began, and she went to the sink, scrubbed her face, and brushed her teeth. Just as she finished, there was a knock at the door.

"One moment!" she called out. She rinsed her mouth, dried her hands, and then went barefoot to the door and opened it.

Harbin stood there. "May I come in?" he asked her.

She closed the door behind him. Harbin walked slowly around the room, glanced at the wastebasket, where she had thrown her shoes and stockings, then at her bare feet. Barbara stood watching him. Then he walked over to her and touched her cheek gently.

"Does it hurt?"

She shook her head.

"Sit down please, Barbara." She dropped into a chair. "Have you had lunch? Do you want some?"

"I'm not hungry, thank you."

He placed his hat on the table where the yellow roses were, then sat on the couch, facing her.

"They called you, and you told them to let me go. Isn't that it?" Barbara asked him.

He nodded.

"Thank you. I was very frightened. I'm grateful to you."

"Yes." Then he sat silently, staring at her.

"About my feet," she said nervously, "the shoes and stockings were filthy. I couldn't stand to touch them. I threw them away."

"I understand. Your blouse is torn. Do you want to change?"

She glanced down. Why hadn't she noticed the tear in her blouse before? Or had she?

"Go in and change," he said tonelessly. "Put on shoes and stockings."

Her torn blouse was off and she was standing in her brassiere and slip when Harbin came into the bedroom. He stopped just inside the bedroom door. "Finish dressing," he told her. "We will talk while you dress and pack."

She pulled on a fresh blouse. "What do you mean, pack?"

"You are leaving Germany. You have a reservation on the four-thirty train for Paris. That doesn't give us too much time."

Strangely, she was not disturbed by his presence in the bedroom. He had erected a wall between them. "No," she said defiantly. "Why should I leave? I have things to do here." Then she added, "Is it because of what happened?"

"On Kurfürstendamm? No, that was childish and impetuous. The other thing was stupid."

She had stepped into her skirt and zipped it closed. "What other thing?"

"Finish dressing. The university."

She was taking stockings out of a drawer, and now she paused to look at him, the stockings in her hand.

"You play the game like a fool, like a child," he said harshly. "Are you a communist?"

"No," she whispered.

"No. Even a stupid communist would know better. What then, a sympathizer?"

"No."

"Well, it doesn't matter now. Did you think you could go to the university and make inquiries about Schmidt and have it end there?"

"I went there to interview him," she said hopelessly.

"What nonsense! Did your editor send you to Berlin to interview a fool who thought that by writing idiotic books he could pull the wool over our eyes? We have plenty of idiotic books, but they are written by idiots and not by quixotic fools. How did you even hear about Schmidt? His books were never published in France. You don't read German. Didn't you think of these things?"

It occurred to her to insist that she had read *Aryan Philosophy* in English, and then she realized that such a protestation would make no more sense than anything else she had done. She bit her lip and finished pulling on her stockings.

"And then you calmly walked to Kurfürstendamm. Luckily, you were arrested before you ever reached Schmidt's apartment. The Gestapo is still searching his apartment, taking it apart bit by bit. Oh, it would have been a fine thing for you to walk in there and ask for Professor Schmidt. Because, my dear Barbara, Professor Wolfgang Schmidt died yesterday. He died after three days and three nights of questioning by the Gestapo. Let me be more brutally frank. He was beaten to death. And the same Gestapo, my dear, is waiting for you to try to contact Professor Schmidt. I am not saying that you would be beaten to death. After all, you are a correspondent and an American citizen and the daughter of a very wealthy family. As yet, they don't know what your associations in Paris were, but they can find out, believe me. And it would be damned unpleasant for you, very damned unpleasant."

He paused. Barbara said nothing, only watching him. "Put on your shoes and pack," he said.

She put on a pair of shoes, and then she opened a suitcase and began mechanically to put clothes into it. Harbin watched her. Then she stopped and turned to him.

"Why are you doing this? Why are you telling me all this?"

"Because unless you open your eyes, you will never survive in this world. You don't belong in Europe. Go home. Or else your insane innocence will destroy you. Don't you have any idea of what I am, of what this place is? Or what kind of a crazy game you are playing? Do you know why they chose you? Because you are an innocent, because it shines out of your eyes, because you are sick with the belief that people are good. Yes! Sick with it! It's no virtue today. It's a sickness. You talk so blithely of interviewing Hitler and Göring. Do you know what they are, what we all are? Do you know where I was yesterday morning? I was watching them finish off Professor Schmidt. That was my amusement for half an hour."

She finished packing, unable to speak, unable to respond in any way. When her bags were packed, Harbin phoned for a porter. Going down in the elevator, Barbara said, "I must pay my bill."

"It has been taken care of."

"No," she protested. "I can't let you—"

"It has been taken care of," he said severely. "We don't have any time to waste."

The same black Mercedes that had driven her from the railroad station to the Adlon was waiting outside the hotel. Harbin held open the door for her and then got in after her. He gave no directions to the chauffeur, who evidently knew where they were going; and when they were on their way, he reached into his breast pocket and handed Barbara her passport and railroad ticket. He said nothing at all while they were in the car. It was only after her bags had been checked through to her compartment and when they were standing on the platform next to the railway car, with no more than fifteen minutes before the train would depart, that Harbin faced her and said, "I am too old to be in love, Barbara, and too cynical and much too cold inside. I try to live with the illusion that I am a Junker, a Prussian gentleman, a person of character and honor. But my honor is a sham, and my pretensions are lies, and I serve a pig in a pigsty—which is not to say that I am any better than the other pigs. But I want you to know that if you had remained here, I would have behaved to you as a gentleman should. For a little while, you helped to feed the illusion that I could still feel, that I could love, that I could retrieve something of what men used to call honor. But that was as much a dream as the rest of my pretensions."

"Will you be all right?" she asked woefully. "They won't punish you for this?"

He shrugged. "I am still useful, I think. I am fifty-two years old, Barbara. I don't find life very enchanting. So it doesn't matter too much."

"It matters to me."

"Thank you for that. Now, get on the train."

He did not try to kiss her, and she could not bring herself to kiss him. She boarded the train and went to her compartment. Through the window, she saw him standing pensively, watching the train as it pulled out.

Part Four

REUNION

Sitting in his office on Terminal Island, staring out of the window at the almost-completed hull of the third yacht he had built for film moguls who were searching for new ways to spend their money, Dan Lavette contemplated his fiftieth year. He had lived half a century, he had been rich and he had been poor, and once or twice he had experienced a sense of comprehending why he was alive. The moments of self-revelation, however, had been ephemeral; discontent was deeper and more lasting. His health was good; he had not put on weight since he had given up mackerel fishing to sit at the desk of an enterprise that was at best modestly profitable and at worst utterly senseless. His wife was the one woman who had ever managed to give him a sense of his own worth or importance, yet he had reached the point where he took her for granted, and lately he found himself thinking more and more often of Jean, who had divorced him ten years before.

He had fathered three children. There was his son Thomas, lost to him. Ten years had gone by since he had seen Thomas. The boy—well, not really a boy anymore, a man now—would be twenty-seven, or was it twenty-eight? Even the birthday had gone out of his mind. Who was he and what was he like, this stranger who was his first child by Jean? What a stupid, hopeless thing that was! The two of them building a wall that became thicker and more impenetrable year by year. May Ling had lectured him on that, on the difference between the hurt pride of a man and a boy; but his own pride or sensitivity or fear was something that eluded him and was beyond his own understanding. He had once tried to explain to May Ling how the mind of a hoodlum, a roughneck, a brawler—as he saw himself—worked, but he had bogged down in the contradictions of his attempt at self-analysis and had given up the effort to make her or himself understand.

By what miracle Barbara had come to love him, he did not know; but she did love him, and she was comfortable with him and May Ling. Since her return from Europe, she had spent most of her time in Los Angeles. They had put a bed in Feng Wo's tiny study, and there, for the past three months, Barbara had been working on her book, spending most of the hours of each day toiling over the typewriter. She had been to San Francisco twice to see her mother, and from all Dan had been able to get from her, the visits were pleasant, although she refused to set foot in John Whittier's house. She too was something of a stranger to Dan, for the girl who had gone away five years before was in many respects very different from the woman who returned. She was still direct and warm and open, and even lovelier than she had been as a college girl; but underneath Dan felt a profound difference, a sense of deep sadness, of unapproachable tragedy that created a wall around her inner self.

"Give it time," May Ling said to him. "She has been through a great deal, and she has suffered. It's not easy for the children of the rich to deal with suffering. For the children of the poor, it's a matter of fact and life. So don't press Barbara. There will come a time when she'll let it out."

The time came. It was Joe who brought it about, during a weekend he was able to spend at home. Joe was the mystery, the reward, the enigma of Dan's life. Dan fought him, resisted him, and worshipped him. They had a terrible battle over what Dan regarded as a wasted summer, when Joe had worked as a laborer at Higate Winery. They fought over the movie people, whom Joe despised, and who, he insisted, used Dan, exhibiting him and his Chinese wife at their homes. Joe resented it that the shipyard had come into being as a way of supporting him through medical school; he was never totally free from Dan's past, the past of a millionaire tycoon, and he was also never entirely free from his guilt at having a father who worked twelve and fourteen hours a day as a mackerel fisherman. He surely did not want him to be a fisherman again, but Dan felt his resentment toward the possibility that he might once again become a man armed with power. Joe was protective of May Ling. Thus they fought and embraced and fought again, with May Ling pleading with Dan to recognize that his son was a man with a will as strong as his own, and to deal with him as a man.

"How do I deal with that?" he wondered now. "They're all strangers." Not to each other; it was he who had sat quiet, inarticulate, that evening when Joe was at home, listening to him tell how a Mexican woman had died in the hospital while the students stood there, being instructed in the symptoms, listening, learning, while a human being died—and then Joe's woeful plaint of hopelessness and helplessness. Why had he resented that? Why had something inside of him said, "God damn it, it's his business to know why and how people die! Why is he whimpering?" And then his anger washed away into mute understanding as Barbara opened up and poured out her heart. She was connected with Joe. She told them the story of what had happened in Toulouse when Marcel died, and for the first time she told them why she had gone to Germany.

"You know," she said, "I heard about all the monstrous things they have done—but nothing was as awful as the sight of that old man, lying with his bleeding face in the sewage, while that brute kicked him and cursed him."

Dan remembered how he had glanced at May Ling. Her face had not changed, but tears were slowly running down her cheeks, and he himself had felt an overwhelming impulse to take Joe and Barbara in his arms, to hold them both and protect them.

Now, in his office at Terminal Island, he came out of his reverie, muttered, "The hell with it. They're good kids. I did the best I could," and then yelled for his secretary. "Bertha!"

She came running in. Her name was Bertha Mendoza, and she was short, stout, and middle-aged. He had hired her as a bookkeeper after Feng Wo's death, with the understanding that she would also serve as his secretary, constituting his entire office force. She was an excellent bookkeeper, a fair typist, and a pretender at shorthand. And she was a Chicano with a violent temper and four children to worry about.

"You yell like I was in San Pedro!" she exclaimed.

"Where the devil's the admiral? You said he'd be here at ten o'clock."

"He's an admiral, Mr. Lavette. You think you push around such a man like you push me? Oh, no. No, sir."

"You're sure this admiral said he'd be here?"

"You think I make up such stories?"

"O.K., O.K.," Dan said. "I'm sorry."

"Always you yell and then you're sorry."

"No lectures. Just bring him in here when he comes."

It made him nervous to sit in his office and do nothing. In the old days, there had always been others to sit in the offices and do whatever had to be done there. He had an almost irresistible craving to be out in the open, on the ways where the work was being done, to see and supervise every step of it, to see things made, to see the miracle of a ship arising out of naked ribs and raw planks.

But he was sitting here, wasting the morning, because a call from Washington, D.C., had told him to expect a visit from one Admiral Emory Scott Land at ten o'clock today. It was already after eleven. When he sat alone and brooded, he chewed the bone of his discontent down to its very marrow.

It was half past eleven before the admiral arrived, a tall, spare, white-haired man in his early sixties. Mrs. Mendoza brought him into the office with a triumphant look, as if to say, "Here, I have produced him." He wore civilian clothes, and he pulled a chair over to Dan's desk and sat down without apology, facing Dan's bleak look with a slight smile. "I'm Emory Land," he said. "You know who I am?"

Dan nodded.

"What are you building out there?" he asked, pointing through the window.

"A hundred-and-ten-foot yacht for some damn fool who has nothing but money."

"That's one damn big yacht."

"As long as they pay for it. There's no Depression in Hollywood."

"You don't enjoy building yachts?"

"They're toys. I don't enjoy building million-dollar toys while San Pedro and Wilmington are filled with men who are starving because they don't have jobs."

"There's an answer for that."

"Tell me," Dan said flatly.

"Tell them to go to hell with their toys."

Dan grinned and shook his head. "I'd like to." He opened his cigar box, but the admiral shook his head. "You mind if I do?"

"Go ahead. You know who I am, don't you, Lavette?"

Dan bit off the end of his cigar and lit it. "I'd like to, Admiral. I sure as hell would. But I got eleven men working on that toy out there. It keeps them eating, and it keeps my kid in medical school." He paused, blew smoke, and studied his cigar. "Do I know who you are? I sure as hell do. You're chief of the Maritime Commission. But what brings you to me, I don't know. I have a lousy little shipyard that hangs on by the skin of its teeth. What I don't shell out for material and payroll goes to meet the payments on my bank loan. I build toys and kid myself into thinking that I serve some useful purpose on this earth."

"I'll be damned," the admiral said softly.

"Why?"

"I didn't expect a shipbuilder to want to serve some useful purpose on this earth. To make money, to build ships, that's something else."

"I'm no shipbuilder."

"Who is, Lavette?" he asked, nettled. "You think you're unique, don't you? Let me tell you something. There's nothing in these whole damn forty-eight states but lousy little shipyards, and you're a jump ahead. At least you build toys. The rest of them build nothing. Nothing. And their bleeding, bleating hearts turn my ass red."

"I'm not bleeding."

"Like hell you're not! You're so god damn sorry for yourself it stinks up the place. Worse than that cigar of yours."

"Is that what you came here to tell me?" Dan demanded angrily.

"Sure. Why not? And I'm not going. I'm at least ten years older than you, but I don't think you could throw me out. Do you want to try?"

Dan burst into laughter. "Hell, no, I don't want to try. What can I do for you, Admiral? You didn't come all the way from Washington to see me."

"Why not. Sure, I'm going to talk to all of you—here, San Pedro, Long Beach, Oakland, Sausalito, right up and down the coast. I spoke to a few already. You call that a lousy little shipyard," he said, pointing out the window. "It's not. It's a damn fine shipyard, rotting away, like every other shipyard in America. Do you know how many ships we're operating in our merchant marine?"

"I could guess. Maybe a thousand."

"Just about that. Ten and a half million deadweight tons. Why, a tiny country like Holland floats more tonnage than that. And how many merchant ships do you think we built last year?"

"None?"

"You're not far from wrong. Tell me something, Lavett, what do you think of this war in Europe? Do you think it's a joke? That's what they're saying."

"No war's a joke. My daughter was in Germany five months ago. Not for long, but it was a nightmare while it lasted. No, I don't think it's a joke."

"We're going to be in that war."

"I hope not."

The admiral shook his head. "Nobody wants to believe it. Nobody wants to deal with it. I have to deal with it. We have one thousand, one hundred, and fifty merchant vessels, and that includes the junk—rusty tramps, the old hulls tied up in the Hudson River, anything that floats and can be called up to make a statistic. I hate to think of what the number would be if we considered the condition of the ships. Now what will happen if we try to send an expeditionary force overseas? We have no army, we have sort of a navy, thank God, but we have no merchant marine. Six months of submarine warfare could just about put us out of business."

"I suppose so," Dan agreed.

"It doesn't bother you?"

"I don't think about it. I operated a fleet of ships in the last war and I became a millionaire. I lost it all. I don't regret that kind of money."

"What in hell are you, Lavette, some kind of damn pacifist?"

Dan puffed his cigar and considered it. "I don't know. I never thought about it that way. I watched the shipping prices in the last war. Every dollar of cargo became thirty dollars. We got fat on the blood of the kids who died. If you're looking for a patriot, you came to the wrong stall, Admiral."

"I'm looking for a man with some guts."

"That doesn't impress me or flatter me," Dan said.

"What in hell gives with you, Lavette? They told me you were some kind of legend here on the Coast. You're one lousy legend, if I may say so."

"Who told you that?"

"Roosevelt."

"I never met him."

"He got it from Al Smith. I gather you met him."

"I met him. All right, Admiral, I gather you're not taken with me. That's all right. Just what do you want?"

"I want you to build ships, not toys. Merchant ships. Steel ships."

"With what?"

"With that shipyard you have out there. You could lay six keels and build something that matters instead of that silly yacht."

"Maybe I could. I don't know. I never tried to build a real ship. Everything I built has been wood. Suppose I did. Who'd buy them? Who'd finance me? Who'd operate them?"

"We'll guarantee the financing and the price and the operator."

"We?"

"My commission, the government. We'll get you the loans, and we'll guarantee the sale."

"You're kidding—God Almighty, you don't mean that?"

"Why don't you try me, Lavette?"

"How many ships do you want?"

"As many as you can build. Put on three shifts. Put that whole yard of yours to work. Enlarge it. I know your situation here. You bought one of the finest shipyards on the Coast for a song because the bank couldn't give it away. I don't give two damns what in hell you believe in. My own belief is that unless we build ships, this whole stinking world is going up in flames. I know about the last war. To hell with that! It's done."

"I told you," Dan said after a long moment, "I never built an iron ship." Then he sat and stared at the admiral, who stared back, his blue eyes cold and unwinking. "I'd need architects, engineers, designers, welders, and specifications."

"We'll help you find the architects and engineers. There's one thing, Lavette, you're short on bullshit. That impresses me—if nothing else about you does. So tell me straight out—if we supply what I said we would, can you build the ships?"

"I can build them," Dan said. "When do I start?"

"Start now. Show me your yard, and we'll get down to facts."

Since she had returned from Europe, Barbara felt unmoored, displaced, as if her being had lost its substance. She had a repetitious dream in which she was old, unloved, lonely and childless in a strange land. One night she awakened from this dream and fell into a fit of half-hysterical sobbing that went on for hours. When at last she sat down to write her book, the dreams ceased.

On her way back from Europe to California, she stopped for a few days in New York. Frank Bradley had arranged a press conference, and in spite of her unwillingness and protests, he insisted that she go through with it. She had become a sort of celebrity, the American heiress who had been arrested and subjected to various indignities by the Gestapo. When she insisted that she had not been arrested by the Gestapo but by the Berlin police and only held in the police station for a few hours, Bradley begged her to allow the story to stand. "For all you know," he said, "the thugs who picked you up were Gestapo. In any case, the publishers are eating it up. I can get you an advance of ten thousand dollars on the book. I put together twenty stories, your best. All we need is the conclusion."

"No," Barbara told him. "I'm not going to publish those articles, Frank."

"Why?"

"Because I'm not the person who wrote them. Because they consist of silly, pointless gossip, and I'm ashamed of them."

"You're crazy. They're damn good writing, and nothing to apologize for. At this point in your career, getting a book published is very important. It's good for you, and it's good for the magazine. I know the money doesn't mean anything to you. That's the curse of being rich. But you've had experiences that should be shared."

"That's just it, Frank. If I write, I want to write about what I felt and what I saw. It's not in those silly stories."

The argument went on, but Barbara remained unmoved. However, since the press conference had been arranged, she agreed to go through with it. It took place at the Hotel Algonquin, in the sitting room of a suite Bradley had provided for her; and the first question, thrown at her by a reporter from the New York *Daily News*, demanded to know "whether it is true, Miss Lavette, that your lover was killed fighting for the communists in Spain?"

Barbara stared at the reporter without replying, and Frank Bradley, standing beside her, whispered, "Don't answer that, Barbara."

She couldn't answer it. A lump was forming in her throat, her heart, her mind. "What were your impressions of Germany?" "Were you expelled, Miss Lavette?" "Did you undergo torture?" "What can you tell us of the methods of the Gestapo—from personal experience?"

She pushed through them and left the room. The action was so unexpected that no one tried to stop her, and then she was out in the corridor with Bradley running after her.

"You can't do this, Barbara! For Christ's sake, you can't just walk out of a press conference like that!"

"I did it."

"Don't you have one lousy shred of consideration for me?"

She stopped suddenly and turned to face him. "Frank, I can't even answer the questions I ask myself, much less what others ask me. Do you know what Germany is? Germany is the final demented horror of what men have created. Do you know what death is, Frank? Do you know what agony is? Have you ever been closer to death than a funeral parlor?"

The reporters had flowed into the hallway, and they stood in a cluster, staring at her. Then the elevator door opened. Barbara bolted into the elevator, and the door closed behind her. A week later, back in Los Angeles at long last, Bradley wrote to her: "What a performance! Did you plan it? And a day later, Germany and Russia sign the pact. I am enclosing the clippings. How do you like that: 'The final demented horror of what men have created— Barbara Lavette.' On the front page of the New York *Times*. My dear Barbara, even when you leap blindly off the curb, you manage to step squarely into a bed of roses. I offer my most humble apologies for unwarrented anger, and in return I offer you any assignment you desire. Robinson has increased his offer to an advance of fifteen thousand and a guarantee of as much in advertising. Let him publish the book, I beg you."

Barbara tore the letter into shreds. She never communicated with Frank Bradley after that and returned his letters

unopened. She had gone to San Francisco, spent a day
with her mother—Tom and John were in Washington—
and then to Los Angeles. On her second day in Dan's
house, awakening from a dream of horror, she sat in bed,
sobbing uncontrollably until dawn brushed the darkness
away.

May Ling came into her room. "Barbara?"

"I'm all right."

May Ling went over to her and took her in her arms.
"Of course you are. Of course."

"Just a bad dream and a miserable night. I couldn't fall
asleep again."

"I know such nights," May Ling said gently. "Do you
want to talk about it?"

"I can't."

"I understand. Barbara dear, I've never interfered or
advised you. If I do so now, will you consider it?"

"Yes."

"Not just to be rid of me at this moment. Do you
promise?"

"Yes, I promise."

"Very well," said May Ling, almost primly. "Take a cold
shower, get out your typewriter, and begin to put it all
down on paper. Your own way."

"Oh, May Ling," Barbara said woefully, "I don't even
know where to begin."

"It doesn't matter. Only begin, and things will fall into
place."

That morning she began the book. The little house in
Westwood was a haven of peace. She was fussed over,
coddled, and adored in a way that she had never truly
experienced before. So-toy, barred from other communication, expressed her affection in the only way she could—in
an endless stream of exotic Chinese dishes. During the day
Barbara wrote, rewrote, corrected, and then destroyed
what she had written in hopeless exasperation. But, bit by
bit, the past five years came into focus. In the evenings, she
sat in the living room with her father and May Ling and
So-toy, reading for the most part, sometimes listening to
the radio or to records. She had no dates, nor any desire
for them; she was totally fixated on the manuscript she
was writing.

The weekends when Joe was home were the best part of
it. He and Barbara became very close during that time. He

was patient, kind, gentle; he never pried and never invaded her privacy, and perhaps because of that she talked to him as she had not talked to anyone else. They had found a bit of beach at Malibu that seemed to be theirs entirely, cupped between two jutting piles of rock, and always deserted. In Southern California, September is the best month for swimming; the water is at its warmest, the days hot and still long in the aftermath of the summer. They would pack a picnic lunch, swim, eat, and then lie in the sun, sometimes in silence, sometimes talking. For the first time, Barbara was able to talk about Marcel, freely, openly. Strangely, this half-Chinese half brother, three years younger, but older in so many ways, had become dearer to her than any other person in the world.

One day, when the two of them were together on the beach, she asked him, "Were you ever in love, Joe?"

He nodded.

"That's the part of me that's missing, and I feel such guilt."

"Guilt? But why guilt?"

"Because I long to be in love even more than I long for Marcel."

"Marcel's dead, Bobby. You can be in love again."

"I don't know. Sometimes I doubt it. I was so alive with him. Everything had a golden glow. I remember the sunsets in Paris, as if the whole city were painted in gold. And then when I went back there, after Germany, the city was dead and colorless. I was alive for a little while, and it was the most wonderful thing."

"I know."

"How do you know?" she asked, smiling suddenly, prodding him. "Who is she? Tell me, Joe."

"It's dumb."

"Being in love?"

"Being in love with a fourteen-year-old kid. Being so much in love with her that I don't think of anything else."

"I don't believe you. A fourteen-year-old kid? Where did you find her?"

"At Higate. She's Jake Levy's daughter, Sally. Why do you think I go there?"

"I couldn't imagine. But then, this whole thing is crazy, Joe. That place has a hold on our lives. You know how Bernie Cohen saved Marcel's life. Years ago, when he was just a kid, there was some kind of rabbi in San Francisco who got the Levys into the business of sacramental wine, and Bernie Cohen used to drive him to Higate. Then he got a job with the Levys and worked there for a while. And now you tell me that you're in love with Clair's daughter."

"That's pretty dumb, isn't it?"

"Oh, no, no. I think it's absolutely wonderful. I told you that I was with the Levys in France. They're great. I like them. But what is she like? Sally, I mean."

He shrugged. "I don't know how to describe her. In some ways she's terribly bright and wise and knowing, and in other ways she's like a crazy kid. She's tall and skinny and freckled, and she thinks she's ugly but she's not. She looks something like her mother, but she's not redheaded. Her hair's more the color of dirty straw."

Barbara burst into laughter. "Dirty straw! Joe, that's the worst description of a woman's hair I ever heard."

"Well, she's not exactly a woman. I don't know what she is, and I don't even know why I've got this crush on her, because she's absolutely crazy. She wants to go to bed with me. Thank God I'm here and she's up there in Napa Valley. Can you imagine if I went to bed with her and got her pregnant, and she's just turned fourteen?"

"It's done." Barbara couldn't stop laughing. It was years since she had laughed like this. "Oh, Joey, darling, I'm not laughing at you."

"You're sure?"

"Oh, don't look at me like that. I'm sure."

"You wouldn't think it was that funny if you had her around you for a whole summer."

"But you said you're in love with her."

"I don't know. I just don't know. It was her idea. It started with her a year ago, the first time I was there. She kept tagging around after me. There's something about her."

"There must be."

"Anyway, she says that if I marry anyone else, she'll kill me and whoever I marry. How would you like to have something like that on your back?"

"If you stay in love with her— Do you think she means it? She can't."

"You don't know her."

"No, I don't." Barbara began to laugh again.

"You don't take it very seriously."

"I do. I do. But it's very funny. And of course that's why you go up there."

"Not entirely. I love the place."

Barbara had been watching a gull taking dainty steps along the lacy edge of the water. She turned to look at Joe now, his dark eyes following a design he was tracing on the sand.

"Tell me about it."

"You were never there?"

"I used to ride near Sonoma. I once had a date with a boy called Clark Addison. Ugh!" She began to laugh again. "He was about five foot two. Came up to my shoulder. He had his father's Cadillac, and we drove up into the Napa Valley. He tried to rape me, and I grabbed him very tightly by both wrists, and do you know, I fractured one of his wrists. He had fragile bones. Oh, heavens, the things one remembers! That poor boy. His wrist was in a cast for weeks."

"How old were you?"

"Eighteen, I think. But I was frightfully oversized. I still am. No, I never saw this Higate place. What is it like?"

"You know the way the valley is, the way the land slopes down and almost makes a V in the middle. Higate's on the left as you drive north on Highway Twenty-nine. Near Spring Mountain. I sometimes think it's the most beautiful place in the world."

Anyplace is when you're in love, Barbara thought.

"There are two big old stone buildings. They're built of the native fieldstone, with high, pointed, raftered roofs, and they're covered with ivy and they look like they've been there forever. One is the house and the other is the original winery, and I guess they were both built in the eighteen nineties. Then there's another stone house, farther up the hill, built into the hillside. There are three wooden buildings that Jake added to the place. The vineyards roll up from the house over the hills, and from where the house is, you can look down the whole length of the valley. There's something about it that gets into you, like making wine is the key to some great secret of life. It's not like being a wino or something, not drinking the wine. It's making it that's the thing, and Clair says that all wine makers are a little crazy—but I guess it's the way they all are, I mean Clair and Jake and the kids, Sally and her brothers. Josh is fifteen and Adam is seventeen, and I don't know, but I have a good feeling when I'm there, and I suppose that if I had my own way, I'd rather be a wine maker than anything else in the world."

"Why don't you?" Barbara asked him.

"Come on. If I ever gave up medicine, it would break pop's heart."

"Hearts don't break that easily."

"No. It's impossible."

When dawn broke, on the first day of September in 1939, the sound Spain heard the year before changed the world. It was the roaring, grinding noise of Adolf Hitler's panzer divisions driving across the Polish border, the sound of the Stuka dive bombers, of the exploding bombs, the sound of a bullet as it penetrates human flesh, the sound of walls collapsing, of roofs falling in, the sound of a child screaming in terror and pain.

"But I am wrongly judged," Hitler pleaded to the world, "if my love of peace and my patience are mistaken for weakness."

Two days later, Great Britain and France were at war with Germany, and Franklin Delano Roosevelt, President of the United States, was reading a letter from Albert Einstein that said, "In the course of the last four months it has been made probable—through the work of Joliot in France as well as Fermi and Szilard in America—that it may become possible to set up a nuclear chain reaction in a large mass of uranium, by which vast amounts of power and large quantities of new radium-like elements would be generated. Now it appears almost certain that this could be achieved in the immediate future. This new phenomenon would also lead to the construction of bombs, and it is conceivable—though much less certain—that extremely powerful bombs of a new type may thus be constructed."

On September 17, Soviet armies marched into Poland. On September 28, Germany and Russia divided the once-soverign nation of Poland between them, and on the fifth of October, 1939, the last regular armed resistance in Poland ceased.

On the eighth of October, Admiral Land dictated a memorandum on West Coast shipbuilding potential, and in the course of it he commented on the Lavette Shipyard on Terminal Island. "It would appear," he said, "that here we have one of the largest and most impressive potentials on the West Coast. It requires expansion and expertise, and much will depend on the will toward cooperation of its owner and manager, Daniel Lavette. Properly organized and managed and creatively expanded, the Lavette Shipyard should be capable of turning out between twenty and thirty merchant vessels a year."

Lunching at the California Club in San Francisco, in the early part of November, Tom Lavette felt more than ever the strength of the ties binding him and John Whittier to each other. However, his assessment of Whittier was slowly changing; almost without an articulated interior decision on his part, Tom had come to think of Whittier, not as a person who was using him, but as someone he would use to own his own purposes, purposes still rather amorphous. The more time he spent with Whittier, the more conscious he became of the man's various weaknesses, his pettiness, and his self-indulgence. The very fact that, at age fifty-one he had transferred so many of his ambitions to Tom proclaimed that he had to a large extent surrendered. He was without subtlety. Tom knew that he was being used because Whittier was clumsy in his usage of the younger man, and Tom was quite content with the relationship. He felt an increasing advantage over Whittier, but he was in no hurry to express it.

On this day Whittier bluntly, almost petulantly, informed Tom that his mother had asked for a divorce. Tom made no comment. He watched Whittier thoughtfully and waited.

"I've been married to your mother almost seven years. I often feel that I am very much your own father, Thomas. I feel that we have a strong relationship."

"How do you feel about a divorce?" Tom asked.

"It should make no difference to our own relationship."

"Then you won't contest it?"

"To what end? Your mother is a headstrong woman. Certainly you know that."

"I like you, John. I think we are good for each other." He had never taken that tone with Whittier before, and now the older man studied him curiously.

"It's nothing I enjoy. It's scandal, and I despise scandal."

"Not today, I think. I mean it's not considered scandal-

ous today, John. I don't want to pry, but did you try to
talk her out of it?"

"I have you to consider, Thomas."

"I don't understand."

"You should. She influences Barbara. And without Barbara's stock to vote, our whole plan falls through. By the
way, have you seen Barbara?"

"No."

Whittier made no attempt to disguise his annoyance.
"She's been away five years and you make no attempt to
see her."

"We were in Washington when she returned."

"And that was three months ago."

"She's in Los Angeles with my father," Tom said. "Are
you suggesting I go to see her there?"

"I don't see why not."

"It's ten years since I've seen my father. I thought you'd
understand that, John. I can't just walk in there, and I
don't want to."

"I never particularly liked Dan Lavette," Whittier said,
"but I saw no reason to hate him."

"You're not his son."

"That's so. Anyway, I spoke to Sam Goldberg. You
know he's Barbara's lawyer. We agreed to a meeting in
December, for the transfer of the stock from the trusteeship to both of you. I hope you don't feel I talked out of
turn?"

"No, not at all."

They went on with their lunch. Tom realized that Whittier was nervous, uneasy. He only toyed with his food. He
started the meal with an old fashioned, and now he ordered
a second one. It had never occurred to Tom to speculate
on whether or not Whittier had any deep feelings for Jean.
His involvement was with himself, not with others; but
now he wondered whether Whittier was not taking the
whole matter of the divorce more to heart than he would
have guessed. After all, Jean was rejecting him. That was
not easy for a man to accept, especially a man like Whittier.

"Tom," Whittier said, finally breaking the silence, "you
know there's no way for us to stay out of this war."

It was apropos of what, Tom wondered. His own
thoughts were far away.

"No, I suppose not."

"I was talking to Senator Lancor the other day. He's on the armed services committee and very close to the navy. We can get you a commission, nothing very fancy, lieutenant junior grade, and then an assignment to my shipping line. They'll want a man of their own with us, and going in now, so early in the game, will look damn good on your record."

"What about training?" Tom asked.

"I don't know all the details, but I think the understanding would be that you're a civilian in uniform. That doesn't change your status or anything for the record. It just places you in a damned good position."

"I'll think about it," Tom said, aware that a very real if subtle change in their relationship had already taken place.

Clair Levy frequently reflected on the fact that life had been extraordinarily good to her. Her husband, Jake, less given to abstractions, reversed her conclusion and pointed out that she was good to life. She was a life giver, not a taker. Life flowed from her strong, competent, life-giving hands. If a grapevine, a dog, or a child were sick, she could cure it. She had three children. The two boys, Adam, aged seventeen, and Joshua, aged fifteen, were like their father in every way except for their flaming red hair. They were large, rather stolid and serious young men, Adam away at Berkeley for his first year of college, Joshua a junior at the local high school. They had grown up in the Napa Valley in a free, easygoing sort of way, barefoot through the summer months, working at the winery when they were old enough, immersed in the half-mystical process of the vine, the grape, and the vats, never questioning the strange fact that to wine makers, the process, more than the making of a drink, was a way of life that approached a religion. They went to a school where at least half of their fellow students lived in wineries. The valley was a world unto itself, a world they accepted without undue resentment or questioning.

Sally, Clair's youngest child, was something else, and the image that sometimes occurred to Clair was that of a wild creature, half doe, half cougar, trapped in the body of a precocious child. Sally never dissembled. She scorned to conceal either her feelings or her desires. She had grown up with two older brothers with whom she was fiercely

competitive, holding that she could do anything as well or
better than they, whether it was playing ball or running
or swimming or fighting. She asked no quarter and gave
none. She was built like her mother, long-limbed, raw-
boned, with the same freckled skin. The well-defined bone
structure of her face, which would one day be the face of
a very beautiful woman, convinced her that she was ugly
beyond reclamation, which only served to increase her de-
fiance of every rule and regulation of female childhood.

She was also, as Clair realized, extraordinarily bright,
certainly the brightest of the three children. She was an
omnivorous reader and read everything, almost without
discrimination. Poetry, novels, technical books, the ency-
clopedia, comic books, magazines—everything was grist
for her mill; and again and again Clair would go into her
room at midnight to turn off the lights and lecture her on
the evils of living without sleep and wasting eyesight that
has to last a lifetime. But Sally's store of nervous energy
was apparently inexhaustible. She would be up at dawn,
racing across the fields, assuring herself that nothing had
changed during the night, and feeding her pets, which included a caged racoon, a turtle, her own special dog that
she had found and adopted, a yellowish indeterminate
breed, and two cats. She lived a full day's life before breakfast, at which she consumed more food than anyone else in
the family. But regardless of how much she ate, she could
not flesh out or fulfill her promise to Joe to become fat and
sexy.

When, at age twelve, she first informed Clair that she
was in love with Joe Lavette and that she intended to
marry him, Clair received the news without concern.
Nothing that Sally did or said was entirely unexpected.
But, watching the progress of this curious infatuation over
the next two years, Clair became somewhat perturbed. Her
attempts to discuss the matter with Jake gave her little
satisfaction. "Leave her alone," Jake said. "Anything you
try to do with that crazy kid will only make matters worse.
She'll grow out of it, and Joe is a good, solid boy who
knows which side is up."

But when Sally—after Joe had left for Los Angeles and
medical school—asked Clair how she would feel if she,
Sally, had an affair with Joe, Clair determined to take
matters in hand.

"Exactly what do you mean by an affair?" Clair asked her.

"I mean if we began to sleep together. You know, mom. If we had sexual intercourse."

Clair swallowed, breathed deeply, took a firm hold on herself, and said, "That's hardly likely with Joe four hundred miles away."

"I could go to Los Angeles. I mean weekends."

"Could you? And how does Joe feel about all this?"

"I haven't discussed it with him."

"Thank heavens!" Clair renewed her hold on herself. There were at least a dozen things she thought of saying, but she restricted herself to observing that Sally was still very young.

"Not really."

"What do you mean, not really?"

"I'm not really very young."

"Sally, you're thirteen years old."

"Well, not really. I've been reading this book on reincarnation, and I've decided that I lived a lot of lives in places like Egypt and China and maybe Norway, because of the way my hair is—"

"Your grandmother had the same hair and she was never near Norway," Clair cried in utter exasperation.

"And maybe Tahiti," Sally went on, carried away by the notion, "because otherwise why would I feel this way about Joe, who's kind of dumb, and anyway, he's a Chink—"

"Sally!"

"Well, I didn't mean it that way."

"I don't care how you meant it. I won't have that word spoken, and to say you care for someone and then call them a Chink is just wretched."

"I didn't mean it that way, mom, please."

"And Joe is not dumb. He's brilliant. He's half Chinese, and a fine boy, and I think," she finished lamely, "I think you ought to forget about all this until you grow up."

"You can't stop being in love just like that! You can't. And all I meant about Joe was that we must have been in love in some previous existence, maybe in China, and I don't mean to cast any impersion—"

"You mean aspersion."

"I know that, and I didn't mean dumb the way you mean dumb. He's dumb about things, and that doesn't mean he's not brilliant. It just means he's dumb. Can I go to Los Angeles for a weekend?"

"No," Clair said flatly.

"Boy, that's great. That's wonderful. That's some way to treat me, like I'm some kind of stupid kid."

"You're not a stupid kid. You're a very intelligent kid, and I do wish you'd use that intelligence at times. Joe will be back here next summer, if he wishes to come, and if you really love him, a year will make very little difference."

"And suppose he stops loving me?"

Suddenly serious, worried, Clair said, "I know Joe likes you. What makes you think he's in love with you?"

"He told me so. Well, don't look at me like that, mom, he never even touched me. You know what I mean. He never touched my breasts or anything like that. He kissed me, that's all. What's so terrible about that?"

When she told Jake that evening about her conversation with Sally, Jake doubled up with laughter.

"I don't think it's quite that funny."

"What breasts?"

"You might take a good look at your daughter," Clair said. "You might even spend some time with her. She is a very unusual child."

"You can say that again. You know, I'd let her go to Los Angeles for a weekend. Joe can handle it."

Clair looked at him and shook her head. "I do wonder about you sometimes, Jake."

Sam Goldberg telephoned Barbara in Los Angeles to tell her about the meeting at his office that would end the trusteeship. She received the news with a sense of shock and bewilderment.

"I had totally forgotten," she said.

"But you will be there?"

"Must I?"

"I think it's best, Barbara. Of course, you can give me power of attorney in this case, but I feel we should discuss the matter beforehand. The meeting's at three o'clock. Suppose you come to my office at noon and I'll take you to lunch, and that will give us plenty of time for a good talk."

"Sam?"

"Yes, Barbara?"

"Sam," she said uncertainly, "how much money is actually involved in this?"

"Don't you know?"

"No. I haven't the faintest idea. I know you spoke to me about it, but that was years ago, and I've just forgotten completely."

"All right," Goldberg said. "Now you listen to me, Barbara. In the two weeks between now and the time you come here to San Francisco, I want you to think about what I'm going to tell you. It's not a question of what you like or what you want, Barbara. That we can discuss at lunch. This is a question of fact, and these are facts I want you to think about very carefully."

"I understand."

"Good. Now the Seldon Bank has a present book value of some forty million dollars. That is a very conservative estimate because the stock is not publicly held. In other words, it is not listed on any market. If it were, the value might be much greater, not less but much greater. Now, your grandfather owned three hundred and eighty-two thousand shares, which represented seventy percent of the stock. Do you follow me?"

"I think so," Barbara said.

"He left this stock in trust for you and your brother, with your mother as the trustee. It was to be held by her for twelve years and then turned over to you and Tom. The income from the stock was hers to use or dispose of as she saw fit. That is another matter, and we'll talk about it when I see you. The main thing with which I want to impress you at this moment is that you will come into the free ownership of one hundred and ninety-one thousand shares of Seldon Bank stock, with a book value of fourteen million dollars. That's a round figure. If you should decide to dispose of it, well, it might be worth a great deal more." He waited. "Barbara, are you there?"

"I'm here. I just can't deal with it, Sam."

"Think about it. Get used to it. You have to deal with it, Barbara."

"I'll try, Sam."

She put down the telephone and tried to deal with the facts that had just been presented to her. The more she thought about it, the more she became prey to gloom and uncertainty, and when at last May Ling came home from the library and poked her head into the tiny room that was Barbara's, she saw a woman close to tears.

"Barbara, what happened?"

"Nothing."

"You look absolutely miserable."

"I am miserable."

May Ling pulled a chair over to the desk. "Do you want to talk about it?"

Barbara repeated the gist of Sam Goldberg's conversation.

"Fourteen million dollars."

"Well, that much money doesn't really have any meaning, Bobby. In any case, it was always yours. You did know about it?"

"I did and I didn't. I always thought of it as belonging to mother."

"Your mother is quite wealthy. She doesn't need that money."

"No. But I don't either, and I don't want it."

"But, my dear, you have it. It's yours."

"I don't want to be anything else but what I am. Do you understand me? All my life I've been trying to find out who and what I am. Now I think I'm beginning to know. It wasn't easy. Do you know that I earned my own living in Paris. I got along on what the magazine paid me. The bank sent me a hundred dollars a week, but I hardly used it. I just deposited it in an account I had there, and I still have six thousand dollars in my account. I don't need any more than that. If I can't prove to myself that I'm a writer, then my life has no meaning at all. I'm twenty-five years old, and the only lasting satisfaction in my life has been the realization that I'm not worthless, and the only proof of it is that I taught myself a craft. Now I'm trying to write a novel that will reflect some of the things I've lived through and seen, and it's the hardest thing I ever tried to do. But if I can do it, and if people will pay money to buy it and read it, then I can have some sense of myself, some justification of myself. I don't want that rotten money!" she cried, almost violently. "I don't need it and I don't want it! How could I live here with you if I were a millionaire? How can I watch daddy break his back in that wretched shipyard? How can I make any sense of my existence? Do you know what was the best thing between Marcel and me? We spoke the same language. I don't mean French or English. I mean that things meant the same for both of us. He understood that I had to live on what the magazine paid me. Once we decided to eat at Maxim's. We pooled all our money and decided on poverty for the rest of the week. Oh, it was a wonderful evening. Not that the food was so great, but the fact that we blew our whole fortune on one posh meal. Do you see what I mean, May Ling?"

"I see exactly what you mean. But you must also understand that nothing has truly changed. My dear Bobby, I don't want to hurt you, but you do see that you were living with a pretense, with the illusion that the money did not exist?"

"But it didn't. Not for me, anyway."

"Bobby, do you remember, during the strike on the Embarcadero, the difference between you and the others down there. Not in terms of love or compassion or strength—but you could leave. They could not."

Barbara stared at her.

"Do you see what I mean? Let me tell you a story, darling. Thirty years ago, I was thirteen years old. I remember it very well indeed. We were poor. I don't say this as a virtue, it was simply a fact. We were the kind of poor where one comes to the end of the rope, and then there's a bottomless pit. We had no money and no hope. There was my father, my mother, and myself. They had not eaten for three days. I had not eaten for a day and a half —nothing, not even a crust of bread. My father was born in this country. He was an educated man, a sort of genius with figures, and once or twice he had worked as a bookkeeper. He had also dug holes for outhouses, cleaned toilets, washed dishes in saloons in the Tenderloin—anything that would bring in a dollar or two. That was when he went to Dan Lavette, who had advertised for a bookkeeper. No one would hire a Chinese. Chinese literally starved to death there in San Francisco. There was no help for them and no hope for them. Well, Dan gave pop a job, and you know the rest, but that's not the point. The point is that being poor is a fact of life in this strange and demented world we live in. You cannot pretend to be poor any more than you can pretend to die. You either are poor or you are not poor, and one of the tragedies of the rich is that they mostly cannot comprehend what it is to be poor. You're very fortunate, my dear, because you have some understanding of what poverty means and of the toll it takes. You are also a talented and healthy and lovely woman. But don't play any games. You're talented enough to make your own way in the world, and you're mature enough to face the fact of the money. I can't tell you what to do with it. That's a decision you must make for yourself."

They sat in silence for a little while, then Barbara nodded. "I'll work it out."

"I'm sure you will."

"Can I give any of it to you and daddy?"

"I'm afraid not," May Ling replied, laughing. "He had his day with Seldon money. No, don't even mention it. Anyway, he has the Maritime Commission behind him now and he doesn't need money. No, dear, this you must work out yourself."

Making the trip from Los Angeles to San Francisco, Barbara had time to think about the decisions that faced her. She tried to acknowledge to herself, to understand that money, which drove and directed and tortured the lives of so many people, had never held real meaning for her. In some ways money had been nonexistent in her life, either as an aspiration or as a subject of conversation. There had always been enough. One had only to reach out or ask. Thinking about what May Ling had said, she now accepted the fact that the years in Paris were, in financial terms, a sort of game, and if the game were to come to an end, it would have to end internally, within herself. She had no prejudice against the rich, no moral generalizations or judgments that motivated her; her thinking was conditioned by her own needs for a structure that would justify the existence of a person called Barbara Lavette, or one that would provide her with some answers as to who Barbara Lavette was and what her business on earth was. More and more, during the days between her talk with May Ling and her departure for San Francisco, she had become convinced that she could not live as a millionaire, that she could not function, as she had to function, as the owner of fourteen million dollars.

May Ling did not bring up the subject again, and since Dan never raised it, Barbara guessed that May Ling had discussed it with him and their decision had been one of total noninterference. The only one Barbara spoke to about it was her brother Joe, and when she put it to him and asked him what he would do in her place, he replied bluntly, "I don't have it, Bobby, so I guess I'd want it."

"Do you want some of it?" she asked, just as bluntly.

"No."

"Well, that makes no sense at all, does it?"

"I guess not. I can't take money from you."

"You take it from daddy."

"Someday I'll pay him back. That's the way I look at it. It's a loan."

"You don't even know whether you want to be a doctor, Joe. I could buy you a winery, any winery."

"You're kidding."

"Why? I have fourteen million dollars. I can buy anything."

He was silent.

"Can't I?"

"No!" he snapped at her.

"Why not?"

"You know god damn well why!"

"I really don't," Barbara said quietly. "I'm trying to find out. I just bought a car, a Chevy. I shopped for a week before I decided to buy it, and then I paid for it out of money I had saved while I was in Paris. I'm not teasing you, Joe. You're my brother, and I have to go up to San Francisco next week and I'm supposed to take possession of fourteen million dollars' worth of stock in the Seldon Bank. I stopped writing. I put the book aside. And I'm so confused that I don't think straight anymore. You know, I grew up with kids in San Francisco who were the way I was then, who never questioned anything and who took their horses and their boats and their cars and the family houses on Russian Hill and Pacific Heights for granted. It's not like here in Los Angeles. We were a tight, beautiful little clique who knew that our wealth and privilege was ordained by God and granted to us by God and never to be questioned. That's why I don't go back there—as much as I love San Francisco, and sometimes when I think about that place, I want to cry—but I can't do what they do. I can't. There's simply no way that I can."

"I know that," Joe said. "I'm not mad at you, Bobby. I'm not jealous. It's just so damn crazy."

"Yes, it is, isn't it?"

But when the time came and she finally set out for San

Francisco, Barbara knew what she intended. The knowledge was fuzzy, and she had decided that she would make no final decision until she had talked to Goldberg, but she was no longer uncertain as to what her decision would be, and that very fact took away a weight that had been pressing on her for weeks. She felt lighthearted and alive, excited to be driving north back to the place that was as wonderful as any city could be.

It was evening when Barbara drove into San Francisco and checked into the St. Francis Hotel. It was a strange sensation to be back here, back where she had stayed before the incredible eruption of "Bloody Thursday." It gave her an almost bewildering feeling of déjà vu, as if she were remembering not only what had happened, but cloudy half-memories of things that had never happened at all. She knew that her mother had moved out of Whittier's mansion on Pacific Heights and was living once again in the house on Russian Hill. Barbara had spoken to her from Los Angeles, and now she telephoned again, found Jean at home, and told her that she was in San Francisco and at the St. Francis.

"Darling, of all places, the St. Francis! Come here and stay with me. There's plenty of room. Just the two of us."

"Tomorrow, mother. I promise. But I want to be alone tonight. I have to think my way out of a few things."

"You think your way into far too much, Bobby. Then lunch tomorrow."

"I already have a lunch date with Sam Goldberg. How about dinner?"

"Of course. And you will stay with me?"

"I'll check out in the morning. You can have me for as long as I'm here," she said, thinking as she put down the phone, Poor Jean—I do feel for her.

Sam Goldberg had not changed a great deal. He was no thinner, no fatter. Now, at the age of seventy-one, he walked more slowly. His thin fringe of hair had turned entirely white, but his blue eyes were alert and bright as ever. He welcomed Barbara with youthful enthusiasm. "My word, but you have become a splendid woman. You know, I read all about you. Front page in the *Chronicle*. San Francisco woman arrested by the Gestapo. That's an honor, my dear. To me, anyway. That is, if you survive it, and I must say that you appear to have survived it very well indeed."

"All of it vastly exaggerated, Sam."

"Well, someday you must tell me all about it, blow by blow, detail by detail. I have bad dreams about that horror over there. What a way for a man to end his life—with a vision of humanity gone insane. But not now. Now we have more pressing things to discuss. Suppose we go to Gino's. Pasta and veal piccata help me to think. I've stopped dieting. It makes no sense at my age."

But at the table, Barbara noticed that he ate very little. He was more intent on her than on the food, observing her, studying her, and at last he said, rather cautiously, "You have a bombshell for me, haven't you, my dear?"

"How do you know?" Barbara asked, smiling.

"Ah, well. Let's say that love is frequently discerning as well as blind, and I love you very much, my dear, not only because you are Danny's daughter, but because you are what you are, which is something very rare and unique."

"Sam, I think that's just about the nicest thing anyone ever said to me."

"I don't believe that, and don't stop eating because I've indulged in a little flattery. Notice I didn't say you're very high on common sense."

"I know. Sam, I don't want the stock or the money, and I don't want you to argue with me or try to persuade me otherwise. I've spent days and days thinking about this and working it out with myself. So that's where I am."

Goldberg didn't comment immediately. He sat back and studied her. Gino came over to the table to ask if everything was all right. "That's a profound philosophical question," Goldberg said. "Mostly things are the way they should be—confused."

"The food is not good?"

"The food is delicious." Gino left them.

"Did you tell Dan?" Goldberg asked her.

"No. He didn't ask me, and I didn't tell him. May Ling knows how I feel, and I'm sure she talked to Dan about it."

Goldberg took a deep breath and pushed his plate away. "I can't eat and think about this at the same time. I am fighting every instinct developed during half a century in the practice of law. I should move heaven and earth to change your mind, and I think that if it were anyone else

here facing me, I would. With you, well, I don't know."
He paused and waited. Barbara said nothing. "You know,"
he went on, "like suicide, giving away money is permanent.
It can always be delayed."

"I know that," Barbara agreed. "But that would delay
other things that are more important to me. I'm writing a
book, Sam, and that's very important to me, and I
must know who I am, and I cannot know that until I am
rid of that wretched money."

"I find that very hard to understand."

"Then you'll simply have to take my word for it."

"All right. Let me tell you that this was not entirely
unexpected. I've been thinking about it. You come to me
and tell me you want to give away fourteen million dollars,
and it may be more. That's not like giving a dime to a
panhandler. I don't equate the problems of the rich with
the problems of the poor, but money is a problem, and
getting rid of it is also a problem. You can't stop someone
on the street and say, 'Here's a million.' You understand
that?"

"Sam," Barbara said, laughing, "I'm not a total fool. I
admit I don't have too much common sense, but I do know
that we must work something out."

"Thank God for that. All right. We accept the presumption that you wish to give this money away. Dan wouldn't
touch it, I know that. Joe?"

She shook her head. "No, he doesn't want it."

"Then he has more sense than a boy of his age should
have. Your mother and Tom don't need it, and anyway,
I don't think you had that in mind. The money is your
responsibility. You can do bad with it and you can do good
with it. You can't just pick something you consider a
deserving charity and give it fourteen million. There's
a whole art to the giving of money, and damnit, Barbara,
there must be, because there are more cheap crooks and
swindlers in the field of charity than you could imagine.
Now, do you know what a charitable foundation is?"

She shook her head. "I have a vague idea, but no more
than that."

"Let me give you a short definition. A foundation is
basically a nonprofit, nongovernmental structure. It has its
own financial base, and it functions for the general welfare,
educationally, socially, charitably. It's a form that has been
developed during the past forty years, in some cases to

evade the payment of taxes, in some cases as a sop to the
conscience of the rich, and in some cases to fill a specific
need that a person of conscience recognizes. I did some
research on the subject. The classic legal definition was
promulgated by Judge Horace Gray, in 1867 in Massachusetts. Quoting him freely, he said that this form must
be considered as a gift to the public weal, consistent with
existing laws, for the benefit of an indefinite number of
persons, either by education or religion, or by relieving
their bodies from disease—he adds to the list then and
specifies the lessening of the burdens of government.
That was quite a novel idea in his time, a time when
government was content to let people suffer, die of disease,
and starve to death. Well, since then, many foundations
have come into being, corporate foundations, community
trusts, family foundations, special-purpose foundations—
all sorts. But they all fall into three well-defined groups.
The first type confines itself to the giving of grants, grants
of money for every purpose imaginable, some good, some
foolish. This is the most fluid, the most flexible category,
and this is the category I would like you to consider.
There is also a type of foundation that organizes it own
research and work, but I don't see that for you. It would
involve you totally, and that's not what you want. And then
there's the type of foundation that runs as a service
structure, with its own people and staff. That too would
involve you deeply.

"So we think about the first kind, a broad, flexibly
conceived foundation for the giving of grants that will
benefit people, to put it most broadly. Now, you must
understand that once you establish the trust, the wealth
is no longer yours. It is irrevocable. However, it is just
possible that we might find a legal loophole that would
give you substantial income from the trust." He looked at
her and waited.

"No. I don't want any income from it."

"You may regret that one day, Barbara. Marriage, a
family, the needs of a family—all that lies ahead of you."

"Sam,'" Barbara said very seriously, "this money comes
from my grandfather. I did nothing to earn it or deserve it.
I don't need it and I don't want it. If you think this
foundation method is the best way to deal with it, then I
agree. But who runs the foundation? Who directs it? Who

decides how big the grants should be and where they should go?"

"It's not simple, Barbara. I think you must play a role in it. That's a responsibility you just can't evade. An organization must be created. Offices must be found. People must be hired to advertise the purposes of the foundation and to pass on the grants. There must be financial management, and there must be a board of directors to make final decisions." He saw Barbara's face fall, and he smiled encouragingly. "This is not your worry. My office can take care of most of it, and I can take a hand in it myself. But I'm an old man, Barbara. I could drop dead tomorrow. Still, we can do all of the mechanics connected with it, and there's no hurry. We can begin functioning next week or next year, whichever is most convenient for you."

"How much would I have to be involved?"

"As a minimum, at least three or four meetings a year. As a maximum, it could involve you completely. You place your own function where you see fit."

She nodded. "You see this as the best way, Sam?"

"Unless you change your mind?"

"No. We'll set up the foundation."

"All right. That's the first problem. Now, I had a talk with your mother. Understand me, Barbara, Danny is like a son to me, but what goes on between a man and his wife is not for anyone else to understand. Your mother is quite a woman, and I don't think she'll give you any grief about what you want to do. But during the twelve years that she has been trustee for yours and Tom's stock, there has been very considerable income. Some of it you used, most of it is untouched, and there's a trustee account in your name at the Seldon Bank that amounts to some-think over a quarter of a million dollars."

Barbara began to laugh. She became half-hysterical, almost unable to stop.

"Are you all right?" Goldberg asked anxiously.

"Yes, Sam, yes." She tried desperately to control her laughter. "It's just a joke. It doesn't stop. I live here in these United States, with millions of unemployed"—her laughter stopped now—"with shanty towns, Bonus March-ers, hunger and misery everywhere, and I get richer and richer and there's no way to stop it, and it's just crazy. It's the craziest thing I ever heard of. I have eight hundred dollars left out of my own savings, and I plan and plot to stretch it out until I finish my book, and living with daddy rent-free and eating his and May Ling's food, and I don't dare buy a new dress, and now you tell me that after all this talk and decision, I still have a quarter of a million dollars that I never knew I had. Well, I don't know whether to laugh or weep."

"Neither. Just face it, and Barbara, don't give that money away. Please. This is a wise old Jew who has seen a great deal of what can happen. Don't give it away. Leave it alone, if you wish. The Seldon Bank is very solid. Just pretend it isn't there. You've just divested yourself of fourteen million dollars. That's enough!"

"Sam, you're upset," she said in amazement.

"Is it any wonder? Now, will you leave that money alone?"

"You'll be terribly disturbed if I don't."

"To put it mildly."

"All right then. For the time being. It's after two," Barbara said. "Is there anything else?"

"One more decision, my dear. It concerns your brother. As I understand it, you have not seen him since you returned from Europe?"

"No, and I feel terrible about that."

"Do you dislike him?"

"No. No, not at all. It's just that, well, we're so different. We went our different ways. Not that we ever had a fight or a falling-out, except the kind of fights that kids have. I guess every brother and sister have that kind of thing. No, I like Tom. I don't know whether I love him. It's been so very long. Five years. That's a long time."

"So much for that. Now, I've had some discussions with John Whittier, whom I gather you don't like."

"It doesn't matter, now that mother has divorced him."

"Well, from what I surmise—and it's no more than a surmise—he and Tom are going to enter into some kind of combination, the Seldon Bank and California Shipping. For a bank to enter into such an arrangement is still not legal in California, but there are ways to get around that, and may I say that such a financial combination will be of enormous strength and importance. The point is that, to control the bank, Tom needs the voting power of your stock—or the foundation's stock, since we'll think of it that way. Both Whittier and Tom have addressed me on this point."

"But when we establish the foundation, could Tom vote the stock?"

"If we write it into the charter, he can indeed. But what I think is more likely is that Whittier will offer to buy enough of your stock to give him and Tom fifty-one percent, which will mean control of the bank. How do you feel about that?"

"I don't care. Should I, Sam? Should I care?"

"That's up to you."

Barbara thought about it for a while and then shook her head. The truth was that she did not care. The load was off her mind and soul. Who controlled the Seldon Bank or any other bank was a matter of indifference to her.

"If we sell them the stock, what then?"

"The foundation will put the money into very solid securities—American Telephone, government bonds, that sort of thing. From the point of view of the foundation, it might be an advantage to have a diversified portfolio of securities rather than all the eggs in one basket, and if I were to advise on that score, I would suggest selling a substantial part of the Seldon stock. And since Whittier will be the buyer, and since he wants it so desperately, we should get a good deal more than the book value, perhaps a million dollars more."

"Is that fair?' Barbara asked.

"Quite fair. We won't go into any details this afternoon. The only question is whether you're willing to sell to Whittier. If you are, I'll tell them that and make the arrangements. There's no need to raise the question of the foundation at this meeting. It would be better, I think, if you yourself told your mother what you plan to do."

Barbara agreed. As they left the restaurant, she said to the old man, "Sam, I'm so very grateful. You've been kind and understanding. You're dear, and I love you very much."

The day before, Jean had dropped into Halleck's on Sansome Street, the small but very expensive couturier where she had been buying things lately. Halleck himself informed her that while war had broken out in Europe, fashion would not bow its head to such mundane forces. The great Paris houses of Worth, Molyneux, and Paquin had alread pulled up stakes and moved to London. And Digby Morton, a step ahead of them, had taken his collection to the States. It might be some months before the Paquin designs arrived, but the Morton clothes were expected momentarily. "Ah, dear Mrs. Whittier," Halleck said—he was a Viennese who carefully cultivated a French accent—"what a pity that in this superb city of ours, which is so much the queen of the world, we have not yet developed a couturier worthy of the name. Ah, that will come." Or, as he said it, "Zat vill come." "But I have information," he added, as if he were imparting state secrets. "The skirts will be straight, always straight. Very high buttons on the jackets. I have some designs; already we are working on them. A pouched and one-sided peplum for day wear. Revolutionary. You are bringing your daughter here, as you said, tomorrow, perhaps?"

"I think not," Jean said slowly. She walked out of the store, indifferent to whether or not she had offended Halleck. She took a cab up the hill to the Fairmont, went into the bar, ordered a Scotch and soda, and then sat at the little table without tasting or touching her drink. Why had she ordered it? She disliked liquor, barely tolerated wine, and the sight of both provoked her. So many things provoked her these days. Her conversation—or rather, Halleck's conversation with her—disgusted her, and for the life of her she could not understand why. Halleck disgusted her. Why had she gone in there at all? But she knew why. She was desperate in her desire to please Barbara, to think of some wonderful thing she could do for her. Then why sit here and perform a charade of drinking? She tasted the drink and made a face.

And then a voice said, "Why, Jean! How delightful! How absolutely delightful!" She looked up, and there was the past, a man called Alan Brocker, fifty-five years old, with the strange, old-man-little-boy face of the very wealthy, workless, pointless Anglo-Saxon. Of all the people in the world, Brocker was the last she desired to meet at that moment, the man whom she had selected—or had he selected her?—for her first extramarital affair. Silly, senseless, mindless Alan Brocker, who had married Manya Vladavich, the model of a third-rate painter called Calvin Braderman; Alan Brocker, who had, as Dan put it, pissed away his life without ever doing a decent day's work or an unselfish act in his life, who had once hired a Pinkerton detective, at Jean's request, to spy and report on Dan's liaison with May Ling. "My dear Jean," he said. "Drinking alone. No woman should be reduced to that, not even after a second divorce, which these days is absolutely nothing. As a matter of fact, I salute you. Manya is in Reno, getting a divorce, so we can drown our sorrows or joys together. Will you ask me to sit down?"

"I suppose I have no choice," Jean said. "Where have you been? I've enjoyed not seeing you for years—how long is it?"

"Ah, Jean, dear Jean. How witty you've become. France, until this stupid war started. What are you drinking?"

"It's sufficient. Whatever it is."

He motioned to the waiter and ordered a drink. "And you, Jean, where has life led you?"

"Would you pay for my drink, Alan?" Jean asked casually.

"Of course."

"I'm grateful. It facilitates things. I've spent the afternoon being disgusted, and I think I've had my fill of it." And with that, she rose and walked out, not looking back, not giving a damn what Brocker felt or thought, only saying to herself later, "You're making quite a habit of burning bridges, my dear Jean. Be careful. You've lived half a century, and there's still a long, tired road ahead."

The next day, Jean went to Sam Goldberg's office at two-thirty, aware that she was half an hour early, but hoping that Barbara would be there already. She had been waiting ten minutes when Barbara and Goldberg returned from their luncheon date. In every meeting with Barbara, Jean anticipated a rebuff that never actually took place, and even now, wanting so desperately to see her, Jean stiffened and held back. But Barbara came to her and embraced her, and Jean held her tightly, thinking, This is all I have left, and the rest is gone, washed out, destroyed.

"Tom will be here any moment now," Jean said. "Did Sam tell you what he wants?"

Barbara nodded.

"Do you care? He has John Whittier's money behind him, and they'll want to buy a controlling interest in the bank."

"Sam and I talked about it," Barbara said.

"It's the way he is," Jean told her. "He has a desperate

need for power and money, the way some people have a need for—well, I don't know, perhaps to be loved. Maybe it's his path to love or hope or just living. Please don't hate him, baby."

"Hate him? Why?"

"I don't know. He's so different."

"Mother," Barbara said, "he can have whatever he wants. I don't care, believe me."

And Jean thought, You really don't, and that's the pity of it.

Tom arrived with Clark Seever, who was the senior member of Seever, Lang and Murphy, John Whittier's attorneys. Seever was a tall, well-groomed, handsome, carefully spoken man in his mid-fifties. He knew Sam Goldberg, as indeed everyone did who was in any way connected with the legal or political functioning of San Francisco, and they shook hands while Tom and Barbara embraced. Five and a half years had gone by since they had last seen each other, and Jean found it strange, almost bizarre, that these, two, brother and sister, were so loosely united, so content to spend a portion of a lifetime away from each other. Jean had been an only child, and like so many only children, she romanticized brother-sister relationships. Yet Tom was not cold or aloof. Too much at stake, and he had obviously structured the warmth and delight with which he greeted his sister.

Barbara, on the other hand, had been anticipating the self-conscious boy she had last seen so long ago. The fact of Tom Lavette was something else entirely, a stranger whom she had difficulty fitting into place and position. At twenty-seven, he was entirely self-possessed, immaculately groomed, his sandy hair parted on one side and swept loosely across his brow; tall, wide-shouldered, his father's height grafted onto the spare frame of the Seldons, he was graceful and meticulous in the niceties of meetings and introduction.

"This is my beautiful sister, Barbara," he said to Seever, "who garnered most of the brains and all of the talent in the family." And then he added to her, "Dear Bobby, it's been too long. Much too long. Well, we'll change that."

The meeting was amiable. Seever brought up the question of control, but almost indifferently. He wondered just how active Miss Lavette desired to be, recalling the role her mother had once played in the affairs of the Seldon Bank.

"I have no interest at all in banking," Barbara said.

"Then you would not be averse to a transfer of sufficient stock to give Thomas the control that the family should necessarily have. Not that I imagine for a moment that you would contest your brother's voting, but then I understand you're not living in San Francisco at the present. Of course, a sale of stock is not the only method, although Thomas has ample capital available for that. There could be an assignment of voting rights if you preferred that method."

"Miss Lavette has no objection," Goldberg interposed, "to a sale of sufficient stock to give Thomas the control he desires, and I think those are details you and I can work out at another time—"

Barbara glanced at her mother. Jean was studying Tom, and then she turned and met Barbara's gaze and smiled slightly. There was a kind of woeful pathos in the smile that cut to Barbara's heart. She had never truly thought of her mother as one who wept, bled, suffered. Even now, at fifty, Jean was an incredibly beautiful woman, and through all the years of Barbara's life, her mother had been the untitled queen of San Francisco society, a sort of magnificent medallion worn by that tight, small circle of wealth and power who regarded themselves as the equal of if not superior to Boston or New York society. She remembered how, in her childhood, she had only to look at the society column in the *Chronicle* or the *Examiner* to find that this or that party or ball or dinner was "graced by the presence of the beautiful Jean Lavette." She had never learned to feel sorry for her, or even to feel for her.

The meeting had gone so smoothly and successfully that Tom was buoyant, satisfied, and sure of himself. "We ought to have a celebration of sorts. Will you join me for dinner?" he asked both of them, Jean and Barbara. "It's been an eternity since the three of us were together."

Barbara looked at her mother. Jean nodded.

"Then I'll pick you up at eight," Tom said. "Black tie. We'll make a real evening of it."

He left with Seever. Still in Goldberg's office, the old man seated behind his desk, watching the two of them, Barbara said to her mother, "He's changed. I've never seen Tom like this before."

"Yes. You do know what you've done, my dear?"

"You mean the stock?"

"You've just given your brother the Seldon Bank. It's a very generous gift. He is understandably delighted."

Barbara shrugged. "He appears to want it very much."

"Oh, very much indeed." Jean turned to Goldberg. "Did you know about this, Sam? But of course you did."

Goldberg nodded.

"And what do you think?"

"Your daughter has a mind of her own, Jean. Also, she has no reason to contest Tom's aims."

"It's Whittier's money."

"I presume so," Goldberg agreed. "Anyway, I'm glad it was all settled amicably. I don't like to see a family squabble over money. The bank remains in the family, and that would have pleased your father, rest his soul. He was a damn decent man for a banker, a part of the old times. They're gone now, Jean. It's a new ballgame, and I'm afraid the rules are a little rough for me. Anyway, it was nice to see the three of you together."

"You're not troubled, are you, mother?" Barbara asked her.

"Not really. Tom is very competent."

It was close to twilight; the air was clean and strong with the scent of the sea. Jean had come by cab. She drove back to Russian Hill in Barbara's car. For Barbara, it was a strange, odd feeling, returning to the house on Russian Hill that Dan had built for Jean after their marriage, where she had been born and spent her childhood. To her, the house had stood there for an eternity, for the beginning years are always an eternity.

They parked, and Barbara took her suitcase out of the trunk of her car.

"No servants, dear," Jean said. "I have a cleaning woman in three times a week."

"Mother, I've been without servants since I left here."

"Tom finds it shocking." She opened the door and held it aside for Barbara to enter.

Barbara's first reaction was of shock and amazement. She had expected nothing to be changed, nothing different. Now all the rooms on the first floor were empty, the walls painted stark white, the polished wooden floors devoid of carpet or rugs. She put down her suitcase and stared, then walked through room after room—all white, all bare, bare walls and no furniture. She turned in bewilderment to look at her mother.

"Darling, I didn't tell you. This is my dream—San Francisco's first valid museum of modern art, or at least the gallery. The art will come."

"But how do you live here?"

"Upstairs I have a very comfortable apartment—living room, kitchen, two bedrooms, office. These rooms down here will be the galleries."

"All your beautiful paintings?"

"Oh, I still have some upstairs. Some I gave to the museum, some I sold. I'm starting fresh, clean. Art is the only passion that still remains to me, Bobby, and thank God for it. If it weren't for that, I should be a very wretched and lonely old woman. But come upstairs now, and we'll change and we'll have a drink and talk. There's so much to talk about."

"Mother, Tom's dressing tonight, and I have nothing but skirts and sweaters and blouses in this suitcase."

"I have enough. We're still about the same size."

Jean opened a bottle of champagne, and they sat in the living room, which had once been the master bedroom, and here at least Barbara found some of her memories—pieces of furniture, a Renoir nude, a Picasso and a George Luks, all of them old favorites Jean would not part with. Barbara told her of meeting Picasso in France. He had kissed her. He had sought her out after reading what she had written about Marcel's death. "What was he like?" Jean wanted to know.

"How can I say it?" Barbara laughed. "The only word is horny, mother. He was absolutely the horniest little man I ever met in my life. Not in anything he did or said. It was just the total effect of him. He reeked of masculine sex. I loved him."

"God, what an opportunity—and I mean for paintings, not for sex. Trouble is, you don't care about paintings."

"I do, but not the way you do, mother. Mother—" She had held off until now. "Well, I must tell you something. I've been putting it off."

"You're very serious. You're not going back to Europe, not now, for heaven's sake?"

"No, nothing like that. This is about the stock, my inheritance."

"Yes?"

"I'm giving it away, all of it. I told Sam to set up a charitable foundation." Having said it at last, Barbara expected all and any reactions—anger, disbelief, opposition, even hysteria—so she was totally astonished when Jean did not react at all, but simply looked at her wineglass and took a sip of her drink. Finally, she said, "When did you decide to do this, Bobby?"

"A few weeks ago, when Sam told me about the meeting."

"Then you've had time to think about it?"

"Yes, I have."

"Did Sam tell you about your account at the bank?"

"Yes."

"Are you giving that away too?"

"No, not at the moment."

"Well, that's reassuring. There are times when one needs money—not perhaps fourteen million, but it helps."

"You're not angry?" Barbara asked.

"Should I be?"

"I thought you would be."

"My dear, beautiful Barbara." She shook her head. "My eyes are wet, and if I rub them, I'll smear my mascara." She refilled the glasses. "I only knew one other person who made a gesture like that. Let's drink to him. His name is Dan Lavette. I loved him very much, but it was a while after he left before I knew how much. The hell with the lousy stock! Do you know what your father would say? He would say that his daughter is one damn fine sonofabitch of a woman—or some such words. Enough of that. Let's talk about other things."

San Francisco had already been a city for many decades when Los Angeles was still a collection of villages connected by interurban streetcars, dozing in the beneficent Southern California sunshine and waiting lazily for something to happen. That was a time that existed as a blurred, golden memory in the minds of a very few, for demographically speaking, there were only a few around to fix it in their memories.

Then two things happened that changed the history of Southern California and fixed the golden memories forever in the past. Film was discovered and oil was discovered. Film, in those days, required maximum exposure to light, and since Southern California had more days of sunshine and more varied scenery than any other part of America that was not out and out desert, the film companies moved to Los Angeles. The industry was young and the companies were fairly small, but both were mushrooming; and while a good deal of Los Angeles County was semidesert, a good deal more of it was lush and beautiful: salt marshes in Santa Monica, broad, fertile fields in Wilshire, snow-covered mountains in the eastern part of the county, green, rolling hills stretching out to the coast, and in the San Fernando Valley, a veritable paradise of orange groves, pecan groves, almond groves, lemon groves, and acres and acres of garden produce—all the elements of which paradise is said to consist, lying in the sun and waiting for man to wreak havoc and concrete and stucco desolation.

The second happening was oil. With the twentieth century came the automobile, and with the automobile an ever-increasing thirst for oil. And beneath the soil of Los Angeles lay one of the largest oilfields in California, with its nexus in an area bounded today by La Brea and Fairfax avenues running north and south and by Wilshire Boulevard and Beverly Boulevard running east and west. In this square mile of land, hundreds of oil derricks arose, but that was only the beginning; and from that center the oil derricks spread out across the county to the sea, to Signal Hill in Long Beach, to Torrence, Baldwin Hills, Wilmington, Venice, and El Segundo. The oil gushed, the speculators went mad, thousands of investors became rich, and thousands more were swindled and became poor; and then the oil, stupidly, greedily poached, ran out, lost its pressure, locked itself away in the ground, and with 1929 and the Depression, the oil bubble collapsed completely.

By 1940, Dan Lavette had been in Los Angeles almost ten years. He had seen the end of the interurban red electric cars, the growth of the freeways, the interlocking of the villages into a sprawling city. He had witnessed the arrival of the poverty-stricken dust bowl farmers from Texas and Oklahoma, partaken of the misery of the unemployed on the San Pedro waterfront, broke and in jail and out of jail and hungry, and then spent years as a mackerel fisherman; and now unreasonably—it appeared to him—he was operating a shipyard where the keels of two merchant ships had already been laid down, with ways being constructed for two more, thanks to loans from the

Maritime Commission, and sitting in the water off Terminal Island was the last yacht that he would build being finally fitted.

Along the waterfront, in Long Beach and San Pedro and Wilmington, unemployment was becoming a thing of the past. Dan had convinced Pete Lomas, turning sixty now, to sell his mackerel boat and come to work at the shipyard as a foreman. Between them, they scoured the docks for shipworkers, welders, cranemen, electricians, posting bulletins, putting ads in the local papers. The Maritime Commission sent him half a dozen young naval architects and a couple of engineers. There was no housing. Piles had to be driven into the mud flats of Terminal Island to extend the base for additional ways, and there were no pile drivers available. Dan's was not the only shipyard lying dormant on the Los Angeles portside. There were five others that Admiral Land had catapulted into life, and the competition among them for workers was reminiscent of the eighteenth-century press gangs of the London waterfront. And not only for workers. The shipyards fought and pleaded and competed and bribed and stole in their desperate hunger for materials, for lumber for the ways and frames, for housing. Dan had platforms built on the mud and rigged surplus World War I tents for the workers to sleep in. He sent the young naval architects out to search for mattresses and blankets, and he threatened to kill the alcoholics he had picked up for laborers who brought their rotgut with them onto the island. It was a miracle that out of the chaos, out of shipbuilders who did not know how to build, out of welders who did not know how to weld, out of carpenters who could not drive a nail properly, out of electricians who lied and bluffed their way into their jobs, out of steamfitters who had never worked on a ship before, out of auto mechanics turned ship mechanics—out of all this somehow two merchant ships were arising and two more were on their way to beginning.

The price Dan paid for this left no room for pleasure or any sense of achievement. There were nights when he never left the shipyard, sleeping on a cot in his office, eating coffee and sandwiches, working until midnight and up again at dawn. He took neither pleasure nor pride in what he was doing. He loathed war, and he felt a sick disgust at the gigantic fact of the profits of war. He had lived through it once, and he had little desire to live through it again. Coming home one night, driven by a desperate need to be clean, to soak in a hot tub, to sleep in his own bed with the body of his wife next to him, he poured out his anger and confusion to May Ling.

"But you're doing it," May Ling said. "Don't you know why?"

"The hell of it is that I don't. All right, I know what it is to be down and out, to need a job, and I'm making a lot of jobs. I'll build ships, and they'll use the ships to run food and munitions to England."

"Which means that people will live."

"It also means that people will die and that bastards like Whittier will be fatter and richer than they are now."

"Danny," May Ling said gently, "have you ever stopped to think about what the Nazis are and what they mean and what they're doing?"

"I've thought about it. I hate those filthy bastards."

"And without the ships, England will die and Hitler will win. It's as simple as that."

"No it isn't," he insisted. "Where does it begin and where does it end? In the last war, the British had a general called Haig, and this bloody bastard sent sixty thousand men to be slaughtered in a single day. They were his own men. Dead is dead. Jesus God, he wasn't fighting for his own land—does anyone know what they were fighting for? I hate those Nazi bastards, but are our own bastards any better? Five years ago, men were dying of hunger out there on the docks at Wilmington and San Pedro—no work, no hope, no jobs, and nobody gave a damn. Now there's money for everything, and Pete and I go and plead with men to come and work. Why? Because there's another stinking war in that stinkhole called Europe, and only war makes those motherfuckers in Washington sit up and take notice."

"Oh, I love your language." May Ling sighed. "All the years I've spent civilizing you."

"Come out and spend a day with me on Terminal Island. One day will uncivilize you."

"I'm sure. Danny, you are a marvelous combination of tycoon, anarchist, and pacifist. Now listen to me."

"I always do."

"Then one time more. When I was twelve years old, and that was not too long ago, there was an anti-Chinese riot in San Francisco. They took two Chinese, Sol Lee and David Jo, and they soaked them with gasoline and then they immolated them, burned them like torches."

"I remember," Dan said. "I saw it."

"And so you wrote off all of San Francisco. Human beings couldn't do such a thing."

"Drunken bastards from the Tenderloin."

"And what about the sober bastards who watched?"

"Yeah."

"So you choose between England and Germany," May Ling said gently. "Anyway, I don't think that's the point at all. I've known you a long time, and you can't live if you don't play their game."

"I gave up their game."

"Did you, Danny? We've always been honest with each other. You wanted the shipyard. Joe would have gone to medical school. I have enough savings for that. But you couldn't stay out of it."

"What are you telling me? That I'm a money-hungry sonofabitch?" he demanded angrily.

"Danny, when did money ever mean anything to you? It's not the money, it's Nob Hill. That's the way they measure things here, Danny. That's the way it is."

"And you're telling me I'm no different than I was thirty years ago?"

"Of course you're different, and you're the same, and I loved you so much then and I love you more now, and you're married to a withered old Chinese lady."

"Like hell I am!"

"Then we're not married. I don't care. Just take me to bed. It's been so long."

For Barbara, Los Angeles was not a city but a place. It was the place where her father lived, a place where she could live and work in quiet comfort, where the gentle presence of May Ling and the old lady, her mother, was comforting and reassuring; and she experienced this amorphous feeling more than ever after she returned from San Francisco. She yearned for San Francisco; it was a measured place where one was properly contained and evaluated. She had looked out of the window of her old bedroom in the house on Russian Hill, and all the city lay beneath her, a unit of high places jutting up from the bay, a thing that men had made deliberately and that they

cherished and loved. It was a proper city properly divided,
the rich in their place, the poor in their place, the social
sets defined and walled in. But her yearning was a memory
of childhood; she could not stay there or live there; and in
the same way, she yearned for Paris, already a hazy dream.

At first it seemed to her that her soul had died with
Marcel, that she could never awaken without a moist-eyed
awareness of the emptiness in her bed, that she could never
laugh or sing or have a feeling of joy again. Even the
incident with Bernie Cohen had not lessened the ghost of
Marcel. After her return from Germany, Paris had been
an empty and desolate city, which she was only too happy
to leave. Now, in the tiny study of the house in Westwood,
she could hide from the real world and create her own
world in the pages of a manuscript. She knew that her
situation was a thing of the moment, that she could not
think of this as her home, that she could not go on existing
without direction. She was full of the memory of love, yet
she could not bring herself to stretch out a hand to a man,
to find a man, to make a date, to relate to a man. On two
occasions, Dan brought one of the young architects from
the Maritime Commission home with him. Obviously, he
was thinking of Barbara, and her reaction was indifference
or cool politeness.

Christmas of 1939 came and went. There was a tree,
which May Ling and Barbara decorated, piles of presents,
and from the Napa Valley, to stay with them for three
days, Sally Levy. Barbara drove down to Union Station to
meet her. Joe had attempted a precise description, but
Barbara was unprepared for the pretty, slender young
woman, her blond hair cut to shoulder length and bobbed
across her brows, dressed in a proper gray woolen suit.

Barbara, after watching the girl stand forlornly next to
her suitcase, approached her tentatively. "You're not Sally
Levy, are you?"

"And you're Barbara," Sally said, throwing her arms
around her. "Oh, I'm so glad to see you. I was sure they
had forgotten, and this is such a huge station. It's very
pretty and Spanish, but huge. You must be Barbara,
because you're just as wonderful and beautiful as Joe said
you were, and you're really glamorous because of all the
great adventures you had, and you know, you're absolutely
my idol, and you mustn't laugh at me. Joe always laughs
at me."

In the car, she was interested in and enthusiastic about everything—freeways, palm trees, mountains, Barbara's car, the style of the houses—to the point where Barbara felt utterly exhausted before they ever reached Westwood. Sally's mind sputtered like a string of firecrackers. She leaped from subject to subject. She flung out a string of questions about Nazi Germany, and then she was off on the subject of love and romance before Barbara had a chance to answer. "You will read my poems," she said to Barbara. "They're really mine. I used to copy Elizabeth Barrett Browning and Thomas Campion and Emily Dickinson because Joe would never know the difference, but then May Ling found me out, and anyway I'm too grown up for that and I write my own now, and they're really very good. Do you think a man and a woman should sleep together before they get married?"

Barbara tried to grapple with this and keep her eyes on the road. "Well, doesn't it depend, Sally, on what kind of a relationship—I mean how old they are—"

"I am too young for anything. Do you realize that, Barbara, I am absolutely too young for anything. I'm surprised that you came for me instead of May Ling. They called May Ling five times before they let me come down here. You would think Joe was some kind of rapist. Did you ever read Havelock Ellis?"

"Good heavens! Did you?"

"Every word. You know, I've necked some, with some of the kids at school. You would understand that. I mean, just to see what it was like. They're idiots, and I hate pimples. Ugh. But I feel that the one man–one woman relationship is most satisfactory. Don't you? I mean when you come right down to it."

"Yes," Barbara said, "you're absolutely right."

Joe was waiting for them, standing in front of the house in Westwood. Sally was out of the car almost before it stopped moving; she ran to Joe and flung her arms around him. He stood there holding her, looking at Barbara hopelessly.

Thus Christmas came and went, and the year 1940 began. The novel Barbara was writing unfolded slowly. She wrote, corrected what she had written, and then as often as not destroyed it. The story was focused on herself: a young American girl leaves college and goes to Paris to study. But even though she had taken up a thread of events that she had already experienced and lived through, it was months before she was able to face this fact. When she did face it at last, she read through the hundred or so pages that she had written with a feeling of unhappiness and distaste. She then said to May Ling, "I've written over a hundred pages and I must have some other opinion. Will you read them, please?"

May Ling read the manuscript in a single evening. Barbara had retreated into her room, where she sat brooding and waiting for a verdict. Finally, the door opened. May Ling came in, put the manuscript on the desk, and sat down.

"You might as well tell me," Barbara said.

"Yes, I intend to."

"It's rotten, isn't it? I want the truth, May Ling. I don't want you to pull any punches. I want the absolute truth."

"I don't intend to lie to you, Bobby. I have too much respect for you to do that. You know, you write very well, solidly and professionally, and I suppose you could finish this story and have it published. A lot worse things have been published, and people are very curious about Paris in the last years before the war. Your descriptions of Paris are splendid, but your character doesn't exist. She's cut out of cardboard. I know she's you. She has to be you. She may look different and have a different background than you had, but she is yourself. But the reader doesn't know who she is or what she is. Why are you afraid to look at yourself and examine yourself?"

"I'm not!"

"Oh, but you are. You've seen things and you've suffered, and you gave your heart to a man and watched him die, and I know how warm and emotional you are, but this is cold and manufactured. Why don't you write about yourself and out of your own suffering? You must."

"I know what I'm doing," Barbara burst out, on the edge of tears. "You don't have to tell me that. I know what I want to do."

May Ling came out of the room to face Dan's curious stare. "What happened?"

"I'm not sure. I think she'll be all right."

"You told her it was no good."

"I had to."

"Jesus, I wish you hadn't. How can you be sure?"

"I think I'm sure. I had to be honest with her."

After May Ling left, Barbara sat and looked at the manuscript. She sat there for over an hour, staring at it, thinking, hurting, trying to deal with her anger at May Ling. Her first reaction was to accuse May Ling. May Ling hated her, she always had, and this was her moment of revenge. How easy it was to read the agonizing work of months—and then to destroy it with a few clever words! She refused at first to remember her own reaction to what she had written. It took the best part of an hour to return to that and to ask herself whether May Ling should have lied? After all, she had made her own judgment, and she had used May Ling in the hope that May Ling would assure her that her own assessment of her work was worthless.

Slowly, methodically, Barbara began to shred the pages she had written. She filled the wastepaper basket with the torn bits of manuscript. Then she looked at her watch. It was just after 11:00 P.M. She felt curiously lighthearted as she put a fresh sheet of paper into her typewriter and began. By two in the morning she had completed three pages, which she now reread with grim satisfaction.

She decided to go on working. She needed coffee. She went into the kitchen, and there May Ling was, sitting at the kitchen table, an open book in front of her. The coffee was on the stove over a small fire. Barbara sat down beside her, and May Ling poured her a cup of coffee.

"I'm sorry," Barbara said. "I just behaved rotten."

"Or normally for once. You had every right to be angry and hurt and heartsick. Months of work gone down the drain. How else could you feel?"

"Oh, no—no, May Ling. You were right."

"What difference does that make? Barbara dear, must you be a saint? Saints are a fraud. People are the way they are and the way life makes them. You're so filled with guilts and self-judgments and self-denunciations that if you go on this way, you will wipe yourself out of existence. You have nothing to atone for. You did nothing evil to inherit that money."

"But that wasn't why I couldn't take it," Barbara exclaimed.

"Do you know why? Barbara darling, I loathe self-abnegation. There's nothing you've ever done or been that you can't face, and you don't have to be proud or ashamed of it, but just face the fact that it is you, and you are what you are. And if you can do that, the book will be good and your life will be good." May Ling rose. "And with that bit of advice, which I don't follow any too well myself, I'll go to bed."

"May Ling?"

Barbara embraced her, clutched the slender Chinese woman in her arms. "Oh, May Ling, I do love you so! Do you think I'll ever grow up?"

"I do. Yes, indeed I do."

The last yacht to come off the ways at Dan's shipyard was the *Isadora*, which had been built to the order of Richard Dyler, the film star. A hundred feet long, twenty feet wide, it was the best thing Dan had ever built, an oceangoing marvel. It had been anchored off the shipyard to be fitted, but a sudden shortage of parts, the coming into being of a thing called priorities, had put off the completion of the ship for months. At last it was done and tied to the dock at Wilmington, and Dyler had decided to celebrate with what he called a boat-warming party, and he invited Dan to come and bring his wife.

May Ling begged off. Her mother was ill in bed with a bronchial infection, and she told Dan that she couldn't leave her alone. Barbara volunteered to stay with the old woman, but May Ling had seized upon her mother's illness as a reason not to go to the kind of a party where she always felt she was a curiosity and an outsider. Dan said that he had an obligation to attend; Dyler still had a final payment of eighty-two thousand dollars to make, and Dan needed the money. May Ling then suggested that he take Barbara.

"It would be good for her," May Ling said. "She does nothing and goes nowhere and sees no one. She's become totally compulsive about that novel of hers. I think that a break would be the best thing in the world for her."

"I've tried before," Dan said.

"Then try again."

This time Barbara offered no objection, but on the contrary was pleased with the idea. She had finished more than half of the new version of her book, and she was satisfied with what she had written. She had come to a point where she was choking on her own presence, and the thought of a glamorous party on a yacht, film stars, and her father as her escort was suddenly exciting. It would be an evening dress affair, and on that score she was totally unprepared. She needed a dress, shoes, and a wrap.

Barbara took three hundred dollars out of her savings account with the delight of a child robbing her piggy bank to buy a new doll, and then she spent an entire day shopping. In Beverly Hills, she found a navy blue pleated chiffon evening gown that could be had for a hundred and eighty dollars. It was sleeveless and backless with rhinestone clips on the shoulders, and she agonized for half an hour before she gritted her teeth and decided to buy it. The saleslady, after telling her, "My dear, if I were as young and beautiful as you, and could look the way you do in that gown, I'd go hungry for a month to have it," then proceeded to talk her into a navy blue satin wrap for ninety dollars more. With the purchase of a pair of high-heeled satin pumps to match, Barbara returned home, penniless, flushed, triumphant, and ashamed.

But when she dressed herself on the evening of the party and came out to be appraised and approved by her father and May Ling, Dan stared at her for a long moment before he whispered, "Baby, you are one hell of a dish."

Her hair was gathered in a bun at the back of her neck, and she wore lipstick but no other make-up. "Let me," May Ling said, pressing a tissue to Barbara's lips until only a shadow of the lipstick remained. "You don't need it. It only takes away." May Ling looked at both of them, Dan gray now, but still without fat on his big frame, the dinner jacket fitted close and well to the heavy muscles on his sloping shoulders, and Barbara like a time-defying recreation of Jean.

After they left, May Ling walked slowly upstairs to her bedroom and stared into her mirror. She touched the wrinkles that had gathered around her eyes and mouth. The once-jet black hair was streaked with gray. She stared at herself as tears welled up in the corners of her eyes, and then she shook her head with annoyance, wiped away the tears, and went into the room where her mother was. So-toy was asleep, breathing heavily. May Ling drew the covers up around her and put out the light and left.

She went downstairs and tried to read, but her thoughts wandered. She concentrated on the page she was reading, and again her thoughts swam away and she dozed off. Then the sound of a door opening awakened her, and

there was Dan. She looked at her wristwatch. It was half
past eleven.

"What happened?" she asked forlornly.

"Nothing happened. Parties like that bore me. You
don't. So I came home."

"Where's Barbara?"

"I left her there. She'll be all right. She was having a
great time."

May Ling rose, walked over to Dan, and put her palms
against his cheeks. "Oh, Danny, I'm so glad you're here."

"Make some of that classy Chinese tea, and I'll play you
jack-o'-diamonds at ten cents a point."

"No, Danny, I want to go to bed, I want you to hold
me."

"All right, if that's what you want. I still can't understand why you skinny Chinese broads are so insatiably
sexy."

"We're an old culture, Danny. We know what good is."

Later, lying in his arms, she said, "Danny, do you know
what I want?"

"Tell me."

"I want to go away with you, just the two of us. I want
to go back to Hawaii, in a freighter, the way we did years
ago. I want you to get a skiff and we'll sail in the islands,
and we'll lie naked on the lonely beaches, and we'll pretend
we're young again."

"Pretend hell! We are young."

"Will you do it, Danny? Will you?"

"Absolutely."

"You're not kidding, Danny? You will do it?"

"It's a promise. I never broke my word to you, did I?"

Barbara was enchanted. For months, she had worked like
a slave and lived like a nun; suddenly, she was like
someone awakened from sleep, rested, alert, totally conscious of herself, of the simple beauty of her gown, of her
firm, strong young body, and of her own beauty. When
she first saw the yacht lying alongside the dock, lit up from
stem to stern, strung with Japanese lanterns, spun in a nest
of music and voices, she said, "Oh, daddy, what a beautiful
thing you built!" There was a note in her voice that Dan
had not heard before, and she was smiling with delight
when he glanced at her. When he led her into the wide
well of the yacht, every eye turned toward her, and Dan

told himself that even here, where beauty was the commodity bought and sold, no one could hold a candle to her.

Now it was an hour since Dan had left her there, assured that any one of half a dozen men would vie for the privilege of taking her home. Alex Hargasey, the director, hovering over her like a butterfly over a flower, had taken on the function of introducing her to what he called "the exotic nobility of Hollywood." The names fell from his lips like titles: Bette Davis, Marlene Dietrich, Spencer Tracy, Gary Cooper, Lana Turner. The women dismissed her; she was a beautiful woman whose name was meaningless, but too disturbingly attractive. The men stared at her, sought her out, projected themselves into rather witless conversation. "Do you like yacht parties?" "But you must be in the theater, not the screen. I would have seen you on the screen." "Top deck over there, but dump Hargasey. He's a rotten old lecher. Five minutes." "But I'm sure we've met. You couldn't be here on the Coast without us having met."

"An actor," Hargasey said to her, "is a little less than a man. An actress, my dear, is a little more than a woman."

"That's very clever," Barbara admitted, wondering whether he would acknowledge its origin.

He merely nodded and shrugged. "You see, I have pleaded with your father to bring you for a screen test."

"He mentioned it. But I'm not an actress. I never could be. I have no talent whatsoever. And no ambition in that direction."

A voice behind her said, "As for talent, I suspect the statement is subterfuge. As for ambition, why not, lovely lady?"

Barbara turned and faced a tall, broad-shouldered man who was disconcertingly handsome, his face tanned, his strong, fine features just rugged enough to save them from perfection, his blue eyes unreal in their brightness. "And you, my dear, where the devil have you been hiding?" he demanded of her.

She was high enough on half a dozen glasses of champagne to giggle with pleasure at this apparition out of her adolescent dreams and to stare at him comfortably.

"Our host," Hargasey said. "Barbara, my dear, this is Richard Dyler."

"Barbara who?" Dyler demanded.

"The daughter of the man who built this toy of yours
—Barbara Lavette."

"Damnit, was Danny here? Where is he?"

"He left. If you had come to your own party on time,
you would have seen him."

"The hell with that," Dyler said. "He left the best
part of him here. My dear lady," he said to Barbara, "what
the devil are you staring at?"

"You. You're much more beautiful off the screen than
on it."

"Beautiful, Barbara, is a term I reserve for women.
You, my love, are beautiful."

"Am I your love?" Barbara asked him.

"The possibility exists. Hargasey," he said to the director, "will you get lost and leave us alone. I have much to
discuss with this young woman." He took two glasses of
champagne from a passing waiter, handed one to Barbara,
and said, "To knowledge of each other!"

"So long as it is not in the Biblical sense," Barbara
agreed, thinking to herself, What a silly thing to say! Am
I drunk? I haven't been even a little drunk since Marcel
died. But everything I say sounds clever when I say it and
very foolish after it has been said. I think I am drunk, and
I don't want to think of Marcel, not tonight.

"We shall see." Dyler took Barbara's arm and said to
the director, "Hargasey, will you please get lost."

Hargasey sighed, spread his arms, and turned away.
Dyler steered Barbara through the crowd of guests in
the well.

"And where are you taking me?"

"High up," Dyler said. "Top deck, where we can look
down at this scum."

"I can't drink when I'm walking, and that's an awful
thing to say."

He stopped and clicked glasses with her. "Drink up."
She stared at the amazing blue eyes and began to giggle
again. "Drink up, Barbara, shipbuilder's daughter."

She drained the rest of her champagne. "Better. I like
that. Shipbuilder's daughter."

They climbed up to the bridge. "Put to sea," Barbara
said. "All the way to China."

"Can't do it. We're tied up. Are you drunk, shipbuilder's
daughter?"

"I suppose so. That was clever the first time you said it."

"The first time I said it was in *The Viking's Revenge.*
Did you see me? My name was Ruric."

"Do you remember all your lines?" Barbara asked in
amazement.

"Only the best. What do you do when you're not going
to parties?"

"I don't go to many parties. I'm a writer."

"What do you write?"

"Do you read *Manhattan Magazine?*"

"Only the cartoons. God damn it, woman, we're in Los
Angeles." Then he took her in his arms and kissed her.

She pulled away and stared at him. "You don't waste
any time, do you?"

"No, I don't."

"You just decide to make love to someone?"

"Not anyone, kid, not anyone."

"Well, doesn't anyone ever say, hold on? Wait a minute?
Let's talk about the weather?"

"Who the hell wants to talk about the weather?" Dyler
said. "I kissed you. You liked it, didn't you?"

"I guess so." Barbara giggled at him. "I never kissed
anyone who looked like you."

"What kind of a crack is that?"

"You're so pretty. I mean beautiful," Barbara added
hastily.

"I told you before, beautiful is for dames." He put an
arm around her, cupped her breast in his hand and kissed
the curve of her neck. She began to giggle uncontrollably.
"What gives with you?" he demanded.

"Champagne?"

"You know, you're beautiful. You're a beautiful dame.
You do something to me."

"What?"

"What do you mean, what?"

"I mean what do I do to you?"

"You're not for real. You're absolutely not for real."

Barbara leaned over the rail and watched the men and
women dancing in the well of the yacht. "Let's dance,
Dyler," she said. "This is the most romantic sight I've
ever seen, all those real movie stars dancing down there in
the moonlight."

"Screw the movie stars," he said. "There's only one
star, and that's me. I don't want to dance. I want to make
love. Come on down to my cabin."

"And then we go to bed?"

"That's up to you, cookie." He pulled her to him and kissed her again.

"Doesn't anyone ever say no?"

"Well, two years ago—aw, shit, honey, you only remember my last name. I'm Richard Dyler."

Barbara burst out laughing.

"What in hell is wrong with you?"

"I want to dance. I want to dance with Richard Dyler. Come on."

"O.K., one dance."

They could hardly move in the crowded well of the yacht. He whispered into her ear, "Did you see *The Last Gun?* That was the first picture I did for Metro. Do you remember the way I died?" A blonde whose face was vaguely familiar to Barbara cut in between them, throwing her arms around Dyler. "Dicky," she said, "where have you been? But where?" Barbara slipped away, leaving Dyler in the clutches of the blonde. Hargasey found her.

"Dyler is an animal," he said to her, drawing her out of the crowd.

"Oh, no, he's delightful. He's very stupid but delightful. And he's so beautiful."

"Beautiful, he's not. So you listen to me. You're an innocent kid."

"All he wanted was to go to bed with me. He's very direct and honest. That's flattering, with all these beautiful stars around."

"To bed he wants to go with everybody, and he does."

"How did he die in *The Last Gun?* I didn't see it."

"The woman he went to bed with stuck a knife into his belly. It should only happen. I want you to meet Bogart. He keeps asking me who you are."

Bogart was charming and interested. He had actually read Barbara's pieces in *Manhattan,* and they got into a discussion about Germany and the war in Europe. He led her out of the well into the lounge. Men joined him. A half a dozen of them gathered around Barbara. One of them said to Hargasey, "Who is she?"

"The daughter of the man who built the yacht."

It was past two in the morning before Dyler emerged on deck again. Barbara was dancing. She waved at him. He stood staring at her glumly, and a little while later the party began to break up.

"Richard," Barbara said to Dyler as they were leaving, "I had the best time ever. It was divine. And you're very beautiful."

Crowded into the front seat of his car, sitting next to a voluptuous dark-haired woman whose name was Cindy, Barbara was driven home by Hargasey. "Tonight," he said to her, "you met some classy people, Barbara, but also some bums. Dyler is a bum. I got a responsibility to your father, so I must tell you that Dyler is a bum."

"It should happen to me," Cindy said.

"I had a wonderful time," Barbara told him.

She let herself into the house and crawled into bed, and lay there aching all over with desire. "I would have gone to bed with him," she told herself. "I would have. Christ, I'm so lonely and wretched." The effect of the champagne had worn off. She began to cry, and that way, weeping for herself, she finally fell asleep.

May Ling's mother, So-toy, died in June of 1940. She was only sixty-two years old. She had never recovered from the bronchial infection that had taken hold of her two months before. She grew weaker; it developed into pneumonia; and she died one night as she had lived, quietly, uncomplainingly, here in a strange land called California thousands of miles from a China she barely remembered. May Ling sat by the tiny, withered body, a meaningless death in a world gone mad with the making of death, and she wept for herself more than for her mother. They laid her to rest next to Feng Wo, her husband.

She had been so silent, so unobtrusive, so gently eager to satisfy Barbara's every want, that it was hard for Barbara to believe that she was no longer there. She had had an enormous respect for the act of writing, the strange mystery that is never so mysterious as to an illiterate, and during the day, when Barbara sat at her desk, struggling with a book that had become a monster that ruled her life, So-toy would enter silently and put down a pot of tea and a dish of small cakes. Now, working on the final pages of the novel, alone in the house, Barbara would look up expectantly and wait for the sound of the old woman's shuffling steps. Other times, Barbara had gone into the kitchen and had sat with her. So-toy always welcomed her with a delicious, slow smile, her wrinkled face trying to express what she could not put into words. They never said much to each other, but there was communication between them.

"I miss her so much," Barbara said to May Ling.

"I know." May Ling was not given to tears. Her hurts were something she dealt with internally.

Barbara finished the book in midsummer. The house in Westwood was silent and empty. Joe, having completed his second year of medical school, was working in a hospital in San Diego for the summer. May Ling was working at the library, and Dan spent longer and longer hours at the shipyard. For Barbara, the completion of the book seemed to bring a whole period of her life to a close. It had been an endless task of writing and rewriting, and still she was dissatisfied with so much of what she had written. She decided to put the manuscript aside for a few weeks and then reread it. Suddenly at odds with herself, restless, filled with a strong sense of aimlessness, she decided to accept her mother's invitation and go to San Francisco.

She took the manuscript with her, planning to go over it carefully and do whatever rewriting she felt was necessary, but in the first weeks with Jean, she hardly glanced at it. "My dear, lovely Barbara," Jean said to her, "you're as pale as a ghost and from what you tell me, you've been living the life of a nun. Well, so have I. But I am old and you are young. Why isn't there a man in your life?"

"Because I don't meet any men. I had four dates with a movie star. That took away my appetite."

"Who?"

"Richard Dyler."

"Well, he is certainly beautiful. Tell me all about it. But not right this minute. We'll talk about that at lunch. We are going to lunch and we are going to dinner—in all the very best places. We are going to the horse show at Menlo Park, and we are going sailing and we are going to the opera and to the theater, and I shall introduce you to fascinating and empty-headed young men, and we shall wander through every gallery in town and pretend we know more about paintings than anyone else—and we will have an absolutely wonderful, delicious time."

But there was no way Barbara could tell her mother all about her four dates with Richard Dyler. "What does one do?" she asked herself. "Does one say, mother, I finally went to bed with him." "Why?" would have to have an answer. "Mother, I just wanted to feel a man's body next to me. It was just too long."

It had happened on their last date, when Barbara finally agreed to go to his purplish-pink Moorish mansion in Bel Air. This time she had only a single glass of wine to drink, so being tight was no part of her rationale, which in any case was not very much of a rationale. She was the only guest. They swam in the seventy-five-foot swimming pool, and then they dined outside on his terrace, in a controlled jungle of palms and cactus and roses. It was one of those warm, gentle evenings that come in the latter part of the Southern California summer and that are known locally as "the Santa Anna effect."

Sitting there, looking about her, Barbara decided that the place was either beautiful or horrible, depending upon one's mood and how one reacted to fake Moorish architecture in Los Angeles.

"Not bad for a kid from Gary, Indiana," Dyler said. "It's kind of pretty in a classy way." Which was as much of a flight of poetic fancy as he was capable of.

"Are you really from Gary?" Barbara asked, thinking that with his face and eyes, he should at least have originated in someplace like Santa Fe or Tarpon Springs, neither of which she had ever been to, but at least they had names that went with the Dyler face.

"You ever been there?"

"Just on the New York train, passing through."

"Don't ever get off. It's a shithole."

"I suppose no one ever told you that your speech is colorful?"

"I never dated a writer before. Are you sure you're a writer? The writers I meet around the studio are creeps."

"I'm never sure I'm a writer."

"No? Well, that explains it."

After dinner, they went into his viewing room. It was a large room, with overstuffed chairs scattered around and a huge couch facing the screen. "I run pictures here," he explained. "You ever been in one of these before?"

"Never," Barbara admitted. "I'm so innocent, I never realized that you could have a small theater in your own home."

"Everyone has them."

"Well, not really. I mean we don't."

"Well, what the hell. I mean people in the industry."

. The lights went down, and Barbara was watching the newest Richard Dyler film, called *Moonlight Bridge*. After about fifteen minutes, Barbara said, "I can't watch the film and be manhandled at the same time. What on earth are you trying to do?"

"You are absolutely the strangest broad I ever met in my life. Didn't anyone ever make a pass at you before?"

"Is that what you're trying to do?"

"I'm trying to make love to you. You're the first broad I can't get any closer to than the senior prom. I seen you four times. For Christ's sake, I want to go to bed with you. Isn't that plain enough?"

"Not here with the projectionist watching."

"It's dark."

"Richard, I'm sure you have a bedroom."

"Baby, eight of them."

"Well, let's pick one."

"I'll be damned," he said.

The bedroom was enormous, the ceiling set with mirrors, the bed covered with a spread of simulated leopardskin, the floor carpeted in white shag that gave underneath like a trampoline, the walls covered with glistening paper of shiny silver and dead black. Barbara had never seen anything like it before, and as she turned, staring at the room, Dyler asked eagerly, "You like it? Botticher designed it. It's got a lot of class, hasn't it?"

"Yes, a lot of class," Barbara whispered, wondering who Botticher was, bereft suddenly of all the passion and desire that had been frustrated for so many months. Dyler had evidently completed his preparatory lovemaking downstairs. Now he pursued the fact of sexual intercourse with simple directness. He undressed with speed and facility, waiting eagerly for Barbara to get out of her clothes. And then it was over in about thirty seconds, and he lay back on the bed, naked and satisfied.

"You got class too," he informed Barbara. "You got one hell of a figure." He glowed with satisfaction, his perfect face more perfect than ever.

Barbara pulled the leopard spread over her and regarded Dyler thoughtfully. "Dyler," she said at last, "do you know what an orgasm is?"

"Don't I ever. What do you think just happened to me?"

"What happened to you was an ejaculation."

"What's the difference?"

She sighed. "Dyler—"

"How come you call me by my last name?" he wanted to know.

"We don't know each other too well."

"You know, that's funny. For a writer."

"Dyler, how many women have you gone to bed with?"

"What a question! I don't get you, I swear."

"Don't you want to tell me?"

"It's no great secret, baby. Maybe three hundred, maybe four hundred. Who counts? I never claimed to be a virgin. Jesus Christ, you knew that."

Barbara nodded. "I guess I did."

"Well, what about you? Fair's fair."

"You're the third. No secrets."

"You know, I respect you for that," he said seriously.

"And with all those women, no one ever mentioned a woman's orgasm to you?"

"Are you kidding? Honey baby, you are talking to a specialist on the subject of women. That's why I picked you. If there's one thing I know about, it's women. A man's a man and a woman's a woman. They are different."

"They certainly are," Barbara agreed.

"You know, cookie, you and me are going to have a lot of fun together."

"I don't think we are," Barbara said.

"Come on."

"I think that in due time I would bore you," Barbara told him gently. "I wouldn't want to do that."

"Hey, you're not going to turn out to be one of those broads who go around working the fact that they went to bed with Dick Dyler? You're not scoring on me?"

"Scout's honor, no."

So it ended. Dyler called half a dozen times before he gave up, assuring Barbara that he respected her because this was the first time a girl had turned him down; and now, lunching with her mother at the Fairmont, Jean said, "But he must be charming. He can't be entirely stupid."

"Oh, no, not entirely."

"And certainly it must have been exciting to date the sex symbol of America."

"Well, I guess it was, for a while," Barbara admitted.

"He's no one to be serious about, I will admit that," Jean said. "Movie stars are not for marrying."

"Who is?" Barbara wondered.

"My dear, San Francisco is teeming with good-looking and eligible young men, and we absolutely must do something about it. You'll soon be twenty-seven years old."

"And I'm beginning to feel like forty."

"What nonsense! You're young and lovely and intelligent, and you can't go on burying yourself in that ridiculous place called Los Angeles." Seeing the expression on Barbara's face, she added quickly, "I'm not talking against your father. I've been meticulous on that point. By the way, how is he?"

"He's well enough. He works too hard. The shipyard has become a madhouse. They've laid the keels of four merchant ships, and he has hundreds of men working there—and he's not happy, not at all."

"Happiness was never Dan's strong point. Is he content, being married—" She paused.

"Don't get into that, mother. May Ling's a wonderful woman. Don't put me in between."

"All right." Jean smiled. "No more of that. Tonight, we dine with your brother. You shall see his handsome new uniform and his very beautiful but brainless girl friend, whom I'm afraid he's going to marry."

"Mother!"

"I know. I'm being nasty. Anyway, Tom is in the navy, the most painless transition imaginable. He has been given a commission, and he is now liaison officer between the navy and California Shipping. Well, I'm pleased about that. Sooner or later, we'll be in this dreadful war, and the navy is the best place to be, especially if you're a shore officer, which I gather is what Tom will remain. He's as thick as thieves with John Whittier, and they have all sorts of plans about taking over California and perhaps the rest of the world too, given time, of course."

"Does he still live with John?"

"No, he's taken an apartment on Jones Street. As a matter of fact, I think he and John bought the building. They've formed some kind of interlocking corporation or something of the sort, and they're expanding or whatever. Suddenly, my dear, the whole thing bores me. You're not envious of him, are you?"

"Good heavens, no."

"And no regrets about all that money?"

"Absolutely none."

"You are a strange girl. I don't mind. I love you very

much just as you are. Now for this afternoon. Krumbach
—he's one of the art dealers here, if you can call them
dealers—well, he's gotten his hands on a Kandinsky, and
he has all sorts of visions of wealth because he knows I
want it. I think I do. Will you come with me?"

"Of course. But what on earth is a Kandinsky?"

"Vasili Kandinsky, a very wonderful Russian painter,
but not very good at getting along with them. He went
to Weimar in Germany, where he worked at the Bauhaus,
and I suppose he's in Paris right now. I've tried to get in
touch with him, but never received an answer. He worked
with another artist called Paul Klee, who just died. I'm
starting with two of Klee's paintings, which are on their
way here from New York. One of your film stars in Los
Angeles had a picture he painted. I tried to get hold of it,
but Krumbach got there first, and now he will try to take
it out of my hide. We'll see. I suspect there are not many
more than twenty people in San Francisco who have ever
heard of Kandinsky, and nineteen of them have no
money."

"Mother, you amaze me."

"Do I? Why?"

"The way you care about paintings."

"I do. They're very wonderful and full of passion, and
they ask nothing but to be looked at and understood.
Which is more than I can say of most people."

Krumbach's gallery was on the second floor of an old
house on Grant Avenue, two rooms, painted white and
hung with paintings of redwood trees, stony beaches laced
with waves only a little less stony, and cowboys roping
cattle in eager but untalented imitation of Frederic Rem-
ington. Krumbach himself was a small, stout man, with
a pince-nez and an indeterminate foreign accent. He welcomed the two women as if they were visiting royalty,
bowed and scraped, and begged them to examine his dis-
play of the most talented new western painters.

"Krumbach," Jean said, "don't waste your breath on me
or my daughter. There are talented western painters, but
you wouldn't dare show one of them. Now, where is the
Kandinsky?"

"Your daughter—as beautiful as the mother. But who
could believe you are not sisters?"

"That's enough," Jean said with annoyance.

Barbara had never seen her in quite that mood, all business, cold, and intimidating. Krumbach sighed, opened the closet door, and brought out a canvas that was about twenty inches square, covered by what appeared to Barbara to be a random arrangement of bright lines and explosions of color reminiscent of fireworks. He put it on an easel and stood back to admire it. Jean barely glanced at it.

"So that's it," she said, looking at her watch.

"It's magnificent," Krumbach said.

"Do you like it?" Jean asked Barbara casually.

Not knowing what was expected of her, Barbara decided to say what she thought. "No, I can't say that I do. I haven't the vaguest notion of what it means."

"What should it mean?" Krumbach cried in pain. "A Kandinsky does not have to mean something."

"I think we must go," Jean said.

"You don't want it, Mrs. Whittier?"

"Not really. You heard what my daughter said."

"But mother," Barbara protested, "I don't know the first thing about modern painting."

"You see, you see!" Krumbach exclaimed. "From her own lips. Modern painting she don't understand."

"I'm afraid I don't either." Jean sighed and put her hand on the doorknob. Then she said, over her shoulder, "What are you asking?"

"Nothing. I'm giving it away. For three thousand dollars, I'm giving it away."

"Come on, Barbara," Jean said.

"Mrs. Whittier, make me an offer!" he cried desperately.

Jean turned and glanced at the painting again. "I really don't know. Oh, well, I don't know what else you'll do with it. Five hundred dollars."

"Five hundred dollars," Krumbach repeated. "And also a pint of blood."

"I don't need the blood. Really."

"Twenty-five hundred, rock bottom."

A half-hour later, they had settled on eight hundred dollars, and Jean wrote out a check while Krumbach looked at her as if his best friend had died.

"Shall I deliver it?" he asked woefully.

"No. I'll take it with me."

Once outside and in a cab, Jean was ecstatic. "I have it!" she cried. "Bobby, I have it. Two Klees and now a Kandinsky, and I have a line on a Nolde. What a beginning! What a grand, exciting beginning!"

"Mother, how could you?" Barbara asked unhappily.

"How could I what?"

"How could you do that to that poor little man?"

"My dear Bobby, that poor little man paid three hundred dollars for the painting."

"How do you know?"

"Because I telephoned the owner. Well, he went down there and got it. Counting his expenses and time, we'll say four hundred. Which means he got a hundred percent profit instead of the thousand percent he began with. I don't think I was too hard on him."

A while later, Barbara said thoughtfully, "I have an interesting mother."

"And I have an interesting daughter," Jean said. "And do you know, my dear, this is the first time in I don't know how long that we've had a chance to be together and do things together, and I intend to make the most of it."

For the next two weeks, Barbara went to parties, dined in the best restaurants, went to a horse show at Menlo Park, read the books she had meant to read, slept late, joined her mother in planning the Russian Hill museum, went to the opera, saw five plays and three films, and spent two evenings with her brother Tom and Eloise Clawson, who was twenty-two years old, very petite, very blond, very pretty, and very well trained. The Clawsons owned a steel-fabricating plant in Oakland and about twelve acres of the residential section of Oakland as well. Miss Clawson said very little, looked at Tom adoringly, and prompted people to observe what a splendid couple they were.

At the end of the two weeks, Jean said to Barbara, "I know you've brought your manuscript with you, Bobby, and I've waited patiently for you to say something about it. But it appears that you won't, and I want desperately to read it. Could I?"

Barbara hesitated. "It's a novel, but it's also me. I'm very naked in it."

"I've seen you naked."

"You're sure you want to?"

"Of course I'm sure," Jean said. "Has anyone else seen it?"

"Not this version. You'd be the first."

Jean spent a whole day with the book, and when she finished, she said to Barbara, "I think it's splendid. Look, my dear, I know a literary agent in New York. His name is Harris Fielding. I met him in London ages ago, but I get Christmas cards from him, and I hear he's quite important. Why don't you send it to him?"

"I'll think about it, mother."

"You don't believe me, do you?"

"You know," Barbara said, "I considered tearing it up and forgetting about it. I've always loved you, mother, but now I've come to like you a great deal. You take it, and send it to him if you wish."

"I don't cry," Jean said. "More's the pity. I'd love to have a good cry now. You're the best thing that ever happened to me. Maybe the only good thing."

A month later, back in Los Angeles, Barbara received a letter from Harris Fielding. "My dear Miss Lavette," he wrote. "Once in a long while, a literary agent receives the manuscript of a first novel that is absolutely fine. Moments like that make the profession worthwhile. I love your novel. It is sincere, uninhibited, and totally gripping. Of course, I know your work, having read your 'Letters from Paris,' so the professional quality of your writing did not surprise me. The maturity of your outlook did, if you will forgive me, in one so very young. I don't think I'll have any difficulty placing this with a publisher."

Moody, at odds with herself since her return to Los Angeles, the letter sent Barbara's spirits soaring. She read it aloud to Dan and May Ling. "I can't believe it," she said, when their delight and excitement had spent itself. "I can't believe that I did it."

Three weeks later, a second letter from Fielding informed her that the novel had been accepted for publication by Halliday, one of the best New York publishers, and that they were paying an advance of three thousand dollars. The check accompanied the letter.

Part Five

DEPARTURE

Barbara was in San Francisco in June of 1941, when Sam Goldberg died. She was there for two reasons: her brother Tom's marriage was to take place on the twenty-first of June, and she had to attend to the final details that would establish the Lavette Foundation. As to the first matter, Tom was marrying Eloise Clawson, which everyone who knew them felt was an excellent match. The Clawsons were an old family, which in California meant that they had arrived there before the turn of the century: they had money, not as much as Tom but very considerable wealth; they were Episcopalian, which was the proper thing to be in their circle, and Miss Clawson was attractive enough for even the newspapers to refer to them as a "handsome couple." In addition to all these evident virtues, John Whittier approved of the match, explaining to Tom that while divorce was becoming increasingly commonplace, a person wise enough to structure a career for the future would do best to make a correct decision at the very beginning. Tom was not in love in the romantic sense, but he was fond enough of Eloise, who said very little and who always agreed with him. But then he had never been romantically in love with any other woman, and he agreed with Whittier that Eloise would make an excellent and advantageous wife. As for Barbara, the comparison between Eloise and Sally Levy could not escape her.

The Lavette Foundation was more demanding than the circumstances of Tom's marriage. Giving away a fortune of fourteen million dollars, Barbara discovered, was a complicated and long-drawn-out process. There was in Goldberg's office a man of thirty-six years who name was Harvey Baxter, who was one of Goldberg's two associates. Goldberg suggested him as one of the board of directors, and potentially as the manager of the fund. He also coopted Jean for the board, a function which she first resisted and then finally allowed herself to accept. With Barbara and Goldberg, the board would consist, at least for the moment, of four members. Baxter found a small house on Leavenworth Street, not far from Jean's house on Russian Hill, and the first financial action of the fund was to purchase the building as its headquarters. At first, Barbara, who was with Jean in the gallery house, felt that the small, narrow, old Victorian house would reduce problems. Then she discovered that there was renovating to be done, new wiring, repainting—a host of problems she had never faced before. She had sketched out plans for a new book, hoping to get started on it before her first novel appeared—certain now that the reviews would be devastating—yet weeks went by and still she was in San Francisco, first with the house, then finding an office manager, then a bookkeeper; and then, having extended her stay to June, she decided to remain for Tom's wedding.

It was on the ninth of June that she had a breakfast appointment with Sam Goldberg at his home. Mrs. Jones, the black woman who had been Goldberg's housekeeper for the past twenty years, looked somewhat puzzled as she admitted Barbara. "Was he expecting you, Miss Lavette?" she inquired. "He's still asleep. He been tired lately, and I don't want to wake him early, because if he don't want to sleep, he sets his alarm."

"He was expecting me," Barbara said.

"Then I go and wake him." She went upstairs and returned a few minutes later, shaken and frightened. "I can't wake him. Oh, God."

Barbara called the doctor, and a half-hour later, he told her that Goldberg had died in his sleep. "Not unexpected," he told her. "Man of his age, seventy-three, bad heart, bad habits, overweight. I warned him, but it does no good to talk to a man like Goldberg—"

"Oh, will you shut up and get out of here!" Barbara cried out through her tears. "Just do what you have to do and get out of here!"

Dan and May Ling came to San Francisco for the funeral, and in the group that gathered around Sam Goldberg's grave were people Barbara knew and loved and others who were only names to her: Stephan Cassala and his mother, Maria, who was Anthony Cassala's widow, and Sarah Levy, who had been married to her father's partner, Mark Levy, dead these many years and Jake and

Clair Levy, and Harvey Baxter, his associate, but not one relation by blood; and because of this, Barbara's grief was even deeper, that the old man whom she had come to love so much should be laid to rest with no blood relative to weep for him. She wept her own tears, feeling that the death of so many of those she loved was overwhelming and more than she could bear.

After the funeral, they gathered at Goldberg's house. Barbara had arranged with Mrs. Jones for food to be cooked and ready for guests, so they all crowded into the old Victorian parlor, with its green plush furniture and its lonely mementos of Goldberg's life. It was a strange afternoon and evening for Barbara, meeting the Levys again for the first time since they had been together so long ago in Paris, being clutched in the arms of Sarah Levy, weeping for herself and her dead husband, and seeing in the flesh the Stephan Cassala she had heard about for so many years. Before he died, Sam Goldberg had suggested to Barbara that Stephan Cassala would be an excellent choice for the Lavette Foundation's board of directors. "You don't know the Cassalas, Barbara," he said to her, "but take my word for it, they are as close as your own flesh and blood."

She had to struggle with herself to comprehend it, to equate her own upbringing with the old Italian woman, a shapeless lump in a black, floor-length dress, whom her father had kissed so tenderly and to whom he was now talking in his very poor Italian. Stephan Cassala was a tall, very thin, and rather good-looking man in his mid-forties. He had a long, thin nose, a mustache, and sad dark eyes. May Ling had told Barbara the story of his tragic romance, if it could be called that, with Martha Levy, who had died in an auto crash years ago. It was so very strange to meet people in the flesh whom one had known out of stories; and when finally she could take him aside and talk to him, she found Cassala gentle and charming.

"I know this isn't the time or the place, Mr. Cassala, but without Sam to hold my hand, the world is a very complex thing. Did he speak to you about the fund we set up, the Lavette Foundation, a very pompous name?"

Cassala nodded. "And call me Steve, Barbara. I can't very well call you Miss Lavette."

"Steve, yes. Then you know about it. If you can possibly find the time, I'd like to have you on our board."

"I'm very touched by that. Of course I'll find the time."

They were like shadows, more memories of memories than actual living people. The Cassalas had once been very wealthy, as had the Levys, as had her father. Now she had asked Stephan Cassala to help supervise a fund of some fourteen million dollars. Was he poor or rich? He was a manager of a bank, but that in itself made no one very rich.

Dan came over and put his arm around her. He wasn't good with words. She would think of him saying, "Poor kid—just too much death." But that was not the kind of a thing he would say. "Poor old Sam," he said. "Funny thing, Bobby, I had two Jews for partners. Nice people; neither one of them ever did a lousy thing. Back then, there were four of us, me and Tony Cassala and Mark and Sam. I was the wild, crazy kid—and there was always one of the others to bail me out. Well, they're gone. Mark's father was a peddler. Drove a wagon clean across the country, selling gewgaws to the Indians and the sodbusters, then he came here and stopped. Sam's father had a grocery or something in Sacramento. Tony was a stonemason. It was all so damn new, and now it's old and gone away forever." It was half non sequitur and half sense, and Barbara felt how much he was hurting inside. She took his arm from around her, squeezed it, and then led him into a corner.

"Daddy," she said gently, "we have to talk."

"Oh?"

"Tom's getting married. In two weeks."

"So I heard."

"Will you never see him or speak to him again? What sense does it make? Our lives are so short."

"Bobby, you're young. You have all the time in the world."

"No one has, daddy. I don't find much sense or reason in life. The God they told me about in Grace Cathedral up there on Nob Hill is either a lunatic or a comedian, and I don't have much rapport with either. The only thing I've found that makes any sense is love."

"That's a good deal, isn't it? Well, Tom is my son, but that's purely genetic. I haven't seen him in twelve years. I haven't been invited to the wedding. My goodness, Bobby, can you see those egg-sucking, ass-licking Clawsons inviting May Ling to their daughter's wedding? And what

would Tom say to her? I know what you're thinking. You'll
talk to Tom and arrange the whole thing. Well, it wouldn't
work. Tom's a twenty-nine-year-old stranger, and I don't
know him very well. It's not pride. Hell, I have nothing
to be proud of. If he comes to me and says, Lavette, I'd
like to get to know you—well, I'd like that. But I can't go
to him."

The following day, Dan and May Ling returned to Los
Angeles. Sam Goldberg's will had turned over his share of
the shipyard to Dan. Everything else, except a cash bequest
to his housekeeper, went to the Jewish Home for Orphaned
Children, the only exception being a string of pearls that
had belonged to his wife, which he left to Barbara.

Tom's wedding to Eloise Clawson took place on the
twenty-first of June. They were married by Father Temple-
ton, who had officiated at Seldon weddings and funerals
for the past thirty-five years, and the ceremony took
place at Grace Cathedral. The reception afterward was held
at the Clawson home in Berkeley, where two great striped
pavilions had been erected on the lawn. Jean wore a gown
of patterned blue-green chiffon with a matching garden
hat, and Barbara decided, with a sense of childish
satisfaction, that her mother was the most attractive
woman there, including the bride. "I couldn't come to the
funeral," Jean said to Barbara. "I know that I should have.
Do you know, I had come to like the old man a great deal,
and he was utterly devoted to you, but I couldn't come,
not with your father and May Ling there."

"I can understand that, but why didn't they at least
invite daddy to the wedding?"

"The Clawsons!" Jean exclaimed, looking around at the
assembled multitude under the striped pavilions. "My dear,
they are the ultimate Philistines. Your father would have
proper words for them. My own vocabulary is limited."

"He did." Barbara laughed. "You are absolutely wonderful. The Clawsons are the most proper people in the world.
And very rich."

"And the rich marry the richer. Of such is the kingdom
of heaven. By the way, have you spoken to your brother?"

"I kissed him."

"He found out that you had given away your birthright.
He is absolutely furious."

"Then I shall avoid him," Barbara decided.

"It would seem to me," Jean said, "that you are also

avoiding the young single men present. Bobby, love, you have the pick of the Bay Area here, and they are swooning over you. You are twenty-seven years old, you know."

"Only too well. Mother, have you ever tried to talk to one of the pick of the Bay Area?"

By the time the reception was over, Barbara had talked to a dozen of them. They crowded around her, first identifying the tall beautiful woman in beige crepe de Chine, then, excited at the thought that this was the groom's famous sister who had been arrested by the Gestapo and who had just inherited many millions of dollars, pleading their cases as best they could.

"But, you see, I live in Los Angeles," Barbara explained repeatedly.

"But no one lives in Los Angeles. That's impossible."

They were not original in their rejoinders, but Barbara felt fortified by their admiration. She said to Jean afterward, "It's my fault, and I don't like myself for it. They were very sweet and nice, but I don't want anything close with them. I can't, mother. I've shifted worlds. I don't know exactly what I mean by that, but it's the only way I can explain it."

The date for the publication of Barbara's novel, the final title being *A Long Way from Home*, was September 30, 1941. The news came in a letter from Fielding, her literary agent, who also informed her that the publishers would like to have a party on that date if she could come to New York. The final proofs of the book were waiting for her, along with the letter, when she returned to Los Angeles. She wrote to Fielding that she saw no reason why she should not come to New York in September; then she went over the proofs, beset with a growing feeling of lassitude and indifference. She felt choked in the tiny study in the house in Westwood. The wonderful sense of elation that had resulted from the acceptance of her manuscript was gone now. After the weeks in San Francisco, she felt isolated and bored. The notes she had put down as an outline for a second novel were suddenly inane and pointless, and she destroyed them one day in a fit of petulance. "Why am I here and what is happening to me?" she asked herself. Joe was gone, drafted, serving an internship in a naval hospital in San Diego. Dan was spending more and more nights at the shipyard, sleeping there. Barbara and

May Ling faced each other alone in the evening, night after night, sharing a kind of lonely despair.

It was May Ling who said to her one evening, "You can't go on like this, Barbara. You've stopped your life. Don't you see what you're doing to yourself?"

"I only know that I'm utterly miserable," Barbara said. "It seems that I want no one and nothing and I miss everyone and everything. My life is absolutely empty and pointless. I don't like the men I meet; I can't comprehend them. I can't write. I can't even want anything very much. And I have the sense of sitting alone in a world that has gone completely mad."

"I'm afraid the madness has only begun," May Ling agreed. "Why don't you go back to San Francisco? Stay with your mother until you go to New York."

"And leave you alone?"

"Oh, Bobby, I'll be all right. And you can do things there. The foundation is a wonderful thing. Make yourself take an interest in it. You can help people, and for the moment, that's the best way to help yourself."

"I'll think about it," Barbara said.

One day she drove out to Malibu and parked by a beach where the surfers were rolling in on the waves, standing, she told herself, like brown mindless demigods on their boards. The world was so easy for some. She kicked off her shoes and sprawled on the sand to watch; and presently one of them, tall, handsome, marvelously muscled, blue eyes under a thatch of sunburned, straw-colored hair, walked over to where she sat and said, "Try it, sis. You might like it."

"No suit," Barbara answered.

"Out here, who cares?"

"Force of habit," Barbara said.

"You're a good-looking dame," he said, sitting down beside her. "What's your name?"

"Barbara. What's yours?"

"Mike."

"What do you do, Mike?"

"In the summer I surf."

"Just that?"

"Sometimes I get laid. How about it? You and me, we could make sweet music."

Barbara laughed.

"Hey, I figured you'd get mad, spit in my eye or some-thing."

"Is that why you said it?"

"Sort of."

"No, I'm not mad. How old are you, Mike?"

"Eighteen."

"Go on and surf. I'll watch."

"You're watching the best," he said.

She watched for a while, then she went back to her car and drove off. The next day, she said to May Ling, "I'm going to drive up to Higate, to the winery. And then I'll stop by and visit with Jean in San Francisco. I hate to leave you like this, but I can't sit still and I can't write. Tell daddy not to worry. I'll call from San Francisco."

With Europe at war, Eloise had agreed to a honeymoon on Cape Cod, and since she was afraid of air travel, they crossed the continent by rail. After the first few hours on the train, in spite of the luxury of a double-bedroom suite, Eloise developed a migraine headache, and when Tom tried to initiate his first lovemaking, she whimpered in agony, the pain being too great to suffer a scream. Tom, who had surrendered his male virginity at the age of seventeen, and who had engaged in sex, either found or purchased, since then, had satisfied himself—insomuch as a man may —that his wife-to-be was a virgin, and he had zealously restrained himself from tampering with that virginity. He had his own concept of who Eloise really was, and he had not tried to test or reenforce that concept with any actual knowledge of his wife. Prior to their marriage, they had danced a great deal, gone riding a number of times, at-tended several dozen dinner parties, a number of beach parties, several picnics, and three Sunday mornings of wor-ship at Grace Cathedral, but they had never actually had a conversation with each other. That is, they had never carried their dialogue to the point where each discovered something deep or genuine about the other.

There were many hidden facets to Eloise's personality more complex and interesting than her migraine headaches —some of which resulted in the migraines; but Tom had no idea of these things, just as he had no idea that to Eloise he was the totally fitting, proper, perfect knight in white armor that she had dreamed about ever since reading, as a child, Howard Pyle's tales of the Knights of the Round

Table. She had never been able to tell him that she considered him the handsomest man she had ever known, and that ever since their first date she had lived and created an imaginary inner life that he and she shared. He never knew that she kept a diary, which she called "Poictesme" after the mythical land of James Branch Cabell, whose novels she had read over and over ever since her teens; and that in this diary were put down her expectations ever since meeting Tom Lavette.

On the other hand, Tom had never revealed any part of his own sexual fantasies. He had a deep-seated suspicion that he had never deflowered a virgin, although several girls he had known had insisted that such was the case; and Eloise's virginity scored highly in his imaginings. He was determined to have intercourse with her their first night on the train. Eloise, her eyes tightly closed against the light, could manage no more than a whisper, and in those muted tones she attempted to convey to Tom what a severe migraine headache was like. "Every jolt of the train is agony," she said to him. "Even the sound of my own voice hurts me."

"Well, God damn it, isn't there anything you can do?"

"I've taken aspirin and codeine and I'm so sick, Tommy. I wish I could die."

Tom left her, went into the lounge car, ordered an old fashioned, and got into a conversation with a well-dressed, rather good-looking woman in her thirties who was sitting in the next chair. He bought her a drink and learned that she was a buyer for Krempel's Department Store in Oakland. They each had two more drinks, and Tom went back to his compartment. Eloise was as he had left her, desiring neither food nor drink. Tom went to the dining car, and since there was an empty seat opposite the buyer from Krempel's, they resumed their acquaintance. She was divorced. He said little about his own situation, except to explain his naval uniform with the information that he was an officer on leave. Since she was to leave the train at Omaha, he felt fairly secure. After dinner, they went to her compartment, had some more drinks, and then went to bed. There was no need on Tom's part to seduce her; the buyer from Krempel's had made the decision much earlier, utterly enthralled by this handsome, slender young man in uniform. Tom, driven by his feelings of frustration and rejection, performed dutifully and without joy; then he made his way back to his own compartment.

Eloise's headache persisted all the way to Chicago, and there, during the few hours of stopover between trains, it finally disappeared. Tom took her to lunch at the Pump Room, and sitting across the table from him, Eloise, with shining eyes, told him how much his patience and consideration meant to her.

"I've been such a disappointment to you," she said. "But I will make up for it, Tommy. I promise you."

"Not at all." He was almost abject in his guilt, which Eloise translated into compassion.

"When we came here," Eloise said eagerly, "I saw how every woman in the room turned to look at you. I'm not a bit jealous, Tommy. I'm so proud. I took an oath last night that I would never again have a migraine—"

"But you can't help it," he said gallantly.

"But I shall help it. It will be mind over matter—only trains are so dreadful. Anyway, I know how lucky I am. I had a chat with Mr. Whittier, and he assured me that I was marrying the man who would one day be governor of California."

"Did John say that?"

"He did."

"Well, that's a long way off. If ever," he said modestly. "Anyway, you look very pretty."

"I suppose that the one good thing you can say about migraine is that when it stops, you just float away with good feeling. Do you like the dress? I feel silly in pink, but everyone says it's becoming."

"It's great."

But on the Twentieth Century Limited, going from Chicago to New York, Eloise's migraine returned; and Tom brooded in the lounge car, smoking too many cigarettes and asking himself, "How in hell did I ever get into this?" and remembering Whittier's warning to him, "For you, Tom, no divorce ever. Make up your mind about that at the very beginning."

Somewhere between Los Angeles and San Francisco, Barbara realized what she was going to do. It was like an idea planted long ago that had grown slowly, as if looking down for the first time in years, she had come to the notion of origin and what it meant; and instead of driving on to the Napa Valley, she stopped in San Francisco and went to her mother's house on Russian Hill. Jean was delighted to see her. The gallery was growing, and Jean bubbled with enthusiasm. The Nolde had arrived, and a quick trip to New Mexico had enabled her to acquire a painting of a buffalo skull by O'Keeffe. "Which ordinarily I would not have, but this one—isn't it splendid, Barbara?"

Barbara regarded it dubiously. "I guess so. Can I spend a few days here, mother?"

"Of course."

"And that money you put away for me, the account in the bank, how do I use some of it?"

"Very simple. Just go to the bank and fill out a withdrawal slip. Good heavens, they know you."

The following morning, Barbara walked to Sam Goldberg's office. She felt wonderful now. It was a clean, cool July morning, and she filled her lungs with the good salt air. This was her place, no question about that, and in all the world there was no other place like it.

At the office, Harvey Baxter welcomed her warmly. He had a wife and two children, the only reason he could contain his unabashed admiration of Barbara; and, mumbling his delight, he drew her into Sam Goldberg's old office, now his. "How very good to see you, Miss Lavette. This time, I hope you'll stay for a while."

"I think so." She plunged right in. "Harvey, I want to buy Sam's house."

"Oh?" He considered it, schooled in the fact that a lawyer should never respond immediately to anything.

"It hasn't been sold?" Barbara asked anxiously.

"Oh, no. No, indeed. The estate hasn't been settled yet."

"And you can sell it to me?"

"As the executor, yes—no reason why not, if you really want it. It's not a very fashionable house."

"Well, I do want it. How much will it cost me?"

"What a pity you never said as much to Sam! He would have left it to you in his will. Well, I can put a fair price on it—say, twenty thousand dollars. We can get you a mortgage for twelve, so that would be about eight thousand in cash." He was aware of the circumstances that had created the Lavette Foundation, and he asked her whether that was too much.

"Oh, no. No, the price is all right. What about the furniture?"

"You know, it's a strange case. Sam had absolutely no one in the world, not a single blood relation. Aside from the money he left to his housekeeper, Mrs. Jones, there were instructions that she could take anything in the house that she wished to have. Very odd, but then, Sam Goldberg was an original. You could say that, couldn't you?"

"I guess so. Where is Mrs. Jones now?"

"Still living at the house. Why don't you go by and see her."

"I will. Meanwhile, Harvey, the house is mine. Agreed?"

"Absolutely. I'll work it out for you."

On her way to Green Street, Barbara could hardly contain her excitement. Somehow, the simple fact that she had made the decision and would own the house changed everything. There was a place that was her own, at last, a place where the books, the walls, the pictures, would be hers. She had always loved the little house. It had been a place of refuge and security when she needed both desperately, and now it was such a place once again, when her need was almost as desperate.

Mrs. Jones opened the door, and her face lit up at the sight of Barbara. "I couldn't wish for no one more," she said. "I didn't think I'd see you again."

Barbara couldn't contain herself. "I bought the house, Mrs. Jones."

"This house?"

"Yes." And when the black woman's face fell, she added, "Oh, no, you don't have to leave—unless you want to."

Mrs. Jones led Barbara into the kitchen, and over coffee, they worked out an arrangement. When the transaction was completed and Barbara moved in, Mrs. Jones would stay on at the same wages Goldberg had paid her. There were a few things in the house that Mrs. Jones wanted as mementos. The rest, except for some pieces of furniture, Baxter would sell, giving the money to Mrs. Jones. At first the black woman refused, explaining that the ten thousand dollars she had received in the will was ample, more indeed than she had ever dreamed of having. But Barbara insisted, and finally Mrs. Jones assented.

That evening, Barbara called Los Angeles and spoke to May Ling and told her what she had done. "Please don't let daddy be hurt by this," she begged May Ling.

"He'll understand."

"I'm not choosing between him and Jean. You must

make him understand that. It's just that I must have a place that is completely my own, a place where I can work and live and be entirely with myself."

"I know." Yet when May Ling put down the phone, she felt a chill of cold fear. It was eight o'clock in the evening, and Dan was not yet home. He might call at any moment and tell her that he would not be home tonight. Joe was in the service, and day by day, the threat of war came closer. It was a time of death—her mother, her father, Sam Goldberg. If anything should happen to Joe, well then, she too would die. She walked around the house from room to room. How lonely it was, how empty, how desolate! The old Chinese superstition states that the spirit of the dead stays in his abode for three years, and even though May Ling disdained superstition, she would not dream of selling the house, even though Dan had suggested it, pointing out that a place like Palos Verdes was adjacent to San Pedro and one of the very best up-and-coming neighborhoods. She could leave her job at the library; the shipyard was making more money than he knew what to do with.

But May Ling would not hear of it. Leave her job? Then she would surely wither away. She could not tell Dan that she must live here, in this house, for at least three years after her mother's death, obedient to a superstition she had always scoffed at. Yet tonight, after speaking to Barbara, even superstition could not people the empty house, cold as a tomb.

It was after nine when Dan returned, and May Ling, as if seeing him for the first time, had an impression of a man close to exhaustion, tired and aging. He had not eaten. May Ling sliced ham, fried eggs, and opened a can of beans, apologizing for not expecting him and not cooking, but Dan said, "Baby, there's nothing in the world in the way of food I put ahead of ham and eggs and canned baked beans. You don't know how many years I lived on that."

"Ugh. Come home tomorrow, Danny, and I'll cook you a great Chinese dinner."

"I may just take you up on that."

"Barbara called from San Francisco," she told him.

"Oh?"

"She bought Sam Goldberg's house. From the estate."

Dan went on eating for a few minutes. Then he said, "For herself or for the foundation?"

"For herself. She's going to live there."

"Well, I had her for longer than I ever dreamed I would. I can't complain."

"I can," May Ling said miserably. "Oh, Danny, I'm so lonely and so unhappy. I suppose it's being Chinese. You grow up with a thing about a family, and there was always a family here. Now they're all gone, mom and pop dead, Barbara up there, Joe in the service, and you away so much. I don't want to whimper about it, Danny. I never have."

"I know."

"Do you still love me?"

Dan burst out laughing, almost choking on his mouthful of food, and May Ling cried out, "Don't laugh at me, Dan. I'm miserable and serious and deeply unhappy."

He swallowed the food, took a long gulp of the beer May Ling had poured for him, and said to her, "Now listen to me. I spent the morning with Admiral Land. He's out here again, and he brought with him two young smart-ass yard managers who were trained by the Maritime Commission and who know more about shipbuilding than I could learn in a hundred years. We have six ways now, and Land wants to put in five more. That's why I get the two yard managers. They'll run the whole works. In the next two months, we'll have eleven keels laid and two hundred and fifty workdays of shipbuilding ahead of us—"

"Danny, you haven't heard a word I said!"

"No? Well, listen. I told Land I was through, finished, that I didn't want the goddamn shipyard."

"You told him that?" May Ling whispered. "Danny, how could you?"

"Isn't that what you wanted?"

"Oh, no. No. You can't do that. Why do you listen to me? Betty Hargrave—she was head librarian and just back from her sabbatical in England—told me how it is. She saw them come back from Dunkirk and then she went through the bombing in London, and Danny, it's that one little island against those monsters—"

"O.K., now listen. You know, I'm beginning to like Land. He's a tough, mean old bastard, but Jesus, he's got the whole world on his back. He wouldn't let me walk out of it, and I'm not sure I really wanted to. He's opened up fourteen yards out here on the Coast, and mine is the best bet. In some ways, the man's a besotted genius. He's lined up over two thousand plants in eighteen states—cylinders, pistons, turbines, sheet steel, winches, compasses, cable—all of them being blueprinted and made and shipped and by God, we're building ships the way no one ever built them before, and this is only the beginning. Well, we worked it out. I'll supervise the building of the ways and the hiring of about three hundred men. That will take maybe eight, nine weeks. Then I'm taking three months off—the first vacation I've had since I started that lousy shipyard."

"Oh, Danny, how wonderful!"

"Hold on. What was the best we ever had it?"

"It's always been the best."

"All right, best of the best."

"Hawaii?"

"O.K. I called Matt Brady at Wilmington Shipping. He runs two cargo ships to Honolulu, big ones, sixteen thousand tons each. They take two passengers, just two, cabin twelve by sixteen, double bed, meals with the captain and ship's officers. Chinese cook who, according to Matt, has no equal. The *Angeles* sails from Wilmington on the twenty-sixth of September."

"Oh, Danny, Danny, is it true?"

"I booked the passage and sent him my check, so it has to be pretty damn true. Then I got on the horn to Hawaii and called Chris Noel—you remember the Noel brothers? We built the hotel with them, and then we lost it when everything crumbled in twenty-nine. Hell, they had no alternative. What do you suppose was the first thing he asked me?"

"Oh, Danny, I don't know."

"Was I bringing that beautiful Chinese gal with me? I told him we're married ten years now. Nothing else to it, but we got to stay with them at that huge plantation house of theirs they call a bungalow. I wasn't calling for that. Hell, we can afford a hotel."

"Danny, we'll stay with them. That wonderful place!"

"No way out of it. I said I was calling to see whether he still owned that lovely yawl of his and could we charter it for a few weeks? Charter it, hell! he said. It was ours. So there it is. I know you're miserable, but could you see your way to enduring your misery until September?"

"I'll try." She came around the table and hugged him.
"I'll try, Danny. I sure will try."

In the four years since he had become president of the
Seldon Bank and chairman of its board of directors, taking
over from Alvin Sommers in 1937, Martin Clancy had
restored his office to the dignity it had once—and properly, he felt—contained. Paint remover had disposed of
the ivory paint, revealing the walnut panels that Jean had
found so depressing. Her Aubusson rug had quietly made
its way to an auction gallery, to be replaced by a somber
and gloomy carpet, and her chintz-covered overstuffed
pieces were replaced by brown leather and dark mahogany.
Jean had removed her bright Impressionist paintings,
which had belonged to her, and now only the portrait of
the first Seldon hung on the wall behind Martin Clancy's
desk.

Clancy, past seventy now, was sitting behind the desk—
and figuratively behind the bank that he had guarded so
zealously all of his adult life—when Tom, a week back
from his honeymoon, entered the office. Clancy had been
expecting him, and he also had a very good idea of Tom's
purpose there. Clancy was a vigorous man, in good health,
a teetotaler and nonsmoker, and he greeted Tom with
enthusiasm, congratulating him on his marriage, his sun-
burn, and his uniform. "Old Tom would have been a
happy man to see his grandson in that uniform, oh, yes,
indeed. Well, Tom, I can guess what brings you here. With
your shares and with what John Whittier has bought from
your sister you're at the helm. A fine man, John. You
couldn't associate with a better one. Of course," he added,
"not literally. But the stockholders own the plant, don't
they?"

"I'm afraid they do," Tom agreed.

"Will you sit down? There's a good deal to discuss—if,
of course, you're interested."

"Oh, I am interested. But not today, Martin. Today I
just stopped by for a few words. I'm calling a meeting of
the board. I want you to step down. I intend to assume the
presidency and the chairmanship."

The words came out with the assurance and crackle of
a whiplash. Clancy had expected, from all he had heard,
a self-assured young man; he had also expected Tom to
suggest a place for himself on the board of directors; but

this kind of immediate demand and arrogance shook him, and it was a long moment before he was able to speak. "Well, Thomas," he said finally, "I can comprehend the legality of your position, and with the voting power of John Whittier's stock, which I presume you have—"

"I have, yes."

"—you have every right. Certainly. But my word, Thomas, you're in uniform, a most honorable uniform, and with the country teetering on the edge of war, surely you realize the responsibility that such a position would entail, the demands on your time—"

"Martin, don't let the uniform trouble you. My assignment is San Francisco, the Embarcadero, and if war comes, few things will outrank the Port of San Francisco in importance. So we can dispense with your patriotic confusion."

Clancy fell silent. He stared at his desk, then sighed, looked up at Tom, and said, "Yes, Thomas, it is your responsibility. I can see that. At least I'll be at your elbow to help you over the rough spots."

"Thank you, Martin, but no. I want you to resign from the board. You're seventy-two years old."

Clancy stared at him, took a deep breath, and said, "Thomas, I have served this bank for half a century, and I have sat on its board for thirty-two years."

"That's a long time. You'll appreciate a rest." And with that, Tom turned on his heel and left. Staring at the door he had closed behind him, Clancy whispered, "You little bastard—John Whittier's running dog. I'll see both of you in hell. If John Whittier thinks he can own this bank and California Shipping as well, he's mistaken. There's still law in this state."

A week later, Martin Clancy had a stroke that left him speechless and paralyzed. Whatever legal steps he might have thought of taking remained locked in his inarticulate skull.

Driving north from Napa, on Highway 29, Barbara saw the hitchhiker signaling for a lift, and she slowed to a stop. Ordinarily, she would have heeded the injunction against picking up a hitchhiker, but even in the glimpse she had driving past, there was something about the young man that made her step on the brake and roll to a stop. He could have been no more than eighteen or nineteen,

wearing jeans and a T-shirt, tall, skinny, a freckled grinning face under a mop of red hair.

"Gee, thanks, miss," he said as he got into the car.

"Where to?"

"About six miles up the road. I'll walk from there. I
should have walked from here, but it got too hot. My sister takes books out of the library at Napa and then forgets
to bring them back, so my father drove me down today
with the books, but then he had things to do, so I told him
I'd hitch back. Only nobody trusts anybody anymore. I
had just decided to give up and walk when you came by."

"Six miles. Well," Barbara said, "I think I'll get you
there. I'm going to a place called Higate, a winery. Do
you know where it is?"

"I sure do. I live there." He turned and stared at her.
"Hey, I'll bet I know who you are. You're Barbara Lavette.
Right?"

"Right."

"What luck! Sure, mom said you'd be driving up today.
I'm Adam Levy. Sally told me all about you. She's nuts
about you, you know. She thinks you're absolutely the
greatest."

"Well," Barbara said, "we're both lucky, aren't we? I'm
very pleased to meet you, Adam. How old are you?"

"Nineteen. I'll be a sophomore at Berkeley when school
starts, and now I'm working my way through the winery.
I get Saturday off. You've never been to Higate, have you?"

"First time. But I met your mother and father in Paris,
when I was living there."

"You bet. You were their interpreter, right? I know
your dad. He and my grandfather were partners, and I
guess you know all about the crazy sister of mine and your
brother Joe."

"Yes, I know."

"Not that I don't like Joe. We're great friends. In fact,
first operation I have—I mean, if I ever have to have one
—Joe is going to do. We got it all worked out. There's
a thing they call spinal anesthesia. You can have an operation and stay awake and not feel a thing, and Joe and I
got an agreement, he's going to give me that and I can
stay awake, and we'll discuss the whole thing, step by step,
and maybe he can rig up a mirror, so I can watch it.
What do you think of that?"

"I think you should stay healthy," Barbara said.

"Sure. But just in case. Anyway, I'm glad you decided to come, but you got to know that all wine makers are crazy. It runs in the family. Do you know what I'm majoring in? Viniculture. I don't care. Like they say, I don't have much ambition, and anyway, I sort of like the wine thing. But my brother Josh—he's seventeen—all he can talk about is getting out of here. You know, mom's father was a sea captain. She doesn't talk much about him. He went down in one of your father's ships off the English coast in the last war. Did you know that?"

Barbara nodded.

"He's Josh's hero, and Josh talks a lot about going off to sea. Mom thinks he'll grow out of it, but I don't know—"

By the time they reached Higate, Barbara had a fairly complete if confused history of the Levy family, and the feeling that the Levy children, if left to their own devices, could talk anyone deaf, dumb, and blind. Withal, Adam was charming, totally outgoing, and without self-consciousness—so much like his sister that Barbara could almost hear Sally in his words. There were moments during the drive when she stopped listening, absorbed by the gentle beauty of the place. She had not been to the Napa Valley since her childhood, and whatever memories she retained of that time only added to the bewitching charm of the place. The rolling, vine-striped hills undulated in the afternoon heat, the hot, midsummer sun beating down either mercilessly or benignly—as one saw it—and then giving way to the cool shade of the great oaks that lined the dirt road to Higate. Barbara understood immediately why the place had such a hold on Joe. The old stone buildings, covered with ivy from ground to roof, stood in happy agreement with the landscape. The vines draped the sloping fields, and on a high pasture, a cluster of cattle stood motionless, as if painted onto the yellow grass background. And everywhere a profusion of flowers, roses and marigolds and zinnias and banks of sweet alyssum.

Jake and Clair greeted her with affection, begging her to stay with them for at least two or three days. She protested weakly, already under the spell of the place, that she had come only for the day, but agreed to remain at least overnight. Sally embraced her with undiluted excitement. "Oh, how keen, how absolutely keen to have you here with us!" She whispered that they must have a private

talk just as soon as Barbara could get away. Joshua, as tall
as his older brother, was quiet, reserved. His greeting
was shy, diffident, and he stared at Barbara with uncon-
scious and unconcealed admiration. He carried her bag up
to her room, stood there staring at her until he remembered himself, and then said to his brother later, "She's
just so beautiful."

Clair came up to shoo Sally out of Barbara's room.
"Later," she said. "Right now, I wish to talk to Barbara
alone." And when Sally had reluctantly departed, Clair
said, "I have something for you, and it's none of my business, but it puzzles Jake and me. We're just so curious."
She took a letter out of the pocket of her apron. "It came
three days ago, and I knew you'd be coming here, so I
held it. I guess you were in San Francisco then. It's from
Sergeant Bernie Cohen, posted in Egypt six weeks ago,
and addressed to you, care of us. The odd thing is that
you asked us about a Bernie Cohen who had worked for
us—in Paris, remember? Did you meet him?" Barbara was
staring at the letter. "Is it the same person?" Clair asked.

"Yes," Barbara whispered. "The same person."

"How on earth do you know him?"

"Can I tell you later?" Barbara asked her. "I'll tell you
the whole story. Right now, I think I have to be alone."

"Of course. Of course. Dinner in an hour and a half.
But take your time, Barbara. We'll wait for you."

After Clair had closed the door behind her, Barbara
sat on the bed, staring at the letter. At last she opened it
and began to read:

"My very dear Barbara," it began. "The fact that I have
not written until now, two years since I saw you, does not
mean that you have ever been out of my thoughts. Let's
say that it took most of that time for me to convince myself that there was any point in writing to you. But don't
misunderstand that. I simply mean that the odds against
my ever seeing you again are so great that for a long time
I felt that the best thing I could do was to disappear from
your life completely. The few hours I spent with you were
the best in my life, and I really don't know of any other
way to put it. In any case, the mails are so uncertain, just
as life is, that for you to receive this letter will be a minor
miracle. That gives me some leeway and I can argue that
I am mostly talking to myself. Although, believe me, mir-

acles do happen. My meeting you was in the nature of a miracle. I don't know of any other way to explain it.

"Now let me say immediately that I am O.K., stupidly healthy, and still unwounded. I struck up a friendship with one of the Indian troops here. His name is Rama Kee, and he talks a lot about a thing called karma. He insists that my karma is something that is taking care of me for some purpose, which to me is a lot of nonsense, but since he's five foot three and I'm twelve inches taller, it's the only reasonable explanation for my not being hit.

"I'm wandering too much, and the best thing for me to do is to begin when I walked out of your apartment that morning. I must admit that I took satisfaction in being dead broke. The only thing I could give you was not to take from you, if that makes any sense. Would you believe that I walked all the way to Villeneuve? Not that I couldn't have gotten a lift, but I had a lot to talk over with myself, and the only way I can do that is to walk. Half a dozen times I started to turn back, because I began to see that I had cut out of myself the only damn thing that was any good whatsoever, but the Cohen strength of character carried me on. It was dark when I reached Villeneuve. I guess I had walked about twenty miles, mostly along the river, with a lot of time off when I sat down by the river and brooded and finally convinced myself that what happened between us was a matter of gratitude on your part and by no means any indication of your being able to actually care about a man like me.

"A Spaniard by the name of Raol Garcia has a café in Villeneuve, and I lucked in there and got to talking about the war, and well, to make a long story shorter, he had a brother who was killed in the Spanish fighting, and when he found out that I was with the Internationals, he couldn't do enough for me. I got a meal and a place to sleep, and the next day, his brother-in-law drove me down to Lyon in his truck. From there, I hitched my way to Marseille. I'll try to be brief, otherwise this letter will have no end, so I'll leave out the details. The thing is that when a Jewish kid finds himself a strange town, he can always get himself a bed and a handout at the local synagogue—which is what I did in Marseille. There I ran into another Spanish vet, a kid by the name of Brodsky, from the Bronx in New York. He had been there for a while and had teamed up with a couple of Marseille men who had bought an old fishing trawler and were running Jewish refugees from Germany and Eastern Europe into Palestine. They needed another hand on the boat, someone who could put together and use a 20 millimeter machine gun that they had bought from a Turkish arms peddler. So right there, I had the kind of a break I had dreamed about.

"For the next three months we ran the boat between Marseille and the Palestine coast. Sleeping people on the deck, we could take anywhere from twelve to twenty, and I guess that during that time we took better than three hundred people into Palestine. It wasn't all altruism on the part of the two French guys who owned the boat, not by any means. For them, it was a damn good business proposition. They took whatever the traffic would bear, and they paid me and Brodsky two hundred francs a month, because, as they put it, we were stupid idealists. They made a bundle, but at least when they were going to turn down someone who didn't have enough for the passage, Brodsky and I could kick up enough fuss to get most of them on board.

"It came to an end when an Italian destroyer put a shell through our hull off the coast of Palestine about ten miles south of Haifa. We had already landed our passengers, so there were just the four of us on the boat. That was the first time I ever tried to use the 20 millimeter, which was just dumb. Brodsky and I made the shore. We never found out what happened to the two Frenchmen. Maybe the Italians picked them up. Funny thing is, we didn't even know that the war had started. And the Italians weren't even in it. They probably figured we were running Jewish illegals and why not shoot us out of the water, or maybe they just wanted target practice.

"We weren't wearing shoes, and we had to hike inland about three miles before we found a kibbutz. I don't want to remember what our feet were like. Anyway, there we were, finally, in Palestine, so if this letter ever reaches you through the Levys, you can tell them that I made it at last, just as I said I would when I went to work for them seventeen, eighteen years ago.

"I'm going to try to get this letter out without putting it through the censorship, but just in case I can't, I won't put down the name of the kibbutz. Things are pretty hellish in Palestine. Many of the kibbutzim are under constant Arab attack. The British confiscate their weapons

and just make it hard all around. This kibbutz was in a
bad way. They had a lot of attacks, and they just didn't
know much about defending themselves, and their whole
armament was four old Mauser rifles and two Webley pis-
tols. Barbara, I know how you feel about war and fighting
and killing, and I think that by now I hate it more than
you do, but there we were, me and Brodsky, and I guess
we knew more about this kind of fighting than anyone
in the British army of occupation. Either we got arms
and ammunition or the kibbutz would be wiped out sooner
or later. So Brodsky and myself, we trained six guys and
we organized what is called a night squad. We would bribe
an Arab to tell us where there was an arms depot, and
then we'd go out at night and raid it. It was dirty, nasty
work, but it served two purposes. It stopped the raids on
the kibbutz, and it gave us the arms and ammunition we
needed so desperately.

"Now, looking over what I've written already, I have to
say to myself that nothing here is going to make you think
very highly of me, knowing how you feel, but that's what
happened, and I suppose we do what we have to do. Then
what happened to me was this. We would have discussions
in the kibbutz about what would happen after the war or
maybe during it, when the Arabs decided that the Jews
had to be eliminated, and hearing all the stories coming
out of Germany and Poland, we decided that there was
no other place in the world for the Jews to come but here
in Palestine. So we had to find a new way to fight and
defend ourselves. Most of the opinion was that somehow
or other we had to have an air force, which is something
to laugh at since there wasn't one Jewish plane in Palestine
and maybe not one Jewish pilot. But anyway, that's the
way everything goes in the Jewish settlements. They talk
about tanks, and there are no tanks. They talk about artillery, and there's no artillery. The same with the air force.
They decide we have to have an air force, so we have to
have pilots, and then everyone votes and I'm elected to
join up with the British and learn to fly a fighter plane.
It sounds crazy, but that's the way everything is done
around here, and they say, Just learn to fly and then we'll
find a plane for you.

"That's how I came to enlist in the British army. The
British recruiting officer tells me, Cohen, you want to be
a pilot, we'll train you. And how I can be stupid enough to

believe anything a British army recruiting officer tells me
is simply the story of Bernie Cohen, and the main reason
why he'll never be rich or smart. The year that followed
is something you must read about. It began with them
finding out about my Spanish war record, so in their eyes
I became a red and a Zionist, which is the worst combination in the world, and for two months I was in a labor
battalion, digging ditches in Eygpt and building pillboxes
and gun emplacements. Then they decided that my talents
were being wasted, and they forgave the past and made me
a rifle instructor. Then I was promoted to corporal and
machine guns, and then I made sergeant, which is what
runs the British army, because when it comes to brains,
their officers are nothing to write home about. I was put
in command of a kind of tin truck called a Bren gun
carrier, and we were going to try to hold Egypt in that
wonderful British kind of dumb desperation against
Graziani. We had about 20 men and Graziani had some
three hundred thousand and a whole air force and maybe
close to a thousand tanks. Well, not exactly. We had three
divisions and a lot of these Bren trucks and a few tanks.
We waited for the Italians until December, and then
Wavell sent out a patrol of some Bren trucks and some
tanks, and we found a hole in the Italian lines, and then
we kept on going. I know this is no way to write about a
battle, but I don't want to write to you about any battle.
You probably read all about it in the newspapers at home.

"I guess the Italians had no heart for the war or for the
fascists, because in the next three months we destroyed
the Italian army and took over a hundred and fifty thousand prisoners. With the karma that my Indian friend
talks about, I was not even scratched. The worst that happened to me was a bout of amoebic, and I'm over that
now. I'm back in Egypt, training men again, and still trying to work my way into the air force, like the kibbutz
elected me to do. But it doesn't look much like it. Anyway, I have plenty of time to think now and to catch up
on a lot of reading and to try to make some sense out of a
life that doesn't make very much sense up to now.

"This letter has been written over three days, and when
I began it I did not intend to do anything more than
satisfy your curiosity. I am convinced you must have
thought about me once or twice and wondered if I were
alive or dead. So I felt that I had a sort of obligation to tell

you that I was alive, and something about how I have been filling my time. Being so very far away from you gives me the courage to write that I think about you constantly, that I believe I love you more than I have ever loved any other woman, and that you are the best and most wonderful thing that ever happened to me in my whole life. These are my own rambling thoughts. For all I know, you may be married. You may have a kid. I won't even ask you to write to me, so if this letter ever reaches you, you can tear it up and throw it away. As for me, I think this war will go on for a long, long time."

Barbara finished reading, and she sat there with the letter in her hands. It was much as if Cohen had transmitted his loneliness to her. How much had she thought about him, how many times? Certainly not constantly. There were times when weeks had gone by without any thought of him at all, but there were other times when his big, slow-moving figure lived in her mind's eye, and she had wondered at those times how he could be a soldier, his movements so slow, almost lazy; and she would remember the rapt attention with which he had listened to all she had said that evening. Well, she was not in love with him; she had never been in love with him. Her heart went out to him, but her heart had gone out to other men, and that did not mean that she loved them. How could she feel anything toward a man who deliberately took up killing as his vocation? She told herself firmly that she would not budge from a conviction as deep as any she had ever held, that killing was the ultimate monstrosity, the ultimate evil, and that to justify it in war or in any other struggle was compounding the evil with the most hideous of sophistries.

The door opened as she sat there, and Sally entered the room very tentatively. "Bobby?"

Barbara looked up at her.

"Oh, Bobby, darling, what happened?"

Barbara shook her head.

"You're crying."

"No." She touched her cheeks and they were wet. "Am I? I didn't know."

"It's that letter, isn't it?"

"This?" She held it out to the girl. "Do you want to read it?"

"I shouldn't. Should I?"

"Yes. I want someone to read it. I think you should."

Sally nodded very seriously, took the letter, and sat down
next to Barbara, who put her arm around her as Sally read.
When Sally finished reading it, she asked, "Bobby, why
did you want me to read it?"

"I had to talk to someone about it."

Sally threw her arms around Barbara and hugged her.
"Oh, Bobby, I love you so much. I do. And I understand.
I do understand. It's a wonderful letter. And he sounds so
sad and so lonely and so far away."

"I'm being absolutely silly."

"Oh, no, you're not."

"I barely know him. The truth is, I hardly know him at
all. I spent one evening with him. I don't love him. I don't
love anyone at all, and that's what's so awful. I feel that
I'm drying up and becoming something I don't want to
be."

"Bobby, you're the most beautiful, wonderful woman in
the world. Don't you believe me?"

Barbara stared at Sally, then suddenly burst into laughter. "You're so good for me," she said.

"Am I, truly? Please stay here. At least for a few days.
This is a wonderful place, and I'll take you everywhere
and show you everything. We all love you, Jake and
Clair, and my brothers are just gaga about you, and
Josh—well, Josh is absolutely swooning over you. Will
you let me show you my poetry?"

"Absolutely."

"You won't laugh at me? You're such a good writer—
you won't laugh at me?"

"Never. You'll show them to me right after dinner, will
you?"

"Oh, Bobby, I do love you."

On the morning of the twenty-sixth of September, 1941,
May Ling pulled down the shades of the house in Westwood, checked the gas jets on the stove, and then turned
the key in the lock. Dan had already stowed their bags in
the cab. Grinning, excited, wearing white duck trousers
and a sport shirt, he stood by the cab and waited for May
Ling. With her back to him, dressed in a simple linen
frock, she might well have been the girl he met a quarter
of a century ago. "Come on, come on," he called to her.
"We go out with the tide at three o'clock."

In the cab, she said to him, "Danny, it's only ten

o'clock. We have five hours. I've never seen you this way before."

"Because I've never been this way. Do you realize that I'm fifty-two years old, and I've never had a real vacation before. Not even that trip to the Islands. That was business. May Ling, I hate this thing called business. I hate the whole rotten rat race. There was a real estate agent in my office the other day. I had to practically throw him out. He wanted to sell me one of those big barns of a house in Beverly Hills. He kept saying I could afford it. Word's around that we're rich. How in hell did that happen? Well, let me tell you this. We may just never come back. Do you remember that beach on the big island?"

"Dodo Beach?"

"Right. A mile of white beach, tucked into paradise."

"That's nice, Danny, 'tucked into paradise.' "

"Well, I may just stay there and never leave it. Live on seafood. Spear fish. Let my beard grow. Barefoot. Naked, God damn it."

"You don't like fish, Danny. And I'm not sure I'd like you with a beard."

"You'd get used to it."

"And all the lovely dresses I bought to wear at the Noels'?"

"Wear them. What the hell!"

The ship, the *Angeles*, had just finished loading when they arrived in Wilmington, and the deckhands were battening down the five big hatches and making fast the booms. Matt Tubman, the first officer, greeted them on the dock and got a seaman to carry their luggage on board. Tubman was a slender, redheaded man in his thirties. "You're on the boat deck, Mr. Lavette, cabin five. If you just trail along after Brady there, you'll find it. None of the amenities right now because we got hung up on late cargo, and we got to go out on the tide. But we'll all get together at dinner. Just make yourself at home on board."

"Do you like her?" Dan asked May Ling.

"Danny, I'd love her if she were a rowboat."

"We're up there," he said, pointing. "This is the main deck. Boat deck next, and we'll have that pretty much to ourselves. Over that, the quarterdeck, and then bridge, topside, and flag-deck. She carries four lifeboats and a couple of rafts, and those big things sticking up are called kingposts."

"Yes, Danny."

"You might as well know. She's home for the next six days."

"Yes, Danny, of course."

The cabin was large and comfortable, opening onto the boat-deck. They were unpacking when the door opened and a short, dark man with an enormous beak of a nose poked his head in and announced that he was Minelli, the purser. "Anything you want, just yell for me, Mr. Lavette. We only carry two passengers, but we treat them better than any ocean liner. You know, I worked one of your ships in the last war, the *Frémont*. I was just a deckhand then." They shook hands.

"By golly," Dan said, after the purser had left, "why didn't we do this years ago. Let's go to bed."

"Danny, we haven't unpacked. The ship is still tied up on the dock."

"Hell, we got two hours before she sails, and I haven't touched you in two weeks."

"Lock the doors," May Ling said.

Naked, she stood in front of him and said, "Do you really still want this withered old Chinese lady? Do you, Danny?"

"Do you know, baby, it's like the first time," he replied, looking at her slight, supple body, the ivory skin, the tiny breasts, as small and firm as when she had first stood before him like that, naked in the hotel room on the Peninsula. "You haven't changed."

"Danny, flattery will get you everything and everywhere."

They were both like kids. They made love as if it had never happened before, and then he sprawled in bed with her body curled up against his stomach, her head in the cradle of his arm, telling him, "How I always loved you the way you are, hard and hairy, a whole, huge, nasty barbarian of a man just the way you are, Danny Lavette, and I guess I am the luckiest woman in the whole world."

"Very true."

"Where are you going?"

"To get a cigar."

"Oh, no, you wouldn't."

"I have two boxes of the best Havana, and sex and a good cigar, my love, are all that any man should dream of."

Later, dressed again, they stood on deck and watched the *Angeles* being warped out of the harbor by tugs. "Do you feel any pangs, Danny, at leaving it—that great, wonderful shipyard you created?"

"Not a pang, not a twitch. I'd give it to the low bidder in a minute."

There were five of them at dinner in the captain's mess—Anson Ulman, the captain, Jack Gordon, the engineer, and Matt Tubman, the first officer. And Dan and May Ling. May Ling wore a white suit and a cotton print blouse. She had used makeup carefully and delicately for the first time in months, and her black hair, cut in bangs across her brow, fell in a rich, helmetlike pageboy cut to her shoulders. The effect on the three seamen delighted Dan, and afterward he told May Ling how Gordon had whispered to him, "That's a young and bonnie wife you got, Lavette." The ship's officers outdid themselves in gallantry, Ulman, a white-haired Swede, telling her that she must make free use of the bridge and that he would be honored to show her the working of the ship. Gordon invited her to the engine room, "When it is your pleasure, ma'am. It's a hot but interesting place down there." The food was plain but good, and while the conversation was not brilliant, it was sparked, as Dan noticed, by May Ling's charm and curiosity.

After dinner, the sun already hull down, as the seamen said, they walked on the boat deck, their own private deck to all effects and purposes, and watched the crimson horizon blend into night.

They fell into an easy, unhurried routine for the six days of the passage. May Ling had chosen a few books very carefully—the collected poems of Robert Frost, Saroyan's latest book, *My Name Is Aram, The Ox-Bow Incident,* and *For Whom the Bell Tolls.* She also brought an old copy of "The Ancient Mariner," a poem that Dan had never heard before. He had no taste for reading poetry himself, but he loved to hear May Ling read; and he was content to lie in a deck chair for hours while she read poetry to him. She had a soft, musical voice, and for Dan, lying in the sun, listening to her voice, feeling the wash of the sea air across his face, was as close to complete happiness as he had ever come.

Other times they played jack-o'-diamonds, but more

often than not they passed hours walking about the ship, chatting sometimes with the seamen, or again just sitting in their deck chairs, side by side, in a comfortable silence.

Just as Captain Ulman had insisted that they be his guests on the bridge, so that he might instruct May Ling on the wonders of the chronometer case, explaining that the nine fine clocks it held were necessary "because there is no clock that is perfect, not to a fraction of a second. But with those nine beauties, we're never off a moment," so did Gordon lure them down into the noisy hell of the engine room, where oil-fired boilers of seven hundred and fifty degrees of superheated steam drove steam turbines, which in turn drove two thick propeller shafts. She was led through the inferno of heat and noise, watching the engine crew checking the guages, studying the dials, opening valves, adjusting the fires, oiling, constantly oiling, the long, smooth propeller shafts. "But it's so clean," May Ling said—or rather shouted—in amazement, her mouth against Gordon's ear.

"Ay, and so it must be. Like your kitchen, dear lady, like your kitchen."

So tight with pressure and tension and the roar of sound was the place that May Ling could not wait to be out of there. "Oh, not for all the money in the world would I work there," she said to Dan when they were on deck again.

"I know, but the oilers and wipers and engineers—they'd work nowhere else."

"And in a war, Danny, what happens when the ship is hit?"

"The boilers burst. And then God help them. To die in seven hundred and fifty degrees of superheated steam, roasted alive—well, it's not something you want to think about. The bastards who make wars don't think about it. You can be sure of that."

"I don't think I can ever be on a ship again without thinking about it. I don't want to go down to the boiler room again."

The days passed. Bit by bit, the knots in Dan's soul and mind unraveled and untangled. People love each other, but no one remains in love, for whatever "in love" is; but bit by bit, day by day, the large, lumbering, gray-haired shipbuilder rediscovered the tiny Chinese woman he had married and fell in love again in a way that he had never imagined possible.

More and more frequently, Jean found that she was altering her first impressions of people. Her first impression of Eloise Clawson, who was now Eloise Lavette, was of an empty-headed fluff of a girl with nothing except her good looks and her people's money to recommend her. At the wedding, Jean had detected a note of fear, a tremulousness, a sense of something sensitive and full of pain that Eloise herself was perhaps only half aware of.

The day after Tom and Eloise returned from their honeymoon, Jean telephoned them at the apartment on Jones Street. Eloise answered the phone. "I thought I might drop by," Jean said. "We could lunch together, if you're free."

"Oh, please, please. Yes, Mrs. Lavette—I mean Mrs. Whittier. I don't know why I said that, but Tom—"

"Don't give it a moment's thought," Jean said. "People do it all the time. You must learn to call me Jean, and then, you see, it won't matter."

Eloise was dressed and ready when Jean arrived, nervously precise and pretty in a pale blue shantung suit and a blue chiffon blouse with a bow at the throat. With her white gloves and her tiny straw hat, she appeared almost unreal, as if she had been dressed by someone else and set to pose. But when Jean kissed her, Eloise clung to her and said desperately, "But you will be my friend, won't you?"

"What is it, my dear?"

Eloise shook her head.

"Tell me about it. You can talk to me."

"I'm so miserable."

"What happened?"

"I don't know. I get these dreadful migraine headaches. I did get them once in a while before I married Tom, but then they began to come all through the honeymoon, one after another. I don't blame Tom. Who wants to be with a person in such awful pain?"

"Have you seen a doctor about this?" Jean asked gently.

"Oh, yes. Mother used to take me to doctor after doctor, and they all said the same thing."

"And what was that?"

"That no one knows anything about migraine headaches.

Some of them said it was psychosomatic, that I did it to myself because I have what is called a migraine personality, but that doesn't do any good even if it's true, because I can't stop doing it to myself. And then Tom just gave up and stopped talking to me, and then another attack would come and I could see that he was furious with me. I don't blame him, but I'm so absolutely miserable—"

"Eloise darling, listen to me."

"Yes."

"We shall go out now and have an excellent lunch, and we will not talk anymore about headaches. I know Tom very well indeed, and I think we can work out some devious plan, just between us. Then I want you to come to my house with me and look at the gallery I am putting together."

"I don't know anything about pictures. I've come to feel so stupid, so worthless."

"Exactly the way I felt for a very long time. The sensation should be called the woman's disease, and the microbe that transmits it is of the other gender. You are not worthless and you are not stupid. You are a very pretty and bright and good-hearted young woman."

"You're not saying that just to make me feel better?" she asked plaintively.

"Of course I am. I want you to feel better. I'm also saying it because it happens to be true. So let's start to get to know each other. I think we're going to be good friends."

William Halliday, Barbara's publisher, was in his mid-forties, recently divorced, and quite attractive, with a long, narrow head, dark eyes under a shock of black hair, horn-rimmed glasses, and a tall, lanky figure. He wore a gray flannel suit, a button-down shirt that was slightly frayed, and a striped tie with the Harvard colors. He was charming, cultured, and protectively possessive of Barbara. He had arranged for her to stay at the Algonquin Hotel, purchased her plane tickets to New York, met her at the airport himself, and saw her settled in her hotel. Halliday's was a small, distinguished, and very successful publishing house; it had weathered the Depression by carefully presenting a small list of talented writers and developing a reputation for literary quality. Several national best sellers had put the firm on a sound financial basis, and now Halliday was convinced that in Barbara Lavette he had found what he had been searching for, a young writer with a clean, lucid style, a sense of the fitness of things, a feeling for drama, and an underlying and intense passion. He had never seen her until he met her at the airport, and having spent most of his adult life in the company of writers, he was hardly prepared for the tall, clear-eyed, beautiful woman who took his hand firmly and greeted him without formality or coyness. He noted with satisfaction that she rejected the silly pompadours that had become all the rage, instead gathering her honey-colored hair in a bun at the back of her head, and he also approved of the blue serge tailored suit and the blue kid shoes. In common with most sophisticated New Yorkers, Halliday regarded the western part of the United States dubiously, and he was excited at the prospect of a potentially best-selling writer who looked like this.

The following day, he took Barbara to lunch at Sardi's Restaurant on West 44th Street. It was the first time she had ever been there, and the place delighted her with its feeling of the theater, its walls covered with framed caricatures of theater people, and its resemblance to European restaurants. Men came to their table to be introduced to her, and Barbara was astonished at how many of them had read a book not to be published for three more days. The praise they offered made her uneasy and self-conscious and one of them, a playwright whose name she recognized, made his plea for the right to dramatize the book as a stage play.

"Time enough for that," Halliday told him. "Anyway, I'm only the publisher, not the agent."

"You see," he said to Barbara, "this is only the beginning. Have a stout heart, a ready smile and believe nothing. It's rather unusual for a first novel to be successful, but our advance sales appear to indicate a very substantial success. That might very well mean a theatrical dramatization and then a movie sale, but that's in the future. Right now we want to sell books, a great many of them. I hope you won't mind being lionized?"

"Is there any way out of it?"

"Oh, yes. You can flee back to San Francisco, if you wish."

"I don't wish," Barbara said firmly. "I've been to New York before, but somehow this is different. I feel that it's so good to be here. I've never really taken the time to see the city, to walk, to look at it the way I would look at Paris."

"Then nothing would please me more than to be your guide. If you need one. Well, even if you don't need one."

"I couldn't impose on you."

"Ah, let me decide that. Meanwhile, here are some of the tasks we've laid out for you. Day after tomorrow, the day before publication, a cocktail party at the Algonquin. Alexander Woollcott is dying to meet you. He'll be there, reporters, celebrities, writers—it will be an ordeal, make no mistake. Tomorrow, interview on WJZ in the morning, WEAF in the afternoon. Have you ever done a radio interview?"

Barbara shook her head.

"Well, the question that will be thrown at you most often is, how much of the book is true? I suspect a great deal of it. Am I right?"

"It's hard to say. I mixed fact and fiction. I suspect that even if one attempts to write very truthfully of oneself, it's so subjective that it is a fiction of sorts."

Halliday nodded. "That's a good approach. By the way, you'll have Hildy Lang with you. She's our PR woman, very good, very competent. She'll smooth over some of the rough spots. The New York *Times* and the *Herald Tribune* both want pictures and interviews for their book sections, and I think they want you to give a talk at Sarah Lawrence College, as a rather famous alumna."

"Good heavens, I'm not famous and I haven't the vaguest notion of what I would talk about and I never even graduated."

"No matter. You'll think of something. Barbara—you don't mind if I call you that?" She shook her head. "Barbara, just say no to anything that feels like a burden. I am a greedy, avaricious publisher, so don't hesitate to reject our notions."

Again and again during the time that followed, Barbara had opportunities to reflect on what the course of things would have been had she been plain, homely, old, or fat; and she felt a growing irritation with a world that dwelt on the fact that she was, according to how they put it, fascinating, lovely, beautiful, sensational—her face and figure rather than what she had written. The first radio interviewer said, "I wish my audience could be here with me in the studio, facing this very beautiful young woman who has written a novel that will surely be one of the most talked about books of 1941. I want you to meet Miss Barbara Lavette."

"What does one say to that?" Barbara wondered.

One says, "How do you do, Al." She had met him an hour before. "We begin with introductions. You call me Al. I'll call you Barbara."

"How much of your book, Barbara, is based on fact? This man who died in Spain, was he actually your lover?"

"How do you feel about the Nazis? Can we live with them? Or must we fight them?"

"Do you feel that there are good Germans?"

"Why does a girl with everything in the world leave home and go to a foreign country? Now that's a part of your experience."

"Do you feel that explicit sex is the wave of the future in novels?"

Hildy Lang, small, dark, efficient, and easily familiar with this strange world Barbara had entered, complimented her. "Great! Simply great! You handled that beautifully."

"I didn't handle it at all."

"Oh, yes, absolutely. Now, Barbara, the Prince Carelli people want to use you."

"Who? What on earth is Prince Carelli?"

"My dear, you have been a recluse. Only the most popular perfume around. They do movie stars and that sort of thing, and now they've decided that a gorgeous author is exactly what they need. They'll photograph you with the book in your hands, and there'll be some little statement about how you love the slop they sell. It's terribly good for the book and they'll pay five hundred dollars, which isn't exactly peanuts."

"Hold on! You're telling me you want me to pose for a perfume ad for something I never even heard of?"

"Darling, it's done all the time. Of course, if you don't want to—Bill says you're the boss."

"I don't want to," Barbara said emphatically.

She stayed up half the night writing her talk for Sarah Lawrence. She had never before in her life spoken from a platform or made a public address anywhere under any circumstances, and now, facing a hall packed with eager, wide-eyed young women, she froze in terror, tried to speak, and discovered that no sound emerged from her paralyzed vocal cords. "Good heavens, what do I do now?" she asked herself. "I suppose I could fall in a faint, but if I did, I'd probably fracture my skull. That would be just my luck. How—how did I ever get into this?"

She took a deep breath, and then said slowly and deliberately, concentrating on making her vocal cords do what they were supposed to do, "You are all wondering, no doubt, why I am standing here in such grim silence. The answer is very simple. Until a moment ago, my vocal chords were paralyzed." Unexpectedly, there was a ripple of applause and a burst of laughter. Barbara took courage. "Strangely, they're the same vocal chords I've lived with all my life, so the reaction was unexpected. But understandable, since this is the first time I have ever made a public address in my life, and if I have anything to say about it, it will also be the last time." Again, applause and laughter. Barbara still had not looked at her written address. She didn't dare to; her memory of it was of a rigid, awkward, and pretentious reflection on writing, youth, and college days.

"I'm a bit afraid to listen to my voice, for fear it will go away, and if I talk rather quickly, it's only to get something said before I go dumb again. I think it was Mark Twain who wrote about the man who discovered, with a good deal of awe and excitement, that he had been speaking prose all of his life. That just about sums up my knowledge of the art of writing. I never did better than a B in Lit, which is a reflection on my intelligence or lack of it, not on the local department, and then, when I was living in Paris, I was lucky enough to be in the right place at the right time, and I was actually paid for writing a weekly 'Letter from Paris.'" She went on, never looking at her notes, just talking.

"This morning, I was being interviewed by a radio announcer, and he asked me where I got my ideas. Being a writer or being interviewed seems to bring out the worst in me, and I replied that I got them from Schenectady, from the Schenectady Idea Service, to which I was a subscriber and to which I paid an annual fee of two hundred dollars. This upset him terribly, and he assured the listener that I was only joking and that there was no such institution as the Schenectady Idea Service." She had to wait until the laughter and the applause died away. "Well, I really don't have much more to say. I made some notes, but I don't think they're any good. It's wonderful to be back here, and I sort of wish I had never left. I'm only half-educated, and perhaps someday I'll have enough courage to come back and finish college."

To Barbara's amazement, her talk was a huge success. Hildy Lang looked at her with new respect, and those of the faculty whom she had once known crowded around with praise and congratulations. Being back there on the campus was like a dream, things familiar and things strange, and the strange and the familiar mixed and haunting. It was only seven years since she had been here last, but they were like an eternity—the students so incredibly young, the faculty so unchanged. A group of students gathered around her; they were here in this lovely place, and the world outside was a threatening, terrifying mystery. They wanted to touch, to speak to, to question, to communicate with someone who had actually been to the lair of the beast, to the place called Germany. She had seen these men called the SS with her own eyes; she had actually walked on the streets of Berlin. Would it ever end? Would England fall? Would we be in the war? Could the Nazis invade the United States?

Barbara realized that she knew so little. She had fled from war and horror. The world was entering into a dance of death beyond the bloodiest dreams of the past, and she could not cope with it. To kill an insect tortured her. She had no answers. She could only say, "I hope for something, some way for it to stop. But I don't know—"

Hildy Lang rescued her. Hildy had no problems with war and peace, with life and death. There was a cocktail party scheduled for five o'clock at the Algonquin, and the car was waiting. "Those kids will eat you up," Hildy told her. "Anyway, that is a crazy place, that Sarah Lawrence, absolutely insane."

Almost a hundred men and women were crowded into the two-room suite at the Algonquin, and Barbara was belly to belly but hardly face to face with a small, fat man who came up to her shoulder, the dean of the literary critics, who informed her didactically that her book was by no means a novel. "And why call it that?" he demanded. "It's a personal history. You lived it and you put down what you lived. That poses a problem, young woman. Where to now?"

"I haven't the slightest idea," Barbara said. She had

downed two drinks with the deliberate intention of getting
drunk—as the only alternative to fleeing the place. She
was a poor drinker. The third drink, in her hand, promised
the desired effect. "San Francisco, I think, but I'm not
sure."

Over her shoulder, someone was saying, "Lewisite—
that's the answer. One can of Lewisite on Berlin and that
does it, every man, woman, and child dead. Then you
build an iron fence around the place and label it: Here
lies Berlin, executed for crimes against civilization."

Barbara squeezed around to see who was speaking. A
stout woman was shrilly defending her position. Barbara
tried to escape, and the dean of literary critics followed
her. "Hemingway," he said, "participates. You observe.
The curse of inherited wealth."

Halliday rescued her. "I want you to meet Bruman. He's
on the *Sun,* and he wants to do a special feature."

"We are beyond Steinbeck," Bruman was saying. "He
is already an anachronism. We are beyond weeping for
the Okies. Hitler has solved the unemployment problem.
Ah, Miss Lavette! Beauty and the brain! Not Roosevelt
and his New Deal, but Adolf Hitler. Bless the ironies of
history. What would a writer do without them? Did you
meet the Führer, Miss Lavette? You must tell me all about
him."

At last it was over, and Barbara and Halliday sat in the
empty room amid the litter, Barbara drunk, sick to her
stomach, tired, wanting nothing so much as to be left
alone. Halliday patted her hand and assured her that she
had performed splendidly.

"But I'm not a performer," she said woefully.

"Let's have some dinner, and then you'll feel better. I
know a place in the Village where they have marvelous
steaks—steak, Bermuda onions, sliced tomatoes, baked potatoes—"

"Oh, no, please."

In the taxi, she tried to think, to put her muddled mind
in order. Halliday was holding her hand, stroking it gently
with his forefinger. "You're a patient, lovely wonder of a
woman," he said, leaning toward her and kissing her on
her cheek, and Barbara said to herself hopelessly, "Oh,
Christ, he's on the way, and the last thing in the world I
want right now is someone trying to make love to me,

and he's my publisher, and I'm so drunk I can't even think straight."

"Mr. Halliday," she said primly, "what on earth is Lewisite?"

"Lewisite?"

"Someone was talking about dropping it on Berlin."

"Really? It's a kind of devilish gas. They say that one canister of it could wipe out an entire city. The trouble is, the Germans have it too. Everyone has it. Good heavens, we don't want to talk about Lewisite. Have you ever been to the Village?"

"Once, long ago, I don't know it well."

"It's a charming place. Not the way it was twenty years ago, but still a charming place. Suppose we stroll a bit and get the cobwebs out of our heads. It doesn't have to be a steakhouse. There are half a dozen good restaurants to choose from."

"I hate to say this," Barbara said, "but I think I must go back to the hotel and go to bed. I'm a rotten drinker, and it's taken every ounce of self-control I have not to throw up right here in the taxi."

It was more than an excuse. It was a reality. "There's always tomorrow," Halliday said, unable to keep the disappointment out of his voice. "Suppose we keep your schedule down to a minimum. Tomorrow is publication day, and I had thought we might wait up for the morning papers. I think there'll be reviews in both the *Times* and the *Tribune*—good ones, I'm sure."

Back in the hotel, feeling stupid and totally disgusted with herself, Barbara hung over the toilet, vomiting up five cocktails and an assortment of canapés. Then she crawled into bed and had a night of restless sleep and bad dreams. It was past ten when Halliday called and said with excitement, "Absolute jackpot, my dear. Listen to this from the *Times:* 'A totally disarming and deeply sensitive picture of Europe in the years before the war. The chapter on Berlin is unlike anything yet written about the Nazis, an understatement that makes the reader cringe with horror. Miss Lavette's command of her material is extraordinary in a new novelist,' and more of the same. The *Tribune* goes even further. Quote: 'Miss Lavette's book is more than a first novel. It's a sensitive, deeply moving record of a young woman's encounter with life and death. The love scenes, while explicit, are never prurient, and throughout the book there is a feeling of tenderness and compassion that is quite remarkable in a woman of twenty-seven. Not for years has this critic read a first novel of such sensitivity and promise.' End quote. There you are. What have you got to say to that?"

"It's lovely. Mr. Halliday, are you pleased with it?"

"Pleased? Barbara, I'm delighted!"

"Then you won't be provoked with me. I'm going home today. Back to the Coast."

"Oh, no. No, Barbara. You can't."

She put down the phone, pulled out her suitcase, and began to pack. She felt wretched, utterly worthless, and could not understand why the glowing reviews were meaningless to her.

Some two decades before, in the early twenties, Dan Lavette had entered into a business arrangement with Christopher and Ralph Noel, two brothers who were large landowners and even larger financial tycoons on the island of Oahu in Hawaii. Together with Dan, they had created one of the first great tourist hotels on Waikiki Beach at a time when it was still a lovely and sparsely used stretch of sand. It was Dan's notion that Hawaii, given the proper combination of cruise ships and hotels, could become a winter sunland for western America that would serve the same purpose that Florida served for the East. With the aid of the Noels' capital, the hotel came into being, and with the Depression, Dan's share in it went down the drain. However, there had been no bitterness in his abdication to the Noel interests, so that when Christopher Noel heard that Dan was coming to Hawaii with his wife, he had insisted that they be his guests.

Noel's chauffeur picked them up at the pier in Honolulu and drove them to the bungalow, a euphemism for the rambling twenty-two-room bamboo and hardwood home of the Noel family situated on two thousand acres of white beach, green lawn, and pineapple fields. The last time Dan and May Ling had been here, twenty years before, a sense of gaiety and relaxation had pervaded the place. The Noels then had a great luau, a Hawaiian feast, with several hundred guests. They had appeared to be living in an eternal now, without care or thought of the future. Twenty years older, the Noels had lost the carefree and bright blush of youth. Their children were at school on the mainland,

and at dinner, the first evening after the Lavettes' arrival,
Christopher Noel expressed their anxieties.

"We're living in a fool's paradise," he told Dan. "Back
there on the mainland, they don't understand how wide
open we are. This war is spreading over the earth like a
disease, and the damn Japs are cuddling up to Hitler. When
I was in Washington a few months ago, I tried to make
them understand that. I spoke to Harry Hopkins, damned
arrogant bastard. Looks at me and tells me, 'We don't
expect Japan to enter the war. It's against her interest.
The Japanese could not fight a major war.' No resources.
Hell, Japan's got half of China for resources, but just try
to make them understand that."

They were dining on the broad verandah of the Noel
house, facing the white beach, the turbulent combers, with
the setting sun turning a lacework of clouds on the horizon
into a fantasy of red and lavender beauty. No talk of war
could rob May Ling of her feeling of peace and beauty.
This place was locked in her memories as the most
wonderful spot on earth, and nothing could change that.

The group at dinner consisted of Christopher and
Ralph Noel, both of them tall, slender, aristocratic-looking
men, their blond hair turned white with the years; their
wives, both of them curiously alike, small, dark pretty
women, carefully gowned, carefully coiffured; Jerry
Kamilee, an enormous, fleshy Hawaiian; his wife, part
Hawaiian, part Japanese; and Dan and May Ling.

May Ling wore an old-fashioned, ankle-length Chinese
gown of white silk, split at the sides and embroidered with
gold thread in a design of pagodas, arched bridges, and
tiny maidens with sunshades. Dan had brought the dress
back with him after a trip to San Francisco, refusing to
reveal what it had cost, and tonight was the first time May
Ling had worn it. "You, little lady," Kamilee said to her,
"have sold your soul to the devil. We grow old and fat
and tired, but you look no different than when we saw
you twenty years ago."

"Ah, if that were only true," May Ling said. "Believe me,
the enchantment is here. I listen to you men talk and
grumble, and I suppose Adam grumbled the same way in
Paradise. The truth is that there is no time here. It stands
still."

"Oh, listen to her," Christopher Noel's wife said. Her
name was Elii, and her family had been four generations in

the Islands. "No, my dear. Time doesn't stand still. I have a mirror that proves it every day."

"She is right about one thing," Ralph Noel decided. "Here is the place. Stay here, Danny. My word, what do you have on the mainland that can compare to this?"

"A damn shipyard, for one thing. We're beginning to build them almost as fast as the U-boats sink them."

"What is the word back there? Are we going into this thing or not?"

"Our problem," said Kamilee, "is Japan. We underestimate them. Half of Hatti's family"—indicating his wife —"is Japanese. I know them a little. They are smart as hell, make no mistake, and damn near anything we can do, they can do better. And they want these islands. Jesus God, how they want these islands!"

"But there's no reason on earth for them to go to war with us," May Ling protested.

"When did reason have any part in making war? As far as they're concerned, it's their ocean. They want us out of it. Manifest destiny. They're sick with destiny. We sit here and grow pineapples and watch the sunsets and get fat and content. The truth is, we couldn't defend these islands against a troop of boy scouts."

"I still want to know what Dan knows," Christopher Noel said.

"What I know," Dan said, "consists of a mud flat called Terminal Island in San Pedro. A few years ago, Sam Goldberg—you remember him, my lawyer in San Francisco, dead now, poor guy—well, a few years ago, we took over a shipyard on Terminal Island. The bank practically gave it to us. Every shipyard on the Coast was dead, decaying, bankrupt, rotting away. Not a ship being built anywhere. Now—well, on our way out here, May Ling read me Coleridge's poem 'The Ancient Mariner.' I met up with my own ancient mariner. His name is Admiral Emery Scott Land, and he heads up a thing called the Maritime Commission, and he's been sitting on my back ever since. He's a man with a single obsession—ships. Now you want to know how insane this world is, I can tell you. A few years ago, you could walk along the waterfront in Wilmington, San Pedro, Long Beach, you'd see maybe two, three thousand men, just sitting, dying, rotting, pleading for a chance to clean a latrine. Now I have two men I pay a wage to, and they have one job. Find men. Find something that can walk and talk. They drive a truck through Orange County and L.A. County, and they stop men on the street, in the fields, anywhere, and ask them if they want a job with good pay. You ask me when we're going into this war? We've been in it. We're feeding England and arming England, and we're creating the biggest damn shipbuilding industry the world ever saw. And there's no way out. Suddenly, the Depression's over, and there's more money around than you can count."

"And Japan, Danny?"

"Before this is over, mark my word, there won't be a foot of ground on this earth that isn't involved."

That night, lying next to Dan, listening to the thunder of the breakers outside, May Ling said, "Danny, it's all changed—here at the Noels'. They've become old and tired and frightened."

"Time passes. People get older."

"But not this time, not here in Hawaii. I don't want to be old now. When we go back to the mainland, I shall become properly old and withered and take up knitting and do whatever an old woman should do."

"You are the strangest damn woman."

"I am. I am indeed. But right now, I feel very young and happy. Let's get away from here, Danny."

"Right. As soon as the yawl is seaworthy, off we go."

But the yawl, called the *Kahana*, had been up on the racks for a year now. It had to be caulked and painted and fitted with new rigging. Christopher Noel would not hear of Dan taking it out until it was completely seaworthy. He was somewhat dubious about Dan handling it without another man in the crew, but Dan insisted that May Ling was as good as any man on a boat. He had no intention of allowing any intrusion into their privacy.

Thus is was three weeks before they were able to set sail. The Noels were marvelous hosts, generous, unobtrusive, placing a car at Dan's disposal, diverting the Lavettes with dinner parties, luaus, theater evenings, and film showings in Noel's private viewing room at the house. May Ling guessed that even after all these years, they were haunted with a certain amount of guilt over the part they had played in the downfall of the Levy and Lavette empire. Dan and May Ling made frequent visits to Honolulu, where he was so insistent on buying anything she approved of or admired that it reached a point where she didn't dare comment on anything she saw in a shop window.

"Dan," she said, "you can't go on spending money like a drunken sailor." He had just bought her a string of ivory beads, each one a miracle of carving, made in China.

"I certainly can," he said. 'Do you know how much money we have?"

"No. I have no idea."

"You might as well know. I own the shipyard outright. Aside from the fact that no one stoops to talk about price these days, my lawyers tell me that the facility itself is worth a couple of million. When Sam and I bought it, it wasn't worth twenty cents.'

"And if they stop buying ships? What happens then?"

"That's up to Hitler and Mussolini. If they stop sinking the ships, the government may stop ordering them. Isn't it a beautiful, stinking thing, May Ling, to get rich because those bastards in the submarines sink more ships than we can build? A ship is a thing of beauty, the result of two thousand years of planning and testing and modifying, a whole, fine precise world in itself, and we build them to be destroyed and get fat on the blood of the men who sail them. It stinks. The whole damn thing we call civilization stinks to high heaven."

"We're here in the Islands. Can't you forget about civilization for a few weeks?"

The day the Noels put the yawl in the water Dan and May Ling spent shopping in Honolulu, returning with their load of canned goods, smoked meat, beer, and wine. Dan bought everything from canned beans to caviar—to the disgust of Christopher Noel. "We have a larder that can feed an army," he informed them. Then he led both of them down to the dock to admire the boat.

"She's a Concordia," Noel told Dan. "Built in 1938 by Howland and Hunt. Essentially, she's a Buzzards Bay boat, built for the Atlantic waters off Massachusetts, which means she can take anything. They don't build boats like this on our side of the world, and there isn't another like her in the Islands. She's almost forty feet and she displaces nine tons, and still she sails like a witch. If worse comes to worst, you can handle her yourself. She has a Gray, four-cycle, thirty-one-horse motor, which won't send you scampering over the waves but will move you very nicely when you're becalmed."

"If I'm becalmed, I stay becalmed. My only hope of heaven is a small boat." Dan grinned. "By God, she is a beauty."

"She'll sleep two nicely, or four if need be. When Elii and I take her out, we spread mats in the cockpit. Plenty of room there if you like sleeping under the stars. She has a two-way radio, refrigerator, stove—everything the heart can desire. God damn it, I envy you. Where are you bound?"

"I thought we'd head southeast, circle the big island, and work our way back. Do some beachcombing. Say six or seven weeks."

"You've sailed a yawl?"

"I had a cutter that was yawl-rigged."

"The way the mast is rigged, she'll handle like a little catboat. And the weather's pretty good at this time of the year. The chartcase has everything you want for the Islands."

"I don't know how to thank you."

"I owe you," Noel said. "Just bring that lovely wife of yours back in one piece. We haven't seen enough of her."

Dan and May Ling left the following day, riding away from Oahu on a gentle easterly. They were in no hurry, and Dan left the small mizzen sail furled. May Ling was a good sailor. The wind held, and they picked up the heights of Molokai before dark.

The next five weeks were a time of peace and happiness and enchantment that Dan would remember and dwell on as long as he lived. They anchored in a tiny cove in Molokai where the sand was white as snow. They swam naked and make love on the sand under the hot sun. Dan let his beard grow. At night, they built fires of driftwood, and May Ling curled up in his arms and watched the colors of the flames. Then they sailed across the Kalohi Channel and found another paradise on the island of Lanai, and May Ling said to him, "Let's never go back, Danny."

"That's an idea."

"We just keep sailing. There's always another island."

"It's Noel's boat. Either we bring it back, or he gets the cops after us."

On Maui, they put in for supplies and stayed for a night and a day with the Jorgensons, who were friends of the Noels. May Ling trimmed Dan's beard, but she declared that he still looked like a buccaneer, burned brown by the sun, wearing sandals, white shirt, and duck sailing trousers. Matching his clothes, her tiny hand in his large paw, May Ling looked like a half-grown boy. Her ivory skin had tanned a deep brown, and there was a spring in her step and a buoyancy in her being that Dan had not seen in years. The Jorgensons were ship's chandlers, and their house in Lahaina was built of volcanic rock. May Ling thought it was one of the most beatiful houses she had ever seen. She charmed the Jorgensons, and they begged Dan and May Ling to stay with them for at least a week and be shown the wonders of Maui, in particular the great volcanic mountain of Haleakala.

"I just couldn't," May Ling said to Dan as they cast off from the dock at Maui. "You get a hunger for the boat. They're such nice people, but all I could think of was to get back on the boat."

"I know the feeling."

"Danny, will we come back here one day—I mean come back and stay?"

"That could be."

But once back on the *Kahana*, it was hard to leave Maui, and sailing easily, tacking, beating into the wind, they circled the island, camped for two days on a tiny beach, and finally raised sail for the big island of Hawaii.

They lost track of the days, and Dan's beard grew thicker. They rode out a wild rain squall, which filled May Ling with delicious terror and with admiration for Dan's handling of the boat. They were becalmed once for almost an entire day. They found a chess set in one of the lockers, and May Ling taught Dan how to play. Once he had mastered the moves, he became enthralled with the game, and they played for hours. They put into Hilo, on the big island of Hawaii, and May Ling found a little bookstore and managed to buy a copy of *Omoo*, by Herman Melville, and a book of Stevenson's short stories about the Islands. While Dan was at the wheel, May Ling read to him, and for the first time Dan heard the story of the bottle imp.

"He must have loved these islands," Dan said.

"Yes, he loved them," May Ling agreed. "He died in Samoa and was buried there. You know, Danny, for me, when I come here, I forget that I am Chinese. It's the only place where no one looks at me strangely and does a double take because my eyes are slanted and my skin is yellow."

"Your eyes are not slanted and your skin is certainly not yellow and you're no more Chinese than I'm Italian."

"I am, Danny, but not here. You know, we've become kids again and we're pretending—and I'm so afraid to go back. I want to be with you, Danny."

"You are with me."

"No. No, you really don't understand. Do you remember that night when you came to dinner, the very first time I saw you, and pop invited you and your wife, but the snow lady would not come, and I was so delighted that she didn't come, because already, before I ever saw you, I was in love with you, and then you came, and you remember how I described the Chinese dishes that mom prepared, and it was just the most wonderful evening of my whole life?"

"I remember."

"Well, since then, Danny, I only wanted one thing from life, to be with you—all the time. I'm afraid that no man could truly understand what I mean, because Joe is my son, and I love him with all my heart, but if I know I won't see him for a month or two months or six months, I can endure it, and it doesn't break my heart. But it's different with you. It's thirty years since you first put your arms around me and kissed me, and that's a long time, but I never kissed another man or loved another man. Do you know what I'm trying to say to you, Danny?"

"It's what Dr. Freud calls a neurotic fixation—and that's pretty damn fancy, wouldn't you say? You found yourself a large, hairy, uneducated hoodlum and decided to make a civilized person out of him."

"Danny, you're dumb!"

"I know."

"Dumb, dumb, dumb. You'll go back to that wretched shipyard and forget that I exist, and I'll sit in that dreary house in Westwood and wait and wait. Oh, sometimes I wish I were large enough to pound some sense into your head."

"Maybe we won't go back. To hell with Chris Noel. I've been reading the charts, and it would be just a lead pipe cinch to take this boat to Samoa. Then New Zealand. How would you like that? I hear it's one hell of a beautiful place."

"Danny, you're crazy."

May Ling would stretch out on the foredeck, her arms hanging over the side. For five days a porpoise had stayed with the boat, swimming on his side, watching May Ling as she watched him. When Dan heard her chattering away in Mandarin, he called out, "Are you talking to yourself, old girl?"

"To Chu Tu."

"Who's Chu Tu?"

"This porpoise. He's been with us five days. We're old friends. I named him after my grandfather."

"And you talk to him in Chinese?"

"Why not Chinese?"

"How in hell would a porpoise understand Chinese?"

She leaped up and ran back to throw her arms around him and kiss him. "Oh, Danny, I adore you."

Dan said to her one morning, anchored off Kiholo Bay on the big island, "Well, baby, it's over. We're going to make sail and head back before Chris gets nervous and calls the cops."

"Danny, do we have to?"

"It's his boat, and anyway, by now Admiral Land must be sore enough to eat his own brass. We've overstayed, and at this point no one knows where the devil we are. I've tried to call in by radio, but either I'm a rotten operator or no one's listening. We've been out a month, and we can figure another five days back to Oahu if the wind holds, longer if it doesn't."

The wind was good, but on the fourth day, they were becalmed at night, and they lay on a glassy sea off the southeastern point of Oahu. Whenever they slept at sea, Dan would awaken frequently. Tonight they slept on mats in the open cockpit. Dan awakened three times, the last time just at the first gray break of dawn. May Ling, curled under a blanket, was sleeping soundly, and Dan rose quietly. There was a touch of wind with the dawn, and he raised the mainsail and locked the rudder on course. Still May Ling slept. He went down into the cabin and began to prepare coffee and toast and bacon.

He was there when he heard the sound in the distance, a bubbling, raging roar of sound. His first reaction was a picture of a volcano blowing its head; then, as the sound continued, he realized that he was hearing the explosion of bombs punctuated with gunfire.

He leaped out of the cabin up to the deck. May Ling

was on her knees, grasping the rail, and from the direction of Oahu the sound was building, increasing.

"Danny, what is it?"

He crouched beside her, putting his arms around her. Now they saw the planes overhead, flying low, wing after wing. Suddenly, one of the planes peeled off and swooped down toward the yawl, a stream of tracer bullets coming from its wings. Dan saw the bullets chop the water; then he heard the impact of them hitting the boat, and May Ling cried out, her body twisting spasmodically. Then the plane was gone, and overhead the planes continued their flight, taking no more notice of the tiny sailboat.

"Danny," she whispered. "Danny, I'm hurt."

He laid her down on the mat. A dark stain was spreading across her chest.

"Danny, what happened to me?"

He knelt over her, his soul rent with the kind of fear he had never known before. "It's all right, baby, it's all right, my love."

Her eyes were open. He pulled out his handkerchief, thinking only that he had to stop the blood, pressing it to the wound.

"Baby, baby," he whispered.

Then he knew that she was dead. He felt frantically for her pulse. He lifted her in his arms, embracing her, pleading, "No, no, no, don't. Don't go away. Don't leave me please, please. Don't go away, May Ling."

He knelt in the cockpit, his arms around her, and began to cry, swaying, kissing her cold cheeks and her lips.

And in the distance, the rumble of obscene sound continued.

Part Six

RETURN

For two days, Barbara had tried to buy an alarm clock. There were no alarm clocks for sale in Calcutta. That struck her as reasonable; it was not a place where an alarm clock was a necessity. But what struck her as even stranger was that in all her shopping excursions, she had come across no such thing as a doll or a toy. Eloise had borne Tom a son, whom they called Frederick Thomas Lavette, and it had occurred to Barbara that she ought to try to send some kind of a gift for the child's second birthday. Calcutta was not a place where they sold toys or alarm clocks.

Very often of late, for a variety of reasons, Barbara had been unable to fall asleep. A morning appointment became a contest between will and fatigue, and usually fatigue triumphed. Thus the search for the alarm clock, and when the search proved futile, she put her problem to Kamil Shee, who was the custodian of the Press Club.

"But it is simple, memsahib. I will awaken you."

"Good. At four o'clock in the morning."

"But four o'clock is not the morning, memsahib. It is still nighttime."

"Then can you awaken me at four o'clock at night?"

"But I am asleep. How can I awaken you if I'm asleep?"

"That's reasonable," Barbara agreed. "Just forget about it. I'll tie a string around my finger."

"You will tie a string around your finger?"

"Yes. That will do it."

By then, in June of 1944, Barbara had been in Calcutta for three weeks, living at the Press Club, which had once been a rajah's palace and which had been converted into lodgings for correspondents during the war. She had been to many other places—North Africa, Burma, Ceylon—since that day in San Francisco when the foreign editor of the *Chronicle* had come to her house and interrupted her writing to insist that they needed a woman correspon-

dent in the China-Burma-India theater, and that no one
was better suited to the job than she. At first she had flatly
refused. She had grown angry. She had shouted at him.
She had apologized, and finally she had agreed to think
about it. Two months later, she was in a C-54 Air Transport plane, taking off from Newfoundland on the first leg
of her flight to the East.

Now, in Calcutta, she was arranging the mosquito netting around her bed and setting her mind on awakening at
four o'clock in the morning. Her appointment with Simil
Chatterjee was for half-past four in the morning, when he
would be at the Press Club to pick her up to show her the
sleeping street at the break of dawn, which was, he insisted, the only time to see it. He felt that this was the
biggest story in India and the story that no one was writing. Barbara suspected that he was a communist, although
he had never indicated this and she had never asked him
directly. He had singled her out and traced her down because he had read her novel, which amazed her, although
by now she was becoming used to the way a published
book could travel into the most out-of-the-way and unexpected places; and because he had read the book, he
felt that she would lend a sympathetic eye and ear to the
situation.

It was never easy for Barbara to fall asleep, and tonight
the pressure of the need to awaken so early made it worse.
It was very hot, and her ceiling fan was broken. She had
long ago discovered that the most prevailing quality of
ceiling fans all over India was that they did not work. She
lay in bed under the netting, naked, trying to compose her
mind. Calcutta was blacked out, but a fitful moonlight
pervaded the room, and Barbara could just barely make
out her body. She had lost weight, and she had a feeling,
by no means based in reality, that she was becoming gaunt
and dry. Actually, her daily intake of Atabrine, a malaria
preventive, had given a golden glow to her skin, and the
few pounds she had lost made little difference in her appearance. For some days now, she had been ready to
leave; she had had enough of the war, enough of distance,
enough of boredom, enough of loneliness, enough of soldiers and officers and correspondents laying their own
hunger and loneliness on her, enough of being the only
woman among a thousand men. Her hatred of war had
once been academic and intellectual; now it was very pre-

cise and pointed and actual. War was waste and stupidity and barbarism, and it seemed to her now that all of her adult life had been caught up in the ever-widening cesspool of war, and that all she had loved had been taken from her by war—Marcel dead in France, May Ling slain by random bullets from a plane that had attacked Pearl Harbor, and it was a war of sorts that had taken Dominick Salone's life too, so very long ago.

She thought of that now, asking herself, "Have I lived that long, truly? Or was that another life in another age? I am only thirty years old, unmarried, childless, with a past that makes me feel as ancient as the old temples in this land."

There was such an ancient temple on the road between Old Delhi and New Delhi, and Barbara, going from New Delhi to Old Delhi in a tonga cart in the burning noonday sun, saw the place with its greenery and its babbling brook, and she stopped there, taking off her shoes to enter. There was one old monk in the temple, covered with a saffron robe and sitting crosslegged, and as she watched him that day, a deep feeling of peace had come over her, the first sense of peace she had experienced in a long time. Now, lying sleepless under the mosquito netting, she tried to remember and to bring back that feeling of peace, to compose herself, not to think of May Ling, not to think of Marcel, not to think of anything at all, not where she was, not where she would be tomorrow, only to sleep.

She awakened suddenly and struck a match to look at her watch. It was half-past three in the morning. She was tired, her stomach was sour, and her whole body was covered with a film of sweat. For a little while she lay in bed, trying to ignore the dampness of the sheet under her body. She was afraid to close her eyes for fear that she would drift back into sleep. Finally, she gave up and crawled out of bed and drew the blackout curtains, shutting out the slight coolness of the night air. To add to the general discomfort, she had her menstrual period, and she felt heavy and bloated and longed for a cool, leisurely bath. She poured water from the pitcher into the basin on the washstand, thinking how odd it was that they should have the same washing facilities here that she had had in her dormitory at Sarah Lawrence, and splashed the water over her face. A cardboard sign over the washstand warned that the water was not to be drunk under any circumstances. She put on her uniform, thinking wistfully of how comfortable a light blouse and a pair of cotton shorts would be. Each day, she disliked the uniform more, and among her fantasies was a shopping trip with Jean, where they bought endless numbers of dresses, each more gossamer than the last—a peculiar fantasy because she had never cared deeply about clothes or paid very much attention to them.

Then she went downstairs, circling the roofless indoor court of the building, with its pool of stagnant water and its tile court where once, as rumor had it, the many wives of the rajah had disported themselves. It was still very dark, the only light coming from the moon and the stars, fitful, reflected in the murky pool. She felt her way through the stygian lobby and stood outside, in front of the building, blessing the light breeze that always came just before dawn. A half a dozen bearers were asleep alongside the building, curled up on the hard brick paving that rimmed it. Barbara was used to the sight of men and women and children sleeping here and there on the streets of the city. Calcutta was enormous but too small for the millions who lived there, and with the famine, hundreds of thousands of peasants had flocked into the city from the countryside.

She had been waiting only about five minutes when she heard the pad and squeak of a rickshaw, and then it came out of the night, with Chatterjee sitting in it. He was a small, skinny man with a black skin, a gentle mouth, and large, dark, luminous eyes. He was very neat, his dhoti snow white, but he himself was always barefoot. He leaped out of the rickshaw and nodded with pleasure.

"How fine, Miss Lavette, to give up a night's sleep for this. You are responsible, very responsible."

"I did sleep a little. But must we ride in a rickshaw? I hate them. The indignity of being drawn by a man as a beast of burden."

"But if the man is a beast of burden," Chatterjee said gently, "he must still live and eat. And if we do not ride in his rickshaw, how will he live?" He said something to the rickshaw man in Bengali. The rickshaw man wore only a loincloth. His body was very thin and hard. Now he looked at Barbara, smiled, and nodded.

Reluctantly, Barbara climbed into the rickshaw, followed by Chatterjee. "But don't make him run," she protested feebly.

"I don't tell him, Miss Lavette. He takes the pace that is best for him."

Barbara sighed. "I suppose that our guilts puzzle you?"

"Ah, yes, certainly. You must have guilts—otherwise the world would be even more obscene than it is. But the guilts of our conquerors are so selective."

"I am not one of your conquerors," Barbara reminded him.

"Oh, no. No, indeed. I fall into generalizations, a bad habit. But you know, Miss Lavette, the Americans have two million troops in India now, many more than the British ever had here, and we are still very much the conquered."

"I know."

For a while they moved in silence through the dark, empty streets of the city. Then Chatterjee said, "I must say, if you will forgive me, that I admire you very much because you are not afraid. To get up in the middle of the night and come with me this way would frighten most women. A city at night like this, blacked out, is very frightening."

"Other things frighten me more."

"The rickshaw man is twenty-three years old. He will be dead before he is forty. I am not trying to be morbid or impress you with our misery, but simply to say that I am aware of his position. But there is no other work for him. He has a wife and children, and they must eat."

"Why will he be dead before he is forty?" Barbara asked slowly. "Is he sick?"

"No. But his heart will give out."

"I see."

The darkness of night was changing in the predawn; the city was coming alive, and the people who lived and slept on the sidewalks were picking themselves up and making their way toward the pools of stagnant water that dotted the city, where they would bathe and perform their rituals of cleanliness. A streetcar clanged past on the first run of the morning, already crowded with riders. The rickshaw man threaded his way among a cluster of sacred white cows that wandered, free to go where they would, through the streets of the city.

"We will be there in a few minutes," Chatterjee told her. "You have seen so many people sleeping in the streets, but they are city dwellers. The streets are their home, the

only home they have. Where we are going is another thing.
You see, the famine has existed for some time now, and
when there is no rice in the countryside, the peasants come
here in desperation. So many thousands of them came
that the government had to set aside certain streets for
them to sleep on. The government is very thoughtful."

"Yes, I know. When I was in Old Delhi, I saw a man
trying to teach children to read under a lamppost. The
light was very dim. I met the governor-general at a reception and I mentioned it to him. He said he would do something. Do you know what he did?"

"Nothing."

"Oh, no. He had a larger light bulb put in the lamppost."

"Ah, how thoughtful. But here we are. Look!" Then he
spoke to the rickshaw man, who stopped.

They were at a spot where the street on which they had
been traveling intersected with a broad avenue, as wide
as the Champs-Élysées in Paris. Now, in the gray dawn
light, Barbara could see far down the avenue, and as far
as she could see, from one side of the avenue to the other,
it was carpeted with the bodies of sleeping people. The
sight was so unexpected—in spite of Chatterjee's preparing her for it—so incredible, so unlike anything she had
ever seen or dreamed of before, that it rendered her speechless. She simply stared, and inside of her, a wave of min-
gled horror and compassion made her feel totally sick and
empty. She could not respond; her universe, badly in need
of repair, crumbled around her, and every belief, every
hope, every dream of a just and equitable world where
God is in His heaven and all's right on earth, came crumbling down along with the universe.

"The sleeping street," Chatterjee said.

Minutes passed while the three of them stood there in a
motionless tableau. Finally, Barbara was able to say, "It
doesn't hurt you to see this?"

"If I let such things hurt me, Miss Lavette, then there
would be nothing left of me and I would not be able to do
my work."

"What is your work?"

"I am a journalist, like yourself. We have a small
newspaper, a single sheet printed on both sides, and we
issue it once a week. Its only virtue is that it tells the truth
about many things that no other newspaper writes about.

When it is printed, I and others take it around to the
villages and the factories. They are illiterate in most
villages, so I read it aloud. Then each villager pays for
the reading with a single grain of rice. Of course, it is
illegal, and recently its publication has been suspended.
That is why I would like to have this story in an American
newspaper."

"I see. Can we go now?"

"Please, a few minutes more. As you see, they are
awakening already. Don't be afraid. They are very gentle
people."

"I'm not afraid. I just don't know how long I can stand
to see this."

"I do understand. But in another moment the sun will
be up. The moment the sunlight strikes the street, they
will begin to leave. They will leave quickly. I want you
to see why."

"I have enough for my story."

"No, no, please, madam, please. You only have half of
the story."

"Very well," Barbara said. In Burma she had seen the
dead brought out of the jungle, bodies stacked on trucks
like cordwood. Why should this be more disturbing?

A single broad shaft of sunlight struck the street now,
and the mass of humanity began to move; the whole thing
undulated, as if the thousands of people there comprised
a single entity. Fascinated, unable to turn her eyes away,
Barbara watched. The street was bedroom, bathroom, and
sewer, and suddenly the mass of people were emptying
out, flowing past the rickshaw, glancing at Barbara and
Chatterjee, and then moving past, men, women children,
infants sucking dry, flat breasts, a slow, sad, silent river of
people.

But not all had awakened. All over the broad avenue
and stretching into the distance were people still asleep,
hundreds and hundreds of them, and here and there around
those apparently asleep was a cluster awake, and now
began a keening dirge of woe.

"What is happening there?" Barbara asked Chatterjee.
"Why are they still sleeping?"

"They are not sleeping. They're dead. Each morning a
thousand, two thousand, five thousand, have died during
the night. There will be six million dead before this famine
is over. Millions died in Hitler's gas ovens, but the world

knows. Six million of my people will die here, and the world doesn't know." He spoke in Bengali to the rickshaw man, his voice harsh for the first time, and they started away. Barbara fought to keep her stomach down, her sense of desolation interrupted by the needs of her own body. She did not have the courage to ask Chatterjee to stop the rickshaw, that she might get out and vomit. Anyway, the city was awake, and they were moving through an ever-increasing flow of people, automobiles, and rickshaws, and if one is a woman and wearing the uniform of an American warrant officer, one does not vomit on a busy street. She fought her body and conquered it, and finally she was able to say to the still silent Chatterjee, "I know what I've seen, and you are right. But this is an act of God or the weather. You can't compare the two."

"God—ah, yes. But there has been hunger in the past, and there was rice put by. This time, the British were afraid that the Japanese would penetrate to Assam, and the peasants would go over to them and welcome them as liberators. So they entered into a pact with the Muslim rice merchants and cornered the market. Millions of people will die, but there are warehouses stuffed with millions of pounds of rice."

"That's a terrible accusation," Barbara said.

"Will you write that story?"

"About the famine and the sleeping street, yes, and my paper will print it. But the other part of it—"

"You paper will not print."

"Without proof. How can they? You accuse the British of millions of deaths, but as you say, there have been famines before when millions died. Even if your accusation is true, the British did not make the famine. Perhaps the dealers are holding rice. That makes the price go up, and it's a filthy, evil thing, but unless you can gave me documented proof of collusion, I cannot make the accusation."

"Miss Lavette, where can I find such proof? I only know what I have heard and that there is reason to believe it. I know there is rice. Why isn't it distributed? Why must so many people die?"

"I can't answer that," Barbara said forlornly. "I don't know. But I can only write what I have seen."

That evening, back at the Press Club, they gave Barbara

a cocktail party. They had heard that she was on her way out, that she had had enough of the China-Burma-India theater, and the American correspondents had organized a farewell celebration. There were correspondents, British and American officers, some nurses from the nearby general hospital, and some Red Cross ladies. Barbara was one of the few people there who did not get drunk; the very thought of liquor on her queasy stomach was utterly revolting, and after her experience of the morning, eating was almost as unbearable. There was a long table in the lounge groaning with food, piles of sandwiches, a great, steaming pot of curry, and mounds of white rice. They toasted her in drunkenly poetic terms. As one wire-service man put it, "Beauty has gone out of our lives." She received at least half a dozen fervent pleas to become a bed partner, and when at last she pleaded total fatigue, explaining that she had not slept the night before, she was mournfully accused of being an unfeeling party-pooper.

Alone in her room, she said to herself, "I must get out of here, or I will surely lose my mind." It surprised her that she had not wept all day, but then she realized that she had not shed tears in over a year. She had lost that habit.

Dan Lavette did not sell the house in Westwood until three years after May Ling's death. He slept there only intermittently, having constructed an apartment for himself with the few facilities he required in the old office building on Terminal Island. But since he knew that Chinese lore had it that the spirit of the deceased remained in the dwelling of the deceased for three years, he held on to the little house. Not that he believed in Chinese superstition, not that May Ling had believed in it, but she had held to the practice, so he would too. At first he told himself that it was Joe's home, which was a reason to hold it, but in June 1942, Joe was shipped out to a base hospital in Honolulu. He tried to explain to Joe why he wanted to get rid of the house, and he thought Joe understood. In any case, Joe tried to understand the grim-faced man who would not let go of his grief. When the three years were over, Dan sold the house and put the money in a bank account for his son. His years there with May Ling had been good years, the best in his life, but to be constantly reminded of them was more than he could endure. When he finally sold the house, he felt the first break in his depression.

He made his life on Terminal Island. Curiously enough, he had no hatred for the Japanese. He could not personalize the thing that came out of the sky and murdered his wife, and his dedication to the shipyard had nothing to do with any complex chain of revenge. He went back to the shipyard because he had nowhere else to go, and he went back to work because otherwise he would have gone mad. At that point he had no future, no dream, no ambition, and in his mind he characterized life as a filthy, senseless, and aimless fraud. While she was alive, he had never actually contemplated May Ling's death. In a society where most women outlived their husbands, he had simply taken for granted that he would die before she did. She had been more than a part of his life; she had shaped his life. With gentle patience and with infinite tact, she had educated him, been his teacher and guide, lived for him, adored him without reproach for anything he had done. He had never dwelled on how much he loved her, yet he had always known that life without her would be untenable.

In June 1944, Dan Lavette still owned the house in Westwood, but he had not been there for seven weeks. As a matter of fact, he had not left Terminal Island during those seven weeks, and when Admiral Land came there to see him, he finally found him, in blue workshirt and Levi's, prowling across the deck of an almost completed Liberty ship. "Lavette," he shouted at him, "will you stand still for one damn moment!"

Dan stood still and waited for Land without enthusiasm, and Land, regarding the heavyset, gray-haired man who stood scowling at him, said almost tentatively, "We have to talk."

"I'm busy."

"You are the most ill-natured sonofabitch I ever knew."

"Thank you. I happen to be inspecting this hunk of tin."

"You've got more damn inspectors than you know what to do with."

"When a ship leaves this yard, I look at it. That's my responsibility. What in hell is yours? To come here and bug my ass off?"

"Sort of," Land said calmly. "What number is this?"

"Two hundred and eighty-one, in the Liberty class." He condescended to shake hands with the admiral.

"I will be damned," Land said slowly and with respect. "I knew it was high. Two hundred and eighty-one. You are one strange, ill-tempered, incredible sonofabitch."

Dan unbent to a slight smile, a mere twitch of his lips, the most he had permitted himself in a long time. He nodded at the ship on which they stood. "How do you like it?"

"It appears all right."

"What in hell does that mean—it appears all right? I don't hold any brief for the Liberty ships. They are a lousy design to begin with, but given the design, we build the best ships in the world."

"Why?" Land wondered.

"Why?"

"You don't give a damn about the war or the country or anything else, as far as I can see. The accounting office tells me that as of now you've grossed six hundred million. You're a millionaire many times over, but you never leave this place. Do you own a suit, or do you sleep in those jeans of yours?"

"I sleep in the raw," Dan said. "Come on over to the office. I'll buy you a drink. We're launching a tanker this afternoon—number twenty-three. I've altered the design, and I'd like you to look at it before we have a congressional investigation."

"You haven't answered my question."

Dan led the way over the side of the ship. "Watch your step, Admiral." They made their way through a jungle of scaffolding, power lifts, cranes, steel plates, beams, and skeletal hulls of ships. "You don't want an answer," Dan said to the admiral. "You want to convert me to this mound of horseshit you call patriotism. Now I'll tell you something, mister. Fourteen years ago, I was sitting over there on the dock at San Pedro. I hadn't eaten in three days. Neither had anyone else within sight of me. I would have worked for a dollar a day—damnit, for fifty cents a day. Now look around you. How many men do you think I got working here right now?"

The men swarmed around them, welders, carpenters, liftmen, laborers, steamfitters, painters. "Over thirty thousand just in this yard," Dan told him. "Over two hundred just in the office. We put them two at a desk. It's easier to get steel plate than desks or typewriters. They work and they eat, and we make a good ship because the only purpose I have in life is to run this lousy shipyard. That's my problem, not yours. But don't ask me to cheer for a system that requires an Adolf Hitler to give men jobs."

"That is one hell of a way to put it."

"That's the way I put it."

"I guess it is. You're the only millionaire I know who sounds like a damn anarchist, but I guess you're the best shipbuilder we have. I wish I had twenty like you."

"God forbid."

"Yes, it would be hard to take, but it would end this rotten war a lot quicker."

They had come to a set of pile drivers, and Land paused to watch the huge hammers drive the wooden piles down into the mud. Shouting to make himself heard, Dan said, "Your boys in Washington wanted three more sets of ways. When we're complete, we'll have driven fifty-nine thousand piles, give or take a few, into this mud."

"I want to talk about that," Land said.

In Dan's office, where the littered, crowded disarray resembled an on-site construction shack more than the head office of one of the largest enterprises on the Coast, Land accepted a whiskey and soda. Dan lit a cigar and said, "You look tired, old man."

"One thing about being an admiral," Land observed, "is that it gives you the right to relegate arrogance and nastiness to yourself. That doesn't work with you, Lavette. How old do you think I am?"

"Seventy?"

"Sixty-five. I'm ten years older than you, and I'll ask you to respect that. All right, let's get down to business. The boys think we're over the hump—at least enough up the hump to begin to build something that we won't have to dump on the scrapheap once the war is over. That means a new class of ship we call the Victory. You'll have the plans no later than tomorrow. Meanwhile, here's a rough rundown. She'll have a displacement of ten thousand tons, overall length of four hundred feet, midship deck housing and a forecastle deck, which will give her a fine graceful swoop up to the bow."

"That makes problems."

"I know. We won't mass-produce it. If you can get out a dozen in the next twelve months, I'll be satisfied. We're giving her good striking power, two gun tubs, fore and aft, platforms sheathed in half-inch steel plate, and that means high-quality steel. The forward gun will be a seventy-millimeter, surface and antiaircraft, and the gun aft will be a five-incher, which means one hell of a big gun and a new concept of mounting and bracing. She'll also carry six smaller tubs mounted with twenty-millimeter multiple machine guns, but that offers no problems. Your power plant will be oil-fired boilers and steam turbines. It's going to cost, but your profits go up at the same time."

Dan nodded without enthusiasm.

"I appreciate a joyful reception when we move forward. We're sending two specialists with the plans. I warned them what to expect. You don't have to be kind to them."

"Kindness doesn't build ships, Admiral. I hate these damn technical reps. Do I need them?"

"I'm afraid you do, Dan. It's a new project. Now listen to me and get off your high horse for a minute or two. We're having a ceremony in San Francisco in August, and the President's going to give you a citation."

"What in hell for?"

"For building the damn ships. What else?"

Dan shrugged.

"You can't refuse. By the way, I ran into your son the other day. Thomas."

Dan nodded.

"Fine-looking boy. You ought to see more of him. Bewails the fact that he's locked into a shoreside job with Whittier's ships."

Dan nodded again.

"And about the citation?"

"I suppose so."

Tom had purchased a house on Pacific Heights, taking advantage of the depressed wartime prices. He and John Whittier had worked out, with the legal aid of Seever, Lang and Murphy, a holding company that combined part of the assets of the Seldon Bank and Whittier's shipping company. The profits of the Whittier fleet could only be described as astronomical. With an entire army to be supplied in the Pacific, with the Hawaiian Islands as a rear supply base that was separated from the American mainland by thousands of miles, the hunger for cargo was insatiable. There were simply not enough ships, and the practice of adding and adding to deck cargo advanced to a point where the danger was exceeded only by the profits.

Tom would have denied that he loved money, pointing out, as he not infrequently did, that a person who grows to adulthood with all the money he requires never truly cultivates a love of money as money. There was a good deal of sophistry in this. Money meant power, and Tom loved power, and with this he enjoyed the feeling that any price, however preposterous, was within his capabilities. The house on Pacific Heights cost four hundred and eighty thousand dollars and would have cost a million to duplicate in 1944—had it been possible to build such a house at that time. It had more rooms, more floor space, and more gray granite than the Whittier mansion, and when Whittier raised an eyebrow at his junior partner's aspirations, Tom was not at all abashed. "I think it fits into my future," he said.

By now, Tom had made his peace with Eloise, and he had begun to believe that in spite of her headaches and certain other inadequacies, she was very much the ideal mate for him. For one thing, she never offered an opinion in company and rarely when the two of them were alone, and at such times, if their opinions differed, she quickly deferred to him. Mostly, she said very little, and days would pass without any conversation between husband and wife except concerning the points where the schedule of one intersected with that of the other. His advance within the navy had been steady if unspectacular, and at this point he held the rank of commander. In all truth, his job was by no means a sinecure, and as liaison between the United States Navy and the Whittier shipping interests, he checked and supervised thousands of tons of vital war cargo. In other times, it might have occurred to someone that as one of the owners of the Whittier line, he had a conflict of interest; but in those years no one bothered to dwell on such niceties. Tom was bright, charming, and wealthy; that in combination with his naval rank took him over all obstacles.

By June of 1944, the new house had been bought and furnished, and Tom decided that even in wartime the occasion called for a reception that would be both a housewarming and a celebration of his third wedding anniversary. He took a reasonable amount of pride in all his possessions, and while he considered Eloise wanting in certain areas, he felt that, dressed and groomed, she was as ornamental as any woman in San Francisco.

"Nothing very big," he told her, informing her of the occasion. "We'll have about sixty people. Do you think you can manage to put it all together?"

"Yes, if you will give me the list of the people you want. Jean will help me."

"I'd rather mother didn't help you."

"Why? She loves to help me."

"I'm not sure I want her to be here. John will come, and that will be embarrassing for both of them. We don't have to have my mother on every occasion."

Eloise took a deep breath. "This isn't every occasion," she managed to say. "This is the first large party we are giving in our new house."

"There will be others."

"No," Eloise whispered.

"No? What does that mean?"

"I don't care if John Whittier comes," she said recklessly. "I know he must come. But I won't give this kind of a party without inviting Jean."

"I'm giving the party."

"It's my home as well as yours."

"By virtue of what?" Tom asked coldly.

"By virtue of the fact that I am your wife," Eloise said desperately.

"I don't intend to argue this. We'll give the party, and mother will understand why she's not here."

"I won't be here either."

"What?"

"I'll stay in my room," Eloise cried, tears in her eyes now.

"You'll do as I say!"

"I will not."

He had not intended to hit her, just as he had not anticipated the wave of burning anger that overtook him. As he lashed out and struck her across the face with the palm of his hand, he was almost as surprised as she. She staggered back, stared at him with her hand pressed to her face, and burst into tears and fled from the room.

He followed her upstairs a few minutes later. She lay on her bed, a damp cloth across her brow.

"I'm sorry," he said. "I lost my temper. That's what you do to me. You make me so damn angry."

"I know," she whispered, squeezing the words out through the pain.

"What is it, one of those damn migraines?"

She didn't reply.

"I just look at you wrong and you get one of those damn headaches of yours. You're doing it to yourself. You know that. Up the guilts. Show Tom what a sonofabitch he is."

"I don't mean to," she managed to say, each word exploding a torrent of pain in her head.

"All right. We'll talk about it when you feel better."

The next day, her head still throbbing, Eloise went to the gallery and poured out her heart to Jean, omitting only the part when Tom had struck her. This she could not bear to communicate to anyone else.

"But my dear," Jean said, "you have invited me and I shall not come. You must not be too hard on Tom. I can't bear to see John Whittier, and to spend a whole evening in the same house with him would be punishment most cruel and unusual."

"Jean?"

"Yes, dear?"

"May I ask you something very personal?"

"Yes."

"How could you marry a man and not know how hateful he would be to you?"

Jean laughed. "Oh, my dear Eloise. There must be ten million women in America to whom you could legitimately put that question, and I don't know what any of them would answer you. It comes down to the fact of being a woman—and the male of the species being what he is, God help him. Marriage is probably the most difficult, delicate undertaking any human being attempts, and we don't have an iota of preparation or training, only the idiotic presumption that marriages are made in heaven and that one lives happily ever after." She paused and studied Eloise. "That frightens you, doesn't it?"

"A little."

"And you're not very happy, are you?"

"I have Freddie. He's darling. He's good and beautiful. I would have brought him over today, but you know he listens to everything, and I don't like to talk in front of him about things like this. People imagine that a two-year-old understands no more than a puppy, but they're wrong."

"Of course they are. But you haven't answered my question."

"No, I haven't. No, I'm not very happy."

"Well, what shall I say? You're a lovely, sensitive young woman. I remember myself at your age. I had a shell of ice, and I didn't hurt too easily. But I was luckier than you. I married a man who was quite remarkable, but he had his own shell. I suppose we were both as hard as nails, or perhaps so soft that we had to pretend to be. It's so difficult to know anything about yourself, and to learn something about another is almost impossible. But we were both of us very tough. You're not. You're gentle, and you hurt too easily. If Tom hurts too much—don't destroy yourself and don't let him destroy you."

"I couldn't leave Tom," she said plaintively. "I know what his plans are. A divorce would wreck his career."

"I suppose it would," Jean agreed.

For thirty-eight hours with no sleep, stimulated by Benzedrine, Joe Lavette had been operating in the base hospital hastily thrown together at Guam. He had amputated arms, legs, hands; separated bits of metal of every shape from intestines, kidneys, lungs, liver, and stomach; probed, dissected, sutured; found himself soaked with blood; changed, scrubbed, operated again; become blood-soaked again— and was finally relieved. Walking blindly, dumbly, he was handed a letter that had just arrived. He went to his tent, sat down on his cot, and stared at the letter, his eyes closing with fatigue. He lay back on the cot and in a moment he was asleep, the letter clutched in his hand. When he awakened, nine hours later, the letter was still there. He sat up and stared at it, unable to remember how it had come to be there. It was from Sally Levy, and as he straightened the envelope, smoothing it where he had crushed it, he smiled for the first time in days.

He placed the unopened letter tenderly on his pillow, and he washed and shaved. It was two o'clock on a hot and damp afternoon. He was ravenously hungry, and he took the letter with him to the mess tent, putting off the pleasure of reading it. There had been no mail for weeks. He filled his stomach with plasticlike scrambled eggs, soggy bacon, sliced white bread, and three cups of black, sour coffee; then, carefully and gently, he opened the letter and began to read:

"My dear, beloved Joe," she wrote. "This is an unhappy letter. Our beautiful, darling Joshua is dead. I write these words and look at them, and they have no meaning. How can it be? He was only twenty years old. He hadn't even begun to live. And he was so gentle and sensitive and kind. I don't think he ever hurt anyone in his life. I thought that I was through with tears, because it is four days since we received the news, but now I had to stop and weep again. I live with my own guilts. I was so vile to him. I used to push him around unmercifully, and when I would lose my temper, I would turn on him and hit him, and he would just stand and grin at me and take it, and I'm writing this because I can't say it to anyone else, but you will understand because you know how horrible I can be.

"The thing is, you have two big brothers and you just accept them. You don't think about it, because there they are and they will always be there. And then the letter came, and mother opened it, and she just sat there staring at it. How does it feel to be a mother, and then you get a letter telling you that your son has been killed in a kamikaze attack and that he has been buried at sea, so you will never look at his face again or see his grave? I know what it feels like to be his sister, but I think that if I were mother, I would have died there. Right there. And she didn't say anything. She didn't even cry at first. She just handed the letter to pop, and he read it, and then he put his head down on the table and began to cry. I had never seen him cry before. I guess I had never seen any grown man cry, and I didn't even know what had happened, but I could guess. And then mom went over and put her arms around him. I think women are maybe stronger than men, or maybe some women, because pop just went to pieces. He was in the first war, so I suppose he felt this terribly, I mean with terrible pain. He hasn't spoken to me since it happened, except he puts his arms around me, and when he does that, the tears start again. Mom won't let me see her cry, but I walked into her room, and she was sitting there, crying as if her heart was completely broken, which I guess it is.

"What makes it worse is that we haven't heard from Adam in two weeks. We believe that he was in the D-day landing on Normandy, and that would account for him not being able to write. He is always very thoughtful about writing. Then we read in the papers that there were heavy casualties among company commanders, and he's a company commander, which just makes everything more terrible. I know that this isn't a pleasant letter, but I can't go on if I don't share everything with you, and the thought that you are out there somewhere in that crazy war in the Pacific just makes me half insane with worry. If anything happened to you, I would die, Joe. That's it. I would just die. I wouldn't want to live anymore. And almost everyone I love is gone now, with Barbara away somewhere in Asia or India or someplace. I tell myself that I have to remain calm and composed. Now mom and pop look at me, and I know what they are thinking. They are thinking that I'm all they have left.

"Dear good Joe, please, please be careful and take care of yourself, I love you so much. I love you more than I can say or put down on paper. Please come back to me just the way you are."

Barbara sent her editor a short cable, very much to the point: "I think I've had enough. Returning. Cable me at the USA PR in Karachi." But it was a week before she could be cleared for a flight to Karachi, the first stop on the Air Transport route back to the States, a week of boredom and misery in the wet heat of Calcutta. A few days before she left, there was news of the Normandy invasion, and Barbara could only reflect with gratitude that soon, perhaps, the war would come to its finish. The flight to Karachi, across the whole great subcontinent of India, was without incident, but at the public relations office in Karachi, there was no answer to her cable. This was provoking but not too disturbing, for she had known cables to take ten days between India and the States. She left word to be notified the moment a cable arrived for her, and she checked into the press hostel.

Once in her room, she discovered with relief that she had her own shower. It had been hot and wet in Calcutta; here it was a hundred and ten degrees in the shade when her plane landed, and dry. She had often wondered which was worse. Showered and with a change of clothes, she went down to the lobby and ran into Mike Kendell, a correspondent for the Washington *Post* whom she had met briefly in North Africa. Kendell was in his mid-forties, fleshy and scarlet-faced from a consistent consumption of alcohol, a city desk reporter who had gotten his first chance overseas during the war. Barbara would not have remembered him, but he fell upon her with joy.

"God in heaven!" he shouted. "A beautiful woman in this pisshole! Don't you remember? Mike Kendell."

"Of course."

"Let me buy you a drink."

"In this weather? All right, tonic water. I don't dare drink when it's this hot."

"Best time. Warms the inside, cools the outside." And seated in the bar, he asked her, "What brings you out this way?"

"Going home, I hope. I've had it—up to here." She touched her throat. "War is for men and idiots. Or are they the same?"

"Come on, baby. Don't be so hard on us."

"Which way for you, Mike?"

"Burma, maybe China, if we get there, if I survive, if I can stay drunk. When do you pull out?"

"I'm waiting for a cable from my editor. Today, tomorrow, the next day. It can't come too soon. I've had eight months of this. It's enough."

"Look, Barbara, you're in for tonight, anyway. No more planes out of here today. The limeys are throwing a party tonight. Come along with me. You know, very posh, regimental headquarters, charge of the light brigade, gunga din, all that Indian crap. You'll enjoy it."

"This is my last clean uniform."

"You look great. Listen, they got a great dry cleaning service here, honest to God. Give me all your stuff and I'll get it cleaned for you. That's paying my dues. Anyway, you're safe with me. By midnight, I'm too drunk to make a pass at Mae West."

"O.K., I'm your date," Barbara agreed.

"Pick you up at eight."

Barbara had been to British regimental parties before, and this one was no different: British officers grasping an opportunity to wear their dress uniforms and pretend that nothing in India had changed, British officers up from the ranks who had never owned a dress uniform, American officers, stringy, dried-out British ladies who had lived a lifetime in India, Red Cross women, a sprinkling of nurses, a few correspondents, a few civilians, but very noticeably no natives, no Indians. The moment she entered the room —a broad, handsome room with a high ceiling and pol-

ished teak beams—she regretted that she had agreed to
come. She would be bored; she would be told by half-
drunk, lonely men that she was the most attractive woman
there; she would spend the evening in a miasma of alco-
holic breath; she would dance with men who grasped her
out of hunger and desperation; and she would be looked
at with envy by other women who were older, tired, plain.
How often she had despised her own beauty, seeing it as an
illusion that separated her not only from the world but
from herself; but those were bad moments. Tonight she
told herself that even this banality was better than another
evening alone in her room, trying to read, trying to sleep,
trying to forget the things she had seen.

Men clustered around her. On these occasions, men always clustered around her. She lost Mike Kendell to the
bar and found herself dancing with a British officer and
trying to decipher the layers of ribbon on his blouse. His
name was Wescott, Colonel Wescott, about forty, very
charming, breaking his back to be charming: "Never could
find the proper words for American women. God's gift,
you know. But whoever thought to find a girl like you in
Karachi. Makes the war worthwhile, don't you know?"

"I'm sure it does." Barbara smiled. "You were in the
first African campaign, weren't you? With the Italians?"

"Reading my ribbons, are you? Bright girl. Quite. With
Wavell. Do you know, that's deuced hard to say. Never
occurred to me before. With Wavell, yes, quite."

"I knew a sergeant who was in it. He was with a gun
carrier. I thought perhaps—"

"Gun carriers, Bren trucks—that is your word, isn't it,
trucks?"

"How clever of you," Barbara said.

"Not at all. What was his name?"

"Bernie Cohen."

"Cohen? He'd be a Jew, wouldn't he?"

"I'm afraid so."

"No, can't recollect any Cohen. Didn't have much to do
with enlisted men, to tell you the truth. Bernie Cohen.
No, can't say that I ever met him. Relation of yours? Don't
tell me you're Jewish?"

"Just as dreadful," Barbara said seriously. "I'm
Italian."

"You're pulling my leg."

"Oh, no. But I've learned to live with it."

When the music stopped, she found Mike Kendell tugging at her arm, and she allowed him to draw her over to the side of the room. "I heard you asking the limey about a Bernie Cohen. Maybe there are fifty Sergeant Cohens in the British army. Who knows? I met up with one in Tunis."

"Let's get a drink," Barbara said, steering Kendell toward the bar. "The hell with the weather."

"You don't think you could get tight enough to look upon me with dewy eyes, as the poets say?"

"Not likely. But I have a deep affection for you, Mike. Do you know, the more I see of the British out here, the deeper my affection for Americans. I used to love the British, but their tight little island suits them better than this place. God, I've had my fill of the mysterious East! When I get back to San Francisco, I'm never going south of Market Street or west of Van Ness, and since I live one block to the east of Van Ness, that about sums up my state of mind; and for six months I'm going to wear nothing but organdy and crêpe de Chine. You know, years ago I met a guy whose name was Bernie Cohen—I won't go into the circumstances—and now he's in the British army, if he's still alive. He's a good friend, and so I ask around. One day I'll meet a British officer who won't do a double take when he hears a Jewish name. What about this Sergeant Cohen?"

He ordered two gin and tonics from the turbaned Sikh behind the bar. "I guess it was about a year ago, maybe a little more. When was it Von Arnim surrendered on Cape Bon?"

"May of forty-three."

"God damndest thing you ever saw. We had these POW compounds, and the Germans marched into them in perfect order, as if they were on parade. There was one battalion that goose-stepped. Would you believe that? Goose-stepping into a prisoner-of-war compound."

"What about Cohen?"

"Right. Well, I'm watching this with a couple of guys from the AP and some British enlisted men. One of them is a big feller, maybe six-foot-two or -three, and that in itself is very peculiar with the limeys. They run pretty small, except among the officers, and this guy has a shoulder patch I never saw before, some sort of a Jewish unit. So I ask him about the patch."

"What did he look like?" Barbara asked eagerly. "Come on, Mike, you're a writer. Describe him."

"Like I said, big, six-foot-two or -three. Hawklike nose—how's that? Blue eyes, very pale blue. I remember that because his skin was burned brown as leather, and the eyes were like blue holes in his head. Very cold, very tough. Interviewing him was like pulling teeth. And an American. Did I tell you that?"

"No, you idiot, you didn't."

"Did you just say you were from San Francisco?"

"Yes, that's what I said."

"So was he."

"It has to be. For God's sake, Mike, tell me about him. Don't just stand there looking at me."

"He fought in Spain," Kendell said.

"I'm going to cry," Barbara whispered. "I tried so hard to find him. When I was in North Africa, I must have asked a hundred people."

"Are you in love with this guy?"

"I can't explain it, Mike. It's very complicated. What else did you find out about him?"

"Well, he was in the African thing from the beginning. It made a good story. They commissioned him in the field, and he was made a second louie, or something like that, and then his captain made some disparaging remark about his being Jewish, and Cohen beat him up and was court-martialed and busted. He would have been jailed, but apparently he was the best weapons expert they had, and, well, there he was at Cape Bon, where it ended. I can't tell you much more than that, because as I said, it was like pulling teeth." He lifted his glass. "Here's to you, lady. Shape up. Because if he's your guy, he is one tough cookie."

Barbara shook her head sadly. "No, Mike. He's not my guy, and he's not so tough. Where do you suppose he is now?"

"God knows! I think they shipped some of them out to Burma, but I imagine most of them went to England for the invasion."

The following day, Barbara's cable arrived. Her editor reluctantly accepted her decision to come home, begging her, however, to turn the journey to use. The Air Transport

Command was setting up an airlift from the China-Burma-India theater for the time when it would be needed to ferry troops back. A series of airfields had been hastily established in Iraq, Iran, Saudi Arabia, and Baluchistan. There was one spot in particular called Sharjah, in Saudi Arabia, and the paper had printed a letter from a local boy stationed there. A background story would be useful, so could she work out a stopover? And finally, the cable read, "I don't know what to do with your story about the famine. It's a hell of a story, but is this the time?"

It was a hundred and five degrees in the shade in Karachi the day she left, and while she knew nothing about Saudi Arabia, she felt it couldn't be any worse than this; but when the C-47 finally dipped down and landed in a blazing, sunbaked expanse of white sand, she began to have doubts, and when she stepped out of the plane, a blast of heat struck her and made her feel that death was imminent. The installation was only a hundred yards from where the plane rolled to a stop, but Barbara knew deep in her heart that she would die before she crossed that space. The young navigator of the plane saw Barbara stagger, and he went up to her, took her arm, and said cheerfully, "It's all mental, miss. This is a regular part of my run. Just think about ice cream and snow. The installation is air-cooled."

Somehow she made it. There was a huge thermometer on the wall on the porch of the installation, and it read a hundred and twenty-four degrees Fahrenheit. "Good heavens," she whispered, "what is it out in the sun?"

"Never took it, miss," the navigator said. "Better off that way."

Half a dozen GIs were unloading cargo from the plane. They wore gloves, as did the mechanics who were fueling it.

"Why the gloves in this heat?" Barbara asked.

"To keep them from burning their hands."

The door from the porch led directly into the mess, where the temperature was no more than eighty degrees, and cool by contrast. The soldiers sitting there, playing cards or sipping Cokes, looked at her bleakly, and it appeared to Barbara that the whole place was depressed to the point of somber madness. The navigator had observed to her that, stationed here, he would blow out his brains in a week. The commanding officer, a Lieutenant Cocoron, in his mid-twenties, greeted her uncertainly.

"You're the first white woman," he said. "You're a correspondent, aren't you?"

Barbara nodded.

"You don't mean to stay here. I mean, I'd like to have you stay, but we haven't got any accommodations for a woman. Jesus, I just don't know. We never had any reporter here before."

"I don't know. What do you say?" Barbara asked him. "The truth is, I think if I step out into that heat again, I shall go quite mad."

Grinning inanely, the lieutenant said, "At least we don't sweat. Dry heat. That's a plus. But why did you come here?"

"I work for a San Francisco paper. My editor cabled that there's a San Francisco kid stationed here, and that I should do a background story on him."

"A San Francisco kid? Jesus, that must be Polchek."

"Adrian Polchek, yes."

Cocoron shook his head. "He's gone."

"Oh? He went home?" she asked.

"No. He's in jail in Cairo. He raped an Arab girl."

"Oh, no!"

"Look, why don't you sit down and let me get you a Coke." She sank into a chair at one of the tables. "Brady," Cocoron called to one of the soldiers, "get the lady a Coke." The GIs in the mess were staring at her hungrily. One or two of them grinned. But most of them just stared at her, bleakly, hungrily. Brady brought her the Coke. It was cold, and she drank it eagerly, realizing for the first time how very thirsty she was.

"Tell me about it," she said to Cocoron.

"You're sure you want me to?"

"Of course I do. I'm a reporter. The only reason I'm here is to get a story on this kid, and now you tell me he's in jail in Cairo."

"Well, you know, we only got two rooms in this lousy installation, this and the barracks." He glanced at the soldiers, who had stopped talking and were listening intently.

"Please," Barbara said.

"O.K." He dropped his voice, but still he could be heard. "I'm Lebanese," he said. "I mean my mom and pop were. Anyway, I talk the language, and that's the only reason

I'm here in this shithole. No. Please. I don't know how to talk to a dame anymore."

"I heard all the words," Barbara reassured him.

"Yeah, I guess so. All right, so you're the first American woman ever set foot in this place. You know what that's like?"

"I know."

"Yeah. Well," he said uneasily, "it's like this. We got two or three Arab girls come from the village to clean up."

"You mean people live here?"

"There's a village two miles away. They got a little well there. Look, I want you to understand. Not Arab girls—I mean, not just Arab girls. These women are slaves."

"Slaves? You mean their situation in social terms—the Arab family and women's place?"

"No. No, miss. I don't mean that." He glanced around the room uneasily. "These are slaves. They still got the slave trade here, black girls they bring in from Africa. Well, Christ, you got to understand how it is here." His voice dropped still further. "Some of the guys sleep with them. Fifty cents, which is more money than anyone in the village ever saw before. Then they turn the money over to their owners. Well, they raised the price, and one of them demanded a dollar from Polchek, and he got sore and wouldn't give her anything, and then this headman from the village comes back with the girl and lodges a charge of rape against Polchek. They know the law, and word gets around, even out here, and there wasn't a damn thing I could do. I had to send him up to Cairo with the charge."

"But why? Why didn't you pay him off? Ten dollars probably would have bought the headman and his village too."

"Don't you think I thought of that, miss? But the way the breaks come, we had two air force captains here, straight out of stateside, and they raised hell and put the kid under arrest."

"And what happens now?" Barbara asked him.

"Christ, I don't know. We're stuck down here in the asshole of creation—forgive the expression, but that's what it is. We can't appear as witnesses unless they call us, and that depends on how much they want to brown-nose the Saudis, which is a lot. The guys want me to go up there, but there's just no way. He could get fifteen years or ten years or five years or just dishonorable discharge, depending."

"Was it rape?"

"No, ma'am, it was not. The girl was a hustler, and the poor dumb kid wouldn't have done anything, but she was scared to death of the headman."

"Well, who will testify against Polchek? The girl?"

"No, ma'am. If the Saudis want to make something out of it, they'll bring the headman up there. But just the charge is enough to get the kid a dishonorable discharge."

An hour later, Barbara staggered through the heat back to the plane, and a few minutes after that they took off for Cairo, Barbara the only passenger, sharing the plane with a cargo of empty Coca-Cola bottles. Once they were airborne, the young navigator came back and asked her whether she was going to write anything about the so-called rape.

"I'll do the best I can," Barbara said.

"Well, all I can say, miss, is that I'd rather be dead than stationed there at Sharjah. That's worse than hell itself. That's just the worst place there is, and some of those guys have been there six months. They don't have any replacements for those jobs, because it's too far back from any front, so they just forget about it for the duration."

"I wonder," Barbara asked herself, "what I would do if I were trapped there?"

The sun was setting when the plane landed at Payne Field in Cairo. Captain Leonard Belton, the Public Relations officer for Air Transport, spotted Barbara as she entered the airport building, grabbed her Valpack, and assured her that he had never believed life could be this kind to him. "How long is it, Miss Lavette? Months. And for a man who adored you—"

"I'm on my way home, Leonard. Nothing, but nothing, is going to get in my way."

"I'm not even married," he pleaded. "How many of these old married bastards have you had to fight off? And my love is a true love. Will you at least have dinner with me tonight?"

Barbara regarded him thoughtfully. He was tall, rather good-looking, and rather nondescript. He had been an assistant to an account executive in a large New York advertising agency before the war, but as he had put it to her when she had been in Cairo earlier, his best years were

the war years. The best of everything. He was describing
the new VIP hostel that had recently been completed. "I
swear," he told her, "that there isn't a hotel in New York
that can offer better service. Kid, it's the absolute lap of
luxury. We have a dining room that would make the Plaza
weep. Maybe not as big, but class. And the food is good.
That, love, is the essential nature of war—it is all on the
house. You don't even need a charge account. When I
saw your name on the transport list, I reserved the
absolute best suite in the place. Bedroom, sitting room, and
bath. Wait until you see that bathroom. And all I ask in
return is to bask in the loveliness of your smile. Well,
maybe a little more—but I'm a good loser. Where have
you been?"

Barbara shook her head hopelessly. "You are wonderful,
Leonard. Absolutely wonderful. You restore my faith in all
the American verities. Now you want to know where I've
been. Without being too specific, during the past few
months I have been in India, in Afghanistan, in Assam,
and in Burma. More immediately, only this morning I was
in Saudi Arabia. I am hot, sweaty, tired, and entirely
exhausted. In ten minutes I will probably collapse. All I
desire now is to sit in a tub for half an hour, and then to
pour cologne all over myself, and then to read some
stateside magazine, like the *Ladies' Home Journal* or
Redbook. So if you will take me to this Shangri-la of
yours, I will be everlastingly grateful."

"How grateful?"

"Dinner tomorrow night. But—"

"All right. What's the but?"

"You bring with you the top public relations man in the
whole area. Who is he, by the way?"

"Oh, no. Don't do that to me. His name is Oswald D.
Ormsbey. Colonel Ormsbey. He's a lecherous old bastard."

"Good. Then you tell him I'm beautiful and reasonably
sexy and he'll come."

"Where does that leave me?"

"You're my chaperon. And do find me a copy of the
Ladies' Home Journal. Please."

Barbara dozed in the tub, then dried herself luxuriously.
The VIP House was all that Belton had promised, and the
magnificence of her two-room suite filled her with guilt.
She had sandwiches and coffee sent up to her room, and
as there were no women's magazines available, the amiable

GI room service sent along a copy of *Yank*. She opened it casually, and read:

Sure there were lots of bodies we never identified. You know what a direct hit by a shell does to a guy. Or a mine. Or a solid hit with a grenade, even. Sometimes all we have is a leg or a hunk of arm.

The ones that stink the worst are the guys who got internal wounds and are dead about three weeks with the blood staying inside and rotting, and when you move the body the blood comes out of the nose and mouth. Then some of them bloat up in the sun; they bloat up so big they bust the buttons, and then they get blue and the skin peels. They don't all get blue; some of them get black.

But they all stink. There's only one stink, and that's it. You never get used to it, either. As long as you live, you never get used to it. And after a while, the stink gets in your clothes and you can taste it in your mouth.

You know what I think? I think maybe if every civilian in the world could smell that stink, then maybe we wouldn't have any more wars.

"I am reading this," Barbara said to herself, "and I am sitting here in a guest house of the United States Army—since you can't let very important people down, especially if they are attractive women—and I am eating a sandwich and drinking coffee in a room that any American millionaire would be proud of, and it's the same war, and I think I have forgotten how to weep. Perhaps nature rations tears. That would be very sensible. You are born with three million, one hundred, and seventy-two potential tears, and you can use them up by the time you are eighteen or you can conserve them. I have been profligate with mine. In Burma, the smell of the dead is worse. I suppose it's the heat."

In any case, the air conditioning in the VIP House was perfect, and Barbara slept as she had not slept in months. She was in bed at eleven, and she slept for fourteen hours. When she opened her eyes, the room was flushed with sunlight. For another hour she lay there lazily, thinking of nothing in particular, dozing, slipping in and out of an elusive dream world, reviewing connections and memories.

She conjured up the sun-drenched, hazy folds of the Napa Valley, the old vine-covered stone buildings of Higate Winery. Both boys were in the army, she recalled, two tall, skinny, freckled, redheaded boys, and her thoughts turned to Sally. She loved Sally, delicious, mad Sally, and that thought plunged her into a haunting nostalgia. How she missed them, how much she loved them—all the bits and pieces and connections of her life, her father and her mother, and Joe off in Hawaii—when she had last heard from him—and Jake and Clair Levy, and the little bit of life called Frederick, her first nephew, and even Tom and Eloise. Yes, she assured herself, she loved Tom, and she would not fault him for having a safe stateside spot, and thank heavens someone in her circle had enough sense to stay away from the lunacy that had overtaken the world.

And May Ling. She would come back to a world without May Ling. It did not seem possible. Three and a half years since May Ling had died; but here, so far away from home and the place of her memories, the fact of May Ling's death lost its reality. Dozing, Barbara saw her again, returned her to life, made everything as it should be, the little house in Westwood unchanged, May Ling embracing her, brewing tea, putting the insane world back to order in terms of her simple, childlike common sense.

She slept and awakened, and the world returned to reality.

Finally, Barbara got out of bed. She bathed again, unable to resist the luxury of the big tub, hot water, and scented bath soap. Then an appreciatively grinning GI brought her toast and coffee and fresh orange juice and crisp bacon.

"It sure beats the infantry," he said.

She resisted the temptation to go out and wander around Cairo and perhaps visit the pyramids again. She had done all that long ago. Instead, she spent the balance of the afternoon writing the story of the Sharjah installation and Private Polchek. It was certainly an odd, strange, offbeat story, but then, most of her stories were. She was not expected to report the battles and the troop movements.

She was interrupted by a telephone call from Captain Belton. "The old bastard is coming," he told her.

"Good. Now tell me something about him."

"What's to tell? He's about fifty, originates in Omaha, Nebraska, and was a captain or something in the National

Guard. He ran some kind of a boondock advertising agency there, and now he's a colonel in PR."

"Does he have a heart?"

"Sure, in his pants."

"Well, bring him along. We'll manage."

"Where do you want to eat? You want some exotic Egyptian food?"

"No, I don't think so. Do you suppose they'd serve dinner for three in my sitting room here?"

"Just tell them it's for Colonel Ormsbey, and they'll serve dinner for a regiment. Sure. That's a good idea. Anyway, it's the best food in Cairo."

Belton and Ormsbey arrived at Barbara's suite at seven forty-five. Ormsbey was a plump, pink-cheeked man with thin, pale hair and glasses. He was effusive and delighted with Barbara. He requested martinis, and sent the GI waiter back to the bar to rectify the proportions of vermouth and gin. "One to seven," he instructed him. "And, soldier, tell Jackson at the bar to send along two bottles of wine. The best. Understand?" Then he said to Barbara, "Now, Miss Lavette, what do you think of this little institution we set up here? Is it class, or isn't it? Not easy to maintain this kind of place with a war on. You got to fight them tooth and nail. But"—he emphasized this with a pudgy finger directed at her—"we carry weight. PR. Public Relations. Everyone wants a good press. That's human nature. Take a woman like yourself. Put her in a barracks? That would be an abomination. People like yourself bring the war home to those we love. I suspect your forte is the human side of war. I haven't read your stuff, but that's what I suspect. Am I right?"

"Uncannily right," Barbara agreed, smiling. "You're a perceptive man, Colonel."

She had anticipated the colonel's taste and ordered steak, fried potatoes, and green peas. Pie and Egyptian melon for dessert. Coffee and brandy. The waiter brought the brandy in deference to the colonel's presence.

Barbara noticed Belton watching her keenly, wondering what kind of game she was playing. Ormsbey had two martinis and most of a bottle of wine, but with no more effect than an increased flush on his cheeks. He ate with hearty appetite, and Barbara poured him a large brandy. He took out a cigar and asked gallantly, "Do you mind this foul weed, dear lady?"

"Not at all. My father smokes cigars. I rather like the odor."

"Ah. Good. A fine meal without a cigar is like life without a woman, endurable, but by no means satisfying." He clipped off the end of the cigar and lit it, a man at peace with the world. "I understand you write for a San Francisco paper?"

"Yes, the *Chronicle*."

"Fine paper. Fine paper." He took another puff. "Of course, with the European invasion on, we're just a backwash. Not too many good stories here. But I'm sure we could find something to entertain your readers."

"As a matter of fact, I did," Barbara said. "I was in Saudi Arabia yesterday, at a place called Sharjah. I'd like to tell you about it—if I may. I don't want to bore you."

"Bore me? That would be the day, my dear. Go ahead."

Barbara told the story of her trip to Sharjah and of the dilemma of Private Adrian Polchek. When she had finished, Colonel Ormsbey was silent for a minute or so.

"Do you know this Polchek?" Ormsbey asked.

"No, I don't."

"Never met him?"

"No."

"Then what's your interest in him?"

"Just that he's a San Francisco boy and that I feel he has been done an injustice. I've spent the afternoon writing the story. I expect it will be picked up by one of the wire service men here. I'd like to end my story by saying that the charges were dropped."

"I know about the Polchek case," Ormsbey said slowly. "We put out a release on him, didn't we, Belton?"

"Yes, sir, we did."

"You know, we've had a lot of trouble with the Saudis. The President's gone out of his way to keep it nice and friendly with Ibn Saud. Very top priority. The Saudis know about this case. Hell, it's not a question of what happened down there. This kid got himself in hot water, and we got to make an example of him."

"But, you know," Barbara said gently, "if I wrote a story headlining this as a grotesque injustice—front page in the San Francisco *Chronicle*—it will be picked up by every paper in the country. It will become a *cause célèbre*. Heaven knows where it might end. And that would reflect very badly on Public Relations here."

Ormsbey puffed his cigar thoughtfully. Barbara and Belton waited. Ormsbey finished his brandy and poured himself another. Then he turned to Belton and said, "Leonard, beat it!"

"Sir?"

"I said, beat it. Get out. Make yourself scarce. I want to talk to Miss Lavette privately."

Belton hesitated, sighed, rose, said good-night to Barbara, and left the room.

"What makes you think I could do anything about this, Barbara—you don't mind if I call you Barbara?"

"Not at all. Oh, I think you carry weight, Colonel. If you let the adjutant general know that this will make a godawful stink, well, the kid will get off with a reprimand at worst."

"And it's important to you?"

"Very important."

Ormsbey finished his brandy. "Tell you what, Barbara, we'll make a trade. I'll get the kid off the hook. You do your end."

"What's my end, Colonel?"

"Leonard tells me you're booked out of here tomorrow. We'll probably never see each other again. You're a damn attractive woman, and I'm not the worst-looking man on earth."

He paused and Barbara waited. "Go on," Barbara said.

"Hell, Barbara, do I have to spell it out? We're not kids, either of us. You've been around."

Barbara regarded him thoughtfully. "What you're saying, Colonel, is that you'd like to fuck me, and if I go along with that, you'll let the kid off."

"You're putting it damn bluntly. I wouldn't use that language to a woman."

"That's commendable delicacy on your part. Are you married, Colonel?"

"Look, Barbara, I put it on the line. Because you struck me as a woman who knows the ropes. You're asking me to stick my neck out. Well, quid pro quo, as they say."

Barbara smiled. "Or tit for tat, as they also say. I'll tell you what, Colonel. Here's a counteroffer. I'll stay here an extra day. If the charges against Polchek are dropped tomorrow, I won't write an absolutely fascinating story, namely, how a colonel in the United States Army offered me a deal, a boy's life for a night in bed."

"You wouldn't!"

"Why not?"

"Your paper wouldn't dare print it."

"You don't know the *Chronicle*."

"I'd sue them for their last cent."

"I bet you wouldn't."

"What the hell kind of a bitch are you?"

"That kind," Barbara agreed. She poured brandy into the colonel's glass. "Have another drink." She smiled at him. "Come on, Oswald, you tried and you lost. A man can do no more."

He sipped the brandy and began to grin. "God damn it, I'm beginning to like you."

"And the kid gets off?"

"No deals. I'll bust my ass to get him off. How about your giving me a break?"

Barbara shook her head. "It wouldn't work. It just wouldn't work at all. We'll just sit here and chat while you finish the cigar and the brandy—and then off you go."

A half-hour later, Barbara steered him to the door, kissed him on his pink cheek, and saw him stagger uncertainly down the hallway. The following day the charges against Private Polchek were dropped, and the day after that Barbara left Cairo on the first leg of her journey home. Colonel Ormsbey saw her to the airport, and she kissed the pink cheek for a second time. "You're a good man, Oswald," she told him.

"If you're ever in Omaha?"

"Absolutely, if I'm ever in Omaha."

At about seven o'clock in the morning, on the sixth of June, Captain Adam Levy leaped into the water off an LST, which stands for Landing Ship, Tanks, and moved in toward the beach. His first impression was the shock of the icy cold water; then he almost fell, telling himself, "Damnit, don't fall. You'll freeze." He was very frightened, but the thought of freezing took his mind off it, and because he felt impelled to do something other than stagger through the cold water, he shouted for his platoon leaders to stay in touch with him. A fleeting thought informed him that he himself could not hear his own voice, so how could anyone else hear it? No one had warned him that he would not be able to hear his own voice. They never briefed you on things like that. The reason was not only the thunderous

bombardment from the ships offshore, but the roar of the
surf and the howling of the wind. Strangely, there were
concrete blocks sticking out of the water. He didn't know
what those were, either.

He saw a man on his right go down, thinking, He must
have slipped. Or could it be gunfire from the beach? He
had no sense of gunfire, and afterward he thought about
that man and wondered whether he had been shot and had
fallen dead in the water before they ever reached the beach.
The thought of death in the cold water horrified him,
even though it couldn't be any worse than death on dry
land.

A minute or so later he was on the beach himself, slopping through the lacy foam and yelling for his platoon
leaders again. Adam had come to learn the art of swearing
in the army and he had embraced it. That was the result of
early deprivation; his mother, Clair, had spent her childhood on lumber ships on the California redwood coast,
and she had learned to swear like a trooper at a very early
age. The result was that she became an absolute martinet
with her children when it came to foul language; and now
Adam, a late starter, was shouting, "Califino, you mother-
fucking second-rate sonofabitch, where the hell are you?"

"Here, Captain." The voice was in his ear. Califino was
right behind him.

"For Christ's sake, Lieutenant, get them up!" Adam
yelled, pointing to where the men in his company had
flung themselves onto the wet sand, the tide wash slopping
over them. "Get them up! Prinsky!" Sergeant Prinsky was
crouching, a few feet away. "Prinsky, get them up on the
beach!"

Califino, big, heavy, phlegmatic, pulled Adam down onto
the sand and spoke into his ear, "You got to stop shouting,
Captain. Voice goes. Sore throat."

"Where's Meyers?" Lieutenant Meyers was his other
platoon leader.

"God knows. I don't see him."

"Thing is, we got to get them up the beach."

"How far?"

"Make it a hundred yards. We'll try to group there and
dig in. Take the right; I'll take the left."

Adam ran down to the left, stooping, kicking the men,
"Up the beach! A hundred yards!" The first dead man he
saw was Oppenheim. He lay on his back, a bullethole in

his head, grinning stupidly. It was his first real comprehension that they were being fired upon, and it came as a shock. Sergeant Duggan rolled over to stare at him and pointed to where small-arms fire was kicking up the sand. Adam squatted. "This is the worst damn place," he said to Duggan. "This is a shithole. Come on, Duggan. Get your guys up there. Up there, a hundred yards."

Duggan began to crawl, waving on his squad. "I'll make a point," Adam said excitedly. "Understand, I make the point." He couldn't crawl. He raced up the beach, counting his paces. The jumping sandspouts of small-arms fire reached out for him, and he began to take crazy leaps, as if doing the high hurdles. Far enough, he decided, and he turned, waving his arms. At least a dozen of his men raced after him, one of them hit and spinning like a top; then Califino reached him and dragged him down.

"That was dumb!" Califino said. "Adam, dumb! That was a crazy thing to do!"

"Fuck it! We dig in, right here."

The men who had run after Adam flung themselves onto the sand around him and began to dig, using their hands, their rifle butts.

"God damn it, use your trenching tools!"

"Schwartz got it," someone said.

Crawling, wriggling, running in spurts, the men of the company reached Adam's point and began to dig in. A fold of dirt protected them. The sandspouts were kicking up behind them. Six bodies lay between the surf and their position. Whistles were blowing, piercing the noise of the bombardment. A shrill voice yelled for medics. It was a bleak, overcast day. Adam could see the big LSTs lurching in the water. Where was the next wave? Where were their reenforcements? Where were the tanks? The orders said they would be supported by tanks.

Lieutenant Sisily from the headquarters company came wriggling through the sand. He was a prissy, spit-and-polish young man. Califino and Adam grinned at each other, and Adam said to himself, "I'm crazy, lying here in a hole, soaked and grinning at that jerk."

"I think it's raining," Califino said.

"Oh, shit on him. Come on, Sisily, you crawl like a fuckin' earthworm." Sisily was shouting to them. They could see the motion of his lips but couldn't hear a word.

He stopped. "The hell with it," Adam said. "Let's get over there." They crawled to Sisily.

"If you stay down," Adam said into his ear, a wave of compassion overtaking him, "that fold of earth protects us."

"I dirtied my pants," Sisily said, tears in his eyes.

"It's only shit. Forget it."

"Where's the command post?" Adam asked him.

"Two hundred yards back. The major wants to know how many casualties you have?"

"I haven't checked. We're just trying to group. I don't think more than ten or twelve."

Sisily closed his eyes and shook his head. Califino touched Adam's shoulder and pointed down the beach. Two more LSTs were discharging men, who flattened out just above the waterline.

"That's a lot of help," Adam said. "Come on, Lieutenant. So you shit in your pants. Life goes on. What does the major want us to do?"

Now, suddenly, mortar fire began. A shell exploded about twenty feet away, showering them with dirt. "He says," Sisily managed, "that there's a bluff, ten, twelve feet high, up ahead."

"How far?"

"He thinks maybe three hundred yards. That's where the fire is coming from. He says we got to get up there and silence it. You're the closest point."

"Ah, shit, come on, Sisily! The major's got more sense than that!" Califino yelled.

"I'll go talk to the major," Adam said. "Get them dug in, Califino, and see if you can find some medics. Come on, Sisily. Show me the way."

The major, a thoughtful man in his mid-forties, was almost as confused as Sisily. "We sort of knew about that bluff," he told Adam, spreading out a sopping wet map in the big hole that had been dug as a command post, "but we didn't expect any resistance there."

"Major, what about tanks? What about air cover?"

The major pointed hopelessly to the leaden gray sky.

"Well, where the hell are the tanks?"

The major shook his head.

"What about those men down there?" he asked, pointing to the water's edge. "Are they staying there?"

"That's our weapons company."

"Oh, shit! Those dumb motherfuckers!"

"Levy, look. We can't use machine guns, and even the tanks can't get up that bluff. You have to go up with men and grenades."

"Why us? My men have no combat experience."

"Because you're there."

"What about those lousy bastards on the battleships? Why don't they lay some shellfire on it? They've been laying their stinking shells everywhere else."

"We have no communication, no fire control. We're trying. But even when we get it, we can't see results until we get up on that bluff."

Adam crawled back and summed it up for Califino.

"Meyers is dead," Califino said. "I told Rondavich to take over. Larry Smith is all right. He's got his platoon dug in over there on the left."

"I'm scared shitless," Adam said. "We been on this lousy beach over an hour, and nothing. No tanks, no air cover, no Germans. All we got is kids being killed. How do you feel?"

"Like Sisily. I'm going to shit in my pants."

"Motherfuckin' stupid bastards!"

"We give it a try?" Califino asked.

"I guess so. We'll be heroes. Thank God my kid brother's on a ship! That's where we should be, on a ship, sitting on our asses behind ten inches of steel. Fuck them. Get Smith and Rondavich and Prinsky and Judson and that new sergeant they gave us, the one who said he was a grenade instructor."

"Finelli?"

"That's him. Hey Bennie," he said to one of the soldiers, then shouted. "Bennie!"

"I hear you, Captain."

"Crawl up there and try to get a look at that bluff we been talking about."

Bennie crawled up to the ridge of earth and very carefully poked his head up. "It's there!"

"How far?"

"Maybe a quarter-mile."

"See anything—Germans, anything?"

"No, sir."

"O.K. Come back."

When Califino returned with the others, Adam repeated the major's instructions.

"It stinks," Lieutenant Smith said.

"I know. The whole thing stinks. I think there's only one way. We spread out and race for the bluff. But let's look. Bennie says you can see it."

They crawled carefully after Adam, who had just a glance; then a machine gun opened up and they came tumbling back.

"It's flat," Adam said. "We just run like hell and hope it's not mined."

"It's wrong by the book," Califino said. "Every way."

"If we crawl, we're sitting ducks. This way, once we're under the bluff we got cover."

"How do we get up there?"

"What about it?" he asked Finelli. "It's not too high. Can we clear it with grenades?"

"Maybe."

"What do you mean, maybe?"

"Maybe."

"Why don't we wait until dark?" Smith asked.

"Tell it to the lousy battleships," Califino said.

"Let's move," Adam said. "Pass the word. We'll take off in precisely ten minutes. And spread them out. We'll regroup under the bluff."

At eleven o'clock, they had taken the bluff. There were only two German machine guns, but it had cost Adam twenty-two more men out of his company. Exhausted, he lay there on the top of the bluff, staring at the green Normandy countryside, the neat rows of trees, the farmhouses in the distance. Fifty, sixty yards away, a mortar shell exploded.

"Let's dig in," he said to Califino. "What time is it?"

Califino looked at his watch. "Eleven."

"God, all I want to do is lay down and sleep."

Barbara's plane stopped at Benghazi to take on passengers; it developed engine trouble during the takeoff, turned around, landed again, and was laid over for repairs. She had a two-day wait before an empty seat turned up on one of the Air Transport planes out of Cairo. She couldn't sit still—she wanted so desperately to be up and on her way—and she talked herself into the loan of a jeep from the motor pool and drove out to the Graveyard. For months, she had heard of the thing they called the Graveyard. When the fighting in North Africa was over, especially after the great battles that had swirled around Benghazi, the army had gathered all the wrecked vehicles, and the place where they were gathered together was called the Graveyard. It was a few miles outside of Benghazi, and the road that led to it ended on a hillock a few hundred feet above the surface of the desert.

Barbara drove out there, came to the end of the rocky road, and halted her jeep. In every direction, almost as far as she could see, the desert was covered with an unbroken carpet of ruined vehicles, tanks and trucks and gun carriers and self-propelled artillery and jeeps and command cars and halftracks, thousands and thousands of the products of man's civilization and ingenuity and insanity. All she had heard of this place paled into insignificance against the fact. It beggared description. There, in that lonely, barren desert, it was a silent, voiceless commentary on a society, a world gone mad.

For at least a half-hour Barbara sat in her jeep, listening to the silence, watching the vultures swoop and wheel over the sea of metal, still searching for scraps of dried flesh; then she drove back to Benghazi.

The following day, she flew to Casablanca; then from Casablanca, in a big, four-motor transport, to the Azores; and then from the Azores to Newfoundland, where the plane dipped down and landed, in midsummer, between banks of unmelted snow eight feet high. Shivering with pleasure, Barbara took handfuls of snow and rubbed it over her cheeks. The tall, dark pines were like a benediction, the air sweet and cold and clean and biting. When the plane took off again, her eyes were wet, and she said to herself, "What a foolish, emotional creature you are!" Five and a half hours later, the big C-54 dipped down and landed at La Guardia Airport in New York City.

Somehow or other, by calling her paper in San Francisco, Bill Halliday, her publisher, had gotten word of her landing time; and he was at La Guardia with Hildy Lang, the head of promotion, to ease her through Customs and to bring her into New York in an enormous, hired black limousine.

"This time, this time, my dear Barbara," he pleaded, "don't run out on me. Just give us a few days."

They had crossed the Triborough Bridge and were rolling down the East River Drive. In the park beside the drive, women in summer dresses played with their children, who laughed and raced thoughtlessly, and no one looked up at the sky. It was unbelievable and impossible, and it seemed to Barbara that only hours before she had been looking at the sleeping street in Calcutta, or watching the trucks roll by with the bodies of the soldiers killed in Burma piled like cordwood, or walking across the blazing white sand of Saudi Arabia, or staring over the Graveyard in Benghazi—and it was impossible, a compounding of the insanity.

"Barbara?"

"Yes," she said slowly, "I'll stay here for a while."

It turned into two weeks, and thus Barbara missed the occasion in San Francisco when her father received his presidential award. As a matter of fact, when she spoke to Dan on the telephone he failed to mention it, and she only knew about it when she read the details in the New York *Times*.

Bill Halliday had saved all her dispatches from overseas, and for most of the two weeks Barbara worked at revising them, rewriting and connecting them. In the course of those two weeks, she spoke to Dan and to her mother, learning that her brother, Joe, was well and stationed on Guam, and that Joshua Levy had died in action in the Pacific.

On July 20, 1944, the Democratic Convention was convened in Chicago, and under pressure from the party politicians, President Roosevelt abandoned Henry A. Wallace, the incumbent vice president, and selected Senator Harry S Truman of Missouri as his running mate. Deciding that Truman should have every opportunity for national exposure, Roosevelt chose him to go to San Francisco and award the presidential citations to the West Coast shipbuilders. While the invited guests were gathering in the main ballroom of the Fairmont Hotel, Truman and his aides met with the shipbuilders in a private suite where, Admiral Land made certain, the whiskey was good and the cigars pure Havana.

Truman shook hands with Dan enthusiastically, and Dan in turn regarded the small, bespectacled man somewhat dubiously. "So this is Dan Lavette," Truman said. "You're a legend, Dan. You don't mind if I call you Dan? Not on the podium, of course. My notes tell me that you're the quarterback of one of the best damn teams out here. You don't mind the designation? Colorful, but appropriate, I think."

"I'm not a quarterback," Dan said coldly. "I'm not a football player: I build ships. That's about it."

Admiral Land pulled him away. "What the hell was going on there?" he whispered.

"Who is that little squirt, Truman?"

"Lavette, I swear to God I don't believe you. That's Harry Truman, candidate for the vice presidency, and he's a damn good senator."

"I haven't looked at a newspaper in months," Dan said. "The *Chronicle* sends me my daughter's dispatches from overseas, and that's all I read. When did they have their damn convention? Why does Roosevelt bother?"

"You are the most painful sonofabitch I ever dealt with. Can you stop hating the world for the next hour or two? Anyway, I'm glad to see you own a tuxedo. It's an improvement over those jeans you wear."

"I don't own it. I rented it. Why in hell don't you get me some engineers who know their asses from their elbows instead of bothering me with these idiotic awards? I shaved this morning for the first time in three days and left the island in the worst mess we've had in months with those lousy Victory ships of yours. I have to get back there tonight."

"And suppose you don't? What's going to happen? You have the smartest bunch of engineers of any shipyard out here. Give them their head. The world won't come to an end. What's it to you, anyway? You hate the war, you hate Roosevelt, and I'm not sure you don't hate me."

Dan allowed himself a thin smile. "Whether I hate you or not, Admiral, you have more balls than anyone else in this outfit, and I wish to God you were out there in the Pacific running this thing."

Dan didn't return to Terminal Island that night. The ceremonies were over, and he was standing at one end of the speakers' table, trying with some embarrassment to unfasten the decoration that had been pinned onto his dinner jacket, when a voice said, "If you'll hold still, I'll do that for you, Danny."

He looked up and saw Jean—the first time he had seen her in the three years since May Ling had died. She had not changed a great deal, nor was she denying her fifty-four years. Her hair was streaked with gray, but worn without dye in a tight bun at the back of her neck, and she made no attempt to conceal the wrinkles. The eyes were still very blue, and her figure was still very much as it had been when he first met her. He noted her simple gray suit with approval, but then, he had never disapproved of Jean's taste in clothes.

"Hello, Jean," he said quietly.

She had unfastened the decoration, and she held it out to him. He noticed that she wore no rings, no jewels of any kind. He stuffed the decoration into his pocket and asked her how she had gotten there.

"Roger Lapham invited me. You remember him, don't you? He's the mayor now. Or didn't you know that?"

"Damned if I did! So he's the mayor?"

"He does it very quietly. Our table was at the back of the hall."

"Where is he now?"

"I told him to leave me on my own. I wanted very much to see you. When I wrote to you after May Ling's death and got no answer—"

"I couldn't answer any of the letters."

"I think I understood that, so I waited. But it's been three years."

"Almost—yes. Look, Jean, I couldn't eat any of the slop they served here tonight. I'm hungry. Let me talk to the people who are waiting to tell me that they always knew Dan Lavette would make it back, and then, if you want to, we'll go somewhere and eat?"

"I'd like that, Danny."

It took half an hour for Dan to disentangle himself from the crowd of old friends and acquaintances who came up to the speakers' table to say that they had missed him, that San Francisco had not been the same without Dan Lavette, and to congratulate him on his presidential citation. Jean sat at a table a little distance away, watching the tall, heavyset, gray-haired man who had once been her husband. If she had not changed too much in appearance, Dan had changed a great deal indeed. He had lost weight; his body had become even more lean than before, his heavily muscled shoulders sloping and uneasy in the dinner jacket, his face deeply lined, his dark eyes sunken under his shaggy brows. He was still an imposing and handsome man, but so different from the big, tough, swaggering, cocky waterfront fisherman she had met thirty-five years before that it was almost impossible to connect the two and make of them a single person. And yet, as she watched him, her thoughts kept going back to the boy, the boy who had sat at the dinner table in the Seldon mansion on Nob Hill, waiting for cues, eyeing the array of knives and forks and spoons so warily, following her lead, looking sideways at her as no one had ever looked at her before. Well, it was all long, long ago, and the Seldon mansion had long since gone the way of the other mansions on Nob Hill, and the boy was this somber, unsmiling man who in four years had become one of the biggest shipbuilders the world had ever seen.

He finished with the well-wishers and walked over to her. She rose, and he took her arm. The very movement was gentle, like the gait of a wild horse subtly broken. They walked out into the cool, bracing night air.

"Are you hungry?" he asked her.

"I couldn't eat, Danny. I hardly touched the food," she replied, not adding that the evening had been a very emotional and difficult one for her.

"There's a place on Jones Street, down near the wharf, an Italian place called Gino's."

The name touched her memory. Long ago, when she had once hired Pinkerton detectives to follow Dan, they reported that Gino's was the place he often met May Ling.

"That would be fine, Danny."

"Cab?"

"I'd rather walk, if you don't mind. It's not too far."

"And downhill, thank heavens. Each year, these hills become steeper and more impossible. God Almighty, do you remember when I used to run up them?"

"I do indeed. I remember running with you."

They walked on in silence for a while. Downhill still had its pitfalls, and when she stumbled once, Dan grasped her arm and steadied her. She took courage from that and grasped his arm; the swell of his biceps under her fingers was good and comforting, and it was good to be close to him, to feel him against her. They could see the bay beneath them, with the fog rolling in, and they could hear the mournful hooting of the ships. The wonderful, woeful old sound brought a lump into Dan's throat. He had been bereft of emotion for a long time; now it filled him and choked him. His voice was thick as he told Jean that he was due back at Terminal Island this same night.

"But can you make it, Dan?"

"The hell with it."

Gino embraced him. Gino had become an old man. "Hey, Danny, Danny, *mio caro figlio,* so long, so long."

"This is Jean," Dan said.

Gino bowed, said something to Dan in Italian, and then took them to their table.

"What did he say?" Jean asked.

"He said you're a lovely woman."

"He doesn't know who I am?"

"No, I guess not."

Dan ordered linguini, with olive oil and garlic, and after that a veal cutlet and salad. Jean said she'd have the same thing. A bottle of red wine. Gino brought the wine and poured it. Jean raised her glass. "To the war's end, Danny. Soon."

"Yes. Soon."

They drank the toast and sat quietly, watching each other. Finally, Jean said, "You miss her terribly. You never got over it, did you, Danny?"

"I miss her."

"You live alone?" Jean asked. Dan nodded.

"In the house in Westwood?"

"No. I sold the house."

"Then where?"

"On Terminal Island. I have a room next to my office. A bed and a bathroom. That's all I need."

"Oh, no."

"Why not?"

"Danny, what do you do with yourself?"

"I build the damn ships."

"But you can't live that way. That's not enough."

"I make it enough. I'm up at five in the morning. The first shift comes on at six. We have our own commissary, so that takes care of my meals. By eight o'clock, I can barely keep my eyes open. I put on the radio. There's a station that plays classical music. I've become damn fond of baroque music. I can listen for about a half-hour or so, and then I'm asleep."

"And you live that way, day in and day out?"

"Just about. If you call it living."

"But why? Why, Danny? Is it because you hate them so much?"

"Who?"

"The Japs."

"Why should I hate them?"

"They killed your wife."

"No. No, I don't look at it that way, Jean. This rotten, sick world we live in killed May Ling, the same way it killed Josh Levy, Jake's kid, the same way it's killing millions and millions of others."

"You mean Mark's grandchild?"

"Yes, he died in the Pacific. You didn't know?"

She shook her head. "How terrible! How absolutely terrible!"

"It's a beautiful world we made, isn't it?"

The food came. Dan tasted the linguini and smiled. "I've forgotten good food."

"It's nice to see you smile."

"Oh?" He stared at her thoughtfully. "Jean," he said, "back in the old days, did you ever sit down and try to figure out exactly how I felt about you?"

"I tried, Danny. Yes, I tried."

He nodded and went on eating. After a moment, Jean said to him, "Danny?"

"Yeah?"

"If you don't hate them, why do you do it? Why do you give your life to building the ships?"

"Because I want it to end. The way I see it, there's only one way to end it—with the ships. Without the ships, it will go on forever. With enough ships, it will end. I have no love for any of these bastards who run governments. If I despise Hitler more than Stalin, it's because Stalin is helping to end it, but to me they're both the scum of the earth, and I put Roosevelt and Churchill only a few rungs higher. They all play the same bloody game, and they all share the same filthy disregard for human life. I make no secret of how I feel. Admiral Land knows. I like Jerry Land. He's tough and he's honest and he put this whole thing together, and when this war ends, he gets as much credit as any of their damned generals—and, well, there it is. I haven't talked so much in years."

"We never talked before, Danny. You know that. In all the years, we never really talked. Barbara asked me that once. 'Did you ever try talking to daddy?' she asked me."

"I spoke to her day before yesterday," Dan said. "Thank God she's all right."

"Did you tell her about the award?"

"No. She would have come. She still has things to do in New York."

"She would have been very proud of you. She's quite a woman."

"Then we must have done something right, Jean."

"A few things," Jean admitted ruefully. "Where is your son?"

"You mean Joe?"

"Yes."

"In the Pacific. On Guam."

"He's a doctor, isn't he?"

"Yes—" Dan's face was bleak.

"We're old friends, Danny. Let's not slip back into the past. Let's try to keep it here and now."

"All right. Tell me about Tom."

"He's a commander, you know. He's John Whittier's partner, and the war has made them both very rich and very important. Not that they weren't both rich enough before, but if you want the whole world, what is rich enough?"

"And that's what Tom wants—the whole world?"

"More or less. When the war is over, he plans to run for the House. After that the Senate. Then the presidency. Presidents are made, I've learned, they don't just happen. Tom is very ambitious. I wish he were a little nicer. There's something we didn't do right."

"And the girl he married?"

"I like her," Jean said. "There's something in her that's very good and honest."

"Is it a good marriage?"

"No, it's a rotten marriage. But Tom won't let go of her, and she isn't strong enough to break out of it."

"I know. Seldons don't divorce."

"That's wasn't called for, Dan."

"No, it wasn't," he admitted. "I'm sorry."

"Candidates don't divorce," Jean said. "Do you have any desire to see him?"

"Of course I do. He's my son. But damnit, Jean, what do I do? Go to him and have him spit in my face?"

"I don't think he'd do that."

"I can't go to him."

"I can understand that."

"And we're neither of us eating, are we?" Dan said.

It wasn't until they were in the cab that he asked her where she was living.

"Don't you know? I'm back in the old house on Russian Hill."

"Yes, of course. I remember Barbara telling me you had turned it into a gallery."

"I had my dreams, Danny. The San Francisco Museum of Modern Art. It was to start up there on Russian Hill, and in no time at all we'd rival New York. Then the war came. I'm just hanging in. It's sort of fun, and it gives me something positive to do. I've had an architect draw up a set of plans, and for two million dollars we could have a perfectly beautiful building. Well, someday, perhaps. Meanwhile, we get a reasonable amount of visitors, and it gives the house a tax-exempt status. That helps. I'm not poor, but neither am I very rich, and I've spent a fortune on paintings. By the way, where are you staying?"

"I wasn't. I was returning tonight."

They were at the house now. Dan paid off the cab. It was strange, very strange indeed, to stand in front of the house he had built for Jean more than thirty years ago, and stranger still to return there with her. He stood looking at the entranceway without moving, and Jean watched him.

"Will you come inside?" she asked softly.

He didn't answer. She took out her key and opened the door and switched on the lights, a blaze of light that lit up the white-walled galleries. Then he followed her into the house and stood there, looking around curiously.

"Well?" She was smiling at him.

"I still can't make head or tail of the paintings you like, but it's damned impressive."

"Shall I boast a little?"

"Why not?"

"I have Braque and Picasso and Kandinsky," she said, pointing to the pictures, "Paul Klee, John Marin, Miró, Delauney, Max Weber, Marsden Hartley—"

Dan laughed. "You've lost me."

She turned to face him, her face suddenly filled with sadness. "I have, haven't I, Danny. I lost the only man in my life who was any damn good." She went over to him. "Danny, stay here with me tonight. Come to bed with me. Make love to me. I'm pleading with you, Danny. Don't say no."

He hesitated, then took her in his arms and kissed her. She clung to him. "I don't even know if I could," he said. "I haven't been near a woman since May Ling died."

"It doesn't matter. Just hold me in your arms. But don't go away." Her voice was filled with fear.

"I won't go away."

They went upstairs. Her bedroom was unchanged, except that the full-length nude that Gregory Pastore had painted was gone. She went to the closet, took out a robe, and handed it to him.

"I'll be damned," he said.

"Yes, it's yours. It's been hanging there ever since."

When he lay beside her, naked, it was very much as if time had reversed itself, and bit by bit the hunger returned, the strange obsessive hunger for Jean that had never left him, that May Ling had always sensed, the arbitary possessor that was first love, that might be crushed and shattered and mutilated but that could never be entirely destroyed. He abandoned reason and surrendered the loyalty to a dead woman that had depressed him and owned him for so long. He was alive. In over three years he had not been alive like this. This wonderful, long-limbed body next to him was his first true love. It did not diminish May Ling. May Ling was dead. He let go of her. He had worshipped May Ling, adored her, honored her. She was his refuge, his teacher, his mother, his consolation; but this woman next to him was his first true love and she was inside of him and she had never left him. She was part of his blood and his bones, and there were times when she had been like a cancer, but the cancer had also been a part of him; and there had been times when he had hated her with animallike ferocity, and he knew that there had also been times when she had hated him; and they had fought each other, cut each other, scarred each other, and while the scars would never go away, the love, the passion, would also remain.

When they finished, shaken by a climactic violence that they had never known in the time of their youth, they lay together, clutching each other, in the dark silence. They sensed in each other the fear that this would dissolve, that it was a rediscovery that could not survive the moment, that all the walls they had broken through would suddenly reassert themselves and separate them in a future that neither of them could conceive. Time passed. They fell asleep, still entangled in their embrace, and then Dan awakened convulsively, dreaming, not knowing of where he was. Jean flicked on the light, and he looked at her, sitting there in bed naked, her breasts still firm and lovely, her long, thick hair falling around her shoulders.

"Are you all right, Danny?" she asked him.

"Sure. What time is it?"

She looked at the clock on her night table. "Two forty-five A.M. Middle of the night."

"Are you hungry?"

"We tried twice—and left it uneaten both times. You want to try again?"

"What can you offer?"

"Scrambled eggs, bacon, toast, coffee?"

They sat at the table in the upstairs kitchen, and they both finished everything Jean cooked. The food was good, and Dan realized that in all the years he had known her, in all the years they had been married, this was the first time she had ever cooked for him. Then they drank coffee and talked. They talked as if they both sensed that the only way to keep down the walls that had separated them was to know each other at long last. Dan talked about May Ling and Jean talked about John Whittier. They talked about their children, about their lives together and about their lives apart from each other; and they were still drinking coffee and talking when dawn came.

"Do you know," Dan said, "all I have with me is that damn rented tuxedo that I wore at the dinner."

"How long can you stay?"

"A day or two. Then I have to go back."

"But you'll come back, Danny?"

"I'll come back."

"All right. We'll go out and buy some clothes. We'll get one of those big, fat, cardigan sweaters that I love. You'll let me pick it out for you. Then you'll change. Then you can take me to lunch somewhere. Then we'll ride the cable cars down to the Embarcadero and walk. Then you can bring me back here, and if you don't feel too old and tired we can make love again."

"I'll manage. But what about the gallery?"

"The hell with it. I'll lock it up. Let's crawl into bed until the stores open."

In bed, their bodies touching, they fell asleep again.

Part Seven

HOMELAND

One day in November of 1945, Eloise Lavette was in the gallery on Russian Hill, waiting for Jean to complete some paperwork in her office upstairs and join her for lunch, when a young man entered and paused just inside the doorway, looking about him uncertainly. He stared at the paintings first with a respectful but bemused expression, which Eloise had noticed frequently on the faces of those who viewed Jean's collection for the first time. Then he saw Eloise, and he smiled. She returned the smile. He then walked over to her and asked whether Mrs. Whittier was in the gallery.

"Yes, she is. She's upstairs. She'll be down in a few minutes, if you care to wait."

"Do you work here?" he wanted to know.

"No, not really. I'm a friend. I help out sometimes."

He was an odd-looking young man. He had a thatch of the brightest orange hair she had ever seen, and under it was a freckled face that was marred by a scar that stretched from his chin to the hairline. The scar, she thought, made his face strange but not truly ugly; it rather blended with the freckled skin; and his blue eyes were alert and alive and widely admiring. He was tall and skinny, with large hands, the backs of which were covered with the same freckles that were splashed on his face. And he was staring at Eloise with such apparent pleasure that she felt herself blushing like a schoolgirl.

"Can I help you?" she asked him.

"Well, I don't think so. No. I'll wait for Mrs. Whittier, if you don't mind?"

"I don't mind."

"I guess," he said, "I'm the only one here."

"I guess you are."

"Well, that's obvious, I guess. I don't always say silly

things. What I meant is, do many people come here to look at the paintings?"

"On weekends we get a fair attendance. And in the afternoons we do get a few people, mostly art students. You see, it's very avant-garde, not the kind of thing that San Francisco is used to. People must be educated to modern art."

"Oh? Yes, I'm sure. Do you understand it?"

"A little. I've learned a great deal from Mrs. Whittier."

"Now that one," he said. "That one looks like two dead fish on a straw mat, only I'm not sure they're fish. Are they?" He was very funny without being disrespectful and so earnestly serious that Eloise burst out laughing.

"I know," he nodded. "That's a really dumb thing to say."

"No it isn't. That's what it looks like to you, so why shouldn't you say so? As a matter of fact, that painting is by Paul Klee, one of the great modern masters. He was a German Expressionist, except that he was Swiss. I mean he was born in Switzerland, but in his painting he was of the German Expressionist school. He was nonrepresentational. I mean he didn't try to paint things as they appear to most people. He changed them into designs that he considered amusing and delightful."

The young man regarded her with awe, nodding, and at that moment Jean appeared and walked over to join them.

"This is Mrs. Whittier," Eloise said. "I don't know your name."

"No, of course. I never told you. I'm sorry."

"I didn't ask you," Eloise said.

"No, you didn't, did you? My name is Adam Levy."

"Mine is Eloise Lavette."

"Oh. Yes. How do you do."

The name jogged Jean's memory. Then she remembered and said, "Of course. You're Mark Levy's grandson. I'm so glad to see you."

He took the hand she held out and nodded. "That's right. Yes. Thank you."

"You see, I did know your grandfather. I don't know your mother and father."

"I understand."

"When did you get home, Adam?" Jean asked him.

"Two weeks ago, luckily, believe me. I could have been trapped there for another year."

"I'm glad you're back, safe and healthy—at least you look very healthy."

"Oh, I am, yes, ma'am."

"And is there something I can do for you? Or did you just wander in?"

"Oh, no. No. Barbara—your daughter—suggested that I come and see you. She said you know every artist in the city."

"Almost every one, yes."

He reached into his jacket pocket and took out a sheaf of snapshots. "These are photographs of my brother, Joshua," he said, handing them to Jean. "He was killed in the Pacific a year ago."

Jean nodded. "I know." She didn't know what else to say.

"Well, I thought it would be nice to have a painting of him that I could give to my mother and father. We don't have anything like that. And Barbara said you might know a painter who could do it for me. I don't know what these things cost, but I can afford it, I think. You know, back pay—"

"Adam," Jean said, "you don't mind if I call you Adam?"

"Oh, no, not at all."

"We're going out to lunch, Adam. Would you like to join us, and we can talk about this?"

"Yes, if you will let me take both of you to lunch?"

"If you wish, certainly."

At the lunch table, Jean watched him with interest. It was not that he was charming; she had known sufficient charming men not to be overimpressed with charm. But this man had a naiveté, a kind of open, boyish simplicity, that was absolutely delightful. Certainly to Eloise. Jean had never seen her like this before, relaxed and chatting away, actually talking. How old was he? Jean wondered. Twenty-three, twenty-four at the most, she thought, trying to recall what Dan had told her. A captain or a major? In the first wave of the Normandy landing, and then leading his company across the breadth of France into Germany. And now he sat at the table with them, apparently enchanted with Eloise, hanging on to every word she spoke. It was all inconceivable. Children went to war. Children witnessed hideous, indescribable things, children killed and burned and destroyed, and then children came back and they were children again.

"But we haven't talked about the painting," he said.

"No, we haven't, have we? Let's get at it," Jean said. "Now, as far as copying these photographs in oils, there are any number of people here in the city who could do that, and quite professionally too. It's merely a question of copying, and such copies are usually flat and lifeless, and I don't think it would bring very much joy to your folks."

"You think it's a bad idea?"

"No, Adam, not at all. The thing is to find someone who can look at these pictures and perhaps go beyond them, someone who can breathe life and joy into the painting, who will create something that is not simply a lifeless copy. I must warn you that such a painting will not be photographic. If it is to succeed, it must capture the essence of this lovely boy. It will not be exactly like him at all, but it may find him more than any exact copy could. Or it may not. You see, you will have to pay the artist even if you don't like what he paints."

"I understand."

"I'll try to find someone if you wish me to."

"Yes, please. How much will it cost?"

"I don't know. I'll try to keep it under a thousand dollars—perhaps a good deal under, perhaps not. Can you afford that?"

"Oh, yes. Yes."

"All right. Suppose you drop by next week—next Wednesday. About eleven. I'll try to have someone there for you to speak to, and perhaps you can see some of his work."

"Sure. That's great." He turned to Eloise. "Will you be there?"

Eloise turned to Jean mutely, and Jean said, "There are days when Eloise helps me, but she has no regular hours at the gallery. Perhaps she'll be there, perhaps not."

"I hope so. I sure hope so," Adam said.

During the fifteen years from 1922 to 1937, the shipbuilding industry of America perished. During that time, in the greatest industrial country in the world, only two dry cargo ships were built. The ways rotted. The companies that made the parts—the compasses, the wheels, the turbines, the speaking tubes, the winches, and the

thousand other items that go into the construction of a
merchant ship—either went bankrupt or closed down, or
clung to life with a skeleton force of a handful of workers.
The thousands of shipyard workers who had found em-
ployment during the years of World War I found other
jobs, or went into the lines of the unemployed. They
became old, and their skills were only memories. The
shipyards were abandoned, and half a hundred unfinished
ships rotted away, rusted, disintegrated.

The first break in this situation occurred in June 1936,
when the Seventy-fourth Congress passed the Merchant
Marine Act and created the United States Maritime Commission "to develop and maintain a merchant marine
sufficient to carry a substantial portion of the water-
borne export and import foreign commerce of the United
States on the best-equipped, safest, and most suitable type
of vessels owned, operated and constructed by citizens
of the United States, manned with a trained personnel and
capable of serving as a naval and military auxiliary in
time of war or national emergency."

Having created this commission and having given it a
mandate, Congress rested. For Admiral Land and his
fellow commissioners, it was another matter entirely.
There were almost no functioning shipyards, no shipbuilders to call upon, no trained workmen—in fact, very
little of anything; and soon thereafter, war in Europe
threatened to engulf the United States. Within this broad
problem, there were two specific situations that called for
solution. On the one hand, there was Dan Lavette as a
prototype. Dan had taken over a bankrupt shipyard that
the bank, which held the mortgage, had been only too
happy to dispose of; and this he had clung to, scraping
together enough money to meet each payroll. He had no
money even to contemplate the building of one steel cargo
vessel, mush less a fleet. On the other hand, the men who
had access to great amounts of capital—the bankers and
the big industrialists—well, they were much too careful
and wise to invest in shipbuilding. The aftermath of the
previous war was still too close. Out of this necessity, the
Maritime Commission was forced into the position of financing the construction of the yards and guaranteeing
the price and sale of the ships—and paying the shipbuilders a bonus for each ship built.

By the end of 1945, with the war over, the construction at the Lavette Shipyard on Terminal Island was winding down to a close. Five ships were still in construction, two of them tankers, the other three Victory-type cargo carriers; but to all effects and purposes the operation was over, and the bonuses had made Dan Lavette a millionaire for the second time in his life. More and more, during the fifteen months since he had met Jean in San Francisco, he was away from the yard. He had trained a group of managers to do everything that had to be done. Joe had not yet returned from the Pacific, but his letters made it plain that he intended to marry Sally and live in Northern California as soon as he came back.

Aside from the bedroom adjoining his office on Terminal Island, Dan had no residence. When he was in San Francisco, he stayed with Jean in the house on Russian Hill. They had fallen into an easy and undemanding companionship. They saw a good deal of Barbara, but they made no plans for the future.

The first meeting of the two of them with Barbara was hardly the way either would have planned it. Barbara had returned to San Francisco and had gone directly to the house on Russian Hill. It was early in the morning, and Jean, still in a robe, let her into the gallery. After their greeting and embraces, Barbara said that she ought to call her father in Los Angeles.

"He's not on Terminal Island," Jean told her. "He's here."

"Here? You mean here in this house?"

"Yes. Upstairs. Probably still asleep."

"You mean he lives here?"

"At times, yes."

Barbara stared at her mother in silence. Then, after a few moments, she asked, "When? I mean—"

"About ten days ago."

"Oh."

"No other comment?" Jean asked her.

"I don't know what to say."

"That's reasonable," Jean agreed. "Why don't we go upstairs and have breakfast. We'll talk about it."

But upstairs, having breakfast with her mother and father together for the first time in more than fifteen years, Barbara could only say, "I'm so very happy to be back—with both of you."

Finally, Dan was forced to admit that he was a reasonably wealthy man, that his life had not ended with the death of May Ling, and that he enjoyed the possession and use of money. Long ago, he had said to May Ling that he would never play the game again—the game that he often thought of as the gunfight on Nob Hill—that he was out of the struggle for boodle that was called American success, and that he was out of it forever. Now he was back in it because it was the only game he knew. He was fifty-six years old, healthy, and vigorous. At that time, the term "establishment" was not in use in America, but if it had been and if Dan had been faced with it, he would have rejected membership with contempt. The word "maverick" was in use, and it fitted him better.

One day, early in December of 1945, having had word that Joe was on his way back and would be arriving in San Francisco in a few days, Dan telephoned Jean and asked her whether she could put him up for a few days. It was a euphemism, an avoidance of the flat statement of a situation, and Jean accepted it, assuring him that she would be delighted.

Driving north, Dan stopped off at Stephan Cassala's home in San Mateo and allowed himself to be persuaded to stay for dinner. It was his first visit to the Cassalas' since May Ling's death, and they welcomed him with a veritable outpouring of love and emotion. Maria Cassala, sixty-eight years old now, had not changed. Her English was almost as bad as when she arrived in America half a century before. She was still stout, her round face unwrinkled, and she still wore her ankle-length black dress of mourning for her husband, who had passed away fifteen years ago. She enveloped Dan in her embrace and exclaimed in Italian, "How can you do this to us? Who loved May Ling more than we did? What is a family for if not for grief? You break my heart. Always, you break my heart. Stephan tells me you are the richest, biggest shipbuilder in America. You think I care about that? You think it impresses me? Make your peace with God. That impresses me. Come to people who love you. That impresses me. You know how many candles I light for you? You know how many prayers I say for you?"

"I know, I know, Maria," he said humbly.

"Even your Italian is no good anymore. Everything you forget. In this country, the children become barbarians. What shall I cook for you? Tell me."

After dinner, stuffed with good food and red wine, Dan and Stephan settled in front of the fire in Tony Cassala's old study, and Dan, looking around the room approvingly, said, "I'm glad you kept it the way it was."

"It's a nice room," Stephan said. "A lot of memories."

"The whole house. It's good you held on to it."

"It isn't easy, Dan. It's a big house, and the taxes have gone sky-high. I'm fifty years old and the manager of a branch bank. Do you know what they pay me?"

Dan shook his head.

"Ten thousand a year. And now the boy's in college. I'm mortgaged to the hilt. There are times—hell, no reason to lay my problems on you."

"Why not?" Dan was regarding Stephan thoughtfully. "Steve, is there anything about finance you don't know?"

"A little."

"How would you like to work for me? I'll pay you thirty thousand a year to start?"

"Doing what? Dan, that's a bonanza, but I don't know one damn thing about shipbuilding."

"That's over, Steve. A year, two years, maybe three, and the only ships they'll be building in this country are tankers. But I won't be building them. I'm going to sell the shipyard. The government owns most of it already, but my equity ought to be worth a million and I think I've got a buyer. No, I've had my fill of building ships. I want to get back to operating them. Hell, there's where the game is, the excitement and the money. Not that I give a damn about the money, but it measures the game, doesn't it?"

"It sure as hell does."

"I've got a million and a half put away out of this shipyard operation, and I'll pick up a million more for the yard. I've already put down an option on a tanker, and I know where there are two more to be gotten at a very decent price. This country is so hungry for oil, now that the war's over, that every tanker's going to be a damn gold mine. I've been talking to Chris Noel in Hawaii, and he's ready to come in with me. I believed in the Islands twenty years ago, and now that this country's lousy with its bloody prosperity, I can't help thinking that Hawaii will become another Florida. And that means oil and more oil. I've been looking at dock facilities in Oakland, and I think I'll open offices there in a few weeks. I want someone to do for me what Mark Levy did in the old days—to run the company, be the comptroller, ride herd over the whole thing—and I think you're the man. Thirty thousand, that's just to start, and I'll cut you in for ten percent of my share of the company. What do you say?"

Stephan didn't answer for a minute or so, sitting and staring at the flames. Then he turned to Dan and nodded. He didn't trust himself to speak.

"Then we'll shake hands on it."

"Thanks, Danny," Stephan finally said.

"Why don't you marry him?" Barbara asked her mother.

"I don't think you quite understand," Jean said.

"You could try me. I'm a big girl now." And when Jean remained silent, she said, "I think I have a right to know."

"Why?"

"My God, mother, does it make any sense to you? For months now, my mother and father have been having an affair. He lives with you—"

"Not really. He does have an apartment in Oakland."

"I truly don't believe this. I don't believe either of you. I love you both so much. You apparently love each other. Or is it just a casual affair?"

"Barbara!"

"All right, forgive me. I certainly shouldn't have said that. I think you love each other. I think he's always loved you. That doesn't mean he didn't love May Ling. The relations between men and women are never very simple—"

"Thank heavens you admit that."

"Still, I never heard him speak a word against you. I know how the past can live in people. But with you two, the past is a long time ago. When I hear people call you Mrs. Whittier, I wince. It's ridiculous. At least change your name back to Lavette."

"And do what, my dear? Send cards to everyone I know, announcing that Jean Whittier is now Jean Lavette? Can you see that? Dan and I are already in the gossip columns—"

"Mother, who cares?"

"I do, for one. You don't discard the habits of a lifetime like an old hat."

"But you do go on with the charade."

"Bobby, darling, try to understand. Your father and I were never happy when we were married. It went wrong from the beginning, in every possible way. Now it is good, just the way it is. We make no demands on each other. When we're together, we're really together. There are men and women for whom marriage is a good thing. I'm not sure Dan and I are in that group."

They were sitting in the little Victorian living room of Barbara's house on Green Street, where Barbara had very properly served her mother tea. Barbara had found the Spode tea service in a little secondhand furniture shop in Oakland and had purchased it with great enthusiasm. She had then spent an afternoon in the library reading up on Josiah Spode (1754–1827) and bone china, and when she informed Jean that she was going to do a piece on bone china for the *Woman's Home Companion* magazine, her mother regarded her with some misgiving.

"Barbara," she said, "what on earth has happened to you? You don't go out. You don't date. You fuss over this little house without end, and now you've plunged headlong into bone china—of all things."

"I've crawled into a cave," Barbara said complacently. "When I've been in it long enough, I'll crawl out again."

"You're thirty-one years old and still unmarried. You live here alone. Why did you ever let Mrs. Jones go?"

"I didn't let her go, mother. She was quite old, and she wanted to live with her sister. Sam left her enough so that she doesn't have to work, and I certainly don't need a servant in this house. An hour a day does it. Besides, I like to live alone. I work better alone."

"Please, find a good man and get married," Jean said wistfully; and it was that muted plea that led to Barbara's suggestion that her mother and father might be married first.

"You see," Barbara said, "we have spun a very tangled web, we Lavettes. Next month, Joseph Lavette is to be married to Sally Levy. Joseph is my half brother and Dan's son. Are you coming to the wedding?"

"I was invited. I've already sent a gift."

"I think you should come."

"I don't know. He's May Ling's son."

"Joe would like you to come. We talked about it."

Jean laughed and shook her head. "More tangled than you imagine. You know Adam Levy."

"Sally's brother, yes."

"He's in love with Eloise. He wants her to leave Tom and marry him."

"Good heavens! When did this happen?"

"It's been going on for quite a while now. It began when he came to the gallery to ask me to find a painter to do a portrait of his dead brother. That's when he met her. You know, Eloise has been helping me two or three days a week. It gave her some diversion and purpose, which heaven knows she needed. She's very bright and quick to learn, and now she's taking a course in art history at the university. Well, he came back, and again, and again. By the way, how old is he?"

"Almost twenty-four, I think."

"He ended up in the war as a major. Do they have majors as young as that?"

"I don't think they do it by age, mother. How does Eloise feel about him?"

"Eloise is older, probably four years older."

"Mother, I don't care whether she's older or younger. How does she feel about him?"

"How would you feel? Apparently the only person who ever gave her a shred of sympathy or understanding is myself, and I'm Tom's mother. I don't delude myself about my son, but he is my son. The poor child is torn to pieces, and just to make it nicer, she's a migraine sufferer. And this Adam Levy is like an attenuated Jewish leprechaun, if you can imagine such a thing. He's absolutely charming and gentle and he worships the ground she walks on."

"Mother, he's only half Jewish, which doesn't matter, and I don't see him as a leprechaun, and he has been through the worst war in human history. He was awarded the Silver Star for extraordinary courage and decision in action, and he was very severely wounded."

"Bobby, don't lecture me," Jean begged her. "I've really become quite civilized."

"You still haven't told me how Eloise feels."

"How can she feel? She has a kind, charming man who desires no more than to be her faithful slave and servant, and she's married to a man who hasn't had intercourse with her in seven months. They have separate rooms,

Bobby. And believe me, if your brother hasn't slept with his wife in seven months, then sure as God, he's sleeping with someone else."

"Then why doesn't she leave him?"

"My dear Bobby, you are a liberated woman. Eloise is a frightened little rabbit. She lives in terror of Tom, in terror of his fits of temper, in terror of having her child taken away from her, and in terror of her migraine headaches."

"He can't take the child away from her. Mother, Tom isn't a monster. He's no Sir Galahad, but he's always been reasonably decent."

"To you and me. We don't see him too often and we're not married to him, and we never ask him for money. Those are three good conditions for decency. Also, this Adam Levy hasn't a bean."

"The Levys aren't rich, but they're not poor. It's one of the best wineries in the Napa Valley, and making wine is all that the boy wants to do. It's not the money that holds Eloise there, is it?"

"Oh, no. It's the whole complex of circumstances."

"I think you ought to help her," Barbara decided.

"I try."

"I mean, you should help her leave Tom."

"I don't think anyone can help her do that."

With some feelings of guilt, Barbara realized that she had more or less ignored her sister-in-law, and later that same afternoon, she telephoned and invited her to have lunch at her house. The house, her home and refuge, had become very much a passion with Barbara. She knew that it was a reaction to the years she had spent abroad, and she also knew that it was in a sense a retreat from reality. It was, as she had said, a cave, a shelter, but the actual cave was herself. She had drawn into herself. Writing required only her own participation. She met no one whom she cared for particularly. The girls of her own age whom she had known were all of them married now and with children. She would soon be thirty-two years old, and for a thirty-two-year-old woman there were only divorced men and that singular species called bachelors, a word that fitted a variety of neuroses. She had overheard a very attractive single woman, only a few years older than herself, referred to as a "fag-hag," and the term had chilled her blood. At least she had some constructive work in her life—aside from her writing—and the more attention she paid to the Lavette Foundation, the more she realized that in her moment of petulance and rebellion she had created something very important indeed. A home for unwed mothers had been funded. A clinic had been opened in San Diego, which catered to the needs of Chicanos, and seventeen scholarships for postgraduate work, medical and otherwise, had been awarded. A grant had been made for research into the history of the Plains Indians, and six additional grants were devoted to research in antibiotics, pneumonia, sickle-cell anemia, and cancer. It had been slow in starting, but to Barbara the results were marvelously satisfying.

Meanwhile, she was successfully operating as an independent person, earning more than enough from her writing to support herself and maintain the house. She loved housekeeping. She had purchased a dozen cookbooks, regretting the fact that during her years in Paris she had never taken advantage of the Cordon Bleu, and she found that it was both pleasant and exciting to have guests to a lunch or dinner that she had cooked and served herself. Today, for Eloise, she had prepared eggs Benedict and fresh spinach and had baked biscuits, and the two of them ate in the tiny breakfast room, with its bay window from which one could just glimpse the harbor.

Eloise was delighted with the house. "It's so small and warm and wonderful," she said. "We live in such a huge barn of a place. Oh, I would be so happy with a house like this! And the food is so good. To me, it's absolutely a miracle when people cook things and have them taste good. I mean, the cooking is one thing, but to have them taste so delicious. And of course, making bread—well, I can't even fry an egg properly."

"It's not real bread. One buys a biscuit mix. It's almost cheating."

"You couldn't cheat," Eloise said earnestly. "You can't imagine how much I've always admired you, Barbara. I read both your books, and they were simply wonderful, especially the one about the war. How many woman could go through all that and experience all those awful things, and then just remain as simple and nice as you are, I don't know."

Barbara was overcome with guilt. To be so admired and praised by someone she had considered to be an empty-

headed doll was mortifying, and for a moment she disliked
herself intensely. However, she could not let the opportunity pass, for she had invited Eloise for a very specific
purpose. "Your friend, Adam Levy," she said, "has been
through a great deal more than I, and he's quite nice, I
think, and very gentle."

Eloise looked at her without responding. Barbara understood Adam's infatuation with her. She was utterly de-
fenseless. The blond ringlets, the baby blue eyes, the
peaches-and-cream skin, the openness— "This is a child,"
Barbara told herself. "It's not a mask or an image she
wears. She is actually what she appears to be—and married
to a barracuda."

"Do you know?" Eloise whispered.

"My mother told me that Adam is in love with you,"
she said bluntly.

"She shouldn't have told you that."

"Why? To be loved by a decent man is a good thing."

"When you're married? I'm married to your brother,
Barbara."

"That means nothing. If we're going to talk about this,
my dear, you must forget that Tom is my brother. Or perhaps you don't want to talk about it?"

"Barbara, if I don't talk to someone, I'll go out of my
mind. I'm so unhappy. I guess I was unhappy before, but
that was different. I was married to Tom, and I never
looked for anything to change it. My father and mother
were never happy. I often felt that they hated each other,
but they stayed together and remained married, and I
simply accepted my own position. I didn't want this to
happen. It just happened. And no one ever treated me
the way Adam does. He makes me feel that I'm worth
something, that I'm important. He lets me talk, and he
listens to what I say. He insisted that I take the course in
art history at the university, and Tom was so furious at
me for doing it, and I just don't know why. And Adam
never asks anything of me. I've never slept with him. But
I feel so guilty and so unhappy—" She shook her head
dumbly. "What am I to do?"

"Does Tom know?"

"I don't think so. He only notices how I feel when I
have a headache, and then he's angry with me. We've had
separate rooms from the time we moved into the house
on Pacific Heights."

"How do you feel about Adam?"

"I don't know. Before we were married, I was so much in love with Tom, and I thought he was the handsomest man in the world, but I never really liked him. Do you understand?"

Barbara nodded.

"And then I stopped being in love with him. I feel so dreadful, telling all this to you."

"But you still haven't said what you feel about Adam."

"I don't know. He's all I think about. I like him so much, and he makes me feel so good. Whenever I go to the gallery now, all I wish is for him to come in. When he does, he takes me to lunch. Jean has been very good about it, but I feel good and I feel wretched too. That's the only time I see him, except for one afternoon when we went to the Japanese gardens—" She paused. "Barbara, he wants me to leave Tom. He asked me to marry him."

"Do you want to leave Tom?"

"How can I?"

"Tom won't take Freddie away from you. He can't."

"Barbara," said softly, "there's one thing I don't think you understand. Tom Lavette and John Whittier are the two most powerful men in this city. They can do anything they want to do."

Most of Tom's evenings were spent away from home. Since his discharge from the navy, he had gradually become increasingly involved in Whittier's company, the name of which had now been changed to Great Cal Shipping. Aside from their vast shipping interests and their interlocking relationship with the Seldon Bank, they owned and operated the West Coast airline that Dan Lavette had pioneered years before; and while still in uniform, Tom had made several trips to Washington, where he obtained franchises into several western states. His evenings—with the exception of those occasions where an attractive wife was necessary—were spent at business dinners or at his club. He felt no necessity to explain to Eloise what the nature or circumstances of those dinners were, nor was she prone to inquire. She was quite content to spend her evenings alone, reading or listening to music—or, now and then, with Jean and Dan.

In Dan, she found the father she had never actually had,

a very large, strong man who gave her a sense of being protected and the feeling of security she needed so desperately. On his part, Dan was absolutely enchanted with Eloise, as if some strange good fortune had given him and Jean another child at this point in their lives. In addition, Dan suddenly realized that he was a grandfather, and he lavished the love and attention on Freddie that he had withheld from his own children—at least, until Tom found out and stormed at Eloise, "No more! I do not want that man in the company of my son!"

"Tom, he's your father."

"I haven't seen him or spoken to him in sixteen years. He's no more my father than he's yours."

"He's still Freddie's grandfather."

"I don't give a damn. Now you listen to me. This ends. I know damn well that he's living with my mother, and I think the whole thing is cheap and disgusting. I don't want him seeing my son."

When Eloise told this to Jean, Jean's reaction was very calm. "I'll talk to Tom," she assured Eloise. "For the time being, do as he says."

Freddie was four years old, a very quiet and strangely knowledgeable little boy. Since Eloise was alone so often in the evening, she fell into a pattern of eating early with her son. During these dinners, they discussed the events of the day—their visit to the zoo, to Fisherman's Warf, their ride on the cable cars, their investigation into the mysterious cable house, where the great master cable spun on its huge wheel, their excursion to the gallery to see grandmother Jean, their ride across the Golden Gate Bridge— or whatever the high point of the afternoon had been.

Eloise was sensitive enough to realize that she was turning to the little boy because there was nowhere else to turn, and she also understood the danger of making a four-year-old child the focal point of her existence. Adam had pointed this out to her when he had asked her to marry him. "You can't substitute a small boy for life. You dear, lovely Eloise, you are destroying yourself—and in the end you'll destroy the boy too."

"How can you say that?" she had pleaded.

"Because it's true, and I must say it. Don't you think the boy will know, that he'll come to understand that you exist only for him? What a burden to lay on that poor kid, and what a way to live your life, married to that bastard and pretending that your son can take the place of all the joy and goodness that life can give you! You're a fine, wonderful woman, and I love you. I loved you, I think, the moment I saw you in the gallery. Oh, I'm no great shakes, but I can give you love and care, and I can give the boy a father. Doesn't that mean anything to you?"

The day after she spoke with Barbara, Eloise finally accepted the fact that it meant everything to her. The dinner she would share with Freddie was still half an hour away. The child was downstairs, playing in the garden, and Tom was dressing to go out. Trembling only a little, Eloise went into his room and said, "Tom, I must speak to you."

"Shoot," he said. Facing his mirror, folding the collar of his shirt down over his tie, he appeared to be in a good mood.

"I want a divorce," she said quietly.

He finished with his collar and turned around to face her. "You want what?"

"A divorce. I've had enough. I can't face anymore."

"What in hell have you ever faced, you silly bitch?" he said, turning toward the closet where his jacket hung. When she stepped into his path, he pushed her aside with such force that she stumbled and fell against the bed. Taking his jacket, he turned to her. "Are you crazy, coming in here like this and telling me you want a divorce?" He put on the jacket.

She got back on her feet. Her head was beginning to throb. In just a few minutes, it would explode with a surge of pain that was like no other pain in the world. The forewarning, the knowledge that the pain was on its way, that it could not be stopped, that it would have to run its terrible, nauseating course, filled her with a dread that equaled her dread of her husband, and she fairly shouted at him, "I am very serious! I will not live with you any longer! I will not!"

"Until death do us part. Those are the words, baby." And he walked out of the room, slamming the door behind him.

At a half-hour past noon, munching a sandwich and sipping a cup of coffee, Barbara sat in her kitchen, correcting a set of proofs. It was a process she disliked intensely, since it always reminded her that the second half of her college education might have been of some small use to her; and when the doorbell rang, she welcomed the interruption. She was not expecting anyone, and she wondered vaguely whether this was the time of the month that the gas and electric meters were read. She opened the door and stared blankly at the man who stood there. He was a big man, dressed in a suit of brown tweed, his face burned ruddy brown by the sun, his eyes pale blue. He stood in the doorway, regarding her questioningly, and she stood facing him, staring at him, and for a long, long moment, neither of them spoke. Then, unable to make her voice do more than whisper, Barbara said, "Please come inside." neither of them spoke. Then, unable to make her voice do more than whisper, Barbara said, "Please come inside."

He walked into the house, closing the door behind him, and very tentatively held out a large hand to her. She took it.

"May I kiss you?" he asked uncertainly.

She nodded.

He bent and kissed her cheek. Then she turned away abruptly, went into the living room, dropped into a chair, and began to cry, covering her face with her hands. He followed her and stood there awkwardly, watching her.

"Do you have a handkerchief?" she asked him.

He took out his handkerchief and handed it to her, and she wiped her face. "I haven't cried in years," she mumbled. "I used to cry at the drop of a hat."

"Are you married?" he said.

She stared at him.

"Well, I had to ask. I got your address out of the telephone book. B. Lavette, so I figured that had to be Barbara Lavette. But then, you're a famous writer, so you might use your maiden name."

"I'm not a famous writer. I'm just a writer."

He nodded seriously. "Are you married?"

"No. Why do you keep asking me that? If you cared about my being married, you might have written me a letter. You might have told me whether you were alive or dead."

"I sent you a letter."

"That was years ago."

"I wrote other letters, but I didn't mail them. I decided you were married."

"Why?"

He shook his head. "You're a wonderful woman. Why shouldn't you be married?"

"I thought you were dead. I'm not married."

"I'm not dead. Thank God you're not married."

"Shall I say thank God you're not dead? Bernie, sit down and let's talk sense to each other." She got up and grasped him by the arms. "You're real and solid and you have both arms and both legs, for which I thank God. Oh, I'm so glad to see you. I wanted so much to see you again."

"Did you? Truly?"

"Yes, truly. You're different."

"Six years."

"Closer to seven."

"Whose house is this?"

"Mine. I bought it after Sam Goldberg died. It was his. Did you know him?"

"Sam Goldberg the lawyer? Yes. And he's dead, you say?"

"Years now." She shook her head. "I don't know where to begin. Seven years since we saw each other—ten years since you left San Francisco. I wandered all through North Africa, India, Burma, asking for you. I found one man who knew you, an American reporter."

"What on earth were you doing in North Africa and India?"

"Writing."

They both began to talk at once, then they stopped and began to laugh. "Did you really write to me?" she asked him.

"I saved the letters. They're my whole history."

"And now?"

"Well, I'm out of the bloody British army, thank God. Got my discharge in the south of England five days ago."

"And you didn't go back to Palestine?"

"Not yet. I had to get back here. I had to see you first."

"Oh, no. I don't believe that."

"It's true. Hell, Barbara, you can say to me, Cohen, be on your way. I don't want any part of you. I'll understand that, and I guess I'll accept it. But I had to hear you say it."

"And for that you came six thousand miles?"

"Well, mostly. I was born and raised here. It's home, isn't it? You get an awful ache to go home, touch base,

feel something you haven't felt in a long time. You don't
have to say it yet."

"Say what?"

"Cohen, be on your way. Let's have some lunch first."

"Shall I make something?"

"No, let's go out. Unless you have something better to
do?"

"I have nothing better to do."

"Then let's walk. I want to smell the city and the bay."
He stepped back to look at her now and said, "The first
time, when you opened the door, it was like looking at a
memory. Now you're real. You look wonderful. You look
so beautiful."

She shook her head hopelessly. She was wearing an old
plaid skirt, brown loafers, and a cardigan over her blouse.

"Let me change. I don't even have lipstick on."

"No, no, just as you are. You don't need lipstick. God
Almighty, don't you ever look at yourself in the mirror?"

"Only too often."

"Wait a minute," he said in alarm, "you got a guy, a boy
friend?"

"No, not a one."

"Well, why? Are they all crazy in this damn city?"

"Only myself. The others are quite sane."

"We'll go down to the wharf and eat crabmeat and
sourdough bread. How does that hit you?"

She nodded. "I think I'm going to cry again."

They sat on the edge of the dock, eating sourdough bread
and throwing pieces of it to the gulls. "Go ahead," she
said to him. "You took eighteen watches from dead
Germans. I think that's pretty disgusting, just for the
record."

"Not dead Germans. Prisoners of war. They were
damn well alive."

"That's even worse. Robbing prisoners of war."

"That's one way to look at it," he agreed amiably. "On
the other hand, I was at that moment clean out of the
milk of human kindness."

"And you sold them for ten dollars each."

"Two pounds—a little less. Then I ran it up to eighty-
five pounds in a crap game. The British can't shoot crap.
They just don't know the odds. I don't know why, maybe
it's a national characteristic. I always did well in the crap

games. The pay is rotten in the British army, but what with this and that, and after buying my air fare, I have thirty-two hundred dollars right here in my pocket. Now that's not too bad."

"For six years of being a British soldier? Five hundred and thirty dollars a year? That's pretty dumb, if you ask me."

"You never used to be that hard on me."

"I never had a chance to. The one time I saw you, I felt sorry for you."

"And you don't feel sorry for me now?"

"It's hard to feel sorry for a dumbbell. The reporter said you got a commission and then you hit an officer and they broke you back to sergeant."

"I'm not officer material," he admitted. "Not in the British army."

"And you carry all that money around in your pocket?" Barbara asked in amazement.

"So far."

"I'd put it in the bank."

"I've thought of that. I don't know how long I'll stay."

'How long do you want to stay?"

"I don't know. How long would you like me to stay?"

"I decide it?" she asked.

"No other reason to stay."

"And you're still going back to Palestine?"

He nodded. "Eventually, or maybe tomorrow. I'd like to stay and see you every day. But that might be boring as hell to you, because when you come right down to it, I'm no more than a faded memory. On the other hand, if I were walking down here and saw you sitting on the dock and eating bread, I think I'd try to pick you up and get to know you. I don't imagine either of us is the way we were. We've been through too much. But maybe the part of us that reaches out toward each other is still there and unchanged. That's the case with me. What about you?"

"I need time. The trouble with a memory is that one adjusts it. There are no checkpoints. It's all inside the head, isn't it? When I opened the door and saw you, I didn't see the man who made love to me in Paris. I was seeing the person Mike Kendell told me about in Karachi."

"Mike Kendell?"

"The Washington *Post* correspondent. I told you about him. Why did you go away, Bernie? That Don Quixote syndrome is the male sickness. It wasn't that you needed me. I needed you. My God, how I needed you at that moment in my life!"

"I was broke," he said desperately. "I had nothing, nothing. How could I stay there and sponge off you?"

"That kind of talk makes me ill. You men have destroyed millions of women by making it legal and proper and admirable, as you see it, for a woman to live as a man's property. Nothing is shared. We're owned, and if you don't have the means of ownership, you don't play."

"I don't think that's fair. You're a Lavette of San Francisco. This is your turf. The Lavettes, the Whittiers, the Seldons—they own this place. I'm Bernie Cohen. I was raised in a Jewish orphanage—"

"Oh, I weep for you!" Barbara said angrily.

They sat in silence for a while, then she broke off a piece of the bread and handed it to him.

"Thanks."

"You're welcome."

He chewed the bread and stared at her. "You're the finest, the most wonderful woman I've ever known."

"How do you know that?" she demanded petulantly. "You don't even know me. You don't know the first thing about me."

"I know the first thing, god damn it! You're a millionaire."

"Then you're making a case for the rich. I happen not to admire the rich as much as you do. Anyway, I'm not a millionaire. I came into a very large inheritance, and I gave it away. I have a little money and I earn my own living. I was earning my own living when we met in Paris, and I still earn it today. I don't know what kind of virtue that is, but just for the record, I am not a millionaire."

Again the silence. They sat side by side. Then he reached out and put his arm around her, and she leaned against him.

"I read your first book," he said. "I bought it in New York. I heard about it in London and tried to get it there, but then we shipped out. And in New York I couldn't find it in any of the regular bookstores."

"Books have a short life."

"I found it in a secondhand store on Fourth Avenue.

I have your new book, but I wanted to read the other one first. I read it on the plane coming out here."

"Did you like it?"

"Most of it. Was it true?"

"The part about you, about Marcel—who knows? Do any of us know what was true and what wasn't true over the past years?"

"And you went into Germany?"

"Yes."

"That was a damn fool thing to do."

"I suppose so. I did a lot of damn fool things."

"I guess you couldn't find two people in the world as different as you and me."

"Do you want any more of this bread?" she asked him.

"No, I've had enough."

"We're not so different," Barbara said. "We're both of us sentimental and arrogant and pigheaded and opinionated—and the funny part is that I've never liked sentimental people, I guess because that's a part of me I don't like too much—and we both live with nasty worms eating away at our guts. By the way, how old are you, Bernie?"

"You don't remember?"

"Forty?"

"That's right. I'm forty, you're thirty-two."

"And for nine years you've been a soldier. It makes no sense, Bernie."

"I suppose not."

"And you were never wounnded?"

"Never. I was with the British Second Army in the invasion, straight through to the Rhine. Never even scratched."

"And how do you feel about the whole thing?"

"'I don't feel very much yet. I haven't had time. Or else I've pushed it aside. I have bad dreams, but who doesn't?"

"I have bad dreams," Barbara said.

"I'm going to stay. Until you tell me to go away."

"And if I don't tell you to go away?"

He was crumbling the remains of the bread into the water. Barbara watched his hands, strong, long-fingered, broad hands. This man, she thought, has only one profession. He has a competence in death. Why on God's earth am I sitting here like this, my body touching his? Why am I at peace with myself?

Almost as if he had read her mind, he reached out and

touched her arm very gently with one of his fingers, tracing a line down to the back of her hand. She turned to him, and his eyes filled with tears. He closed his eyes and shook his head.

"I don't want to remember. I don't want to feel any way about it. And I don't want to forget, either. You don't forget. That's an illusion, and I don't need any damn illusions. We liberated a concentration camp. There was an open mass grave that they hadn't had time to cover. Their last killing. There were eight or nine hundred bodies in that grave—skinny, emaciated bodies, men, women, small children. When I was a kid, I caught a butterfly and handled it, and when it died, I cried. The other kids laughed at me. I'm trying to keep from crying now. That's what you were talking about before, isn't it? Men don't sponge off women and men don't cry. Only you'd be surprised how many men cry. I watched them cry in Africa and in France and in Germany. It was a big killing, and the whole world was crying. Oh, Jesus, I don't even know what I'm saying. If I had a brain in my head, I'd get up and walk away and leave you here."

"That's bullshit," Barbara said coldly. The rejoinder was so unexpected that he simply stared at her.

"Let's just sit here quietly for a little while," Barbara said, "and look at the water. We're here and it's today and it's nineteen forty-six. It's only four o'clock. We've had a strange few hours. I was correcting some proofs when you rang my doorbell. I have to finish that later and get them in the mail tonight. You can come home with me. It won't take more than another hour. Then, if you wish, we'll go out and have some dinner. Or I can cook something at home. But let's not push this anymore."

"O.K. Then are you going to tell me to go?"

"Bernie, shut up for a while."

"O.K."

They sat there in silence for about fifteen minutes; then they walked back on the Embarcadero and took the cable car up the hill. It was a process of getting used to him. He wore his clothes well. He stood very straight and he walked with ease. "I suppose," Barbara said to herself, "that if he weren't so tall, you wouldn't think of him as a good-looking man. If he were short, that huge nose would be ugly. It's amazing what height does." She found herself thinking of his body, trying to remember it.

He sat in her living room, reading newspapers and magazines while she finished correcting the proofs. Then she mixed a batch of martinis.

"First drink," she said, after she had filled the glasses. "What do we drink to?"

"*Shalom.*"

"Oh?"

"Peace. Hebrew."

"All right. *Shalom.*"

"You know, Barbara," he said, "I figured to wait until we got to know each other a little better. But either people know each other or they don't."

"You can't argue with that."

"In one way. In another way, I don't know whether I'll ever really know you. I don't know if it matters. Myself, I'm a fairly simple character."

"Heaven help us." She began to laugh.

"You don't believe me?"

"No."

"Well, perhaps you're right."

"Don't give in to me," she said.

"Why?"

"I keep thinking about the way Mike Kendell described you, very cold, very tough, blue eyes cold as ice."

He shook his head. "I'm not tough. I'm not very bright, either. My word, Barbara, I really don't have one bloody thing to recommend me. That's why I don't see much sense in waiting. I mean waiting around until we got to know one another better. I thought maybe a week or two, and then I'd ask you whether you'd marry me."

"You thought that a week or two would do it?" she said, smiling.

"Well, you know what I mean."

"Yes. You put it to me now, and if I say no, you haven't wasted any time and you can bug off to wherever you're bound for."

"Oh, no. Come on, that's not what I meant at all. Does that mean no?"

"Bernie, are you asking me to marry you?"

"Yes."

She sighed and filled their glasses again. Then she sat quietly, watching him.

"Let's give it some time."

"You're not saying no?"

"Let's give it that week or two," Barbara decided.

"Can I ask you one question?"

She nodded.

"Did you ever think about marrying me?"

"I thought about it."

"That's enough. I'm not going to push. Let me go back to my hotel and shower and change clothes. That's a touchy point with me."

She found herself giggling.

"And then I'll call for you properly. What would you like to do tonight?"

"Suppose I have a date tonight?"

"But you said—"

"No date. I'm teasing you, Bernie. I think that tonight I'd like to get a little drunk."

"Eight o'clock?"

"Eight o'clock," she agreed.

The Great Cal Building was the first of the great postwar skyscrapers to loom up over San Francisco. Built in record time, it defied earth faults and the threat of earthquakes, and while there were those who complained that it broke the symmetry of the flow of buildings over the hills, most commentators welcomed it as the beginning of a new era. Jean made her first visit there about a week after Tom had opened the new offices of the Great Cal Corporation, informing Tom that she would arrive early in the afternoon and would require only a few minutes of his time.

"I realize how busy you are," Jean said. "But this is important."

Tom had lunched with Whittier that day, in the private dining room on the floor above their offices, and Whittier guessed that Jean's business concerned Barbara. "Just who is this Jewish feller she's been seeing?" he asked.

"God only knows," Tom replied. "Someone from overseas. Apparently she met him during the war."

"On the other hand, Jean might just be here with your father's blessing."

"And what does that mean?" Tom asked.

"He's operating three tankers out of Oakland. I don't like that. I don't like him being on the bay at all. I don't like your father, Thomas. I don't like him one bit."

John Whittier was aging rapidly. He had become nervous and petulant, and he had developed a habit of whining. He made frequent visits to his physician, and his loss of weight made Tom suspect a malignancy of some kind. More and more, Tom felt it would be a relief to have Whittier out of the way. Illness had made him supercautious. He complained endlessly about the cost of the new building, and he had become obsessed with over-spending and waste. Now, with a seamen's strike looming over the shipping industry and with cargo falling off, he was worse than ever.

"Don't worry about my father," Tom said soothingly. "He's a very small potato. And if the seamen strike, he might just go under."

"That's it with you youngsters. Don't know the meaning of a strike. Don't remember the last big one. That sister of yours—she played a cute game with me." He went on and on while Tom said to himself, "Old man, I'm tired to death of you."

For his part, he felt quite certain that his mother did want to talk about Barbara. He had no strong feelings about her, one way or another. They met very infrequently, and when they did, their exchange was polite and impersonal, as were his increasingly rare exchanges with his mother. Her relationship with Dan Lavette was embarrassing to him. It made him uncomfortable and uneasy, and the circumstances that had brought it about were beyond his understanding. His growing dislike for his natural father had increased over the years; his mind had altered the memories to suit his needs, and his distaste had turned into loathing. He had never spoken of it to Jean, and he was determined that this time, too, the subject would remain undiscussed.

However, he welcomed the tall, handsome, meticulously dressed woman who entered his office that afternoon with enthusiasm. It was a point of pride with him that Jean remained attractive at an age when so many women surrendered to dowdiness. "Do you like the offices?" he asked her eagerly. "Lionel Smith decorated them. I don't suppose it's entirely to your taste, mother, but it's the wave of the future. Clean, simple lines—well, you've been waving the flag for modern art. You should like it."

"Perhaps it's too antiseptic for my taste, but very nice.

Tom, can we be alone? I don't want to see John Whittier."

"You won't. I've arranged that."

"Good." She looked around the office—the marble slab that served as a desk, the contour chairs, the couch of leather slung on chrome, the fake Mondrian wall—thinking that it was quite tasteless and uninspiring. On the other hand, she had not offered to help, but then, neither was she an interior decorator. "Please don't sit behind that enormous desk, Tom." She seated herself on the couch and pointed to one of the contour chairs. "That would be better. This is rather intimate."

He seated himself and sighed.

"I want this to be a quiet, civilized discussion, Tom. I came here to ask you to give Eloise a divorce."

He was taken completely aback. He stood up, walked to his desk, and lit a cigarette. Then he turned back to her and said, "I don't think this is your province, mother. I'd rather not discuss it."

"Please sit down, Tom."

"I prefer to stand."

"Very well. It is my province. You are my son. Eloise is my daughter-in-law and a dear friend."

"That's just the trouble."

"What does that mean?"

"I mean that if she spent less time around that damn silly museum of yours and more time at home—"

"Tom! Why don't we talk sense? You know the situation as well as I do."

"I'm not going to talk about it at all."

"Then I shall have to insist that you do."

"There is nothing to talk about. There will be no divorce."

"I had hoped you would be more sensible," Jean said quietly. "You are my son, and believe it or not, I care for you—as much as you let me. I don't want to pressure you, and believe me, I can. I am asking you as earnestly as I can to let that child go. Live your life, but let her live her own life and find whatever happiness she can."

"I told you, I will not discuss it."

"Then you force me to. Alan Brocker was a friend of mine in the days when I had such friends. He subsequently married Manya Vladavich, who was Calvin Braderman's model—"

"Damnit, mother, what has this got to do with anything? My work is piled neck deep. I happen to be the chief of one of the largest corporations in California. I will not have you interfere with my personal life, and I will not waste an afternoon standing here and listening to you babble nonsense!"

"But, Tom, what can you do? Have me bodily removed?" Jean asked.

"I can damn well leave. If you wish to spend the afternoon here talking to yourself, you have my blessing!" He started toward the door.

"Tom, just hold on! I mentioned Manya because Manya loves to whimper on my shoulder. A year ago, Lionel Smith, your decorator, was having an affair with Alan Brocker."

Tom paused and turned to face her.

"Alan had just turned sixty, and I suppose he required stimulation. He is also very wealthy, and he has always bought what he fancied. Manya came to me with this delicious gossip, but the romance was short-lived. Manya also has a loose and spiteful tongue."

"That bitch," Tom said.

"Please sit down," Jean said gently, telling herself, "What a rotten way." She was filled with pity. His arrogance was crumbling. As much as she knew about such things, it was her doing as well as his. "I didn't want to say this, Tommy. Believe me, it makes no difference to me."

He dropped into a chair. "No, not at all."

"Not at all. I don't understand such things. I don't condemn them, either. I've lived too long and hurt too many people to sit in judgment. If you have a relationship with Lionel Smith, that's your affair—only yours—not mine, not anyone else's. I told Manya that if she ever spoke of this to anyone else, I'd slit her throat."

"Thank you for nothing."

"Perhaps," Jean agreed. "But I do think I bullied her into silence. As I said, I don't judge. With all our power and money, people like ourselves have messed up almost everything in this land, sex included. I have no opinions on that score, and I don't know what is right and what is wrong. I do know this—Eloise is being destroyed. Do whatever you have to do, but let her go."

He stared at her in slience.

"She doesn't know about this, and as far as I am concerned, she never will."

"Your concern overwhelms me," he said bitterly. "Does my father know? Did you inform him of your brilliant discovery?"

"Do you care?"

"Yes, God damn it, I care!" he shouted. "Oh, you're both of you two gorgeous characters! First he dumps you and runs off with this Chinese floozy, and now the two of you live together in that so-called museum of yours with the whole city snickering at the spectacle, and then you come here and sit in judgment on me!"

"Dan doesn't know," she said evenly. "I will see to it that he never knows, if you are reasonably circumspect. But if you carry on this charade with Eloise, then sooner or later she will know and so will others. I can appreciate the fact that a divorce does not fit in with your plans, but if you believe that your marriage is a mask you can wear, you're mistaken. Quite the reverse."

"What about Freddie? He's my son."

"He'll remain your son. There's no malice in Eloise, not a shred. She would never do anything to hurt you. Eloise is expecting me this afternoon. I want to take her and the boy to my place, and they will remain with me until arrangements are made."

"You've thought of everything, haven't you?"

"Tom, I wish to God there had been an easier way to do this. I wish everything I said could be unsaid."

"Do you? Do you really?" he asked, his voice quivering. "You haven't enjoyed this at all, not one bit, have you, mother?"

"No, I have not."

"Like hell you haven't!" He covered his face with his hands.

"Tom." Now she was pleading. "I'm your mother."

"Are you? The way he's my father—oh, yes, you're my mother. Always by my side, always helping me, always loving—what kind of crap is that!"

"Tom, please."

"Are you finished? You've done it all. There's nothing more you can do to me. Nothing."

"Tom, I'm sorry."

"So am I." He was in control of himself again. "I am

also very busy. I have work to do." He turned away and sat down behind his desk.

Jean rose and looked at her son for a long moment; then she left. He remained seated, staring at the papers on his desk.

She drove to the house on Pacific Heights, seeing it as if for the first time, the enormous pile of stone and wood that her son had bought as a fortress against his fears and agonies? And who else but she and Dan were responsible for the fears and agonies? She remembered a stand-up comic who once chortled, "I've been rich and I've been poor, and rich is better." She no longer knew. Like a housewife picking up pieces of broken glass and clumsily stepping on the pieces and crushing them in the process, she was trying to gather together and reconstruct the bits and pieces of her life. She was fifty-six years old, and almost nothing made a shred of sense. She had lost all of them, husband, son, and daughter. And now she was frantically trying to repair the rents and tears she had caused in the lives of others, telling herself that she made amends by helping Eloise.

Well, she thought, one does what one does. It was not much of a philosophy, but she admitted to herself that she was not very much of a person. It was, perhaps, the first time she had examined herself without obstruction and made such an admission, and she felt better as she went on into the house.

On the morning of the day of Joe Lavette's wedding to Sally Levy, Barbara and Bernie Cohen drove up to Higate. Barbara drove her 1946 Ford, the first of the postwar vintage; and Bernie contrasted it with the ancient Chevrolet in which he had driven Rabbi Blum on their first trip to Higate, when the rabbi had rescued Jake and Clair Levy from impending bankruptcy with a contract for them to manufacture sacramental wine.

"Over twenty years ago," Bernie said. "That Chevy was a miracle. I had put it together out of seven different junkyards, and the miracle was that it worked. Well, cars were simpler then. The old man was terrified. Did you ever meet the rabbi?"

Barbara shook her head. "No, but I wish I had."

"He was an amazing character—long white beard, beautiful blue eyes, a skin as pink as a baby's, he looked

as if he had stepped right out of the Old Testament. You
know, he took me out of the orphanage when I was
twelve—closest thing to a father I ever had. That was
after his wife died. There's a strange story about him, and
I wonder how many people know it? You know, his
father wasn't even Jewish."

"Then how on earth could he be a rabbi?"

"Listen and learn, dear woman. His father was a Dutch
seaman named Blum who jumped ship in eighteen fifty
and went into the diggings. He never found any gold,
but in the course of looking for it he met and married a
dance hall girl who was Jewish, whose name was Rosie
Katz. Then, a few years later, Blum the father jumped
back on a ship and was never seen or heard from again.
Now, in Jewish law, the descent is through the mother,
so the child was technically Jewish, just as the Levy kids
are technically not Jewish because Clair isn't Jewish.
Well, believe it or not, Rosie became a very successful
madam in the old Tenderloin, retired reasonably wealthy
in eighteen sixty, married again, this time a Jew, and the
rabbi was raised as a Jew, sent east to the seminary, and
then he came back here as a full-fledged rabbi. How about
that?"

"It's incredible," Barbara said, "When I think of how
new we are here. Mother had a bit of doggerel that she
used to impart to me as a great secret. It went like this:
Granddad worked in the placer mines, Daddy's on Nob
Hill. If it weren't for Sutter and Sutter's gold, I'd still be
sucking swill. Mother said that grandma once heard her
saying it and became perfectly furious. How granny ever
permitted mother to marry an Italian fisherman, I'll
never know."

"From what you tell me of your mother, it was not a
question of permission."

"She's quite a lady. You'll meet her today, and daddy
and everyone else. It's going to be a rough day for you,
Bernie, so gird your loins."

"And how will you introduce me?"

"Ah, we come to that. Well, I suppose I could
introduce you as a bloody mercenary who seduced me one
night in Paris long ago."

"Come on, Bobby."

"Or I could explain that this is an old friend who was

staying at the Mark Hopkins until three weeks ago, when he moved into my house."

"Why did you take him in?"

"Pity, I suppose."

"I evoke pity?"

"I think you do. When you look at me in that beseeching, plaintive way"—she took her eyes off the road to glance at him—"like now. Sort of like a camel."

"Oh, Jesus Christ, no! Not like a camel."

"Camels are dear beasts."

"Camels are the ugliest, stupidest, foulest-smellest animals God ever contrived. You know, you never say anything nice to me."

"That doesn't mean I'm not fond of you."

"Since we sleep together and eat together and spend most of our days together, that's a reasonable assumption. Why won't you marry me?"

"Did I say I wouldn't?"

"You never said you would."

"I'm not sure I would. I'm not sure I wouldn't."

"That's just great."

"It takes time."

"Seven years?"

"That's one way of looking at it," Barbara agreed. "On the other hand, you have no visible means of support. You're footloose and fancy free. You remind me of my father, which may be why I'm taken with you, but that's a minus as well as a plus. You've spent much of your adult life at war, which is nothing I am enamored of, and you also confuse me. Jews are supposed to be intellectual, introverted, and abashed."

"Who said so?"

"Well, I've sort of accepted that. Maybe I'm wrong. But as far as Palestine is concerned, it's the last place in the world I desire to go. I love San Francisco. It's my home; it's the place where I'm most comfortable. I don't ever want to travel again, and I don't ever want to live anywhere else."

"Bobby, what would I do here?"

"What would you do in Palestine? You're forty years old. From what you tell me, it's a bleak, inhospitable desert, a ruined land that has to be made over foot by foot. I'm a writer and I'm a woman. I want to have children, and I want them to grow up here. With all its faults, with all the lying and the cheating and the dirt and the misery, it's the best place in the world that I have ever seen. I am sick to death of this Jew and gentile, black and white, Chicano and Anglo—God Almighty, won't we we ever grow up and become people?"

"The six million Jews who were murdered by the Nazis, the children among them, they won't ever grow up, Bobby."

"And six million Bengalis died in the famine in India, and I saw a street where the dead were laid out like a carpet. Bernie, I love you. I'm trying to drive a car and think and talk, and it's not easy. But I love you. You and Marcel. Two men in my life, like the two sides of a coin, because you're as different from him as day from night, but you're the only two men I ever wanted. Bernie, what do we do? Do we spend our lives trying to atone for the dead? I know something about Palestine and the Jewish settlements there. But I will not put a gun in my hands and kill—not if my own life depended on it, not for anything, not for any dream or ideal. I've lived through the worst bloodbath this world ever saw, fifty million dead, and that's not the way and I won't go that way."

"What would I do?" he asked miserably.

"It doesn't matter to me. What does any man do? You studied agriculture. Look around you." They were in the Napa Valley now, driving north on Highway 29, the vineyards rolling away and up the hillsides on either side. "We'll buy a piece of land if you want to. Farm it. Make wine. Anything. Bernie, I wasn't going to tell you, but damn it, I will. I think I'm pregnant."

"What?"

"I'm one week late. Usually, that doesn't mean anything, but I'm as regular as clockwork. Anyway, I've got a feeling about it."

"That's wonderful!" he burst out. "Bobby, that's great, just absolutely great. We'll get married."

"Just hold on. Not so quick."

"You wouldn't get rid of it?"

"Oh, no, my lad. I'm going to have this kid, come hell or high water. I'm thirty-two years old, and I'm going to have this kid and others while I still can, even if I have to resort to artificial insemination. And I don't want one. I want three or four. But you and me, Bernie, we're two people. Maybe we're not so different. I think we both

spent our lives expiating some kind of guilt. I grew up
rich and you grew up lonely and poor, and I think that's
some kind of cement that binds us together now. I'm
not looking for bliss. I think you're a little crazy and kind
of intractable, and we're going to have a lot of misery,
but maybe we can work it out so that we have a lot of
happiness as well. I'm willing to give it a try, but you've
got to see me as a whole person, not just as a woman and
not just as a mother, but as a whole human being who
is half of your life. I'm not saying I wouldn't go to Palestine someday or even live there for a while, but my
roots are here, and I think yours are too. Whatever we
were in the beginning, it's this war that's made us what we
are today. So I'll reverse the question. Will you marry
me and live here with me?"

He didn't answer until they had turned into the dirt
road, with the old stone buildings of Higate before them.
Then he said, "O.K. I'll give it a try."

When Barbara came into the room where Sally was being
dressed by her mother and by Sarah Levy, her grandmother, Sally broke free of them to throw her arms around
Barbara. "Oh, Bobby, how perfectly wonderful to see you!
And you're so beautiful! Why can't I look like you?"

Barbara felt quite foolish in the flowing shell pink organdy dress that had been decided upon for the maid of
honor. Pink was decidedly not her color, but pink was
what Sally would have, and Barbara's satin slippers were
pink, and the broad-brimmed straw hat she carried and
now tried to protect from Sally's embrace had a dripping
garnish of tiny pink roses.

"Sally," Clair said, "if you don't get back here and let
me finish the hem, you won't look like Barbara. You'll
look plain silly."

"Do you like it?" Sally asked, turning, stepping back,
swirling the folds of white organdy, to her mother's annoyance. "I think I look like granny did when she was my
age. Don't I, granny? I saw a picture—only my hair's like
straw. I don't know what to do with my hair. I wish I
could cut it off, only Joe would kill me. That's because
he's Chinese. He has a fixation on yellow hair."

"Sally," Clair said sharply, "no more of that. Joe is
Barbara's brother. He is not Chinese. Heaven help me,
what do I do with her?" Clair asked Barbara.

Barbara laughed. "In one hour, she'll be off your hands."

"Poor Joe."

"Poor Joe indeed," Sally said.

"You look very beautiful," Barbara told her, thinking that the years had changed very little of Sally. She still had the tiny breasts she had bemoaned; she was taller, but still very slender, and with her yellow hair falling over her shoulders, in the white organdy wedding gown, with a veil of tulle and a white Juliet cap, she looked like something out of a Mucha print, an illustration for an unlikely tale of a time long ago.

"Bobby," she exclaimed, "we are truly going to be sisters. Isn't that wonderful? And Adam is Joe's best man, so it's brother, sister, brother, sister, and if only Adam would marry you. No. I forgot. You have that marvelous, romantic soldier. I remember the letter so well, and he's here. I caught a glimpse of him through the window. Bobby, why don't you marry him? We'll have a double wedding. I mean, Adam is impractical. He's totally gaga over his Eloise. Peaches and cream. Well, if that's his taste, it's his taste. She's all fluff, if you ask me."

"If you ask me," Sarah said hopelessly, "you'll talk Joe to death. Please stand still."

"Are you going to marry him? Barbara, how did he ever find you?"

"In the telephone book."

"Of course. No one ever thinks of telephone books. Don't you think he's marvelously romantic, Bobby? You know, he looks like Spencer Tracy, except that he's a foot taller and his nose. Well, I like a man with a good nose. It shows character. Poor Joe. Mom's right. Mom you're right," she told her mother.

"Thank you. Now hold still."

"I mean," she explained to Barbara, "that poor Joe never had a chance. I threw myself at him. I confess it."

"I think Joe loves you very much. I wouldn't feel sorry for him. He's lucky."

"Do you think so, Bobby? Bless you. I'm so happy, but quite nervous. Do you know, we've never had intercourse."

"Sally!" her grandmother said sharply.

"Granny, don't be shocked. If I said we had, then you'd have good reason. He's hopelessly old-fashioned. Can you imagine, here it's nineteen forty-six and I'm twenty years old and I'm a virgin."

"Sally," Clair said, "if you wish to discuss your virginity, you can take it up with Barbara later. Right now we're trying to fit this dress. I suggest you hold still and be quiet for five minutes."

"Anyway," Sarah said, looking out of the window, "Dan is here with your mother, Barbara."

Barbara ran downstairs to greet them. A slow stream of cars, bumper to bumper, was coming up the road to the winery. On the lawn, facing the main house, a green-and-white-striped pavilion had been erected, with chairs set up on a dance floor. Another huge tent housed the tables, and beyond that, Chicano winery workers were preparing the barbecue under the careful eye of Rudy Gomez, Jake's foreman. Jake himself, already resplendent in a white dinner jacket, was greeting the guests, and when Barbara appeared, Dan was introducing Jean. Joe stood at the other end of the garden, talking to Judge Henderson of San Francisco, who was to perform the ceremony. Barbara looked around for Bernie, and not finding him, walked quickly over to where Joe stood. Joe introduced her to Judge Henderson.

"Well, young lady, your mother's daughter, true enough. She was the belle of the city at your age, and you do her proud."

Barbara begged Joe's presence, "for just a few minutes, please, sir." She took Joe aside and said to him, "Joe, my mother's here. Whatever you feel deep inside, it was a great act of courage for her to come here."

"I know."

"I want you to meet her now."

She led Joe over to where Dan stood with Jean. "She's a beauty," Joe whispered to her. Jean, in a simple beige chiffon dress, her face shadowed by a wide straw brim, was indeed an imposing and handsome woman.

"Mother," Barbara said, "this is my brother Joe. I want you to meet him and know him and love him—as I do."

They stood looking at each other for a long moment. Joe appeared at a loss. Then Jean walked to him, put her arms around him, and kissed him. He stepped back, looking at Jean and then at Dan. He nodded, not trusting himself to speak. Finally he said, "I'm glad you came. I'm very glad." Then he turned and walked off.

Barbara took her mother's arm. "It's all right, mother. Give it time. Everything's piled together today. Joe's scared. Sally's scared. These are all good people, but I think the only time they see each other is at weddings and funerals."

"I shouldn't have come," Jean whispered.

"You damn well should have," Dan said.

"I shouldn't have kissed him."

"Thank heavens you did," Barbara told her. "Nothing today is going to be easy. This place is dripping with emotion, and I don't know whether I can stand it myself. I've been so long without family, and now they're everywhere I look."

"Where's your soldier?" Dan asked her.

"Don't call him that, please. He's around somewhere. Now listen to me, both of you. He's Jewish. He has no job and he has no real prospects, and he's been living with me in my house these past three weeks, and I'm going to marry him. That's it, flat and straight, and I'm glad I got it out before you meet him. So both of you digest that, and you'll meet him as soon as I can find him."

With that, she ran off, and Jean said to Dan, "Well, this is certainly going to be a day."

"I think you can say that again."

Adam Levy, with Eloise and her small son, had climbed up the hillside to a point where the wedding party, the houses, and the guests were below them. They had gone up steps, so it had not been a hard climb, and now, a hundred feet higher than the gardens, they could look out over the whole vista of Higate, the stone buildings, the gently rolling vineyards, the pastures where cattle grazed, the line of cars crawling up to the main house, and the swirl of guests eddying into the gardens and the pavilions.

"I can see the whole world," Freddie said.

"My whole world when you and Freddie are in it," Adam said to Eloise. "There's a real mixing of the Levys and the Lavettes. It began forty years ago."

"Adam, I'm frightened," she whispered to him.

"That's normal. I mean that one gets used to it and lives with it, and then it goes away. This is a strange place to you, filled with strange people. Like most people, we'll have our ups and downs. We'll work it out."

"Can I go down there?" Freddie asked her.

She looked at Adam, who nodded. The little boy ran down the steps.

"It was good growing up here," Adam said, "making wine, growing grapes. It's not the greatest thing in the world, but it's a good way to live. You'll unwind here, and then you'll never be afraid again. We'll have more children, if you want to."

"He won't get lost?" she asked nervously, pointing after her son.

"No, he won't get lost, Ellie."

"I think I'm very happy, but I'm not sure," Eloise said. "I keep waiting to be scolded. I keep waiting for Tom to find me and be very angry. Then I begin to die inside."

Adam drew her to him and kissed her. "Do you know," he said, "all the time overseas I waited for it to be over, day after day, waiting for it to be over, and I always told myself that when it was over, something good would happen. I can remember sitting in cold wet mud and eating cold, miserable C rations, and telling myself, another meal, another day, and one day it's going to be over and then everything will be fine. But I never dreamed it would be you. I never dreamed that anyone like you existed. No, I think I did, but it was only a dream."

"You won't get tired of me and angry at me? I'm not smart and I can't do things. When I see women like Barbara and Sally and your mother, I just want to crawl away and hide."

"Then I'll crawl away and hide with you. And now we'd better go back. They're beginning to go into the pavilion, and I'm the best man, for the moment. You talk about being afraid, poor Joe is paralyzed."

Looking everywhere for Bernie Cohen, who had disappeared, Barbara finally went into the old stone aging-building. Here, out of the warmth of the noonday sun, it was cool and damp and suddenly silent, the big metal tanks looming strangely. Bernie stood inside, in the dim light, motionless. As she entered, he turned slowly to face her. After he had stared at her for a moment or two, he said wonderingly, "I've never seen you look like this before. God, you're beautiful."

"If you like pink."

"Don't laugh at me now."

"I never laugh at you, Bernie. I only giggle a little." She walked over to him, went up on her toes, and kissed him lightly. "You're full of regrets and doubts, aren't you,

Bernie? You've sold your birthright for a mess of Barbara.
What a strain it must be to be Jewish, to spend two thousand years trying to teach the world to be civilized, and
then to give it all up and discover that even a Jew can become a practiced professional killer."

He pulled back. "That's a hell of a thing to say!"

"Good. I'm glad you can get angry with me. I want a
husband, not a willing slave. You know, I was in Germany. You were too, but you came there with a gun in
your hands. So we saw it differently. I'm not laughing at
you, Bernie. And I'm not trying to hurt you."

"You do a damn good job without trying."

"Then perhaps I have to. I'm trying to say something
very important, and I want to get it said before we go out
there into the sunlight, where Joe and Sally will pledge
to live happily ever after. No one lives happily ever after.
Happiness is the pie in the sky we're fed from the moment we come out of the womb, and the little bit of decent human understanding we could hope for falls by the
wayside. Well, what I'm trying to say is this. There's a
moment in life when something hits you over the head.
It's like waking up after you've been asleep for a long time,
and what happens then is that black and white are no
longer black and white. It happened to me in Germany
when a German Junker saved my life. Possibly that's not
very much in the large scheme of things, but it's my life
and the only one I have, and it's nicer to be here talking
to a man you love than to be beaten to death by the
Gestapo. Does any of this make sense to you?"

"Go on," he said coldly. "Finish your lecture."

"Oh, I will, you can be sure of that. When we walk out
of this building, we will either know something about each
other or we won't. You see yourself as a dedicated fighter
who trained for years to liberate Palestine as a Jewish
homeland. I see you as a frightened little boy, motherless
and fatherless, who was rescued from an orphanage by a
kind man and given a burden of debt you've spent your
life trying to repay."

"Spare me the psychoanalysis."

"Why? Because it's true? Didn't it ever occur to you
that you've paid your debt, that you fought those wretched
fascists for nine years? What else must you prove to
yourself? That all the slanders thrown at the Jews for a
thousand years are lies? That the only virtue is to kill or

be killed? That's the male curse, the male abomination
that has filthied this beautiful world for centuries. I'm a
woman, and I don't buy it and I will not buy it. A bullet
has no conscience or judgment. You've been lucky. Josh
Levy was not lucky. May Ling was not lucky. Fifty million others were not lucky. I want you to live. It's as
simple as that."

He sat down on a wine barrel and put his face in his
hands. Barbara waited. Minutes passed, and still she
waited. Finally, he looked up at her and said, "I give up
the fight. Is that it?"

"No. We never give up the fight. We give up the guns."

He stared at her thoughtfully. Then he said, "You're
quite a woman, Barbara Lavette."

"And you're quite a man."

"Then maybe we'll work things out. Like I said, I'll
give it a try."

"A woman could ask no more. Now, like I said, gird
your loins. You're going to meet my father and mother."

They shook hands, Bernie Cohen and Dan Lavette. They
were the same size, Barbara noted, the same bulk. Jean
regarded him judiciously, thinking that she and Barbara
were not too unlike, their taste in men not too dissimilar.

"Dan Lavette, my father," Barbara said, "and this is
Jean Whittier, my mother. They're not married, but they
do live together occasionally, and they get along and
they're legitimately my father and mother. They're nice
when you get to know them."

There was no time for much more than that. The place
was full of the past, a crowd as mixed as the lives of the
two families—Chicanos and Chinese and Italians and
Jews, lawyers, politicians, trade union leaders, Mexican
music, and the smell of roasting lamb and beef, men in
uniform, an admiral, a mayor, women in pink and yellow
and white, great jugs of wine waiting to be drunk, tears
waiting to be wept, laughter waiting, and Joe Lavette
standing uneasily in front of the stone house with Adam
beside him as the seats under the pavilion filled up.

"What do you think of him?" Jean asked Dan.

"I think he'll do."

"He reminds me of you."

"That's no accolade."

"It all depends on how you look at it," Jean said.

Judge Henderson said to him, "Do you, Joseph Lavette, take this woman to be your lawfully wedded wife?"

"I do."

"And do you, Sally Levy, take this man to be your lawfully wedded husband?"

"I do."

"Then, by the authority vested in me under the laws of the State of California, I declare you wed as man and wife."

Clair Levy, finally, at long last breaking out of the shadow of her son Joshua's death, was able to laugh through her tears and tell her husband exuberantly, "Just see what we have put together, Jake. Sally is Jewish and Irish and Scotch and English, and Joe is Chinese and French and Italian. What damn wonderful kids they're going to have!"

Sarah Levy, Sally's grandmother, had used up her tears, and now she sat with Dan and fondled her memories. They went back forty years together, to the time of the great earthquake. She was only nine years older than Dan, but after her grandson's death she had become an old woman. Dan could remember when she was as like Sally as a sister, the same yellow hair, the same slender figure. But death had touched her too mercilessly—her daughter, her husband, and then her grandson.

"Still," she said, "I'm glad to be alive. I guess we're both of us lucky, Danny. I tell myself that God runs the world stupidly, but today I refuse to think about that."

"I suppose He does His best. That's what we all do."

Barbara watched Bernie Cohen dance with her mother, and afterward she said to him, "I didn't know you could dance. We've never danced."

"Would you like to try?"

"Why not? My belly's still flat."

"It's an old trick, to tell a man you're pregnant."

"I'm full of old tricks, as you will discover."

Dancing with Barbara, Bernie said, "There's one thing you can be sure of. I worship the ground you walk on."

"That's too extravagant. I don't want to be worshipped, not myself or the ground I walk on."

"O.K. It's one of those phrases you pick up reading. You'd be surprised how much reading you do during a war. What I mean is that after I met you, I never thought of myself in terms of any other woman. Only I was never very sure how to pull it off."

"You worked it out."

"Funny thing is, I didn't. I still don't know exactly how it happened. I only know that I love you, I think, as much as any man can love a woman. I don't know why you want to marry me, but I'm not going to dispute it."

"I have my reasons," Barbara said.

"This is a hell of a good wedding," he said a few minutes later.

"It has its points," Barbara agreed.

The

The third chapter in the triumphant saga that began with *The Immigrants* and continued with *Second Generation*

Establishment

The Lavettes—a special breed. A powerful and passionate clan. Swept up in the McCarthy witch-hunts, struggling to help a new-born Israel survive, they would be caught up in a turbulent saga of war, money and politics. All would fulfill their magnificent destinies as their lives became a stunning portrait of their times.

A Dell Book   (12296-1) $3.25

Howard Fast

At your local bookstore or use this handy coupon for ordering:

Dell	**DELL BOOKS** THE ESTABLISHMENT (12296-1) $3.25 **P.O. BOX 1000, PINEBROOK, N.J. 07058**

Please send me the above title. I am enclosing $ _____
(please add 75¢ per copy to cover postage and handling). Send check or money order—no cash or C.O.D.'s. Please allow up to 8 weeks for shipment.

Mr/Mrs/Miss _____

Address _____

City _____ State/Zip _____

ARENA

NORMAN BOGNER

"Another *Godfather!* It has virtually
everything!"—*Abilene Reporter-News*

**The spectacular new novel by the
bestselling author of *Seventh Avenue***

Four families escaped the Nazi nightmare with
dreams that could only come true in America.
For Alec Stone, the dream was a boxing arena.
For Sam West, it was a Catskill resort—a refuge for
his beautiful, speechless daughter, Lenore.
For Victor Conte, it meant establishing a west-coast
talent agency.
And for Paul Salica, it meant a lasting committment to
another family—the Mafia.
But to young, gifted Jonathan Stone, no dream was
big enough. Obsessed by love for Lenore, he would
risk all they won—again and again.

A Dell Book   (10369-X) $3.25

At your local bookstore or use this handy coupon for ordering:

Dell	**DELL BOOKS** ARENA (10369-X) $3.25
	P.O. BOX 1000, PINEBROOK, N.J. 07058

Please send me the above title. I am enclosing $ _____
(please add 75¢ per copy to cover postage and handling). Send check or money
order—no cash or C.O.D.'s. Please allow up to 8 weeks for shipment.

Mr/Mrs/Miss_____

Address _____

City _____ State/Zip _____

Dell BESTSELLERS

☐ **TOP OF THE HILL** by Irwin Shaw $2.95 (18976-4)

☐ **THE ESTABLISHMENT** by Howard Fast........$3.25 (12296-1)

☐ **SHOGUN** by James Clavell $3.50 (17800-2)

☐ **LOVING** by Danielle Steel $2.75 (14684-4)

☐ **THE POWERS THAT BE**
by David Halberstam $3.50 (16997-6)

☐ **THE SETTLERS** by William Stuart Long $2.95 (15923-7)

☐ **TINSEL** by William Goldman $2.75 (18735-4)

☐ **THE ENGLISH HEIRESS** by Roberta Gellis....$2.50 (12141-8)

☐ **THE LURE** by Felice Picano $2.75 (15081-7)

☐ **SEAFLAME** by Valerie Vayle $2.75 (17693-X)

☐ **PARLOR GAMES** by Robert Marasco $2.50 (17059-1)

☐ **THE BRAVE AND THE FREE**
by Leslie Waller $2.50 (10915-9)

☐ **ARENA** by Norman Bogner $3.25 (10369-X)

☐ **COMES THE BLIND FURY** by John Saul $2.75 (11428-4)

☐ **RICH MAN, POOR MAN** by Irwin Shaw $2.95 (17424-4)

☐ **TAI-PAN** by James Clavell $3.25 (18462-2)

☐ **THE IMMIGRANTS** by Howard Fast $2.95 (14175-3)

☐ **BEGGARMAN, THIEF** by Irwin Shaw $2.75 (10701-6)

At your local bookstore or use this handy coupon for ordering:

Dell **DELL BOOKS**
P.O. BOX 1000, PINEBROOK, N.J. 07058

Please send me the books I have checked above. I am enclosing $ _____
(please add 75¢ per copy to cover postage and handling). Send check or money
order—no cash or C.O.D.'s. Please allow up to 8 weeks for shipment.

Mr/Mrs/Miss _____

Address _____

City _____ State/Zip _____